KEEP ME CLOSE

CONJURING FASCINATION SERIES

KEEP ME CLOSE

JM PAQUETTE

4 Horsemen
Publications, Inc.

Published By: 4 Horsemen Publications, Inc.

4 Horsemen Publications, Inc.
PO Box 417
Sylva, NC 28779
4horsemenpublications.com
info@4horsemenpublications.com

Cover Illustration by Oxford
Cover Typography and Typesetting by Autumn Skye
Edited by Kate Klocek

Library of Congress Control Number: 2022931344

Paperback ISBN-13: 978-1-64450-398-0
Hardcover ISBN-13: 979-8-8232-0666-2
Audiobook ISBN-13: 978-1-64450-395-9
Ebook ISBN-13: 978-1-64450-397-3

For Vanessa, who insisted that demons need love too.

(Don't worry—there's a happy ending for everyone!)

CONTENTS

PROLOGUE

THEO

"**C**OME TO ME, THEODORE." The voice of his Maker is deceptively soft and utterly undeniable. Theo freezes mid-sentence, all thoughts of the plan to find the Greater Demon or research the magical dagger vanished. His mouth hangs open as Jolena's will wraps around him. His body obeys immediately, turning abruptly to move toward the speaker, but not before Theo sees Oren's expression, his friend's normally expressive face blanking in defense as his eyes dart to the direction of the call. Though the command focuses on Theo, all three vampires can feel it. Against his will, Theo walks out of the kitchen, abandoning Oren who stays seated on the counter. Harald takes a few steps behind him but lingers inside as Theo reaches the sliding glass door to the rooftop terrace. He catches a glimpse of Harald's calculating expression in the reflection of the glass, and the shock is almost enough to make him stop moving.

Why can I see his reflection? None of us should be able to—

Theo cuts the thought off, never quite sure just how complete Jolena's hold over them is. Sometimes, he is convinced she can literally read their thoughts, but other times, it just seems like she's really good at reading their body language. She may be able to compel their bodies, force them to her will with her power as their Maker, but she cannot change how they feel about it, and Theo is never very good at schooling his expressions, not like Oren and Harald.

Then again, everyone always assumes Harald is simply the muscle of their group, a pretty face blessed with a strong body, but Theo and Oren both know better. Harald sees everything, and if one of them could regain the ability to be seen in reflections, it would be him.

Theo's body doesn't miss a beat, stepping outside to face the woman he once worshipped as a goddess. He had been young and foolish then, always a sucker for a pretty face, but he's learned what Jolena is over the centuries, and he knows better than to be excited to see her.

That doesn't stop the breath from catching in his chest at the sight of his mistress—her long dark hair unbound and falling in perfect waves around her face and down her chest, her smooth skin and wide eyes, always so pleased to see him that first moment after an absence.

"My lady," he breathes, sinking to one knee before her as he knows she expects, moving before the compulsion can force him down. He knows she will appreciate the gesture, seeing it as evidence of his loyalty to her. It may have been two hundred years since he last saw her, but Theo will never forget what she likes.

Of course she would show up now, he thinks ruefully, *when we're in the shit.* The image of Sylvia flashes in his mind, and he wonders how much Jolena knows about his human lover. *How long has she been watching us?* He doesn't think it's a coincidence that his old mistress would arrive as they struggled to contain a powerful artifact. It's been almost two months since Charlie Wagner left the dagger in a pool of his blood, and they are still no closer to figuring out what to do with it—naturally, Jolena would want it.

I would enjoy watching her face as she tried to pick it up, Theo muses, keeping his face down so that she can't see his expression. *How long has it been since something could hurt her?*

"Theodore," she croons, and her voice raises goose-bumps on Theo's skin. He hates his body's response to her presence, to the sound of her voice, and he bites his lip, very aware of his fangs extending in his mouth, the stirring of desire he cannot stop.

"Mistress," he replies, still looking down. He can see her lower legs, feet covered by dainty heels, her coffee skin exactly the same as that first night so long ago when she first saved him and then seduced him. She wears a green dress with delicate gold beading in a pattern on the top layer, the fabric drifting slightly in the wind, fluttering around her shins. Theo knows that if he looks up, he will lose more of himself, unable to stop it. He always was more susceptible to Jolena's power than Oren or Harald. He doesn't know if it's because she made him first or she wanted him more, but they seem to retain more of themselves when under her spell. Theo remains aware of himself but is trapped, unable to control his body or his words, fighting only in his mind against her control. Jolena seems to know this, and she loves tormenting him, abusing him every chance she gets until she eventually bores of his resistance and leaves them alone again.

Sylvia, Theo thinks again, frantic this time, wishing he could tell Oren and Harald to take care of her. He knows he doesn't need to say the words, that they know what he wants, but the idea of his Sylvia without his protection with a Greater Demon loose in the world is terrifying.

They will keep her safe, he reminds himself. *And if they fail, Pilkington will protect her.* The thought stabs uncomfortably, but he knows it is true. He's seen how the demon looks at Sylvia, and he is no fool.

"Let me see you," Jolena commands, and Theo's body jerks to his feet. He is taller than she is, his face hovering above her, and he keeps his eyes averted, studying the skyline behind her, relishing his last moments of freedom. She reaches out to stroke his cheek, her nail leaving a red line of pain on his skin, and she leans forward to lick the tiny drop of blood her touch has drawn. The cut is small, less than he would have received while shaving, but the pleasure that shoots through him is both wonderful and terrible. Jolena is here to play, and she will not tire of him any time soon.

Theo wills Oren and Harald to stay inside. Perhaps she will forget about them if she can't see them.

"Look at me," she orders, and Theo's eyes slide to her face, meeting her golden gaze, and something inside of him turns liquid, everything that he is drowning in the overwhelming need to serve her, to be what she wants of him.

Please let her be satisfied with just me, he thinks in a disjointed voice.

"You are different, Theodore," she croons, a hand brushing his hair behind an ear, fingers stroking his skin the way she knows he likes. "Where is the loyal warrior I know?"

"Still here, Mistress," he replies, body jerking to attention, every nerve focused on her touch. "Always here."

"You'd better be," she snaps, then tilts her head, looking around his body to the door beyond. "And where are your little friends?" She snaps her fingers, and Theo feels the magic burst past him, calling his companions outside. She sighs at their appearance, never as interested in them as she is in Theo. Wrapped in her will and close to her mind, Theo can feel her appraisal: Oren is mildly interesting when she wants a verbal sparring match, but she only uses Harald when she wants a fuck, leaving the big man to his own thoughts.

For a woman who so clearly understands Theo, he has always marveled at her lack of insight regarding Harald. *Still waters run deep*, he thinks, *and one day, her casual dismissal of Harald will be her downfall.*

But not tonight. Now, she has all three of them under her power. She shakes her head, releasing the others, returning her attention to Theo. "I'll be borrowing this one for a time," she declares. "I trust you will manage his affairs, whatever they are these days."

For all that she delights in torturing Theo, she is always careful to leave his life undisturbed. Theo used to think it was because she cared about him, truly cared enough to safeguard whatever life he had built. Now, he knows it is only because she wants to be able to drop him back into that life periodically, enjoying his struggle as she loosed his bonds only to yank him close again, allowing him to see how his behavior hurt those around him. Jolena's hold over him is most of the reason why he has never tried to maintain a relationship with a mortal over the years. Breaking the hearts of friends was hard enough—he didn't want to risk a lover.

Until Sylvia.

"Yes, Mistress," Oren agrees in a faint voice. Harald doesn't speak, but Theo imagines that his big friend has nodded. He wishes he could see his friends before Jolena makes them leave.

I should have planned for this, he thinks ruefully. *We should have talked about the possibility.* In the past, they've always had a general plan for Jolena's appearances—the others cover for whomever she takes— but they haven't talked about it since Theo met Sylvia. They've been too wrapped up in figuring out the magical dagger before the Greater Demon returns.

But I told her about Jolena, so at least Sylvia will understand. He pauses, and if he could smile, he would have, imagining his human's expression at that conversation. Sylvia might understand that he has to go, that the magic that made him a vampire is beyond his power, but she definitely wouldn't be what he called understanding about it. She'd fuss, and fight, and demand he find another way.

I will, he promises himself. *I will break free as soon as I can, and I will come back to you.*

Meeting Jolena's gaze again, Theo hopes he can keep his promise before it's too late.

CHAPTER 1

SYLVIA

"**J**OLENA."

Sylvia stands up, taking a step toward the vampires who have just crawled through her window from the fire escape. "What about her?" she asks, the sinking feeling in her stomach growing as Oren sighs, the motion lifting his shoulders as he frowns.

"She showed up outside Theo's apartment," Oren explains. "She has ... borrowed him for a time."

"What the fuck does that mean?" Sylvia snaps, hating the desperate sound of her voice, the spinning sensation in her gut. "How can she just borrow my boyfriend?"

Oren shakes his head, his expression bordering on apologetic. "She's our Maker, Sylvia. She can compel us at will."

Sylvia spares a glance at the demon in human form still sitting at her small kitchen table. He would understand compulsion. Pilkington hasn't moved, but the frown on his face is quickly replaced by thoughtful calculation.

Good, Sylvia thinks. *He's already working on a new plan.* They have worked on several plans over the last months, considering and discarding multiple options. Sylvia immediately discounted some—like Oren's suggestion they relocate to a hidden cabin in the wilderness until they can find out more about the dagger—but others had promise. Pilkington is still working his way through his library in the demon realm, so they may yet find answers there. Oren and Harald have been hunting for signs of the demon released by Charlie Wagner. Theo has been watching for signs of Adam, Sylvia's ex who had escaped the disastrous summoning. Theo is sure that Adam wouldn't give up on the dagger or Sylvia so easily.

All of our plans involve Theo, Sylvia thinks. *All of my plans involve Theo. Why did she have to choose* now *to come back?* Sylvia considers the dagger hidden inside her apartment, shoved in the top shelf of her medicine cabinet. *I need a better hiding place.*

"Do you think she's after the dagger?" she asks, wanting to get the question over with. If someone as distant as Jolena has caught wind of the artifact, they have bigger problems. Every creature in the city would be after them if someone in another country had heard about it.

Oren shakes his head. "I don't think so. I mean, she would want it if she knew, but I can't imagine she would know."

"If Jolena knows about the dagger," Harald says in his soft voice, "we would have been attacked. This apartment is known. We haven't been hiding. Others would have been here by now."

Oren nods, running a hand through his shaggy dark hair. He sinks onto the chest at the foot of her bed, one hand tapping out a nervous rhythm against his jeans as he contemplates. Harald hovers near the window. He never gets comfortable in her apartment, always one step away from looking like a guard on duty. His clothes may be modern now, the simple t-shirt and shorts, but he would never not be a soldier. And with Theo gone, he would take her safety very seriously.

"It could be coincidence," Oren agrees. "Not that it matters. Theo is gone."

"Maybe she just wanted to talk to him about something," Sylvia suggests. "Just a conversation, and that's all. He could already be on his way here."

Harald and Oren exchange a look, but it is Harald who speaks. "He is not coming back here," he says. "Not for some time."

"How long?" Sylvia asks, trying not to imagine what kinds of things a Maker would do with their vampire progeny to pass the time. "When do you think she'll ... let him go?"

Oren bites his lip, expression damning, and Sylvia's gut tightens again. "I don't know."

"Well, when was the last time she showed up?" she prompts.

Oren glances at Harald, who meets Sylvia's gaze straight on. "It was the summer of 1803," he says, "and he didn't return until the winter of 1812."

Sylvia staggers, sitting down hard in the kitchen chair. "But ... that's nine years," she says weakly.

"She held all three of us for the entire 14th century," Harald adds. "And it has been some time since she saw him." He frowns, then says gently, "She will not release him, Sylvia. We should plan for his absence from here."

"Like hell," she snaps, staring in turn at the three men surrounding her, two of whom seem all too eager to abandon Theo to his fate. "Don't we have a demon-controlling dagger? I can just go get him."

Oren starts to object, and Harald opens his mouth to speak, but the demon beats them both, reaching across the table with a hand to touch Sylvia's arm. "The dagger is powerful, but the only reason we still have it is because no one else knows we have it." He pauses, releasing her, then admits, "Well, aside from Adam and the Greater Demon. If you use it to hunt Jolena and retrieve your vampire, others will sense it, and they will come looking."

"So, what then? I just sit back while Theo has been kidnapped?" She looks around the room again, meeting their eyes until both vampires look away. Pilkington does not shy away, but his face is careful. "You can't agree to just leave him there," she says to the demon. "I can't leave him trapped like that."

"Believe me," Pilkington says, "I do not envy the Muldavian's predicament, but there are more important things right now. Stealth and secrecy have been our allies until now. We shouldn't risk them until we absolutely have to."

Sylvia hears his words and knows that he is speaking sense, but she also knows that she will not leave Theo trapped by his Maker for a moment longer than it takes for her to find him. "Would you leave me trapped?" she asks. "To keep your precious dagger secret?"

"That's not the same thing," the demon snaps, "and you know it. You are the only one here who can wield the dagger. The rest of us are just pawns."

"I won't sit idle while Theo suffers," Sylvia declares. "I'll hunt him on my own if I have to. We have to find him."

Pilkington shakes his head, studying her face. "I knew you would say that." He turns his attention to the vampires. "Well then, the lady has spoken. How may we obey her commands this time?"

Sylvia stiffens at his words, realizing that she is treating them as servants, just like Jolena, but she doesn't change her mind. Theo would try to free her. She can only try to do the same for him. "Do you know where she took him?" she asks.

Oren shrugs. "They were still at his apartment when she ordered us to leave. They may still be there, but I doubt it. Jolena's taste runs a bit … higher than ours."

"She's a fancy lady?" Sylvia asks, recalling what Theo has said of his Maker in their few conversations about her. "So, she would stay somewhere nice." She pauses. "Do you think she has an apartment in the city?"

Harald is the one to speak. "Unlikely," he says. "Jolena isn't one to wait, to watch from afar and gather intel. She's spontaneous, acting in the moment. An apartment would require too much planning. I expect she only arrived in the city a day or so ago."

"Would she have human servants with her?" Sylvia asks.

Oren raises a brow, face thoughtful. He exchanges a glance with Harald, a silent conversation between old companions, then Oren speaks, "Mirrikh will be with her."

"Mirrikh?"

"Her companion. Bodyguard. A wolf shifter. She doesn't go anywhere without one of them nearby." He frowns, then adds, "She probably has two humans with her as well, probably a man and a woman. She doesn't like to be alone or without food. She'll also need a place to hide from the sun."

"So, a hotel ... maybe for the night, but then somewhere else to hide during the day. Somewhere fancy." She nods, an idea hitting her. "How modern is Jolena? Does she keep up with trends or is she stuck in the last century?"

Oren considers, sharing another of those looks with Harald. "She enjoys new technology. I imagine she probably knows how to drive and use the internet. She always was a woman ahead of her time."

"Yeah, she sounds great," Sylvia snaps. "I bet she's using an Airbnb."

"A rental house?" Oren asks.

"Yeah," Sylvia nods. "She wants something nice, but that she can hide from the sun in, so that's not likely a penthouse apartment. Then again, if she has human servants, I doubt she sleeps in a coffin underground somewhere like Theo."

Both Oren and Harald glance sharply at her at the last words, eyes darting to the demon in their midst. A vampire's resting place is a closely guarded secret. For all that she and Theo are close, Sylvia does not know where Theo's coffin rests, but she knows it must be underground somewhere. *But somewhere with Wi-Fi,* she realizes, recalling Theo's addiction to the zombie game on his phone.

"Do you think she has a phone? Will she need Wi-Fi? Or will she leave that to her humans?"

Oren nods, seeming to follow the line of her thoughts. "She likely has a phone," he says. "Okay... we're looking for somewhere rentable for a short term, somewhere she can be alone with Theo, but also close enough to civilization for Wi-Fi, somewhere she can also hide underground."

Harald nods in agreement. "It's a start," he agrees.

"So, we're doing this, right?" Sylvia prompts. "We can at least start looking for him."

Both vampires nod, and Sylvia turns to Pilkington. "What about you?" she asks.

"What about me?" the demon echoes.

"Will you help us?"

Pilkington pauses longer than Sylvia likes. "I will continue to help you by searching for information about the dagger," he says. "We still need to learn what it does and how it works."

"We know what it does," Sylvia snaps, regretting her tone almost immediately, but the fear in her gut rises again. "It lets me control creatures."

"*Demons*," Pilkington reminds her, "and *these* vampires." He nods at Oren and Harald. "That does not mean it will work on a vampire like Jolena."

"Why wouldn't it work? Aren't demons even stronger than vampires?"

"Some are, yes." Sylvia senses there is more beyond his words, but he doesn't add anything.

"Like you," Harald says, and Pilkington glares at him.

"Yes, like me, but think of your vampire. He's a thousand years old, right? Jolena must be twice that. We don't know that the dagger will work on an ancient vampire like her."

"But it works on Greater Demons," Sylvia argues. "Of course it will work on a vampire. It's all magic."

Pilkington shakes his head, and both vampires seem to lean in a fraction to listen to his next words. "Yes, it's all magic but very different kinds of magic," he explains. "Your vampire is strong, but only in comparison to some. If the dagger is designed to control demons, it may only work on lesser vampires by accident. It may not work on a shifter at all. We need more information before you just walk in there expecting the dagger to save you."

"Theo is a thousand years old," Sylvia reminds him. "That's hardly a lesser vampire."

Pilkington raises an eyebrow, then glances at the other vampires in the room. "Do you not talk of such things with the Muldavian?"

Sylvia's face heats at the question, and she stiffens, looking awkwardly away. It's true that she and Theo haven't had many conversations about his nature—they spend more time enjoying each other's company in other ways. The demon must sense her desire, for he scoffs, shaking his head.

"Your vampires are strong compared to humans, yes, but they are still babies compared to other creatures."

"A thousand years old is a baby?" she echoes, turning to see the vampires' reaction to this observation.

Oren rolls his eyes, but he nods at the demon. "Jolena was old when she made us, Sylvia. If the dagger is made for demons, it may not work on her at all. He's right."

"Don't forget Mirrikh," Harald adds.

"It has been some time since I tangled with a shifter," Pilkington admits. "I'm sure I can take him, but not if I have to make sure you're not doing something foolish." He gives Sylvia a pointed look.

"What?" she asks, raising her hands to her chest. "What did I do?"

"Besides trying to die with a body full of vampire blood?" he asks. "Nothing."

"Wait," she asks, the idea jumping into her mind. "If I died, would Theo be able to compel me like this? Control me?"

All three men look uncomfortable, but they all nod.

"I see," she says, the idea sending a shiver up her back. She hates knowing that she can compel them with the blade—thinking about being under such a compulsion herself is terrifying. "But it doesn't matter now. I'm not full of Theo's blood."

"Exactly," the demon says. "If you get hurt now, you'll just die, and I don't want to face the Muldavian in a decade and tell him about it."

"I'm not going to die," she insists. "But I'm not going to sit here either." She sighs and bites her lip, running a hand through her hair. She knows that even for all the danger she hasn't changed her mind. "We have to find him." She turns to Pilkington. "I'll keep researching with you, but we're also going to start looking for Theo, and if we find him before you learn anything..." Sylvia lets the words trail off, her meaning clear.

Everyone is silent for a long moment, but it is the demon who speaks. "He is a vampire. His Maker will not damage him."

"Won't she?" Sylvia whirls on him, her anger finding a convenient target. "And how dare you talk about being damaged? You've been held captive before," she snaps. "I'm pretty sure that left a mark on even someone like you."

Pilkington blanches, and he looks at her, eyes hurt at her harsh words. He had mentioned captivity to her during one of their many conversations, but she can see that he didn't expect her to throw out his secret in front of the others. "I'm sorry," she says quickly. "I shouldn't have said that." She sits down, slumping onto the table with her head in her hands. "I'm just worried about him."

"I know," Pilkington murmurs, a gentle hand rubbing her shoulder, but she doesn't miss his quick glance at the vampires in the room. For all that they are working together to solve the mystery of the dagger, the demon doesn't trust the vampires, and without Theo to keep his friends invested, Sylvia wonders how much they trust the demon. They hadn't been there when Sylvia had nearly died, hadn't seen the demon keep her alive long enough for Theo to arrive, and while he has told them what happened, centuries of distrusting demons has not made them eager to embrace their new companion.

Harald looks out the window, and for a moment, Sylvia catches a glimpse of something in the glass pane, a reflection there and gone. The vampire turns to look at her, seeming to sense the direction of her suspicions, and he steps away from the glass, standing next to Oren. "We will look for Theo," he says, "but if things go badly, we need a backup plan. What happens if this place is attacked?"

Pilkington sighs. "We've talked about this. If something happens during the day, I will keep her safe." He pauses, then adds, "And the dagger."

"Yes, but where will we find you the next night? We need another base."

Sylvia nods. "How about Viking Times?" she suggests. "We can hide backstage so no one sees us." Oren looks surprised, so Sylvia asks, "What? Too obvious?"

He nods. "Actually, no. It's a good idea. No one would think we'd be so foolish. And you can come in the back door, so no one on the street will see you."

"Good," Sylvia says. "It's a plan." And though part of her screams at the idea of inaction, at the thought of sitting in her apartment while Theo has been captured, she calms herself with a deep breath before looking at Pilkington. They still have a mystery to solve. "Are we still up for reading more books tonight?"

The demon nods, getting to his feet and moving to the small space in front of the refrigerator. His hands glow blue, the light of his magic lighting up the long sleeves of his Henley as he reaches into the air and returns holding a stack of ancient books. He puts them on the small table, then reaches into the air to retrieve another pile. Sylvia looks at the vampires, neither ever eager to help during this part.

"We'll start looking," Oren says, standing up and moving to the window. "I'll be in touch." He taps the pocket of his jeans and the phone he carries. Harald says nothing as they climb through the window to her fire escape, but he gives the demon a long look before he follows Oren.

"Thank you," Sylvia tells them, watching until both vampires have jumped off the edge: Oren into the sky to pursue Theo that way and Harald to hunt the streets below. She closes the window, turning to face the demon at her kitchen table.

Normally, she and Theo pore through the books with Pilkington, she and her vampire sprawled on the bed while the demon occupies the table. She leans against the window for a moment, closing her eyes and trying to calm her speeding heart.

Theo is safe, she reminds herself. *He may be captive, but he's alive, and Jolena may be mean to him, but she won't actually hurt him. Not really.* She tries to ignore the memory of Theo's voice as he hinted at what his Maker enjoyed doing to him. An image forms in her mind, her vampire entwined with a dark-haired goddess, and something in her chest breaks a little. *He can't help it,* she tells herself. *She's his Maker. He can no more resist her than you can stop gravity making you fall off a building.*

At least you know he won't enjoy it.

He's a vampire, an awful voice whispers. *If there's blood involved, you know he'll enjoy it.*

Stop, she tells herself, forcing her eyes open. *There's nothing you can do about it right now. Focus on what you can do.* She looks up to see Pilkington studying her carefully, a finger to his chin.

"I feel like tonight is going to need more than just tea," he comments, though he stands and fills the kettle from the sink, preparing to boil the water. "Say the word, and I'll add the required lubricant." He reaches into the air, pulling out an amber-colored liquor bottle and setting it on the counter with a clink.

"Maybe later," she tells him, settling herself at the table and sliding the top book over to her side. "I'll start with tea for now."

As the demon readies their mugs, Sylvia can't help but wonder what Theo is drinking at that moment.

She knows it isn't tea.

An hour before dawn, the vampires return empty-handed with solemn faces, Oren scowling while Harald continues to glance out the window, seeming unable to keep himself focused on the moment. Sylvia wants to ask the quiet man what has him so distracted, but the impulse passes as quickly as it comes.

He's worried about Theo. We all are.

She closes the book she has been reading. *St. Alloucious's Treatise on Arcane Artifacts* is filled with interesting descriptions of magical items, but it is a little dated. Sylvia wonders if someone has created an updated version—something a little easier to get through for a modern reader—with an index and images. *Someone should write a guidebook for all this,* she thinks. *Just a quick overview to give a modern reader the gist.*

Sighing, she rubs her eyes. Despite her research, she has found nothing like the dagger she now possesses. She has a rough sketch of the artifact on the table for reference, the swirls on the blade outlined in faint pencil since they only appear when she holds it—something she tries to avoid at all costs. She wouldn't mind one of the magic wands the saint describes instead—a swish and flick of her wrist, and Theo would be back in her apartment.

"Nothing?" she says, though she already knows the answer.

The vampires shake their heads.

"So now what?" Her question hangs in the air as the demon and vampires exchange long looks. Without Theo to connect them, their fragile alliance is teetering.

Surprisingly, Harald is the one to speak. "We keep looking." Sylvia nods, but Harald isn't finished. "In the meantime, you need protection."

Sylvia looks behind her at the demon before realizing that Harald is speaking to her. "Me? Why?"

Both vampires stare at her, and she turns away from them to see the demon is also watching her with an exasperated expression. "Because I have a magic dagger that everyone wants," she says slowly, rubbing her temples and trying to clear the fog from her brain. "Got it." She turns back to the vampires with a shrug. "Well, I've been fine the last months without you guys during the day. No one bothers me. Granted, I don't go anywhere…" She sighs, shaking her head. She recalls the argument with Theo right after she acquired the dagger—her mentioning that she needed to get another job and him insisting that he pay her expenses for the time being. She had given in, after a few well-timed kisses and a look from those big pleading eyes, but it was the idea that all of this was temporary that had caused her to agree. Now, it looks like temporary is going to last a bit longer.

"Things have to change now," Oren says. "Jolena is here—and she may know about the dagger. That means others may know—creatures who can strike during the day." He looks over at Pilkington, who has not said anything yet. "You've been here most nights. Can you guard her during the day as well?"

"I don't need someone guarding me!" Sylvia snaps before the demon can reply. "You're just drawing attention that way."

"I can," Pilkington agrees with a long judgmental look at Sylvia, "but there are times when I cannot be here. I have other obligations to attend." She knows he must be thinking of their time underground, when she had nearly bled to death in his arms, and she wishes she wasn't always the weak link, the most fragile one in the room.

"Tell me about it," Sylvia moans, falling back into her kitchen chair. "My life has revolved around this stupid dagger since I got it."

"Perhaps one of you could stay here during the day," Pilkington ventures.

"You know better," Oren replies, and the two men hold a long silent staring contest—vampire and demon sizing the other up. "Besides, we are not mere guard dogs to be ordered about."

"I wouldn't order—" Sylvia begins, then stops herself, thinking of the dagger's ability to command both vampires and demons.

But Pilkington snaps his fingers, a delighted smile crossing his face. "Excellent idea!" Sylvia and the vampires watch him as he moves over to the empty space before her refrigerator, reaches out his hand into another dimension, and pulls it back out—along with a very large black dog. "Meet Tengo," he says, gesturing at the animal. He addresses the creature, and Sylvia senses something silky in his voice, a command she hasn't heard him use before. "Guard her," he instructs, "and leave the baby vampires alone."

"Baby vampires?!" Oren exclaims.

"Fine," the demon sighs. "Protect the young vampires and keep them all safe."

Sylvia stares at the dog, which seems both frightening and adorable all at once. Her instincts war with her common sense. She knows better than to pet a strange dog, let alone one conjured by a demon to protect her, but her instincts insist that cuddling this creature will be the best part of her days. "Tengo?" she echoes. "Bingo was taken?"

Harald takes a slow measured step away from the dog, moving closer to the window. Oren hasn't moved, still offended. Sylvia holds out her hand, and Tengo trots over to her, body language exuding happiness. His head hovers at her mid-thigh. He sniffs her palm, licks her hand, then pushes his considerable head at her, the universal dog sign for "Pet me."

"I didn't know you had a dog," she tells Pilkington, scratching Tengo behind his ears and around his neck. The dog sits at her feet, resting his head on her lap.

The demon shrugs. "I have a lot of things," he says simply.

"Is he a regular dog?" she asks, then shakes her head. "Never mind. Obviously not. But does he eat and have to take walks and stuff? I didn't put down a pet deposit for the apartment."

Pilkington shakes his head. "He is a dog in appearance only. He can take care of himself—and you. You needn't trouble yourself over him."

"Does he understand me?" she asks, looking down at the deep red eyes looking up at her adoringly. A pink tongue lolls out to lick his lips before tucking back inside behind huge teeth.

"He is clever," the demon replies. "A loyal companion." Tengo lifts his head to look over the table at the demon, huffs, and returns to her lap.

"Let me guess," Oren comments. "He made a deal with you, too?"

Pilkington raises an eyebrow at the vampire. "Of course," he says. "Everyone deals with me."

CHAPTER 2

Oren

OREN HAS BEEN STANDING ON THE ROOFTOP FOR THIRTEEN minutes when Harald finally arrives. His friend is flushed, normally smooth hair mussed, his mind clearly on something else as he climbs the ladder to the roof. Harald can slow his descent from high places, but he doesn't possess Oren and Theo's ability to fly. Harald's skills lie in other areas. The vampire doesn't speak when he reaches the rooftop, simply nodding at Oren, who tilts his head and narrows his eyes at his old friend.

"You decided you needed a haircut but changed your mind midway?" Oren asks, voice thick with sarcasm.

Harald reaches up to fix his hair, a slow wave of red creeping up from the collar of his shirt, but he still says nothing, glancing around to make sure they are alone.

"It's fine," Oren assures him. "Trust me. I've checked this entire place. Twice. You know, while I was waiting for you." He narrows his gaze at his old friend. "Did you suddenly forget how to tell time? Do you need a new watch?"

"I'm here now," Harald says, avoiding Oren's eyes.

"You know, this would be a lot easier if you'd just tell me what the hell is going on with you," Oren snaps, glaring at his old friend. "And don't you dare tell me it's nothing because you've been gone three times now, not where you said you'd be—and you're always where you say you will be, Harald. Lying is not in you."

"Only in you, is it?" Harald asks, turning those bright eyes his way, his quiet voice filled with menace.

"When have I lied?" Oren demands. At Harald's raised eyebrow, he adds, "To you?"

"Am I not allowed to have secrets?" Harald counters, the big man looking down to scan the street again, unable to break centuries of protective instincts.

"Secrets, yes," Oren agrees. "Lies, no." Harald says nothing, and Oren shakes his head in frustration. "I'll leave it for now," he promises, "but this conversation is not over." He turns back to the streets below, scanning the crowd milling between the clubs that populate this part of town. The sound of music drifts up to the rooftop, echoing from one of the bars below, but no one seems spooked or bothered.

There is no evidence of either a Greater Demon or their Maker, neither creature leaving a trail for them to follow. Theo has been gone for four weeks, and Oren doesn't have much hope of finding him, but that hasn't stopped them scouring every fancy hole in the city. Jolena could be long gone by now, Theo in tow, back to one of her many pleasure palaces around the world. Oren knows how small their chances are of finding him, but he keeps hoping for a break, if only to see a different expression on Sylvia's face when he sees her each evening. Theo's human is a strong woman, not unlike his Morena, but Oren knows she needs to focus on the bigger picture. Morena would never lose sight of her target, never let her love for him distract her from what needed to be done.

That's why you never saw her again and she died as a human.

The thought raises a possibility, and he gives Harald a sidelong glance. *Could Harald have found someone? Could that someone be why he hasn't been where he should be over the last few months?* It has only been a minor matter, and Oren would be thrilled to know his friend has found a companion, but with Theo gone, Harald's unreliability has become a liability, one that Oren cannot afford.

"Look, I need you right now," he says, voice strained. "I need to know I can rely on you. Between Theo being gone and the demon and the dagger..." He shakes his head. "I need to know that you will be here with me."

Harald gives him a long look. Someone who didn't know him might think he is slowly comprehending Oren's words, but Oren knows his friend, knows that Harald is considering his options, examining every detail with the precision and attention that has kept them all alive through the years. He waits a few moments, scanning the crowd below for any signs of alarm, sensing any magic in the wind. When Harald looks up, Oren turns his full attention to his friend. "Are you with me, Harald?" he asks, the same question they have always asked one another.

"I'm with you," Harald replies, dipping his chin. "I will be here when you need me."

"Good," Oren says, closing that line of discussion for the moment. "Now, any new ideas on how to find Theo?"

Harald shakes his head. "But I do have an idea about the demon."

Oren gestures. "Go on."

"Think about the demon Pilkington," Harald begins. Oren wants to stop him, to remind him that Pilkington is their ally, despite his demonic origins. He has just as much reason to destroy the dagger as they do. Oren isn't thrilled about cooperating with a demon at all, but he trusts Theo's judgement. Plus, without the demon, Theo and Sylvia would both be dead, and a Greater Demon would have a powerful artifact. Oren isn't sure why the demon didn't just take the dagger when it left, but Theo didn't address that—focusing on how he had found his human nearly dead in the arms of a different demon who had apparently kept her alive with his magic long enough for Theo's blood to rescue her.

Oren still doesn't know what to make of that. Demons aren't known for their healing magic, aren't known for healing anything, period, so Pilkington's ability and motivation are a mystery. Though, having seen the demon's face as he watched Sylvia sometimes, he has started to guess at motive.

Sylvia is a lovely woman: smart and funny, pretty if you're into blondes.

Another face swims into Oren's memory, a dark-skinned woman with hair black as night, and his fingers brush the silver chain around his neck, the metal burning as always, but he ignores the pain, connecting to Morena in the only way he can now.

What would she say? He thinks about it, considers their situation from her perspective. She would focus on the dagger, of course. It's the greater threat to the most people. Morena would insist that is the priority. *And she would be right,* he admits.

Much as he wants to find Theo or even the Greater Demon, he knows that finding out more about the dagger is critical. Research isn't his strength, though, and fighting a Greater Demon would be a great way to burn off his nervous energy—but he would likely die in the process. The Morena in his head says nothing, but he can picture her expression—judgy, disappointed, frustrated. *Just be patient*, she would say.

As for Theo, he knows that even if they do find his friend, Theo will not be himself, not while Jolena is still around. Last time, it had taken Theo years to recover from his time with her. And he was single then. Now, with Sylvia, Oren doesn't want to think about what Jolena is doing to his old friend. Oren had been subjected to Jolena's jealousy right after Morena died—and he'd been damn lucky that his Maker hadn't known about the human before she died, or it would have been much worse. Oren had used the reminder to get him through her attention. Unfortunately, Theo wouldn't have such comfort. And Jolena's hold on him is far greater than on either Oren or Harald.

Oren is not looking forward to the Theo he will get back from Jolena, even though he knows that, with time, his friend will return. Part of him wants to find him right away, to rescue him before the damage is done, but he knows better. Until Jolena willingly sets him free, Theo will be her creature. And Oren doesn't want Jolena anywhere near the dagger or demons.

Oren glances up, realizing that Harald has not said anything else, allowing Oren's mind to spin as it will. Harald sees that his attention has returned, and he continues, "Have you noticed a certain ... scent around him?"

Oren narrows his eyes, considering. He doesn't think Harald is suggesting the demon stinks, but he recalls his memories of those evenings at Sylvia's apartment. *Is there something about the demon that marks him as different?*

"Maybe?" he replies, details flooding his mind. He nods slowly, tasting the scent in his memory. "But it's connected to Sylvia somehow, so I just thought it was her apartment."

"Yes," Harald says, "and no. It's more than just location bleeding into him. Though, that is definitely part of it."

Oren purses his lips, conjuring his memory of Sylvia's scent. "She does have a hint of the same smell on her," he says, "though I'd need to see her outside of her apartment to tell for sure." He looks at his friend. "You think she smells like Pilkington?"

Harald nods, then looks down, scanning the crowd again before continuing his speculation. "Theo said he kept her alive at the circle. Perhaps he did so by joining them somehow, bonding her to him."

"And him to her?" Oren asks. "There is definitely a connection there, but the girl nearly died. It's normal to bond with the person who was there with her for that. It doesn't have to be demonic." He pauses. "Maybe it's just friendship."

"Maybe," Harald allows. "But think of the Greater Demon, the one that wounded her. What if there is some connection there as well?"

Oren considers the idea. It's not completely impossible—just highly unlikely—but Oren doesn't know enough about how demon magic works. *Not my skill set,* he reminds himself with a grin. *Just point me at the danger, and I will figure it out as I go.* "Do you think that's possible?" he asks. "Do demons leave a mark on their victims who survive?"

Harald nods. "Some can."

Oren decides to ignore how Harald knows that. "So, we could follow Sylvia's scent around the city to track the demon?"

Harald nods. "Perhaps. She hasn't left the apartment a lot lately, so her actual scent shouldn't muddy the trail."

"Should we talk to the demon first?" Oren asks. "Do you think he will tell us anything?"

Harald frowns. "Maybe." After a long pause, he nods. "Yes."

"Alright," Oren agrees, "but I'm going to let you do the talking since you suddenly know so much about demon bonds."

Harald ignores the comment, slipping off the roof and heading into the night.

CHAPTER 3

PILKINGTON

"**W**HERE HAVE YOU BEEN?" PILKINGTON ASKS, GLARING at Sylvia as she dumps an armload of grocery bags on the tiny counter. His tone is sharper than intended, and he schools his face into a calmer demeanor. He had only returned home to his realm for a few hours that morning, long enough to make sure nothing needed his immediate attention, and he hadn't expected Sylvia to leave her home while he was gone. He doesn't want her to feel like a prisoner in her apartment, but the idea of her wandering around makes his human stomach hurt in a way he doesn't want to think about. It is daytime, so she needn't fear vampires, but the Greater Demon could attack at any time. Tengo would protect her, but Pilkington doesn't think he could defeat a Greater Demon in his current form.

He spent twenty-six nerve-wracking minutes waiting on her fire escape, knowing that she was fine because he can always sense his arusha, but ready to fly into action the moment he sensed something wrong. She is fine, of course, his worries unnecessary, but the knowledge doesn't soothe him as it should.

This is why I didn't want an arusha, he reminds himself. *I have enough to worry about in my own life—and now all I do is think about her.* He studies Sylvia in her kitchen, her long blonde hair unbound and running over her shoulders and down her back, covering the black hooded sweatshirt she has on over her usual tank top. *All you did before was think about her,* he admits. *There is nothing new here.* She is wearing jeans today, her feet tucked into her battered black boots. He would get her new ones if she asked.

And so would the Muldavian. The thought makes him look away, and when he speaks, his tone is softer. "You shouldn't go out alone."

"You sound like my mother," she snaps, pulling a half gallon container of milk from the bag and moving to the refrigerator. "And I wasn't alone. Tengo was with me." She reaches down to give the large dog some scratches. Tengo leans into her hand for a moment, then gives the demon a pointed look before returning to his accustomed place before the front door, blocking it should someone try to force their way inside. "Well, he waited on the street when I went inside, but yeah, I wasn't alone." She pauses, turning back to her bags and pulling out a red box of dog treats. She opens it and tosses one to where Tengo guards the door. "Good boy," she coos. "Sweet Tengo."

The demon tries not to scoff at the notion of the hellhound being called sweet and eating dog treats, and some of his tension fades. When the Tengo regains his voice at the close of their arrangement, Pilkington is going to get an earful.

Sylvia returns to her bags, adding in a soft voice, "Were you waiting long? I had to go food shopping."

"Long enough." He releases a long sigh, recognizing the frustration in her tone and understanding how she may be feeling trapped in her own apartment these days. Still, it is a foolish risk for her to take given the circumstances. "You know I can provide whatever you require," the demon reminds her. "I want you to be content." He ignores the true meaning of his words, wondering if she senses his desire and dismissing the thought as quickly. His arusha is still pining over her captive vampire lover.

"I know," Sylvia says, continuing to put food away in the cabinet, "and so can the apps on my phone." She returns to the next bag for a carton of eggs and a small container of half and half. "Besides, your food tastes weird, especially the creamer. I wanted real food."

"My food is real food," Pilkington insists, slightly offended at the idea that he isn't adequately providing for her needs.

"Yeah, real interdimensional food," she quips, retrieving a few boxes of frozen food from the bottom of the final bag and shoving them into the mostly empty freezer. Pilkington wonders if the Muldavian has cooked for her, and she is compensating for his loss with processed food.

"It's real food," he repeats, sitting down in her accustomed place on the windowsill, his back to the closed window, his long human legs crossed at the ankle across his boots. Today, his Henley is pale grey matched with dark pants, the clothes conjured by his magic when he returned to this realm, but just as real as anything he could purchase here. He does possess an actual closet of human clothing on this plane, but sometimes he doesn't arrive near enough for that to be practical. His magic can make things real here, a power that should only work in his own realm—and doesn't—another unwelcome gift from his father.

He can feel Sylvia's eyes on him as he looks at his feet. Perhaps one day he will be comfortable enough in her apartment to remove his shoes, to settle in as the Muldavian had done when he was here. He doesn't look up to meet her gaze, not wanting to see that look on her face—the one where she remembers that he is the one here with her now and not her vampire lover.

"Where does it come from?" she asks quietly. He looks up to see she has finished putting everything away and is folding the cloth bags before she jams them into a kitchen drawer. She kicks her boots off with a swift motion, and they thump near the front door. Pilkington stares at her purple socks. "Your food. Is it real food from here, or is it from your home or what?" She moves to the refrigerator and pulls out a pitcher of iced tea, gesturing at him with it to ask if he wants some. Pilkington doesn't want to admit how much he loves that little gesture, the motion one between friends close enough to not need words for all things. He nods in acceptance, and she turns to pull down two glasses from the cabinet.

"It's real food from this realm," he replies, watching her pour the tea. "I just move it here from wher-ever it is."

Sylvia puts the pitcher away, then grabs his glass, taking the three steps across the small room to hand it to him. "So, what—like someone else's gallon of milk just vanishes from their fridge?"

Pilkington laughs. "Something like that, though I tend to take things from stores, somewhere they won't be missed." He takes a sip of the tea, savoring the taste as he does all flavors on the mortal plane. Food doesn't taste bad back home, but food on the mortal plane is exotic, like being on vacation. "Does it really taste different?" he asks.

Sylvia takes her own sip, considering. "Meh. Maybe it's because I know where it came from, so my brain insists it should taste weird." She gives him a small smile. "You know I appreciate everything you're doing for me, right? I don't mean to seem ungrateful."

"I do," he says, recalling the fight she had given the Muldavian when he offered to pay for her apartment just until they sorted out the business with the dagger and the Greater Demon. She had argued fiercely that she needed to take care of herself—and that meant getting another job—but the four of them had finally managed to convince her otherwise, eliciting an angry promise that she would not put herself in danger by going outside the apartment more than necessary until this was over. The Muldavian had done most of the persuading after the rest of them left, and Pilkington has an idea how he managed it. His arusha had been angry when she agreed—but satisfied.

She is neither now—only wistful on the edge of defeat.

"I'm glad you're here keeping me safe," she tells him, gesturing with the glass. "I know you must have other things to do instead of spending your nights and most days here. It's just..." Her words trail off as she leans back against the counter, forgotten glass held against her chest as she stares at nothing. He knows what, or rather who, she is thinking about, the desire for her lover spooling out until the demon can practically see the longing surrounding her like a cloud. He has seen humans like that before, many times, but seeing his arusha heartbroken is too much. Getting to his feet, he closes the distance between them in two steps, putting a comforting hand on her shoulder.

"What can I do?" he asks. "How can I make it easier?"

Her eyes come back from wherever she went in her head, and she looks down at his hand with a warm smile. "You're doing it," she assures him, and the taste of her desire shifts subtly from longing to something else. Pilkington recognizes it, but part of him refuses to believe it even now.

She likes having him near her.

Of course she does, he snaps at himself. *She's your arusha. She can't help it.*

"Where did you go?" she asks suddenly, looking up at him. "Earlier, you said you had things to look after. What did you mean?" She pauses, then concern darkens her expression. "Are you hunting the Greater Demon too?"

Pilkington shakes his head. "No. Not today anyway." He moves his hand away and steps back, taking a sip of tea to clear his mind of ridiculous ideas. "I went home."

"Home?" she echoes. "Like back in the demon realm?" He nods, and she cocks her head, curiosity sparking her eyes. "Can I ask about it?"

Pilkington shrugs, moving back across the apartment to sit on the chest at the foot of her bed a few feet away. "What would you like to know?"

"I know you have a ... house there, right? You said it was big. And I know it has a library. But what is that world like?"

Pilkington thinks of the colorful skies of his home realm, the variety of demonic buildings there, each one constructed according to the demon's taste. He has seen her sketches of the Muldavian, and he has a momentary flash of Sylvia in the large space at the back of his house, a canvas propped before her as she paints the sky of his world. Paint smears the sides of her white shirt. His shirt. He shakes his head to clear the image. "It's big," he tells the human, focusing on the world instead of his home in it, "bigger than your realm by far, with vast empty spaces."

"Are there not a lot of demons?" she asks. "Why is it so empty?"

Pilkington smirks, not wanting to get into the cesspool that is demonic culture. "Let's just say that demons prefer their space." He glances out the window at the city around them. "Not like here where everyone piles on top of one another."

"There aren't cities there?"

He scoffs. "None that any respectable demon would live in," he says, and Sylvia laughs.

"What?" he asks, not understanding the look on her face.

"I knew it," she tells him. "The clothes made it obvious, but now I know it."

"Know what?"

"You're a fancy demon," she says. "A rich guy."

"My estate is respectable," he defends, "but I'm not exactly a rich guy the way you're thinking. My world is not like this one."

"No?" Sylvia narrows her eyes. "Demons don't segregate by social class there? Let me guess—it's a power level thing. You're a powerful demon. I know that much. Are there hordes of lesser demons living in some small apartments like this one in your world?"

Pilkington sighs. "Your vampire has explained power levels then? Good." He is about to continue, but something in Sylvia's expression makes him pause. Something that he said has upset her, but he isn't sure what it is.

"Do those other demons come here then?" she whispers. "Escape that world for this one?"

"Some do," he says carefully, not sure where she is going with these questions. From her tone, he might think she was sympathetic to those lesser demons— but one of them had hunted her and two others nearly killed her vampire. She shouldn't have any sympathy for them at all.

"Are they ... like you? Or like the other demons?" At his cocked head and curious expression, she adds, "You look ... and act human. The other demons, like the ones hunting me and Theo—they were nothing like you. They were monsters."

"Demons *are* monsters," he reminds her. "Have you not been paying attention?"

"But you aren't a monster," she insists. "I know you're not ... human... but you're not like them. You're ... different."

Did you say that to your vampire too, arusha? Insist that he is different, not like the rest of the vampires who live for drinking blood?

Pilkington ignores the uncomfortable frisson of what must be jealousy that runs up his arms at the searching look on her face, the hopefulness in her words. He will not hurt her by speaking his thoughts. "In appearance, certainly," he admits. "Perhaps in some behaviors. But we are all subject to the same constraints, the same impulses. Most demons have not had my freedom to travel the realms and see what I have."

"Can they not move like you do—back and forth freely? Do they have to be summoned here? Are they always under a compulsion when they are here?"

The demon doesn't answer right away, knowing that he cannot tell her too much without breaking the rules of the geas that allows him to visit the mortal plane. The Marquis of the Realm, his patron Lord Forneus, has allowed him free reign to travel between worlds until he sorts out the mystery of the dagger—a process he hopes will take many more weeks. Pilkington hadn't been thrilled about telling the demon lord about the dagger's existence, but frequent trips back and forth without a reason would have raised questions in the end. It was better to come forward immediately, report the fallout from his investigation of Charlie Wagner, and request special permission to travel both worlds until he found some answers. Forneus agreed, but Pilkington knows the demon lord's patience will only last for so long. When he thinks of it, he will need answers—and Pilkington needs to have them ready. Forneus may favor him, but that can shift in an instant if Pilkington fails to give him what he wants.

And if he ever finds out I have an arusha on the mortal plane... Pilkington lets the thought trail off. Thinking of such things only allows fear to grow. He cannot control what the demon lord will do; thinking about it will change nothing.

Sylvia has been watching him, no doubt drawing her own conclusions from his silence, and sensing his reluctance, she asks another question. "How are you able to go home and then come back here again so easily? I know you were originally summoned and then freed when Charlie died," her voice doesn't stumble on the magician's name, and Pilkington swallows the pride he feels for his brave arusha, "so are you still here on that ... visa or spell or whatever?"

"No," he says, not wanting to lie to her. "I am here by permission to investigate the dagger."

"So, when this is over... when we figure this out and find that demon... will you go home again?"

He nods. "Of course." Her face falls. He doesn't realize the power of his words until he sees her sag against the counter, shoulders hunching as she bites her lip.

"Oh," she says, staring at the floor.

There is an awkward silence as neither says anything. Tengo lets out a soft huff, red eyes shifting to glare at the demon. Pilkington watches his arusha, trying to decipher the wash of conflicting desires he senses in her. "What is it?" he asks quietly. "I've upset you."

Sylvia says nothing at first, then takes a deep breath, puts the glass on the counter behind her, and stands up straight, meeting his eye. "Are we friends, Pilkington?"

The demon bites the inside of his cheek to keep the broad grin from crossing his lips, not wanting her to see how happy the question has made him. "Yes," he says immediately.

"What does that mean then? Being friends with a demon?" she pries.

He leans back, hands sinking into the soft mattress behind him. He knows what his arusha does on that bed, at least, was doing before her vampire was reclaimed by his Maker, and he sits up, not wanting to think about it, hands clasping on his lap as he draws his feet close to the base of the chest he sits on. His reluctance is strange, another aspect of his growing attraction, and he tries to ignore it along with everything else he feels. "It means I enjoy your company," he says boldly, taking the risk. "I like you."

"Do you like many humans?"

Pilkington laughs. "Some. It depends."

"On what kind of deal you've made with them?"

Ah, he thinks. *There it is.* "What is it you are asking me?"

"We've made no deal, no demonic bargain. You insist I don't owe you anything, though you did save my life, and you don't owe me anything. We are friends by choice, right? So, when all this is over, will I still see you, or will you go home and return to whatever your normal life is?"

Pilkington allows the smile to cross his face. If only she knew that his normal life involves checking up on her every time he visits the mortal realm. "I will always come see you," he promises. "Not because you owe me anything at all."

"Have you had human friends before? Like this? Without some kind of bargain?"

Pilkington shrugs, considering the question. He has not had an arusha before, so that answer is a resounding no, but he's known she was his for years now—ever since he first stared into those blue eyes under a wooden roller coaster when he inhabited a foolish teenage body. But has he had other human friends?

Do I have friends?

"I... I'm not sure," he replies honestly. "I know humans," he tells her, "but are they friends? Do they tolerate me for my powers, for what I can give them, or do they value me for myself?" He pauses. "I don't know."

"That sucks," she says quietly. "I guess I never thought about it that way." She pauses, then adds. "I like you for you," she tells him. "Just so you know. I don't want anything from you."

He chuckles. "Just my library," he says, but the joke falls flat between them.

Sylvia frowns, then crosses over to stand in front of him. She isn't tall, so her head isn't very far above him while he sits looking up at her. "I like hanging out with you," she says, reaching out to gently poke his chest. "You." She laughs, the motion moving her shoulders. "If we weren't always researching ancient daggers, I'd enjoy spending time with you doing something else."

"Like what?" he asks, not wanting to seem needy but unable to stop the question. "What would we do?"

"I haven't watched a movie in I don't know how long," she says, a small frown playing on her lips as she considers the options. "I'd drag you to see something. Or we could watch a series on my phone." She glances around the apartment. Sylvia doesn't own a television or a computer, so her only access to media is through her phone. "Hell, I'd sit down and play a board game with you. Cards. Whatever." She smiles, leaning down to put a hand on his shoulder. "I'd enjoy just sitting at the table drinking a pot of tea with you."

She smirks, recalling the night he'd procured the finest Japanese tea for their mugs. "Even regular old Lipton tea. I don't need fancy tea."

"What do you need?" he asks, the words a whisper. Her touch on his shoulder sends odd chills down his human body, and he knows he should stop this, that she is confessing her friendship for him, but his body refuses to obey him.

"I don't *need* anything," she replies, putting her left hand on his other shoulder, trapping his face between her arms. "I just want to spend time with you." She stares into his eyes for a long moment, willing him to understand her, and the demon is suddenly aware of something else creeping into her, the slow curl of desire across her skin, and her eyes skate to his shoulders where her hands rest. "Is that weird?"

"No," he breathes, very aware of the heat of her hands on his body.

Two emotions cross her face as she looks at him—fear followed quickly by guilt—and she stands abruptly, her hands leaving him as she steps back. She lets out a soft breath, then cocks her head. "Come on," she says suddenly, holding her hand out to him. "Come with me."

The demon obeys, standing up. "Where are we going?"

"We need to get out of here. Let's go see a movie."

CHAPTER 4

SYLVIA

SYLVIA AND HER DEMON WALK DOWN THE STREET, THE fading afternoon light bronzing her blonde hair golden. She pulls it back into a quick ponytail, glancing at Pilkington's hair, the color reminding her of another companion from years ago. The image of Phil flashes across her mind, his hair wet as they splashed in the ocean, and she pushes the memory away, for once, not wondering what happened to her old friend.

"So," she addresses the demon at her side, "what did you think?"

"Of the movie," he asks, raising an eyebrow, "or the friend date?"

Sylvia snorts, jostling him with her shoulder. "Both," she demands.

"The movie was acceptable, though foolish in some ways," he criticizes, taking her arm as they cross a busy intersection. His attention is focused on her, but he never stops looking around, ever aware of their surroundings as they head back to her apartment.

Sylvia narrows her eyes at him, trying not to notice the strength of the arm touching hers. "A critic, huh? What was foolish?"

"The star-crossed lovers could have been together at any moment," he says, stepping aside as she uses the key to open the door to her apartment building. Lately, her protectors have made sure the door is always shut and locked, despite the efforts of some neighborhood residents to leave it partially closed, the door appearing closed but the lock disengaged. Sylvia knows a simple lock will not help keep a determined creature out of the building, but she has learned that open doors are invitations to demons while locked doors imply an inhabited domicile. Neither demons nor vampires can enter an inhabited home without an invitation. Granted, someone else could easily open this door and allow creatures to enter, but every level of security helps. At least no one but Sylvia can invite a creature into her apartment—that space is solely hers.

"But if they got together right away," Sylvia says, speaking over her shoulder as she walks up the stairs in front of him, "what would the story be about?"

"Defeating the resurrected sorcerer who damned them in the previous life?" he suggests, stepping ahead of her as they reach the top of the stairs to make sure no one else occupies the hallway. When he sees they are alone, he gestures for her to go ahead and move to her apartment door. "Getting to know one another? Building their relationship into something more than love at first sight?"

Sylvia laughs. "I didn't peg you for a cynic," she says. "You don't believe in love at first sight?"

Pilkington gives her a long look before his lips twist into a handsome smile. "I believe in … friendship," he says as she opens her door. Sylvia tries to ignore the rush of pleasure washing over her at that smile.

"Flirt," she teases, flinging the word over her shoulder as they enter. She kicks off her shoes, flinging them against the wall next to the door, and hangs her purse on the hook next to the door. The wall around the peg has been repaired, the hook clearly remounted after being pulled free. She lets the demon close the door behind them, making her way to the stove to fill the kettle with water for their tea. "Hot or cold tea?" she asks, not looking at him.

"How can you drink more liquid right now?" he asks. "That soda was enormous."

She laughs again. "It's the movies," she tells him. "Soda and popcorn are required for the experience." She pauses, then asks, "You have been to the movies before, right?"

The demon nods, settling himself on the chest at the foot of her bed, his new normal spot when he isn't at the table. "I attended some of the earliest moving picture shows."

She pauses, setting the kettle on the burner and facing him. "But you've been back since then?"

"Oh yes," he tells her. "But never with a friend."

Sylvia smiles, happiness warming her chest, and she turns to light the burner, not wanting Pilkington to see her expression. She has gone to the movies with her friends so many times—especially with Miriam and Jeremy when they were growing up—but sitting in the dark with the demon has awakened something else in her—and she isn't sure how she feels about it yet.

Being with Pilkington feels right. Comfortable. Easy.

The way it should feel when I'm with a friend, she reminds herself. *It's just been so long since I've been around anyone except Theo. I've forgotten how to be around normal people—how to be normal around people.*

Pilkington is a demon. He isn't a normal person. Or is he? What does that even mean anymore?

She watches the burner catch, the flame whooshing, and she tries to calm the rising emotion in her chest. *It's nothing,* she assures herself. *Just the attraction of the normal life I left behind. That's all.*

And if part of her wanted to hold his hand while they sat in the dark, it is only because she misses Theo and needs someone to reassure her that things will work out.

"So," she says, turning around to face her friend, "more research?"

The demon sitting at Sylvia's table pours her more tea. They have graduated to the teapot this evening, giving up on single cups as the night wears on, and Sylvia is happy to sample the new box of loose leaves and mesh strainer. The black tea has enough caffeine to keep her going, and Pilkington has dressed it with a splash of milk and a smidge of sugar, just enough to keep the bitterness at bay. She takes a sip with a sigh.

The demon pauses in his reading, looking up at her, a small smile creasing the corner of his lips. "Good?" he asks.

"Yes," she nods, setting the mug down next to the huge book open in front of her. "I need something to perk me up," she admits. "This," she pauses, lifting the book to glance at the spine, "McGilvery person isn't exactly stimulating."

"What kind of reading would stimulate you?" Pilkington asks, and Sylvia tries to ignore the frisson that skids up her arms at the question. The demon has an uncanny way of saying innocent things in a way that makes her shiver. It doesn't help that his human face is pleasant to look at. She's been studying it the last few nights, detailing all the ways he is different from Theo.

His hair is shorter, framing his face, dark and smooth, perfectly in place, completely unlike Theo's wild red hair that curls and kinks when wet. A brief flash of Pilkington soaking wet invades her mind, and she quickly looks down at the book, intent on studying again.

I'm awful, she thinks. *Theo is being held captive, and I'm sitting here imagining other men naked.*

You're human, she reminds herself. *And he's handsome. A fool could see that. Appreciating Pilkington's good looks is like appreciating fine art, a classic painting.*

Yeah, of a fallen angel.

The idea sparks something in her memory, and she looks up at him. "Hey, did you fall?"

Pilkington looks around the small apartment, confusion on his face. "What?"

"You're a demon, right? Does that mean you were an angel, and you fell somehow? Is that a thing? Where do demons come from anyway?"

Pilkington chuckles, the sound transforming his face as the sound grows, and soon he is really laughing. "What do they teach these days? A fallen angel? Hardly."

"Where would they teach such things?" Sylvia asks. "Hogwarts? It's not like there's a class at the community college on supernatural creatures."

"Not at the human college," Pilkington agrees, taking a sip of his tea, "but you can still take History of the Species at the Lyceum."

Sylvia stares at him. "The Lyceum?" she echoes, trying to place the name. "You mean the language school?"

Pilkington smirks. "Is that what they're calling it these days?" He scoffs. "I suppose it fits. They do teach the old tongues there."

"Are you saying that the Lyceum teaches classes on this stuff? Magic and creatures and everything else?" She sits up straighter. "There's a freaking Brakebills in the city?"

The demon nods, taking a sip of his tea. "It doesn't have dorms or anything. They only offer theoretical classes. Though many creatures find tutors that way to hone their own skills. I thought your vampire would have told you this."

Sylvia ignores his last comment. "So why aren't we over there asking one of the professors about this dagger?" she asks instead, her mind spinning with new possibilities. Pilkington cocks his head, considering her question. "Do you know anyone there who might be able to help us?"

"Maybe," the demon replies. He reaches his hand out and through the worlds, pulling it back a moment later with a laptop. The sight still amazes Sylvia, who should be used to the demon's ability to pull objects from other places with ease. He closes the book in front of him, resting the laptop on top of the cover. He opens it, typing with a speed that surprises Sylvia again.

"Seriously?" she asks, scooting her chair around the table to see the screen. "Where did you learn to type so fast? Lots of things to write in your world? I always pictured you with a quill pen or something."

"We do use ink in my world, but I spend a lot of time in this one. Keyboards haven't changed in a century," the demon tells her. "I spent a lot of time on typewriters. Christopher required input on the key layout." At Sylvia's blank expression, he shakes his head again, fingers flying across the keys as he tries to find a Wi-Fi connection in her building. "What did you actually learn about in your schooling?" he muses.

"Not typewriters," she tells him. "Mostly algebra and European explorers, to be honest."

Pilkington smiles. "Also important subjects." Sylvia wonders if the demon has met famous historical people. Not for the first time, she wonders how old he is. Before she can ask, he adds, "Christopher Sholes invented the typewriter after a minor deal." He grins at her shocked expression. "Though he would come to regret the arrangement."

"Why?" Sylvia asks, suddenly wary of the demon beside her. "What did you demand in exchange for the idea? His firstborn child?"

"Please," Pilkington scoffs, and the tension between them evaporates. "I do not deal in children."

"I'm glad," Sylvia says, laughing as Pilkington correctly guesses the password to her neighbor's Wi-Fi. "Backstreet4eva?" she repeats. "How did you guess that?"

Pilkington shrugs, quickly navigating to the Lyceum's website. "Marcus bargained for front row tickets some years ago," he explains.

Sylvia blanches, the thought of her straightlaced neighbor singing along to the boy band an unexpected vision. She turns to the demon sitting beside her. "Do you make deals with people often?"

Pilkington meets her gaze, sensing the depth behind the seemingly offhand question. "I am a demon," he says simply. "Making deals is what I do."

"And what do you do when people can't deliver on their end of the deal?" Her face is open, waiting for his answer before rendering judgement.

"It depends," he replies, and she can feel the truth in his words.

"Have you ever..." Her voice trails off as she realizes that maybe these are questions she doesn't want to know the answers to.

"What is it you would like to know?" the demon asks, abandoning the keyboard and turning to face her.

Sylvia looks down, biting her lip as her mind races. She and Pilkington have grown close, their friendship immediate and comfortable. He has settled into her life with a surprising ease, much more easily than the vampires climbing through her window. With Oren and Harald, she had to establish ground rules, especially about barging in when she and Theo were alone.

The demon had required no such negotiation, always seeming to respect her boundaries without her having to say a thing. She looks up at him now, the comfortable nature of their relationship sinking in. She's not sure she wants to know the darker side of him, a side she had embraced when Theo confessed himself a vampire. But her relationship with the vampire has never been like this, not quiet companionship. Sparks and fireworks and wild pleasure, yes, but in quiet moments alone, Sylvia wonders what they will talk about in five years' time. Or ten.

Though, if it takes Jolena ten years to release him, perhaps we will have plenty to talk about then.

Pilkington is still watching her, patiently waiting for her tangled thoughts to sort themselves out.

"I don't know if I want to know," she says bluntly, voicing her thoughts. "I like you, and I want to keep liking you, and if you're anything like those other demons, I don't think I want to know." She looks at him, boldly meeting his dark gaze. "And I hate that I'm a coward."

The demon reaches out to take her hand gently, his skin warm against hers as he moves it slowly to his chest, pressing her hand over his heart. She is reminded of Theo's skin, so warm when he first arrived full of a stranger's blood and slowly cooling by morning. Not that her vampire is chill to the touch, but there is definitely something otherworldly about the vampire by the end of the night. Pilkington's skin is warm through the shirt he wears. She can feel the slow steady thump of his seemingly human heart. "Do you trust me?" the demon asks quietly.

Sylvia nods immediately. "I do. And I wonder if I'm a fool for it."

The demon nods in understanding, his fingers softly thumping over her hand in time with the heart she can feel in his chest. "You feel that?" he asks. When she nods again, he continues, "You know me. I have done terrible things, and I have done wonderful things, but I will always strive to deserve the trust you have in me."

Something warm and comforting fills Sylvia's chest. "I know you," she echoes, her voice soft in wonder. "You're so familiar and ... right. Why?" She stiffens, and Pilkington releases her hand. She tucks it close to her own chest, still feeling the echo of his heartbeat in her skin. "Why do I feel so close to you?" She frowns, recalling Theo's attempts to use his powers on her when they first met. "Is it real?" she asks. "Or is this part of your demonic powers?"

"It's real," the demon says softly, "and it's also my powers. They are part of me, so whatever you are feeling is partly because I'm a demon. I cannot not be myself, even in this body, and part of you will always respond to what I am."

"Who," she says clearly. "Not what. You are more than your demon self." She reaches out to him slowly, and his own hand moves to meet hers between their bodies, palms pressing flat against one another.

"We are all more than one part of ourselves," he says softly, lips curling into a smile as her palm touches his, and something inside Sylvia jumps in response. She gently pulls her fingers from his, hating how much she doesn't want to let go of him.

"Are you doing something to me?" she whispers. *Or am I doing this to myself?*

The demon's eyes are very dark when she looks into them, and she can sense the magic in him, the depths of his power, the creature lurking beneath the human form he wears. For an instant, she can see another shape lightly outlined over him, the hulking blue form with long hair and small horns, dark lines swirling across his bare chest, a slightly smaller version of the demon he was during their first encounter. She knows the demon can wear different forms, part of his magic, but this one seems real somehow. "Is that what you truly look like?" she asks, eyes wide as she tries to focus on the demonic shape hovering just out out of reach of her human senses.

Pilkington yanks his hand away from where the tips of her fingers still brush against his and scoots his chair a few feet back, hitting the refrigerator. The demonic outline vanishes, and he is human again, but Sylvia can't unsee the image. The air between them echoes with magical energy, and Tengo looks up from his spot near the door, a low growl humming in his chest as he looks at the demon.

"What the fuck, Pilkington?" Sylvia asks, annoyed now as frustrated desire coils in her gut. "What is going on?" She remembers asking Theo if he was doing something to her the night they met, and she doesn't want to think that her connection to Pilkington, her comfort in his presence, is because of some magical aura. She wants something in her life to be real, not magical, but staring at the demon at her kitchen table, she wonders why she thinks magic isn't real.

Why is my life always like something from a dream? A nightmare? She stares at the demon in her kitchen, his eyes wide, a hint of his teeth visible as he bites his lower lip. *He really is a handsome man,* she admits again.

Different from Theo in so many ways, and yet, I think I am as close to him in some ways as I am with my vampire.

My vampire, she thinks. *That's what he calls him.* She has noticed that Pilkington never calls Theo by name, only the vampire or the Muldavian.

He never uses my name either, she realizes with a sigh. As a demon, Pilkington has a healthy respect for names, not using them unless it is necessary. For him, names have power, and he doesn't like to wield such control—not over her. Or Theo. *Two sexy men in my life,* she thinks, a soft smile playing on her lips. *This is like a dream.*

Maybe everything before this was the dream, she considers. *I feel like my life didn't really start until I met Theo.*

Liar. Your life started the day you met Phil.

And stopped again the day he left, she replies, the voice in her head bitter. *And now Theo is gone as well. How long until Pilkington joins them and abandons me too?*

"I just..." she says, trying to quiet the competing voices in her head. "I just need to know if it's ... real," she finishes.

The demon stares at her for a long time, and the world shrinks to his form, then his face, and then his eyes. A flash of memory bursts into her mind. A face surrounded by a shock of dark hair and a soft voice. *"I am yours, arusha."* But instead of Phil saying the word that taunted her for years after he disappeared from her life, it's another face, an older face looking down at her.

Pilkington's face.

"Who are you?" she asks, feeling the power in her words, somehow knowing that the demon must answer her now if she allows him to. If she wants the answers.

"Who are you ... to me?" Pilkington opens his mouth to speak, his body tense but his eyes defeated.

Sylvia is vaguely aware of Tengo's low growl, and then a voice cuts through the moment like a sword.

"It's a bond, isn't it?"

Sylvia turns to the sound of the voice, seeing Harald standing just inside the window, the vampire having crept silently into the room while they were distracted. She glances behind him, looking for Oren, but the fair-haired vampire seems to be alone for the moment.

She looks from the vampire to the demon, Harald's words sinking in. "Bond? What bond?"

Pilkington looks distinctly uncomfortable, the moment ended, the demon getting up and moving to the counter, suddenly very interested in the few dishes in Sylvia's sink.

"Was it when you healed her?" Harald asks quietly. The demon stiffens, but he doesn't move to face them, instead turning on the water and reaching for the sponge.

"Harald, what are you talking about?" Sylvia asks. When her words are met with silence, she glares at the vampire, the only one whose face she can see. She doesn't want to think about the demon's face in her memory.

My mind is playing tricks on me, she assures herself. *My memory of that night is unreliable in so many ways. Trauma does that.* Her hand skates across the scar on her belly, and she rallies, focusing on Harald, the one who seems to have some answers.

"If you don't start talking right now, you won't like what I do next." Sylvia doesn't know if she would really use the dagger to get the answers she seeks, but in the moment, she needs one of the supernatural creatures in her apartment to give her something.

"Sometimes, demons form bonds with other creatures," Harald says slowly, not taking his eyes off the demon. "When they use their magic on a creature, it connects them." He pauses, then adds, "I understand it makes it easier to track them."

"What do you mean—it connects them? Track them? What—like for hunting?" Her head whips to the demon standing perfectly still before her sink. She can feel something pouring off him, powerful magic that she can drown in if she allows herself to soak it in. She takes a deep breath, steeling herself for a hard conversation. "Are we bonded?"

Pilkington's shoulders jerk at the force of her words, and he replies immediately, "Yes."

"What the actual fuck?" Sylvia takes another deep breath to calm down, counting slowly to three and then to ten. "Pilkington," she says quietly, using his name as she rarely does, "please tell me what this means."

The demon shuts off the water and turns around, wiping his hands on his pants, his face more serious than she has ever seen it, not even in her hazy memories of the time between when the Greater Demon left and Theo arrived, when she nearly died in his arms. "It means I always know where you are," he says quietly.

Sylvia nods. That doesn't seem terrible. Having a demon GPS could be useful given the way things have been going. If Charlie kidnapped her now, Pilkington would be able to find her right away. *And rescue me? Would he?* Looking at his solemn face, she knows he would. She knows he would do anything for her.

The knowledge is equally terrifying and exhilarating.

She is acutely aware of Harald in the room with them, and she thinks carefully about her next question. If she were alone with the demon, she knows what she would ask about—the way touching him sends hot shivers across her body—but she can't ask about that with the vampire in the room. She is very glad that Oren isn't there for this conversation. He would take one look at her and know exactly what she is thinking—and he would judge her for it.

And rightly so. *What are you doing thinking about bonds with a demon when Theo is being held captive by his Maker?* Sylvia rallies, trying to organize her thoughts, redirect them to safer questions.

"What else?" she prompts, her voice gentle now. "Is this like a demon possession type thing?" She thinks of movies featuring possessed people. "You ride me like a puppet?"

There is an awkward pause after her question, and Sylvia realizes how it sounded. "Not ride me," she backpedals. "I mean..."

"You are no one's puppet," Pilkington says. "You are your own self."

"My own self bonded to a demon," she snaps. *And not a vampire. Not Theo.* Frowning at both the demon and the vampire, she asks the first question that pops into her mind, "How long does this last?" When she drank Theo's blood, the effects lasted a week or so. This seems more permanent.

The demon looks down at his feet, but Harald's expression remains stony as he shrugs. "Demon bonds do not fade," he explains. "They are broken when the creature dies."

Sylvia does not miss his use of the word "creature" and not "human." *Not my death*, she thinks. *His.* "When the demon dies?" Sylvia asks. A shudder runs through her at the thought of Pilkington's death, and suddenly there is a warm doggy head beneath her hand, nuzzling against her leg, offering comfort. She pets Tengo without thought, soaking in the dog's reassuring affection as she struggles to understand.

"Demons don't die," Harald answers, watching the way she pets the dog with interest. "They simply return to their plane of existence."

She turns her head to stare at Pilkington, the idea that he cannot die reassuring. The image of Theo's face, slack-jawed and empty as he lay bleeding on her bed fills her mind, and she shakes her head. The memory fades, replaced by Pilkington's face in the same condition, and her heart begins to pound. She cannot help the demon with her blood. She wouldn't be able to save him if he is hurt.

"You can't die?" she asks him, needing to hear the words to calm herself. "Like … ever?"

"Of course I can die," he snaps. "Just not here."

The roiling in her gut loosens a fraction, then tightens again as she realizes what he means. "So, it lasts until I die then?"

The demon nods, a quick jerk of his chin. "Your death will free you from the bond."

"But not you," she says slowly. "You will never be free until I am gone—or even after that?" She tries to understand what his words mean. She has learned a great deal about demons from their months studying the books, but this is something she hasn't read about yet. *Has he somehow tied himself to me for the rest of his existence?* "Pilkington," she whispers, "what have you done?"

The demon looks at the vampire, clearly debating his next words, then says quickly, "Forgive me. It was not intentional."

Sylvia follows his glance to Harald, and she understands the meaning. They will talk about this—but not here—not in front of the vampire.

She frowns, trying to put everything together from what she's learned of demonic powers from her research on the dagger to push the conversation in another direction. She focuses on the practical aspects. "So, you know where I am," Sylvia ponders, "but what do I get from this? Do I get some of your powers?" She knows a traditional demon bond involves an exchange of some kind, a bargain.

The demon jerks his head. "Perhaps."

Heat floods her chest at the implications of his word. "But when I said we had no bargain between us, no deal, nothing owed or exchanged but friendship, you agreed with me. You said yes!" Her voice reveals her hurt over the betrayal of her trust.

"There is no bargain between us!" the demon insists, his own voice raw with emotion. "Our bond is not like that!"

"Then what is it like?"

"It's ... complicated."

"Simplify it," she grits through her teeth.

Pilkington glances at Harald, clearly not wanting to have this conversation in front of the vampire. "We are connected," he says finally, clearly deciding how to answer her questions. "And our connection offers you certain protections from other creatures."

"Like what?" She glances down at Tengo. "Like your demon dog?"

The demon nods. "Tengo is a bonus," he says. "He's nothing to do with this." He glances at Harald, clearly grasping for another topic. "You may be less affected by his abilities than a regular human," he says.

Sylvia frowns. "What, like Theo when he tries to whammy me?" Both creatures stare at her, and she raises her shoulders innocently. She doesn't want to explain how Theo had tried to use his powers on her when they met and failed—until she had agreed to let him in her mind. "Do it now," she tells Harald. "Try to get into my mind and calm me or whatever."

Harald glances at the demon for a second before focusing his gaze on Sylvia. She can feel the push of his power, and it is strong, but it is an alien thing, nothing like Theo's sultry caress against her mind. Harald's intrusion is cold, clinical, and Sylvia easily pushes the magic away. As his power retreats, she sees a flash of a face in his mind: a shock of white hair around an elfin face. She can sense his need for the woman, a connection that makes his attempt to pursue Sylvia merely perfunctory. He doesn't want to invade her mind because he is bound to another. Using his power to subdue Sylvia feels like a betrayal.

"Wow," she breathes. "Who is that?"

Harald jerks in shock, stepping away from her even though several feet separate them. Sylvia glances at the demon still standing at her counter, knowing that she would not want anyone else to listen to their conversations, to know their secrets.

"Nevermind," she tells Harald. "It's none of my business." She takes a deep breath to settle herself.

Realizing that Pilkington has no idea what has happened, she looks at the demon. "Oh, it didn't work," she tells him, "but it could be because he didn't want it to." The image of Theo floods her mind along with a wash of guilt. Before the demon can ask questions, Sylvia continues, "Does this mean I can resist anything Jolena would do?"

Harald frowns, considering for a long moment. He nods at Sylvia, a subtle acknowledgement of her respect for his personal life. "Maybe," he replies. "Maybe not. Jolena is stronger than I am." He looks to the demon. "Perhaps she is stronger than your bond."

"Doubtful," the demon says quickly. "Even an ancient vampire is no match for my powers." The demon is boasting, and Sylvia sees the moment he regrets his words. *If he's so strong, then what have we been waiting for all this time?* She has so many questions for him the moment Harald is gone.

I will be alone with him, she thinks, the idea both thrilling and terrifying. *Alone with a demon I'm bonded to.* Thoughts of bonds make her think of Theo again.

"So, we can go after Theo," she says suddenly, clinging to the plan that had been her focus until she started talking about friendship with the demon. "I may be immune to her powers, and if not, you can definitely take her."

"Possible immunity to her vampire powers," Pilkington says, shaking his head. "Not her physical strengths or her companions. I have not lived as long as I have by running off to face ancient vampires whose abilities are unknown to me," Pilkington complains.

"But you just said—"

"I know what I said," he snaps. "That doesn't make it any less foolish to pursue your vampire."

His refusal annoys Sylvia, and she allows some of her fear to shift to anger. She wonders if the demon has been procrastinating, biding his time with her when he could have freed Theo at any moment.

You weren't complaining, a small voice accuses, and the guilt adds to her fury. She glares at the demon. "You weren't going to tell me about this," Sylvia accuses, raising her eyebrow at him. Her voice is cool as the enormity of their connection sinks in. "You would never have told me if you didn't have to."

"Are you happy to know it?" Pilkington replies, his voice sharp with brutal honesty. "To know that you are connected to me for the rest of your life?" His words send a sharp thrill through Sylvia's chest, and she pauses to think about her response.

Being connected to a demon should be terrifying, but she only feels ... relieved. Knowing that Pilkington will be part of her life for as long as she lives—forever as far as she will know it—is satisfying in a way she can't explain. She knows what her therapist would say: *Of course you are happy about it. Important people in your life keep leaving you behind. It's reassuring to have a strong supporter who will never go. Who* can't *go.*

Her anger fades, replaced by something comforting and far too intimate. Sylvia tries to run from it.

"Are you able to affect my emotions?" she asks suddenly. "Can you make me feel things?"

Pilkington's face twists in disgust, but his voice is steady. "I could. But I will not. You have my word on that."

"So, you could control me the way a Maker controls a vampire?" she asks, the idea frightening but still seeming hypothetical. She doesn't know why, but she believes the demon's promise. Deep inside, she knows he would never abuse her that way. "If you wanted."

"Probably," Pilkington admits. "But I do not want to know for sure, and I will never try." He looks at the vampire when he speaks next. "Losing one's free will is the worst experience, and believe me, I've experienced a great many things."

"Pilkington," Sylvia asks, studying the demon's middle-aged face, "how old are you?"

"Old enough to know better," he sighs, then a rueful smile crosses his lips as he turns to the vampire. "How did you stumble on the bond, Harald?"

Harald sniffs for a moment. "The scent. She smells like you, and you like her." He glances at the window, and Sylvia catches the brief hint of a reflection in the glass again. She is about to ask him to stand still, but he continues, "I wondered if the other demon might also have bonded with her. Theo said it used magic on her too."

Sylvia freezes, remembering the cold spiraling through her as the Greater Demon leaned over her, its voice making her teeth ache and her head throb. Her hand slides up to curl in the center of her chest where the echo of that cold remains. Pilkington considers the point, scanning Sylvia with a careful eye, no doubt recalling what he had seen that day. "The Greater Demon healed her spine," he comments, "but it left no trace of itself with her."

"Wait, what?" Sylvia sputters, hand flattening against her chest. She imagines her spine, attaching her faint memories of that time to specific points on her body.

"Healed?" Harald echoes. "I was not aware that demons had any healing abilities at all. I thought yours an outlier."

"It's not healing the way you think of it," Pilkington explains. "When Sylvia was hurt, I simply held her together until the Muldavian arrived. His blood healed her."

"But my spine?" Sylvia asks weakly, her body curling over her hand protectively, shoulders hunching in the seat. Tengo whines softly, demanding her attention, and she returns to the room again, hand abandoning her chest to pet the dog.

"You were damaged by the Greater Demon," Pilkington explains. "When you freed it, you could have collected a boon, a gift of equal value to its life and freedom. But you were dying, so it undid the worst of the damage in exchange, giving you life and freedom— for a few moments anyway." He frowns. "I'm sure he thought you would die soon enough, or he would not have left you there." Sylvia pauses, taking that in. She shudders, the idea of making a bargain with that creature for anything, even her life, a repulsive idea.

Yet you don't mind a bond with Pilkington? He too is a demon. She rallies, trying to follow the logic of his words. "How can you just undo damage like that? What is this—time travel?" Sylvia asks, images of Superman flying backward around the planet filling her mind.

"Perhaps that's one way to explain it. It's part of demon magic, an ability to reset a creature in certain ways to the way we initially found them." He pauses, then adds, "It is a common practice to restore those possessed after the demon departs."

"Can you bring someone back from the dead?" Sylvia asks, fascinated. Questions fill her mind, the possibilities a welcome distraction from the revelations of the night.

Pilkington frowns, an eyebrow raised. "I don't know," he admits after a moment. "I've never tried. I've heard stories, of course, but I've never seen it happen. I have seen damaged creatures returned to a previous state of being, though never after they had died."

"So, when you die here," Sylvia says, recalling what Harald said earlier, "you go back to your home realm?" The idea of the demon's death makes the hairs rise on her arms, and she wraps her arms around herself to hide her reaction.

The demon nods, already knowing what she will ask next. He waits for her to say it though.

"Then, when I die..." she begins.

"You leave your body and go elsewhere," the demon says quickly, clearly not wanting to continue the discussion. Perhaps the thought of her death affects him the way the idea of his upsets her.

It must be the bond. She wonders about the limits of their connection. "Wait, could I go to your realm? After I die?" she pushes.

The demon cocks his head, considering. "Probably. There are many spirits in my world." He pauses, then adds, "Though I'm not sure why you would want to spend eternity there."

"Maybe I want to see this fabulous library firsthand." Sylvia tries a small smile to lighten the mood.

"You don't have to die for that." The demon laughs, the tension in the room broken for the moment. "I'll show you sometime when we aren't chasing rogue demons and captive vampires."

"And researching artifacts," she adds, smiling fully at him now, feeling that connection again. She catches the look on Harald's face as he studies both of them, and guilt pricks at her conscience. She steels her spine, pushing the feeling away.

Why should I feel guilty? For being bonded to a demon? For having a friend? I don't even want to think about what Theo is doing right now.

Against his will.

Staring at the demon in her kitchen and then over to the quiet vampire near her fire escape, Sylvia wonders if her will is strong enough to do the right thing when the time comes.

CHAPTER 5

HARALD

HARALD FAIRHAIR HAS ALWAYS KNOWN HE ISN'T THE smartest man, but what he lacks in intelligence, he makes up for in cunning. Because he is easily dismissed as a mindless buffoon with big muscles and no brain, Harald is often overlooked—a fact which makes it much easier for him to observe—and Harald is very good at seeing things, details that others miss.

So, when he sensed the witch following him that first night so many months ago, he pretended not to notice, waiting for the right time to confront her. It was easy enough. After that first night when he seemed not to notice her presence, she grew careless—as he knew she would—letting herself be seen in quick glimpses.

Harald has never been a particularly romantic man, preferring to take his pleasure when the mood struck and opportunity arose, but spending the last few centuries with Oren and Theo has made it very easy for him to disappear into the background. Women notice Theo's red hair, Oren's quick wit. They may ogle Harald's muscles, but they never stop to talk to him, not with Oren nearby. And that has been fine with Harald.

Until now.

The first time he saw the white-blonde hair of the witch following him, he knew he was lost. He had been sensing it for a while before then—feeling the connection burning between them—but he didn't completely fall for Suren Tallardy until that first time he cornered her before dawn, surprising her on her way back to the apartment she was renting.

"Oh," she said, a hand raised to her chest in shock at his appearance, then quickly relaxing to fall to her side. "It's you. Finally." She sniffed, running a hand through her short hair and tugging it tight at the base of her neck—a nervous habit he now recognized—and raised a pale eyebrow at him. "So, we gonna talk about this mate bond or what?"

By the end of that question, Harald was a believer in bonds. By the end of the conversation, he was a believer in much more.

His faith in Ula, as she preferred to be known right now, is unshakeable, as certain as the stars above. Harald hadn't known such certainty could ever exist in the world, but here he is, consorting with a witch— and a Tallardy witch, no less, a family known for deceit and depravity. But the power of the bond is undeniable, just as the old stories have said. He remembers Oren teasing him about never falling in love back when Theo first met Sylvia. He had remained silent then, not yet willing to share his newfound joy with his long-time brothers.

But now he has waited far too long—and Ula's secret presence feels like betrayal. Harald can tell by the look on Oren's face as his friend stares from Ula's blank expression back to Harald's attempt at encouragement.

"I'm sorry," Oren says, "but I thought we were here to talk about demon bonds—and now you're telling me this witch is your mate."

Harald nods, taking Ula's hand in his and stepping slightly in front of her. He knows that she will move again, determined to face Oren's reaction without using Harald for a shield. Ula is a powerful witch, gifted with great abilities, but most of her magic requires preparation. She is not a fighter—and she will not win a fair fight with a vampire. "She is my mate," he says again. "Oren, meet Ula."

Oren stares for another few seconds, then shakes his head, bringing a hand to the bridge of his nose with an explosive sigh. He sniffs, then looks up, exasperated. "Lovely to meet you, Ula. Do you mind giving me a moment alone with Harald here? I think my friend may have gotten into some bad blood."

Harald does not let go of Ula's hand, though she gives him a questioning look, following his lead in dealing with his friend. "I am here, Oren, and she is with me," Harald declares. "You can speak freely."

Oren bites his lip, closes his eyes, then opens them and lets his frustration loose. "You know what? Fine." He gives Ula an apologetic look before continuing, "Ula, forgive me, but this isn't about you." He returns his focus to Harald, who stands, ready to take his friend's judgement, whatever it may be. "Dude," he says carefully, "you have lost your goddamn mind—and now is not the time for this shit!" He runs both hands through his hair, trying to calm down. "There is too much going on right now for you to suddenly find a mate! Odin's tits, Harald! You have no idea who the hell she is!"

"I know exactly who she is," Harald replies calmly.

Oren narrows his eyes at Ula, studying her with his vampiric senses. "A witch," he observes. "How do you know she hasn't just spelled you?"

"Because I know," Harald replies in that same calm tone. He knows that Oren may take a little time to come around, but in the end, he will support Harald's claim.

Oren snorts, throwing his hands up in disbelief. "I give up!" He frowns, the expression out of place on his normally cheerful face. "Everyone around me has lost their goddamn minds!"

Now, it is Harald's turn to frown. "Who else has lost their mind?" At Oren's face, Harald takes in a breath, something in his chest easing for the first time since Jolena strolled back into their lives and stole Theo away. "You found him?"

Oren nods. "She has him at the penthouse. She brought him back there. And he's just as crazy as you are."

"Why do you say that?"

"He told me to leave him alone, to pretend I didn't find him, like that's possible. I can't do that, not after looking at Sylvia's face each morning when I tell her we still didn't find him." Harald recalls Sylvia's face as she stared at the demon in her apartment, the human clearly trapped by conflicting emotions, but he doesn't contradict Oren.

"Is he ... well?" Harald asks, knowing that Oren will understand the question.

Oren nods again. "A few marks but nothing cata-strophic. He must be obeying because he was loose on the rooftop when I saw him. She would never let him walk free if she thought he might run."

Harald nods. "I see." Jolena is his Maker as well, but her hold on him has never been as strong as hers over Theo or even Oren. She had turned Harald because he was their friend, not because she wanted him. She has certainly abused him in his turn over the centuries, but in the end, Harald just isn't her type, and he knows it. Usually, staying quiet in her presence is enough to escape her attention. Harald is glad that he has some freedom from his Maker, but he hates that his freedom comes at the expense of his friends' well-being. Oren has never spoken of his time with Jolena, withdrawing into himself afterward.

But Theo. Theo was not the same... not for a long time. Luckily, as vampires, his friends could wait for him, but with a human lover, Theo doesn't have the luxury of time.

Harald glances at Ula, who gives him a reassuring smile, her presence a comfort. *Could I stay away from her?* He wonders if, set free on a rooftop, anything could hold him back from reaching Ula's side.

No. I would fight to my dying breath to return to her.

So, what is Theo doing? How is he not fighting every moment to return to Sylvia?

The answer arrives quietly, as most solutions do in Harald's mind.

Because she is not his mate.

The knowledge makes Harald a little sad. He wishes for his friend to know the happiness he has found, the satisfaction in finally connecting with the partner fate intended for him all this time. And Sylvia... she will be heartbroken, no doubt.

Though if Harald's suspicions about the bond with the demon are correct, she may not mourn for very long. Perhaps, Sylvia already understands some of what Harald now feels, except not for his friend Theo, though loyalty would keep her patiently waiting for the vampire's return.

"Seriously, dude," Oren tries again, looking over at Ula, "I didn't think you even believed in mate bonds."

"I didn't," Harald admits, "until I found her." He knows only one thing will convince Oren that the bond is real, so he releases Ula's hand and steps closer to the vampire. "Walk with me," he says, continuing to move slowly across the rooftop where they have met to stand on the edge. A huge glass skyscraper is across the street, a few lights still glowing in higher floors, but the glass across from them is dark. "I want to show you something," Harald says, then gestures to the building.

"I've seen the Times building before," Oren says dismissively. "The view from the roof is great. Humans love it. There's a restaurant up there."

"No," Harald says, and Oren stops talking to look at his friend. "Look." He points to the floor directly across from them, a sheet of dark reflective glass—where Harald can clearly see his own reflection standing alone on the rooftop. In the distance behind him, a smudge of white shows where Ula has lingered on the far side of the roof.

It takes Oren a moment to register what he is seeing, and when he does, his face does a weird cartoon bounce between where Harald stands next to him and the figure reflected in the glass across the street.

He moves his hands, and part of Harald's chest disappears, hidden behind the magic that keeps Oren from having a reflection.

"How?" Oren manages, for once at a loss for more words.

"I know," Harald says, then uses one of Oren's favorite phrases. "Pretty cool, no?" He grins, letting his happiness shine through for the first time since the night he met Ula. "I can finally shave properly."

"Jerk," Oren smacks his arm, but then his fingers reach for the silver necklace he still wears. Small tendrils of smoke wisp from his fingers as the material burns his skin, but he doesn't let go, no doubt thinking of the woman who gave it to him so long ago.

Gave him a necklace—but not a reflection.

"So, she's really..." His voice trails off.

Harald nods proudly. "Yep. My mate."

"But why here? Why now?"

Harald sighs. "That, you may not like so much. She's here because of the dagger."

Oren's head snaps back to his, magical mate bonds forgotten. "She's after the dagger?"

Harald nods. "When we're done with it, yes."

"But...?"

"It belongs to her family. They sent her to find it," he pauses, letting that sink in before he finishes, "but she isn't going to bring it to them."

"Why not?"

"She wants to destroy it," Harald explains. "It's too dangerous to just lock it up somewhere—someone will just steal it again. That's how it was let loose in the world in the first place. Creatures keep stealing it and end up unable to wield it, so it just shifts from hand to hand, wreaking havoc along the way."

Oren nods. "That I do believe. We should tell Sylvia … and the demon."

Harald nods in agreement. "But not yet," he suggests. "Let us go speak to Theo and see if we can reason with him." He pauses, wanting to make sure Oren understands. "But if he doesn't want to leave, we can't make him. And neither can she."

Oren blows out a heavy breath, then rolls his eyes. Finally, he looks at his friend, a grin crossing his face. "I have to hand it to you, man. You have the absolute worst timing, but I'm happy for you." He claps both hands on the outside of Harald's arms, an ancient gesture of good will. "Come on," he says, wrapping an arm around Harald's shoulders. "Introduce me to your lady properly. Then we'll go talk some sense into our friend."

CHAPTER 6

PILKINGTON

AFTER THE VAMPIRE LEAVES, SYLVIA IS SILENT FOR A LONG moment, stealing quick glances at him but unable to meet his gaze.

"So," he says finally, to break the tension. He has finished washing the few dishes, dried them, and returned them to their places in the cabinet, and he turns around to face his arusha.

"So," she echoes, then sighs, her shoulders lifting with her breath. Her fingers twist the ties escaping from the neck of the hoodie she wears, and she bites her lip nervously. She takes another long breath, gathering her nerve, and then she sits up straight. "I have questions."

"I imagine you do," he says, moving away from her to sit on the chest, giving her space.

"Do you have questions?" she asks, raising an eyebrow.

Pilkington frowns. "About this? Or in general?"

"Either," she says, clearly stalling. "You start then."

Pilkington nods, willing to take the first few steps. His arusha is uncertain, bordering on afraid, and he doesn't like knowing he has unsettled her so. He wanted her to learn about the bond eventually— maybe—but not like this. Not now when so much else is unknown. "Very well," he says. "Would you like to know more about how the bond works?"

Sylvia huffs, but she gives him a relieved smile. "That's not what I meant, and you know it—but I'll take it. Yes. Tell me more about the bond."

"Bonds form when a demon forges a connection with a human. You know that much," he begins, carefully choosing his words now. Sylvia believes they bonded when she was captured by Charlie Wagner— and she is right in a way—just not the most recent time she was caught by him.

Too much, he reminds himself. *Just tell her what she needs to know. More will come … in time. The right time. Not now.*

"A bond allows the demon to find the human, to protect her from the influence of other creatures, and to share some of his powers with her."

"I don't know what that means," Sylvia says. "How can I share your powers? What powers? Making deals?"

Pilkington pauses, wondering if she is ready for this. His arusha is strong. She will understand. "As a demon," he begins, "I have certain abilities. For instance, I can sense the emotions of those around me."

"Really?" she scoffs. "How am I feeling right now?"

"Nervous," he replies immediately, feeling the emotions wash over him as they always do when he allows himself to feel them. "A little afraid. But also excited."

He pauses. "And satisfied—but threaded with guilt." He peers at her. "Why do you feel guilty, Sylvia?" He knows the answer, but if they are to get past this, he knows she has to face her feelings truthfully.

She glares at him, then cocks her head. "Can I feel your emotions?" she asks.

Pilkington nods, ignoring the way she has avoided his question. "Yes." Now it is his turn to take a deep breath. He lowers his defenses, allowing her to sense him. "Close your eyes," he tells her, and when she obeys, he whispers in his demon voice, "Now reach out to me; find me in the darkness."

"I know where you are," she says tartly, then gasps as she no doubt realizes that she does know where he is—where he is *exactly*.

"Now see me," he continues, feeling the soft brush of his arusha's senses against him. "Feel me."

"Calm," she whispers. "Careful. But only on the surface." She pushes deeper, pressing into him, and Pilkington allows her to get closer, forcing himself not to react, not to push her away as his instincts demand. "Excitement," she says, her voice soft in wonder. "Eagerness. Pride, but also a tiny hint of … fear?" She pauses. "Why are you afraid, Pilkington?"

"Because I do not let people get this close to me," he replies honestly, the words pulled out of him by her closeness, "and it is terrifying." *And wonderful*, he realizes, allowing himself to feel the joy of his arusha's touch, something he has denied himself until now.

"Why are you letting me in?" she whispers, and Pilkington shudders, his need to tell her everything nearly overwhelming his common sense.

"Because you are my—" He stops himself before he says the last word, cutting the connection, opening his eyes, and standing up abruptly, crossing to lean against the window and look out onto the street beyond. His chest heaves as he breathes, trying to steady his racing human heart. It has been a long time since anyone got so close to him—to the truth of him.

He hears her stand up and take the few steps across the room to him. She presses her body against his back, her arms wrapping around his middle as she buries her face against him. He wants to sag into her embrace, to lose himself in the offered comfort, but he knows that every step closer to her is dangerous—and doomed. "You don't have to fear me," she tells him, her words muffled in his shirt.

Pilkington's heart aches at the promise in her words, and he whirls around in the circle of her arms, looking down at her, his arusha who still pines for another. "Don't I?" he asks, a hand reaching out to hold her chin.

"What are you afraid of?" she asks him again, looking up into his eyes now, lost in his emotions.

"You," he whispers.

"Why? I'm nothing to be afraid of. I'm just me."

"You are everything," he whispers, "to me." His words seem to jar something loose in Sylvia, and she shakes her head, eyes clearing as she fumbles her way through the fog of emotion surrounding them both. He feels the moment she returns to her senses—the guilt washing everything away with bitter clarity. "Why do you feel guilty?" he asks again, raising an eyebrow at her as he looks at her arms still around him.

She seems to realize that she is holding him and lets go, stepping back awkwardly. "I..." she begins, but nothing else comes out.

"I know," he says, sparing her the effort of explanation as he sinks down to sit on the sill, emptiness filling the place inside where she was moments ago. "Believe me. I know."

"This is ... not friendship," she says, frowning. "This is ... more."

The demon nods, waiting for her to say what he knows she must. *I'm a fool,* he reminds himself. *I didn't have to push her here. Now she will pull away from me.*

As she should. You let her go years ago. Stop trying to undo the good thing you did back then. She is not for you. Not like that. Never yours.

Always mine, he argues, but he knows it doesn't matter. His arusha may want him now, may feel something for him, but she will never act on it. She is loyal to her vampire even now, despite the pull of his magic, the draw of their bond. It makes him want her even more.

"I'm such an idiot," she says quietly, pulling away. "I can't do this. I'm sorry. I can't do this to him."

Pilkington nods. "I know," he says again. "I understand."

"You really do, don't you?" she asks, shaking her head. "I'm so sorry."

"Don't be sorry," he tells her. "Never apologize for how you feel. Never apologize to me for the truth."

"Why are you so perfect?" she asks. "It's like you were made for me—and it's not fair." She looks down. "I'm a terrible person. I can't believe I'm even thinking such things right now, never mind saying them out loud to you."

Pilkington lifts her chin with his hand, forcing her to meet his gaze. "You are a person," he says. "You are not terrible." A tear slides down her cheek, and Pilkington wipes it away.

"Don't," he tells her. "I understand."

"I know you do." She sighs, wiping her face as she gathers herself, then looks up at him again. "Please tell me this emotion thing isn't all the bond does?"

"Oh no," he assures her. "I just needed you to know ... that part."

"Is that what you always feel?" she asks, then rallies. "I mean, can you always feel me like that?"

The demon shakes his head. "Not unless I look, like I just did." He doesn't tell her that he can always sense her desire, but some things aren't meant to be shared— especially not if his arusha desires someone else.

"Good," she breathes. "That can be ... overwhelming. Distracting."

The demon nods. "Very."

"So, what else can the bond do?"

Pilkington considers the hours left before dawn. "We can definitely cover a few things before you need to sleep. Let's start with the basics, though."

"What about that grabbing-stuff-through-the-worlds thing?" she prompts. "That seems super useful."

The demon laughs. "Let's start with something a bit easier first, shall we?"

CHAPTER 7

SYLVIA

THE NEXT AFTERNOON, SYLVIA AND PILKINGTON STAND IN the open space in the Student Services building at the Lyceum, studying the campus map to find Professor Dilmun's office among the sprawling buildings. Students surround them: teenagers wearing backpacks coated in pop culture patches carry ornate staffs as they hurry by on one side, clearly late for class as they hurry to the stairs; a group of middle-aged women cluster on stuffed chairs around a low table holding an ancient book, all of them whispering excitedly while one holds a stack of index cards, clearly quizzing her companions; and a few limp bodies stretch out on the various couches and chairs, books abandoned on bellies or over faces as they catch a few winks of sleep.

Sylvia knows that the city holds all manner of humans in all stripes of behavior, but she has never seen so many obviously otherworldly people in one place.

"How does no one recognize this place?" she asks, watching as a tall man in a black leather jacket leans down to talk quietly with the blushing woman behind the glass window marked "Registration" in bold letters. "How did I not know this was here?"

Pilkington shrugs. "Humans see what they want to see. Unless you come looking, this is a language school, specializing in Ancient Greek, Latin, and Sumerian. Very few people come to a learning annex in a city to brush up on their classic language conjugations."

"I can't believe I didn't know about this place, though," she marvels, unable to watch as many people as she wants to. She lowers her voice. "Are they humans, though? Or are there ... creatures here?"

Pilkington pauses his study of the map to stare at her. "These are mostly creatures," he tells her. "Close your eyes and reach out with your senses," he says. "You can feel them."

"Feel them?" she echoes, not sure what he means.

"Yes. Creatures have a magical aura that can be sensed." He nods. Glancing around, he gestures to an empty couch a few feet away. "Take a seat, close your eyes, breathe, and let yourself feel your surroundings." He smiles at her, but something in his eyes is sad for a moment. "Like the emotions, but not so personal. Give it a few minutes and tell me what you discover."

"Okay." Sylvia obeys, settling into the seat and closing her eyes. She is glad the room is busy, everyone focused on something else, so no one will stare at her for sitting with her eyes closed. This is not a pose she would ever think of adopting in a crowded public space if she were alone, but with the demon nearby, Sylvia knows no one will harm her.

She takes a deep breath, settling herself with the breathing technique she learned in therapy. When her mind is clear, she opens her senses, just a little, to see what she can feel.

A brush of heat wafts over her face, and she opens her eyes to locate the source. Pilkington is watching her from several feet away, and as she looks at him, the heat returns, a slow press of warmth against her cheek. "Demon," he mouths at her, then jerks his head slightly to his right. Sylvia follows his gaze to spy a young woman with short dark hair and glasses at a table. She has a book propped up on the surface before her, but as Sylvia looks at her, she catches the woman's eye.

Sylvia frowns. The woman seems perfectly human, but then the flash of warmth presses again, and Sylvia catches a hint of red hovering around a necklace the woman wears. Noticing Sylvia's attention, the woman quickly jams the necklace back under her shirt with a frown, then slams her book closed and begins gathering her things.

Sylvia turns to ask Pilkington a question, but he is already standing next to her. He leans down to whisper, "She carries a red demon with her, an incubus, and he noticed you." Sylvia makes a mental note to ask him what that means later—*and how can someone carry a demon with them?* She focuses on the more important question first.

"Why?" Sylvia asks. "There are so many people here. Why would he look at me?"

"Because you're with me," Pilkington replies, and there is a world of meaning in his words that Sylvia is not ready to explore.

"What else is here?" she blurts, changing the subject. "I mean, who else?" She's trying not to think of vampires and demons as alien creatures, something other than human, and calling them who instead of what helps with the division in her mind.

"Take a look," the demon urges.

Sylvia spends the next few minutes playing spot-the-creature. Demons feel warm, though she doesn't get to explore the sensation because the only other demon in the building quickly leaves when he spots Pilkington. She is surprised to find a cold spot, an absence of light and heat in a place that should be full of something else.

"Vampire," the demon whispers, and Sylvia cocks her head.

"But it's still daytime," she says. "How?" She studies the young man in question—he looks like any other college student: an unzipped gray hoodie over a plain shirt and jeans, seated at a table with a stack of books next to an open laptop, sipping a coffee as his hands moves the mouse.

"Look at his hand," Pilkington says, leaning close. "He wears magic to protect him from the sun."

Squinting, Sylvia makes out a gold ring around his middle finger, and suddenly, it's the only spot of heat in the empty space the vampire occupies. She frowns, not liking how the vampire feels, and she worries what will happen the next time she is close to Theo.

Will this emptiness fill the space between us?

"How am I able to do this?" she breathes. "And why can I do this now? What changed from before?" They spent part of last night experimenting with their newly shared powers, but Sylvia still doesn't quite understand everything.

Pilkington shakes his head. "You've always been able to tap into my powers," he tells her. "You just never tried before." He pauses. "Not like this anyway."

"What do you mean?"

The demon takes a breath, clearly contemplating his explanation. "You have a sense of people, right?" When she nods, he continues, "You have a general idea of whether they mean you good or ill or if they notice you at all."

"Yeah," she agrees, "but everyone has that. It's called intuition. I should listen to mine more often."

"True, some humans are more susceptible to the subtleties than others, but your ability to gauge others has always been something more than the average human."

"Always?" she echoes. "Why? If we only bonded a few months ago..."

The demon's face closes, and Sylvia wants to ask, but something makes her hesitate. *I don't want to know,* she decides. *Not yet. Not now. One magic ability at a time is enough.* "So, I'm a super senser," she says. "I can deal with that." She turns her attention back to the room, knowing that she is a coward for not pursuing the details.

A prickling sensation, like her fingers have fallen asleep, signals the presence of what Pilkington calls shifters, creatures able to change their form to an animal. There are many of those at the school, some in groups that Pilkington identifies with a low howl under his breath, and others alone at tables with headphones and laptops.

The final creature she senses makes her open her eyes immediately. The scent of the ocean fills her nose, and memories of a childhood spent near the sea swirl into her mind. "Witch," Pilkington mouths, watching as the tall man notices Sylvia, stops dead to stare, then moves toward her with deliberate steps. She knows the demon is about to intervene, placing his body between Sylvia and the stranger, but then she is standing up, her eyes wide with surprise.

"Jeremy!" she squeals, stepping forward to give the man a long hug. "It's been forever!"

"Copland?" Jeremy asks, looking Pilkington over with obvious surprise. "What the hell are you doing here?"

"I'm doing research," she says vaguely, staring at him, feeling the soft waves of the ocean breeze tingling on her skin. "What are you doing here?" She looks him up and down. Jeremy is tall, mid-20s like Sylvia, with wavy brown hair and wire-rimmed glasses. Sylvia hasn't seen her childhood friend in months, though they stayed in touch with occasional texts and emails. "I didn't know you were back in town." She doesn't mention how the last time he had been in town, Amanda had called off their wedding and broken his heart.

Stepping back, Jeremy runs a hand through his hair, grimacing. "Yeah, I meant to tell you so that we could get together, but I've been pretty busy with the new students."

Sylvia's mouth falls open. "Students? Jeremy, you teach here?" She stares hard at him, trying to identify the scent pushing at the edges of her memory. "What? How?" She runs out of questions, and Pilkington leans down to whisper in her ear.

"Witch," he repeats.

"You're a freaking witch?" The question comes out louder than she intended, but no one seems to notice her explosion.

Jeremy narrows his eyes, clearly confused. "Yeah." He gives her a once-over. "What are you, though? I mean, other than..." he gives the demon a long look, "...with him." Pilkington's face darkens, and Jeremy recovers quickly, no stranger to dealing with demons. "I mean, what are you doing here?" he asks instead. "You taking classes now?"

"No," Sylvia tells him. "Actually, we're here looking for a professor." She turns to Pilkington, waiting for him to supply the name.

"Professor Dilmun," the demon says. "Anthropology?"

Jeremy nods. "Officially, yes. But really Artifacts and History. Yeah, I know her." He glances down at his watch. "I think she has class now, but she has office hours at 4:00. She's on the fourth floor, third... no, second office on the left. Her door is covered in all sorts of fun stuff. You can't miss it."

Pilkington nods, then looks at Sylvia. "Perhaps you can stay here with your friend and catch up while I go see if she is available?" Sylvia does not miss the odd emphasis he puts on the word "friend" and has to hide a smile. She and Jeremy are actually friends—nothing more.

You're friends with Pilkington.

Yeah, but there's more. We're bonded. It's demon stuff.

She looks at Jeremy, glad to see a familiar face from before the craziness took over her life here. "You have a few minutes?" she asks him.

"Sure," he says, offering an arm for her to take. "The coffee here is amazing. Let's get some." He looks at Pilkington. "We'll be over there." He gestures down a hallway in the center of the building. "The coffee is on the other side." He pauses, then adds. "We won't leave the building." His words seem to satisfy some need in Pilkington, for the demon nods, stepping away from Sylvia and heading for the stairs without a word.

"Wow," Jeremy breathes after the demon has disappeared into the crowd of people milling up the stairs. "What did you do to that one?"

Sylvia scoffs, raising a hand to her chest. "Me?" she asks. "What are you talking about?" She shakes her head. "Don't answer that. First, I need to know everything: who you are, how you got here, and why this is the first I'm learning that you are Harry freaking Potter."

"I can't believe you didn't know," Jeremy says. He has told her about growing up as a witch, discovering his powers—his strengths involve water and the ocean, so that's why he smells like the beach—and his life spent learning how to manage his abilities. He's finally learned enough that he is ready to teach others how to use their skills, passing on the gift his own teachers had given him over the years. "I really thought Amanda told you."

Sylvia shakes her head. "Not at all. She never said why she broke things off." She scoffs. "I mean, what could she say? 'I broke up with Jer because he's a witch'? She just told me you guys weren't getting married, and she was leaving for a few weeks." Sylvia wonders what she would have said if her friend had told her the truth. Probably freaked out. Before Theo, she would not have welcomed any supernatural creatures into her life—not after what those witches did to her in the cemetery that night.

Jeremy sighs, and Sylvia can still see his pain, though like anyone who has been left behind, he tries to hide it. "I should have known better than to try to marry her. She tried to accept my life. I know she did." He looks around, face falling for a moment. "But this... it's just too much for a normal person to handle." He looks up at her, startled and embarrassed, the sadness fading as his normal sunny disposition returns. "Not you, of course," he adds quickly. "You've always been ready for this world. Haven't you?"

Jeremy doesn't know the specifics of what happened that night when she was fourteen, but he knows that she spent some time recovering in the hospital before he returned that summer. He has never asked her about it, and she has never volunteered the story, comfortable with their friendship without that part of her history filled in. People looked at her differently when they knew—the way Miriam sometimes looked at her—with pity. Sylvia never wants that—and certainly not from Jeremy.

The moment passes, and her old friend leans in, face giddy like a schoolgirl ready to gossip, and Sylvia smiles, glad to be around her friend again. She pictures Jeremy when they first met—he was a shy kindergartener, and she ran over to show him the shells she had unearthed in the playground. He's come a long way from that awkward boy.

"Now," he begins in a low whisper, "tell me how you found him again. I always wondered if he was a creature and that's why he left suddenly." At her blank look, he continues, clearly guessing. "Wait, did he find you? Of course he did. That bond is like a magnet. I can sense it, and he's not even here. Seriously, Copland, well done. Who knew he was the famous Mr. Pilkington after all?"

Sylvia puts a hand on his arm to stop him. "Jeremy, what are you talking about?" She decides to leave the famous Mr. Pilkington issue for later. Jeremy isn't making any sense.

Isn't he?

Sylvia ignores the voice, the low thrum in her body that knows exactly what Jeremy is saying.

"Who are you talking about?" she asks in a tiny voice, needing him to say it out loud, to make it real.

"Phil, of course," Jeremy says. Her face must be terrible because he reaches out to grab her hands. "Are you okay? What's going on?"

"Phil?" she echoes weakly. "What about him?"

Jeremy gives her a long look, one reserved for the really drunk or the really old. "You're with Phil," he explains slowly. "Did you find him, or did he find you?"

Sylvia grips his hands, a wash of fear followed by anger rushing through her. "What makes you think Pilkington is Phil?"

Jeremy scoffs, still eyeing her like she's an idiot. "Your drawings, for one. When I got back after that first summer, you were constantly sketching his face on everything. Every notebook had his eyes, his hair, those hands... like a character sketch you never tired of." He sighs. "I wasn't there that summer he left, but I always hoped he'd come back. You were so lost without him. Of course, seeing that bond, I get it." He grins. "I know he can look like whatever he wants when he's here. Pretty sweet that he stayed the same human so you'd know him, right?" He raises an eyebrow at her, but his expression shifts in the middle as he realizes the effect of his words. "Copland?" He peers at her carefully. "You okay?"

"I..." She lets the words trail off, unsure of her answer. Her mind wants to race. She can feel the words building inside, an avalanche waiting to release, and she struggles to hold herself steady. Phil's face fills her mind, but not that day at the beach like she often thinks of him. This time, Phil stands above where she is tied to the slab in the cemetery, frozen in place, face scary blank as that witch continued to speak.

He wasn't there. It's my memory playing with me.

In her mind, Phil says something, and the woman strikes him... slashing his arm...

With the fucking dagger... she realizes slowly. She can see it now, the designs crawling up the blade glinting with the demon's blood, catching the edge of moonlight. Blood sprays across her legs, Phil's human body easily cut.

But it was my blood, she insists, remembering the warm wetness pooling in her middle. Her hand slides down from the table to press against her belly, unable to feel the scar through the layers of shirt and hoodie, but she knows it's there.

Yes... later... when he came back ... as the other.

As Pilkington.

In her memory, her Phil stands frozen for a moment, saying something she can't recall, then turns and runs straight through the graves, not pausing at all as he leaps over the low wall along the cliff's edge. He doesn't make a sound as he falls, but she can hear the splash as he hits, the sound loud and terrifying because she is alone now, trapped without any allies.

But he came back, her mind reminds her. *In a stronger body. Not in his demon form but as this man.* A flash of his face as she lay cradled in his arms. *"I am yours, arusha."*

Motherfucker.

"Jeremy," she says quietly when her ability to speak returns, "what is an arusha?"

CHAPTER 8

PILKINGTON

BY THE TIME PILKINGTON GETS BACK DOWNSTAIRS AND across the building, his arusha has calmed herself. He doesn't want to admit how much he had wanted to bolt to her side when he felt the rise of her panic, but it only lasted a moment, followed by a frightening hollowness that slowly settled into a cool distance.

She's fine, he assures himself. Her friend must have said something that alarmed her.

I'll kill him.

The demon takes a deep breath to calm down. *You will not kill him*, he promises himself. *He is her friend. Her old friend. Her long-time companion. One who has known her longer than you have.*

Perhaps he confessed his love for her, the demon muses. Why wouldn't he adore her? His arusha is quite lovable: funny, smart, radiant when she smiles, loyal...

Of course she is loyal. To the Muldavian.

Pilkington slows his pace, knowing that she is fine and needing to settle before he returns to her presence. This used to be easier before the Muldavian was reclaimed by his Maker. Pilkington could sit in her presence, enjoying the satisfaction on her face when she spoke to her vampire lover. His arusha was happy. Content.

But then the Muldavian had gone, and every time he sat across from her at the table, ostensibly researching while they drank pots of tea, Pilkington found his attention wandering, his desire growing into something quite impossible.

Even with the bond pulling her steadily in his direction without the distraction of her vampire nearby, Pilkington knows that his arusha will not betray her lover. Even though the Muldavian isn't with her, she won't stray.

So this Jeremy can hardly pose a threat anyway. Though he thinks of the familiar way they had hugged, the embrace of good friends, and he wishes he could have that with her.

She said she was my friend. No bargains. No deals. But that was before she found out about the bond. Before she knew she was tied to me with magic.

He reaches the central corridor on the ground floor and makes his way through the crowd to the coffee shop on the far side. Other creatures give him a wide space, knowing he is powerful even if they don't know exactly who he is.

Jeremy recognized him, a detail that Pilkington is not about to dismiss but decides to explore another time. Some witches would know his reputation—and this Jeremy is a professor. Part of his job may involve knowing about powerful demons who frequent the area. Pilkington chuckles at the idea of his name on a syllabus somewhere, required reading of his early exploits fodder for young mages.

He wonders if Sylvia would ever read about him—if she would want to. If the Muldavian would allow her to when he eventually returns. Vampires are not known for their charitable nature, and Pilkington knows that Theo will not appreciate the bond the demon shares with Sylvia. He wouldn't appreciate it if their roles were reversed—not anymore. Would the vampire want his lover to learn more about her demon friend's history?

Do I want her to know?

Not all of his adventures on the mortal plane have been successful, and though he generally tries to avoid murder and mayhem, preferring to collect useful items from his dealings, sometimes he has to collect in other ways—and it is never pretty to disappoint a demon. Pilkington wonders if he will ever be close enough to Sylvia to explain such things. If she will still call herself his friend when she learns more about him.

She accepted the Muldavian, flaws and all.

Yes, but she was blinded by lust and caught in the vampire's powerful pull.

You know better. She hasn't been subject to anyone's pull except yours since that night on the Ferris wheel. The night you claimed her as your own.

I didn't intend to claim anyone. Ever.

The demon lets out a breath, hearing echoed variations of that claim over the years of his existence. *No one intends for things to work out the way they do sometimes. And yet, they still do. The world moves on.*

Except there is no moving on this time.

He is just as bound as his arusha, caught in the pull of her allure, unable to sever the link between them. And when her mortal life ends, he will keep her in his realm just as he keeps his soul-servant Billy—though he is still foolish enough to hope that she may want to be there with him.

Her other option would be to venture into the unknown that takes all mortals, but she no longer has that choice. The demon will not allow her to leave him. He cannot. Her bond with him is stronger than anything she can ever have with her vampire lover, though the demon will never force her—not if he can help it.

But Pilkington has been around long enough to know that some things are beyond his control, and it is easier to move with the winds of fate than to struggle against them. He looks up, conscious of his surroundings again, realizing that the crowd has quietly pulled away from him, people giving him a wide berth as they move down the hall. He pulls his power back into himself, conscious of the effect he is having on those around him.

The hallway opens into a large open area dotted with couches and seats at his end but slowly transitioning into chairs and tables. He spots his arusha sitting across from Jeremy on the far side of the room. He can see her back, all that blonde hair tied back into a messy braid, the rope reaching down her back over her black hoodie. She is leaned down over the table, a to go cup of coffee forgotten at her elbow. Jeremy's face is concerned as he speaks quietly. Pilkington is not at all ashamed to pause for a moment to listen in.

"...powerful connection stuff, but it's not really my area, so I don't know any more than that." The witch pauses, then reaches out to touch Sylvia's arm in a comforting gesture. Pilkington bites the inside of his mouth but forces himself not to move. "You're really in the shit, Copland," Jeremy says with a small laugh. "And you seem like you belong here—in this world. Maybe I should have married you instead."

Pilkington stifles his reaction, but a choked sound still makes its way out of his throat. Two witches on his left immediately take two big steps away from him, skittering quickly down the corridor behind him.

You have to calm down, he tells himself. *You have things to do. Stop behaving like some lovesick fool and get it together.* He is helped by the sight of Sylvia's hand reaching out to playfully smack Jeremy on the arm for his comment. "No way, Jer. You are not at all my type."

"Too bad." Jeremy smirks. "I know you would never run out on a promise like she did."

Sylvia pauses a little longer than Pilkington thinks she should before replying. "Yeah, I definitely wouldn't have left you like that." Her voice is softer as she continues. "You deserve so much more, Jer. You know that, right?"

Jeremy shrugs, and Pilkington sees the witch has dimples when he smiles. Actual dimples. "I know," he says. "It's just hard to remember it when..."

"When people keep leaving you behind," Sylvia finishes for him. Her words hit the demon harder than he expects, and he knows that someday he will have to explain everything to his arusha.

Not yet though. Not now.

Deciding that he has spied on them long enough, Pilkington makes his way across the room. Jeremy looks up at him first, but Sylvia's body language shifts as he draws nearer, her shoulders straighter, her breathing calm. She knows he is near without seeing him. The demon stands beside the table, looking down at them.

"Any luck?" Sylvia asks.

"Yes," he tells her. "Professor Dilmun will be back in her office any minute now."

Sylvia smiles, but there is something brittle about the edges of the look. "Really? That was easy."

"Easy enough to talk to someone," the demon reminds her, not willing to reach out and identify the mood she is in. "We don't know if she even knows anything."

"You're looking for information about an artifact, right?" Jeremy says, ever helpful. Pilkington wonders how much Sylvia has told her old friend—and how much they can trust the witch. "If anyone here is going to know anything, it's Nin—Professor Dilmun." He leans back, gathering up his bag and coffee cup. Sylvia stands as well, stepping around the other side of the table to give Jeremy another hug. "It was good to see you, Copland," Jeremy says quietly, giving the top of her head a soft kiss. "Let's not wait so long next time." Sylvia steps back with a nod. "And besides, I'm going to need all of the details once the shit settles, deal?"

Sylvia laughs, comfortable with her old friend. "Of course, Jer." She pauses, then adds. "You know that anyone here would be glad to be with you, right?"

"Just not you," he reminds her.

"God no," she replies with a laugh, "but seriously. You're surrounded by your kind of people. Take a chance."

Jeremy gives her a meaningful look that makes Pilkington wonder what they were talking about when he arrived. "You too." He turns to the demon, sticking out a hand. "Nice to meet you, man," he says casually, but Pilkington can sense the apprehension in the gesture. This witch knows who he is, his reputation at least, and though he is safe enough as Sylvia's friend, one can never be too polite to demons.

Pilkington returns the handshake with a little more force than necessary and hates himself for being petty. "The pleasure is mine, Jeremy Vedder." The witch's face pales a little at Pilkington's use of his full name, and he pulls his hand back. When the demon turns to Sylvia, she is narrowing her eyes at him.

"Seriously?" she says, then scoffs and snatches her coffee cup from the table, heading back to the hallway. "Is it this way?"

CHAPTER 9

SYLVIA

THE TRIP TO THE PROFESSOR'S OFFICE DOESN'T TAKE nearly as long as Sylvia needs it to, but she tries to rally, focus on the issue at hand and not the fact that the demon she has been drinking tea with for the last few months is actually Phil, her childhood companion who disappeared from her life the summer she was sixteen. She tries not to stare at his face as they go up the stairs side by side, knowing that the demon will sense if she behaves differently around him. She doesn't have to stare though. She knows his face, has even sketched it a few times when the demon returned to his home, leaving her alone with Tengo.

I'm such an idiot, she thinks. *How did I not notice?*

Because you were traumatized and try not to think of any of that stuff.

Surprisingly, the voice in her mind isn't her own, nor even the therapist she saw for years afterward. It's her best friend Miriam who talks her off the ledge, and Sylvia smiles, grateful for her friend's reassurances. Miriam would understand. She would also squeal at the idea that the "new guy" Sylvia has been hanging out with—Sylvia has told Miriam nothing of the supernatural turn her life has taken in the last few months—is actually Phil, the boy she had a terrible crush on during those summers when Miriam went away with her family.

And I'm bonded to him, she reminds herself as they crest the stairs and turn to head up another flight. Jeremy's scant knowledge of arushas is still bouncing around like a pinball in her mind, not quite finding any purchase, and she focuses on her surroundings instead. Sylvia is glad that her apartment is up a flight of stairs, and the exercise doesn't bother her at all. On their way up from the third floor, she passes what must be a professor, the older woman red-faced and huffing as she steps triumphantly onto the landing of the fourth floor, her arms weighed down with books and two bags slung over each shoulder. Sylvia pities her.

"You need a hand?" she offers the woman, holding out a hand to take the pile of books.

"Oh, hell yes," the woman exclaims, chest puffing as she takes in deep breaths. She dumps the pile into Sylvia's arms. Sylvia almost stumbles, the weight surprising, and she reconsiders her assessment of the woman's health. A strong hand on her lower back steadies her, and Pilkington is behind her.

"Allow me," he says, reaching out to pluck one of the bags from the professor's shoulder. The woman's black sweater straightens as the weight of the bag is lifted, settling back next to a pile of necklaces resting on her chest.

"Oh, you are awesome," the woman breathes. "I'm heading to my office. Do you mind carrying them the rest of the way?" She points with one hand while the other readjusts her remaining bag, this one clearly more manageable. "It's just round the corner."

She leads them away from the staircase and down a smaller hallway to the left, pausing to rummage in her remaining bag. She pulls out a red and white lanyard with the words "I like big books and I cannot lie" embroidered on it attached to a large ring holding keys of all shapes and sizes. Sylvia stares as the woman flips through the keys easily, searching for the one to the door she approaches—the second one to the left. She wants to recognize some of the keys, but her brain refuses to identify them—nothing looks like a car key or a house key, and even the key she uses to unlock her office door is oddly shaped, a large silver gothic monstrosity more at home in a Victorian mansion than a college campus.

"Dr. Dilmun?" she asks.

The woman gives her a surprised look, then swings her gaze back to her door, where the name "Dr. Ninian Dilmun" appears in fancy gothic script on a placard to the right. The nameplate is almost covered by the papers taped to every available surface—pictures of gothic swords, golden wands, and elaborate staffs are mixed in with mystical waterfalls, old maps with unrecognizable names, and oddly, a picture of a beach that Sylvia would swear is the view from beneath the pier back home.

"That's me," she says. "You need something?" She shoulders her door open, revealing a large room covered in so many contrasting shapes, colors, and textures that Sylvia has to blink for a moment before everything settles into place. The walls are covered in pictures, tapestries, hanging strings of beads, and shelving of all kinds. One corner bookcase holds rows of skulls, but Sylvia can only identify about half of them. Sylvia wonders about the one with huge black horns and can't help her gaze from glancing quickly over at Pilkington. He is also staring through the doorway into the jammed office, but he seems to take the professor's style in stride.

Sylvia stands in the doorframe for a long moment, feeling a little like Alice or at least a companion on a strange journey through time. She restrains the urge to glance down the hallway to the next door, reassuring her brain that the room is the right size for the space. It does seem bigger on the inside, even with all the stuff jammed inside. A worn couch covered in pillows rests against one wall beneath a variety of pictures snug against one another. Sylvia takes a moment to realize that what she has taken for another picture is actually a glimpse of a window nearly covered by the edges of other pictures. Bookcases are filled with books—paperbacks shoved next to leather-bound volumes and stacked near rolls of parchment—amid other items—several wands, a small jumble of bladed weapons, and bottles and pottery. Several staffs lean into another corner, with random umbrellas looped over the visible edges. Dr. Dilmun makes her way across the room and around a desk, dumping her bag on a chair to her left. She turns to Sylvia, plucking the stack of books from her arms and plopping it down on what is probably a table, but it is hard to tell from all the stuff piled atop it. The woman doesn't pause, reaching for her bag as the demon holds it out. She tosses it casually onto the same chair as her first bag, then slumps into a large chair behind her desk.

Sylvia opens her mouth to speak, but the professor raises a finger in her direction. She reaches behind a stack of books on her desk and pulls out a delicate teacup. Taking a small sip, she frowns, then runs her hands in a series of complicated gestures beneath the cup. Sylvia watches as steam begins to rise from the contents. Dr. Dilmun takes another sip, sighs in satisfaction, then gestures for both of them to enter and have a seat. Sylvia walks in first, aware of the scent she has been smelling since they encountered the woman on the stairs—cinnamon and spice, fall leaves and cold mornings.

She's a witch. She reminds herself to ask Pilkington why witches smell—and smell different from one another—after this is over.

Pilkington enters after her and, with a nod from the professor, eases the door shut behind them. The couch is the only place not covered in clutter, so they take a seat there. It is surprisingly comfortable, and Sylvia makes herself sit up straight, not wanting to appear rude by slumping over on the sofa.

"So," the professor begins, "you've found me. How can I help you?"

Sylvia looks at Pilkington, not sure how much he plans to reveal.

"We are seeking information about a dagger," he says.

Dr. Dilmun takes a small sip of her drink, then sets the cup down. "You're in the right place." She gestures at the pile of weapons leaning in the corner. "You want to find a specific dagger? I have a few over there. Tell me which one you seek."

Pilkington shakes his head. "We don't want to find it," he tells her. "We want to find out more about it."

The professor nods. "I see. You found a dagger and want to know more about it." When the demon doesn't reply, she continues, "Well, then, tell me about it."

"It's 10 inches long, silver, with carvings up the blade," Pilkington begins, but Sylvia stops him, reaching into her pocket and withdrawing one of her sketches of the weapon. She hands the folded paper to the professor, then leans back to watch as the woman opens it up, smoothing the folds flat on her desk. Her eyes skim the picture with bored disinterest at first, but then her eye catches on a detail, and then another, and soon she is leaning close to the image, mumbling to herself. "Is it—? No, it doesn't have—wait, there it is. Could it be the...? No, too early for that. Handle is third century, but it's added after. It's that blade though..." Her words trail off, and she looks up at them with wide cautious eyes. She glances at the door, as if checking to see if it's closed. "I'd have to see it to confirm, of course," she begins in a low voice, "but I'd bet my tenure that this is Sophia Ardy's cursed blade."

A shiver runs up Sylvia's spine, and Pilkington follows it with a comforting hand on her back, keeping her steady. "Cursed?" she echoes.

Dr. Dilmun stares hard at her, and that smell of cinnamon fills Sylvia's senses. For a moment, the wave almost overwhelms her, but then it is gone, the magic parting over her as if she is protected by a sheet of glass. The witch stares at her, then nods, shifting her attention to the demon. "You have nothing to fear from this blade," she tells Sylvia, "but you, of course, cannot abide such a thing." The rest is directed at Pilkington, and he sits up straighter on the couch.

"I can abide many things," the demon says. "I can do so with much more ease when I know what I am dealing with."

"The blade is not for you," she says. "It is a witch's tool." Her attention slides back to Sylvia. "But you are not a witch," she muses, "yet there is something there. Something more. You are surrounded by power, girl."

Sylvia rolls her eyes. "Story of my life," she says. "Tell me what you mean. What is a witch's tool?"

The professor leans back in her chair, taking another sip of her drink before speaking, clearly moving into lecture mode. "Witches use tools to focus their power. They come in many shapes, but weapons are common enough since people used to carry them everywhere. The ancient world was a dangerous place."

"This world is dangerous," Sylvia interrupts, not needing a lecture. "Tell me about this dagger."

Dr. Dilmun leans forward again, tapping a finger on the sketch sitting on her desk. "This tool has a story. A history. A myth, even. It is said that long ago, a witch bargained with a demon." Her eyes drift to Pilkington, but she says nothing. "A poor bargain, and it ended badly as these things sometimes do. The witch's family was destroyed in the aftermath, all but one, the youngest daughter, a virgin who swore revenge on the creature who killed her family." She pauses, looking up at the ceiling. "Who knows why she thought she could ever be strong enough to take her revenge—a witch against a demon? Very few can beat those odds. But Sophia was a canny witch, and instead of trying to grow her own power, she started gathering power into a blade instead."

"You make it sound like she was charging a battery," Sylvia says.

"You can look at it that way," the professor says. "Except Sophia charged her battery with the powers of other witches."

"Witches can do that? Is it like donating blood? Sharing power?"

The look on the professor's face makes Sylvia realize she needs to take a lot more classes about the supernatural world she has joined. "Witches do not willingly share power," Dr. Dilmun says. "Sophia stole it from those she felt had wronged her—those who had failed to help them escape the wrath of the demon—and then later, those who tried to check her path or reason with her."

"So, she killed witches and stored their power in the dagger?" Pilkington asks, nodding. "That makes sense."

"Does it." It is not a question. Professor Dilmun clearly does not approve of the witch's tactics, but she continues. "Eventually, she gained enough power to control certain creatures. Not all of them, but enough that demons and vampires joined forces to take her out of the equation. They separated her from the dagger—and her head from her body, of course—though some say she was also trapped in the blade with the others. The dagger was supposed to be held in safekeeping by the Klaviger."

"The what?" Sylvia asks.

"The Klaviger runs the vampires," Pilkington explains. "They make sure vampires don't get exposed."

Sylvia nods. She vaguely remembers Theo hinting at such an organization, but he had never told her the name or what they actually did. "They had the dagger then?"

Dr. Dilmun laughs. "Of course not! It was almost immediately stolen. It's been bouncing between factions for centuries." She pauses, then gives Sylvia a quizzical look. "The problem, of course, is that the dagger can only be wielded by a virgin who bonds to it with blood—and we all know there are few demons or vampires—or even witches—who can claim that virtue. Sophia Ardy was not a fool when she created the blade, limiting who could use it and for what purpose."

"I know no tales of Sophia Ardy," Pilkington says, "nor even of the Ardy family."

Dr. Dilmun laughs again. "Of course not. Sophia was an Ardy, her family were the Ardys, but Sophia was always tall. So when she was hunted, she earned a new name: the tall Ardy."

Pilkington smiles. "Tallardy," he muses. "I'll be damned."

CHAPTER 10

PILKINGTON

SYLVIA SAYS NOTHING ON THE WALK BACK TO HER APART-ment, and the demon doesn't ask any questions, allowing her time to work through her thoughts. He can sense the upheaval inside his arusha, no doubt a result of learning the dagger's sordid history.

Pilkington doesn't realize anything is wrong with her home until they open Sylvia's apartment door. Her gasp is the first clue that anything is amiss, and he stares over her shoulder at the wreckage inside the room. He immediately moves in front of her, shielding her from any danger as he reaches out to sense if anyone is still in her room.

The place is empty. Ransacked, but empty of any residue. No trace of the intruder remains, and Pilkington curses as he steps inside, moving aside so Sylvia can take in the chaos that was her apartment.

The table lays on its side, the chairs scattered—one leaning against the wall in front of the refrigerator and the other on its back alongside the wall to Pilkington's left. Clothing is strewn across every available surface, the door to Sylvia's wardrobe hanging askew from one remaining hinge. Her nightstand has been flipped over, the books piled there laying on the floor. Her lamp is shattered in a heap on the floor next to the bed. The rocking chair that normally holds her extra clothes has been pulled into pieces, the wooden struts splayed out on her bed and the seat resting in the middle of the small bathroom. The intruder must have thrown it through the open door. The medicine cabinet hangs open, bottles and tubs haphazardly laying in the sink, some smashed on the floor. The smell of perfume is strong in there, the remains of a bottle still idly dripping from the edge of the counter.

Her kitchen hasn't fared any better, her few plates shattered on the counter and floor. The drawer has been pulled free and dumped on the floor in front of the sink. The cabinet door is open at an odd angle, but Pilkington's gaze strays from Sylvia's shattered expression to stare at the cabinet above the refrigerator. She had moved the dagger there a few weeks ago, hiding it out of sight and more securely than her medicine cabinet could offer. He gives Sylvia a look to make sure she isn't going to faint on him, and satisfied that she is stable for the moment, he steps over the wreckage to peer into the empty cabinets. He runs a hand over both just in case, his fingers picking up traces of remaining tape and a sticky residue from where Sylvia had taped the artifact to the ceiling of the cabinet.

"It's gone," he whispers. He looks over to his right to the shattered window from the fire escape. The intruder clearly entered there and searched the place until finding the dagger above the refrigerator and leaving with it.

Nothing to be done for it now, he thinks, though his stomach plummets at the idea of someone else wielding the dagger, forcing him to do anything they want with a word. For a moment, he allows himself to regret not leaving Tengo behind to guard her apartment, but it hadn't seemed necessary, so he had sent the dog on a daytime mission to retrace the steps of the vampires the night before. He's caught hints of another trail mingled with theirs a few times—a witch's scent—and he wants to find out what Theo's companions have been up to. He calls Tengo, and the dog returns immediately to his side, abandoning his tracking. When he appears in the room, he moves to stand next to Sylvia, allowing her hands to rest atop his large head, offering his support amid the chaos.

Pilkington looks over to Sylvia, determined to comfort her after this terrible intrusion into her home. Instead of the broken look he expects, however, Sylvia is smirking. With an oddly upbeat chuckle, she steps past him and moves to the refrigerator. She kicks the chair out of the way and opens the top half into the freezer. A full laugh escapes her now as she reaches inside and pulls out a small rectangular box. Pilkington can read the label: Hungry Man Fried Chicken Frozen Dinner. She gives the box a little shake and lets out a relieved sigh as the box emits a soft thunk from side to side.

"At least that's one thing," she says, then sinks to the floor on wobbly legs. Pilkington is there to ease her down, sitting next to her with his back to the stove—the only undisturbed item in the apartment. She rests the box across her knees and gives him a watery smile.

Pilkington pauses, not wanting to upset her further but totally confused. He raises an eyebrow, then says carefully, "You have a sudden desire for fried chicken?"

"Yes," she says, "that's exactly it." She looks at him as if there is something he isn't quite understanding.

The demon nods. "Very well," he tells her. "Let's pack up what belongings you need and then we can get you whatever you want to eat." He gives her a hard look. "Somewhere else."

Sylvia cocks her head to the side, narrowing her eyes at him. "You really think I want to eat right now?" She shakes the box at him. "Pilkington," she says slowly, "this is a frozen dinner."

"I know your opinions about frozen foods," he replies.

"Frozen dinners," she continues, "go in the microwave." She gives him a pointed look.

The demon stares back, not understanding what she is telling him. He knows how TV dinners work.

"Seriously?" she asks, then gestures with the box to her tiny counter space—one small section between sink and stove on their side and another small section between the other side of the sink and the wall. Pilkington follows her gaze, studying the debris of plates, cups, and glasses strewn across the Formica surface. His eye catches the glinting remains of her teapot, and he vows to get her a new one as soon as she is settled again.

"Do you see a microwave?" she asks. Pilkington's eyes widen again, and he glances back at her counter, as if somehow the device could have escaped his attention all this time.

"No," he breathes, then looks back at her. "But you can put those in the oven."

Sylvia scoffs. "No one puts these in the oven. Wait 50 minutes for bad fried chicken? Please."

The demon stares at her. "So why...?"

Sylvia snorts, then holds up the box, tipping it sideways. Pilkington's eyes widen more as the dagger slides out, the pommel landing solidly in her hand. He looks up and over to the empty cabinets, then touches his thumb and forefinger together, the tackiness of the tape residue sticking them together with an audible sound. "Then what...?"

"A decoy," Sylvia says proudly. "I thought this might happen, so I got a fake dagger and hid it up there." She narrows her eyebrows at him. "Remember when I went shopping that day and you got worried?" When he nods, she adds, "I started wondering what would keep someone from breaking in and stealing the dagger if I wasn't home, and I decided to hide a fake so they could find something and leave feeling victorious. Besides, no one looks twice at frozen dinners inside a freezer."

"The freezer?" he echoes, still reeling.

Sylvia smirks. "I worked in an ice cream shop one summer. We used to keep some cash in the freezer overnight since no one knew the safe combination. It belonged to the previous owner." She shakes her head. "Sometimes it's easier to ignore the obvious."

Pilkington has to forcibly restrain the urge to take his arusha in his arms, hugging her fiercely and then kissing her senseless. The relief flooding his system makes him foolish, and he leans forward, a hand reaching out to cup her chin. "You are brilliant," he tells her, nearly unable to comprehend the wave of gratitude he has for her in the moment. His fears of being compelled wash away. "I cannot ever thank you enough." His magic gathers at the words, and he tries to hold himself back, to avoid giving his arusha any more promises, but the words are out before he can stop them. "I am eternally grateful to you for this," he tells her, "for safeguarding my free will." He feels the magic spill forth with his promise, his demonic power encasing them both. Sylvia reaches up to cup his hand with her own, and she smiles at him.

"I don't need your eternal gratitude," she says, and just like that, the magic shifts, waiting for her next words to settle the contract. "How about you just keep your free will eternally instead, huh?" The promise seals into Pilkington's soul with a zing, and he jerks at the force of it, letting go of her face in his surprise and confusion. "A thank you will do it," she adds with a laugh, then seems to notice his shock. "You okay?" she asks, setting the dagger on the floor and reaching out her other hand to touch his face.

Pilkington takes a breath, sinking back into his human body again, the magic draining away now that the agreement has been made. He has made many contracts over his long life, and all of them involve similar magic, but none has ever felt like that—no contract ever jolted him to his core. *What was it she said? Keep your free will eternally?* His eyes skirt to the dagger now laying on the floor, and he wonders what the artifact has done to his normal magic. Her words felt like a contract—but also like an order, something he cannot disobey even if he wishes.

"I'm not altogether sure," he says quietly, mind frantically considering the possibilities.

Can she wish me to retain my free will? Is that even possible?

"Will you do something for me?" he asks.

Sylvia's eyes narrow, but she nods her head. "What is it?" Something inside Pilkington warms—his arusha knows not to blindly promise things—unlike him sometimes.

He nods to the dagger on the floor. "Use that on me."

Sylvia frowns, her hand dropping from his face to her lap as she leans back. "Why?" Her voice drips with disgust.

"I need to know something."

Sylvia sighs. "Okay, but I want to know why you need to know this." Her hand reaches reluctantly for the dagger. "And I'm not doing anything dangerous," she insists. "After all, I just gave you eternal free will." Grinning, she lifts the dagger as she finishes her sentence, and Pilkington feels the echo of that power again. She frowns at him, then sighs heavily, her shoulders lifting with the movement. "Lift your right hand," she tells him with a grimace.

Pilkington looks down at his hand—which has remained resting on his leg.

Sylvia cocks her head. "Lift your right hand," she says more forcefully.

Nothing happens. Pilkington waits for that telltale pull, his body obeying without his control, but there is nothing. He can lift his hand if he wishes, but he doesn't have to.

Sylvia shakes the dagger, like it's a remote control on the fritz, and tries again. "Lift your right hand." When Pilkington's hand doesn't move, she stares at the dagger in her own. "Fuck," she says. "Do you think they somehow switched the dagger?" She peers at it, bringing the blade close to her face as she studies the markings. "It looks real..."

"It's the real dagger," Pilkington says softly.

"But it doesn't work," she says. "What happened? Did being in the freezer break it somehow?" She looks up at him, eyes wide with fear. "Did I seriously break an ancient artifact?"

Pilkington reaches out to touch her hand, comforting her. "It's not broken."

"Then what is going on?"

"You have broken me," he explains. "I am free from that artifact's control. Eternally free." He breathes the last few words, the depth of his gratitude overwhelming him.

"What? How?"

Pilkington wants to tell her, wants to tell her everything, but something holds his tongue, and he finds himself staring at her face instead, his eyes drifting to her mouth. He catches himself and snaps his gaze back up to her eyes, but he can tell she has seen his desire. "I..." His words trail off, and he doesn't know what to say.

"Kiss me," Sylvia says suddenly, hand gripping the dagger tight.

Pilkington stares at her, unable to believe what he is hearing. The compulsion he expects does not follow her order, and he finds himself staring into her eyes instead, not daring to look at her lips because he knows he will obey her. The moment stretches out, and slowly, Sylvia nods.

"Holy shit," she breathes. "It really doesn't work on you anymore." She frowns. "Will it still work on the vampires then? The other demon?"

Pilkington nods, slowly coming back to himself after the intensity of the moment. "It should," he says, getting his head back in the moment. "You freed me from the dagger, not the other way around. It should still work as is."

"We'll have to test it though," she says.

Pilkington bites his lip. "Will you be asking Oren or Harald to kiss you then?"

Sylvia smirks, smacking his arm with her free hand. "Neither, thank you very much."

"Is that not your test, then? Why ask me?"

She shrugs. "I'm not sure," she admits. "It just felt like the right thing to say." She tilts her head. "If it was truly broken, you wouldn't do it, though I guess part of me wanted to see if you would use the opportunity."

"I would not steal a kiss from you," he says, slightly offended.

"I know that," she says. "And I knew that before I asked you. But now I'm sure." For a moment, Pilkington thinks she is about to say something else, something important, but then her gaze lands on the shattered glass on the floor beyond where they sit. She sniffs, glancing around her at the destroyed apartment, then out the broken window at the afternoon light. "So now what?"

Pilkington stands, reaching down a hand to help her to her feet. "Now," he says, "we—"

He is interrupted by a sharp gasp as Sylvia stands up, and he looks down to see a small line of red appearing on one of her fingers. She cut herself on the blade while standing up. Wincing, she leans over to set the dagger on the counter behind Pilkington, then brings the finger to her mouth, sucking the cut. She pulls it out after a moment and examines her finger. More blood wells to the surface, and she puts it back in her mouth. "This is a problem," she says around her finger. After another moment, she pulls it out again, examines it, then grabs the towel from the oven door behind the demon and jams her finger in it, turning her back to him. Pilkington wonders why she is being so careful with her blood, then remembers that she is accustomed to spending time with a vampire. Cuts that bleed can be a problem. He reaches out to touch her arm.

"It's fine," he tells her. "The blood doesn't bother me." He watches the realization dawn in her eyes as she faces him, another reminder that he is not her vampire lover, but then she smiles.

"Perks of a demon," she says, then looks in the direction of the bathroom. "The Band-Aids were under the sink. I wonder if they're still there."

The demon is moving immediately, heading to retrieve the bandage. The bathroom is disheveled, but the box of adhesive bandages is still undisturbed beneath the sink, and he pulls one from the box. "Neosporin?" he asks from the bathroom, seeing the small tube laying in the sink nestled beside a red bottle of Tylenol.

"Sure," she replies from behind him. "Never know where those magical daggers have been."

Pilkington swears she glances at his forearm as he rubs a small amount of the healing ointment on her cut, then applies the bandage. "We need to get a scabbard for that if you're going to carry it around with you."

Sylvia snorts. "I'm more likely to stab myself with it than anything else," she scoffs. "Hey, if you're immune, can you hold it now?" She offers the dagger. Pilkington takes the pommel carefully, then immediately hands it back as pain throbs though his fingers. Small wisps of smoke escape from his red fingertips.

Sylvia winces. "Now it's your turn for Band-Aids." But as she watches, the skin heals, his powers easily repairing his body. "That's a cool feature," she comments.

Pilkington nods, recalling several times when his healing ability has come in handy. "Come," he tells his arusha. "Let's pack a bag of things you need. Then we can get you a scabbard for that weapon."

"Where do you get a scabbard?"

"I know a guy," he tells her.

"You have a scabbard guy?" she asks, then shakes her head, resting the dagger on the edge of the bed. "Never mind. Of course you do." She picks up a shirt from the floor and tosses it on the bed, starting a pile of clothing. Pilkington says nothing as she moves across the small room, kneeling to slide open a drawer in the bottom of the wardrobe that somehow remained untouched in the chaos. She retrieves two battered sketchbooks, then turns around and begins digging between the top of her mattress and the broken back of the futon. She pulls another sketchbook out, this one in much better condition. A quick scramble locates a handful of pencils, and she wraps them up in a cloth designed to hold her drawing tools. Pilkington knows that Sylvia is an artist; he has imagined her painting in the empty room in his house he created for her, knowing she'd never use it. But she has never shared her art with him beyond the sketch of the dagger that she kept on the table when they researched. He hopes that one day he will be worthy of such trust.

Standing up, she gives the room a sad smile, then returns to gathering more practical items: clothes, toothbrush, shampoo. She places the art supplies carefully in the bottom of a battered duffel bag she pulls from beneath the bed. It says "Carland Beach" in faded letters on the side and Pilkington hides a smile. He was with her when she bought it, along with...

As he watches, she unearths a familiar skirt from beneath the remains of the rocking chair, chuckles fondly, and puts it in the bag. Pilkington's chest warms as he realizes that she has kept the things they bought on the pier that last summer before he left for good. "One condition though," she says as she finishes gathering her belongings.

"Yes?" Pilkington asks. She is calm now, but he knows an explosion is coming, her wrath at the loss of her home too new to face.

With a final glance around, her hand reaches up to hold the necklace she wears—the compass he left on her windowsill long ago now. She didn't wear it when Theo was here, the silver burned him, but since he left, she hasn't taken it off. She holds it up now, the arrow that would seem to point north sliding slowly to point directly at him. She lets out a breath, following the arrow to him, but says nothing, letting the necklace drop to her chest. For a moment, he is sure that she is going to ask him who he is again—*Who are you ... to me?* But instead, she sighs, giving the room a final look.

"I was promised fried chicken."

"Lady's choice," he breathes, reaching out to take her hand and lead her away from her home.

CHAPTER 11

SYLVIA

SYLVIA AND PILKINGTON STAND OUTSIDE A SHOP WINDOW covered in ancient papers, obnoxious paintings, various hangings made of beads and crystals woven with frayed threads, and other items so peeled that Sylvia can't identify how they originally started life. A battered sign above the door reads "Raya's Relics." Sylvia gives Pilkington a nervous glance.

"This place?" she asks. "It looks like a front for human trafficking."

Pilkington raises his eyebrows, then nods. "I can see that." He takes her hand. "No one will harm you while I am here," he promises.

"I know that," she says, giving his hand a squeeze. She takes a breath, steeling herself. She doesn't want to admit how much his touch soothes her.

Of course it does, she tells herself. *It's Phil. He always made everything feel better. Safer.* She sneaks a peek at

116

him, but the demon is still studying the shop, lips pursed in thought.

Why didn't you tell me?

She knows this isn't the time for such questions, and she also knows that she is making excuses to delay the inevitable. She will have to ask him eventually, to know the truth of why he left.

With her free hand, she adjusts the strap slung bandolier-style over her shoulder and chest, the bag resting against her hip. The dagger is inside, lying flat against the bottom, but Sylvia is cautious of the sharp edge, worried she will stab herself in the leg as she walks. She's wearing jeans and a long hoodie for layers of padding between her skin and the blade, but she is still nervous. The sight of this store hasn't reassured her, though she's not sure what she expected the shop to look like. This is a contact who can provide a scabbard for a magical dagger on short notice. Sylvia is still new to this world and doesn't know how big of a deal this should be.

"So," she says, looking up at the store name again, "Raya, is it? Let me guess: you made a deal with her?"

Pilkington smirks. "No. I'm not sure who Raya was, but she was long gone by the time I made this deal with Chet. He … acquired this store soon after our agreement ended."

Sylvia does not ask how this mysterious Chet acquired a store of magical artifacts. She knows that she's been ignoring many questions like that lately, and she doesn't enjoy the feeling. She tightens her grip on Pilkington's hand instead, thinking about what he just said. "Wait—your agreement with him ended already?" At Pilkington's nod, she asks, "So he doesn't owe you a favor? How will we get the scabbard then?" She glances down at her purse with a frown. "I don't have any money."

"Chet won't need money," the demon assures her. "His tastes are more ... particular." He smiles at her. "Don't trouble yourself over it. I have what is required." He nods at the door, reaching out to pull it open. "Ready?"

"I think so," Sylvia says.

"Stay behind me," Pilkington tells her, releasing her hand to enter the store first, "and say nothing unless you have to speak. The less he knows about you, the better."

"Got it," Sylvia agrees and follows him into the store.

The smell hits her first, and she nearly stumbles. It's not unpleasant—rather, the scent is everything she has ever loved smelling in her life invading her senses all at once.

It's magic, she realizes. *I don't know why, but now that I'm paying attention, I register magic as smells, and this place is filled with magical items. What else have I smelled in life that was actually magic?* Chocolate wars with jasmine and vanilla candles flirt with fresh cut grass while underneath everything is the smell of the ocean breeze. Surprised, she stares up at Pilkington's broad back before her.

Is that what he smells like then? Home? She shakes the thought away, studying her new surroundings instead.

The store isn't very big, the front room jammed with a variety of bulky furniture and odd sculptures. Tapestries and paintings line the walls, some leaned up from the floor which is covered in layers of thick competing rugs. Lamps and sculptures jockey for space on every flat surface. Decorations with moons and stars dangle from the ceiling. Pilkington contorts his body sideways to avoid one; the long tendrils smell of cinnamon as they move past quickly. The back of the room has a small opening, and Pilkington heads through it without pausing. They enter another room, but this one is lined with shelves and glass cabinets along the walls. There is enough space behind the counter for a person to walk, and sitting on a ragged stool is a middle-aged man with long blonde hair. He is leaning on the counter, peering at a bracelet on a velvet square of cloth through a special lens on his glasses, and he sits up when they enter the room, the extra glass slotting into place among four other glass circles that rest above his regular frames. He narrows his eyes at Pilkington, clearly trying to place him and failing, but his nod is friendly enough.

"Hey," he greets in a deep voice, and Sylvia wants to cross her arms in front of herself, to hide from the creepy vibe he gives off. She is very glad that Pilkington stands between them. "Looking for something specific?"

"Yes," Pilkington says, and his voice is slightly different from the warm tone Sylvia recognizes. This is Pilkington the demon, ready to do business—not the friend she has come to know. "I need a scabbard for a dagger," he explains. "Seven inches long with a bridge."

"I see," the man replies, and Sylvia doesn't miss the ways his eyes skate quickly to his right and back again. She follows the glance to the doorway behind him. It seems to lead into a back room of some kind. Sylvia wonders what's back there.

Wait, she reminds herself. *I can try to … see.* Pilkington was able to show her how to use some basic abilities, like sensing the truth of her surroundings. She reaches out with her newfound senses, and the smells nearly overwhelm her again. This room reeks of magic, some of it coming from the man behind the counter. His glasses have a soft glow that she can see now, and she tries to focus her attention on the room beyond them. The items in the cases clamor for her attention, knives glowing yellow and red and blue, and she squints, trying to see behind them. The doorway itself has no visible door, but as she stares, a low golden haze fills the empty space.

Is that a … spell? Maybe only certain people can go back there. That kind of security makes sense. This place is filled with valuable items. She tries to push through the doorway, but it resists, though for an instant, she gets a flash of something odd—sunscreen and aftershave—a familiar combination that must signify another kind of witch she hasn't identified yet. The smell is so familiar, though. She knows she should remember what it is.

She pushes against the barrier again, and an angry hiss interrupts her efforts. She looks up to see that both the shopkeeper and Pilkington are watching her carefully, the man through intrigued eyes. He flips one of his lenses down and scans her from toes to hair, grin widening as his gaze moves. Sylvia feels suddenly naked despite her layers. His gaze hovers at the bag at her hips for a moment, but not long enough. *If he's looking for magic,* she thinks, *he must see it—like I can see it—but he doesn't want me to know he sees it.*

The man flips the lens back up and looks at Pilkington. "You should know better," he says menacingly. "Bringing a witch into my shop so she can scan my security."

"I'm not a—" Sylvia snaps. Pilkington widens his eyes at her, a reminder to stay silent, but the words are out before she can stop them. She isn't a witch. She doesn't know what she is anymore—but she isn't a witch. She's nothing like witches.

Witches did this to me.

"Curious," the man comments, turning his attention back to Pilkington. "Scabbards you say?" He sniffs, then climbs off the stool, stepping over to the doorway. "I think I have what you need, but I need to dig it out. Give me a moment." He steps through the door, arms dragging against both sides as he passes, and Sylvia gets a weird image of magic swirling, the golden color shifting darker at the edges, almost red now. She watches the spell shift for a moment, the colors swirling again so the entire space shifts red, and something inside her issues a warning.

"The door," she whispers, turning to face Pilkington, but the demon's face has gone still. He is staring into the empty space like a man obsessed, leaning forward like he doesn't quite believe his luck. "Hey," she says, reaching out to touch him. Something tries to bat her hand away, some foreign power, and Sylvia reacts with annoyance, pushing harder to reach him. "Hey!" she says again, louder this time. Her hand connects with Pilkington's arm, but the demon is still staring at the doorway, transfixed by something she can't see. The colors are lovely, the pattern pleasing, but it's not worth zoning out for. She gives Pilkington's arm a little shake, but the demon remains frozen.

Oh hell no, she thinks, feeling the strange power in the room pulse, growing stronger as it layers itself over Pilkington. *No way. You can't have him.*

She steps forward, putting her body between the demon and doorway, and reaches up to grab his face with her hands. The demon jerks as she touches his skin, eyes unlocking from whatever he sees to look down at her. "There you are," she whispers. "Come back to me."

"Where did I go?" he asks, his voice dreamy.

"I don't know," she replies, "but you're back now." She stands on her tiptoes, tugging his face down to give him a kiss on the cheek. At the last moment, Pilkington's eyes shift to the doorway behind her, and he moves his face, just enough for her kiss to land on his mouth instead. Sylvia doesn't have a chance to be surprised or embarrassed because a voice she didn't expect to hear again echoes through the doorway behind her.

"Seriously, Sylvie? Every time I see you, you're kissing someone else."

A chuckle bursts from her lips, and Sylvia spins around to see Adam McGibbs standing just beyond the doorway, the shopkeeper a few feet behind him in the back room. Adam holds a silver rod in one hand, and he points it at the demon behind her.

"You," he orders, "hold her."

Sylvia gasps as Pilkington's hands close on both sides of her hips, his grip firm but not painful. She glances behind her, but the demon's face is blank—a look she has seen before. But that was on a different face with blue skin and dark swirling tattoos and small black horns beneath a riot of black hair—his demonic form—and it had been when Charlie Wagner compelled him. Her face snaps forward to stare at Adam through that soft red haze in the doorway, her ex holding the silver rod like a weapon.

It must be another demon artifact, she realizes. *It must suck to be such a strong creature and then be subject to stupid random artifacts all the time. Well, not all the time,* she admits. Demon artifacts seem to be fairly rare—and not surprisingly—demons can't enjoy being compelled by items as well as their names.

She recalls the dagger in her bag, a weapon of her own, but Adam is a human, and magic like that won't work on him. *I can always try to stab him with it.*

She remembers the fight in her kitchen so long ago when he had attacked her and only Theo's arrival had saved her. She may be strong—but Adam is bigger and faster and stronger—and she doesn't know how to fight him. Not to mention Pilkington's hands on her hips holding her in place. She begins to squirm, and for a second, it feels like Pilkington will release her, but then the body behind her tightens, steadies, and the grip remains.

Wait—is he faking it? Did I really free him from all compulsion magic?

She looks up at Adam. "It's none of your business who I kiss," she snaps. "What the hell are you doing here?"

He laughs. "I thought I was selling a very valuable dagger," he admits, stepping forward to grab something from a surface beyond her view through the doorway. He keeps the silver rod pointed at Pilkington, but his other hand appears with the decoy dagger from her cabinet. "Imagine my surprise when Chet here told me it was fake." He studies the bag at her hip. "But you came here for a scabbard. Let me guess—you brought the dagger, too." He tosses the fake aside, and it lands with a loud clatter behind the door. "Get it for me."

"Fuck you," she says, determined not to let him have it.

Adam ignores her, looking behind her at Pilkington. "Bring her closer," he demands, and Pilkington takes a slow step forward, propelling Sylvia before him. There is an opening to their left that will let them behind the counter; a few more steps will bring her back there. "Closer," he says when the demon pauses. "Closer."

Sylvia allows herself to be pushed closer, frantically considering her options. She can still see the swirl of red on the doorway, a sheen that colors everything behind it—like Adam—a ghostly pink.

I need to get Adam to come through, Sylvia realizes. *Pilkington can't go through that door. I can, but he can't.* She doesn't know how she knows that, but she does. Just as Theo can't pass through a doorway into a residence without an invitation from the occupant, Pilkington will be held outside by that red spell. She remembers how Chet touched both sides with his hands as he walked through, no doubt activating the anti-demon spell.

I need paint, she thinks suddenly, *or a marker. Something to break that pattern.* Her bag thumps her hip as Pilkington takes another step, taking them both behind the counter. A turn to the right and they will be standing before the doorway. A small burst of heat thrums up her leg where the artifact rests beyond layers of fabric. She isn't touching it now—but she can feel it, the power calling out for her to use it somehow.

I have the dagger, she thinks suddenly. *I can use it to scratch the doorway.* That's not what the dagger wants her to use it for, and she's not even sure if a scratch is enough to disturb the spell, but she recalls the circle she had been trapped in in the old subway station and the way Pilkington's casual swipe along the drawings had caused a dent in the magic—enough for the Greater Demon to escape.

And how do I know what the dagger wants?

Pilkington pauses as they draw even with the doorway, his feet slowly moving so both of his shoes rest against her boots on the left side, his right leg slightly between her legs.

"Now," Adam commands, "push her through to me."

Pilkington's hands slide up her hips to her shoulders, but in the moment when he would push her forward, he instead shoves her to the side. Adam reaches for her instinctively, his hand reaching through the barrier and brushing the strap of her bag, and it is enough. As she lands hard on the floor to the demon's right, she looks up to see Pilkington snatch the rod in Adam's right hand, jerking the man fully through the doorway. Adam's mouth opens in horror, shock freezing his expression as he looks down to see the demon holding the anti-demon artifact.

"Sto—" he tries to say, but the demon is already moving, pulling the rod free and snapping it easily between both hands. In the same move, he jams the broken end through Adam's chest, a spray of blood arcing from his back and spattering the doorway.

Droplets hit Sylvia's face, and she scoots backward. The demon allows Adam's body to fall, and he stands glaring through the doorway. With the broken end of the rod, the demon pushes gently against the magical barrier. Sparks erupt at the connection, but the rod will not pass through from this side.

"We seem to be at an impasse," the demon calls through the doorway. Sylvia hardly recognizes the sound, her eyes frozen on Adam's slack face where his body has fallen on the floor. "Give me what I came for, and I will be merciful."

She can hear the fear in the shopkeeper's voice when he replies, "I need your word, demon."

"Make your claim," the demon demands.

Sylvia can hear noises that must be the man getting to his feet in the back room. "I will give you this scabbard," the man says, "and in exchange, you will not hold me accountable for that man's behavior." The demon above her nods, and the man in the other room continues. "I don't even know him. He just came in before you with a dagger that he claimed was magical. I didn't know what he would do."

The demon nods again. "Agreed," he says, and Sylvia feels something brush against her skin, a soft brush of demonic power.

Is that what a demon contract feels like? She had felt something like it back in her apartment sitting on the floor, but it was so much stronger.

There is more shuffling, and then she can see the man as he approaches the doorway. He holds a black scabbard in one hand, and he looks through the door carefully, avoiding the body lying on the floor between them. Sylvia can hear dripping, and she knows it's blood. No one here cares though. *No one here is a vampire,* she realizes.

Only demons and men.

She puts her hands on the floor and touches something sticky. Adam's blood has begun to pool, sliding its way to her. She scrambles a bit, getting awkwardly to her feet, and when the demon reaches out to help her, she backpedals, slipping away and hopping over the counter rather than let him touch her. She doesn't know what to think. Of course, Adam was going to hurt them. He needed to die.

But it had all happened so fast. And Pilkington had barely blinked at the violence. And though he is negotiating now with the shopkeeper, Sylvia has an awful feeling in her gut, something telling her that they will not be leaving anyone alive in this place in the end.

From the far side of the counter, she watches the exchange, not really following the words. The man hands the scabbard to Pilkington, who turns to hand it to her. Sylvia takes the length of leather, then stares at it dumbly for a moment.

"Test it," the demon says quietly. "Make sure it fits."

"Oh," she mumbles, then reaches into the bag with her other hand to retrieve the dagger. Heat blossoms in her hand at the touch, and a sense of quiet satisfaction fills her as she lifts it free. A tiny hint of red coats the tip, and Sylvia realizes that she must have cut herself with the blade again when she scooted away from Adam's body. She drags the blade across her thigh to clean it, the tiny line of red caught on her jeans, and she wonders if her purse is totally ruined or if a few stitches will save it.

She doesn't see the shopkeeper's face as she reveals the blade, but she does look up in time to see him hide his greed as she slides the dagger home. There is a small bump on one side of the scabbard with a hole in it. A leather thong trails down. Pilkington steps away from the doorway and makes his way around the counter to her. He takes the scabbard, careful not to touch the pommel or her fingers as he takes the leather thong and wraps it over the top and ties it, securing the blade inside. He hands it back to her without a word, then turns around to face the shopkeeper, who still hides behind his magic doorway. Sylvia feels that heat again, the sense of power beckoning, but she ignores it this time, dropping the dagger into her purse and shifting the bag so it rests against her back, out of sight and easy reach.

"Our bargain is complete," the demon says in that sweet soft voice.

"Yes," the man agrees. "Don't come back here."

"I won't," the demon replies, then cocks his head, and something in his body language warns Sylvia to turn away. He looks at her over his shoulder. "Wait outside a moment," he says quietly. "I need to speak with him. Alone."

Sylvia nods, backing out of the small room and into the front room. She wants to continue, to leave through the doorway and never think about Raya's Relics again, but something stops her.

You need to see this, she tells herself. *You need to know.* She pauses, standing in front of a small mirror. She has a spatter of blood on one cheek, and she scrubs it away, eyes filling with tears.

From the front room, she can still hear Pilkington. "Tell me," he says conversationally, "what you want, Chester Masterson." There is a pause, and then his voice turns silky. "Tell me what you want to do now."

The man's voice is odd when he replies, dreamy. "I will call Sal," he answers.

"And what will you tell Sal?" the demon presses, his voice a thread of darkness now.

"I will tell him that I saw it. That it's here. That the Tallardy dagger has been found."

"I thought so," the demon comments. "Come here. Look at this. Don't you want to see it closer? Come here and look at this."

There are no more words, but Sylvia knows the gasp and soft gurgling sounds are the last sounds that Chet will ever make. She flees the store onto the street, and though being on the sidewalk in the dark brings its own host of fears, she is ready to face those rather than the demon who will exit the shop after her.

She walks quickly down the street, pausing only when a large warm head presses into her palm. Tengo appears at her side and nudges her to pause against the wall of a building. She senses Pilkington before she sees him, the demon standing a few feet away from her, respecting her need for space. To let her get used to him, he waits a moment before stepping forward, and she flinches away. His hand hovers between them for a long moment, then falls to his side.

"You killed him," she says quietly.

The demon nods.

"Why?"

"He would have betrayed us. He had to die."

She nods, numb. "I know that." She pauses, her true feelings rushing to the surface. "But you were going to kill him all along, weren't you?"

The demon sniffs, rubbing his hand against his pants, then looks hard at her. "I was."

"But you made a bargain. You said you wouldn't hurt him."

"No, I said I wouldn't hold him accountable for Adam's actions. And I did not. He died for his betrayal of our secret, not for being a bystander."

Sylvia sighs, thoughts swirling. "I think... I think I need a moment," she says finally. When he opens his mouth to speak, she says quickly, "A human moment. A me-time moment." She frowns.

"But—"

"Please don't tell me about my safety. I have Tengo." She pats the demon dog's head. "I just need to sit somewhere without all this. Somewhere quiet. Alone."

The demon lowers his head. "Very well." After a pause, he adds, "Tengo will let me know when you need me."

Sylvia begins walking down the street, not sure where she is going, but needing to get away from him. She knows she will need him, but she wonders if she will ever want him again.

Sylvia sits on one side of a diner booth, a warm cup of coffee between her hands, staring down at the cracked Formica tabletop as if it could answer all of her questions. She feels stuck, trapped in place by forces beyond her control, but at the same time, things seem to be moving too fast, dragging her along in the wake of the current while she scrambles to stay afloat.

Take stock, Copland. Where are you?

Normally, Sylvia would use this moment to create a list. She likes lists, the neat rows of her messy handwriting allowing her jumbled thoughts to become clear. But her sketchbook is in the bag with her belongings—and that bag is stowed wherever Pilkington puts things when he doesn't want to carry them. He explained it as an extraplanar space, a pocket in space-time, but when she laughed and asked him about the TARDIS, he only gave her an odd look.

"That's time travel; I'm just storing things so I don't have to carry them," he had explained. When she asked him about time travel, he had simply shaken his head, neither dismissing her question nor answering it. The demon has a tendency of doing that. He doesn't distract her like Theo will when she asks questions that he doesn't want to answer—usually with a kiss. Instead, the demon lets her feel his reluctance and allows her to decide if she wants to pry. Sometimes, she will press him, and the demon does answer her—though she doesn't always like his replies. She knows that he would tell her what arusha means if she asked him instead of dancing around the question with everyone else.

Sitting at the diner, drinking lukewarm coffee, she wonders if Theo's approach is better.

Maybe I don't want to know, she admits. *Maybe that's why I'm sitting here now, wondering how I somehow managed to trade one monster for another.*

Because she knows that Theo is a vampire, that he kills people to survive—or at least feeds on them, willing or no. And she's done an incredibly good job of ignoring how much that bothers her—just like she's managed to ignore the little voice within that reminds her of all the reasons why her relationship with the vampire is doomed. *You're not Elena*, she reminds herself, *not Yuki, not Mina, not Sookie, not Buffy—nor anyone else who ends up with the vampire long term. And they are all something special*, she continues, *fairies, witches, slayers, secret vampires—and you are ... not.*

You're just Sylvia.

She always wondered why Theo would want to be with her, doubted her value, but then he would look at her—and she just knew. She knew that he had chosen her, despite their differences, despite their difficulties. He chose her knowing it would be hard.

And isn't that what love is? Choosing to stay together despite the obstacles? Choosing that person every day. No one said love wasn't hard.

But do I love Theo? She stares into her cold coffee, swirling the liquid around. *I definitely like him, and I like being with him. And I want him—of course, I want him. He does amazing things to my body. But is that love?*

She doesn't want to admit it, but another face has wandered into her mind, a young face with bright eyes and dark wet hair slicked back as the wave crashes over him again. The face shifts in her mind, the cheekbones widening, the lips growing, the boy she knew transformed into the man she knows, and she wonders if that could be love. *Bonds aside. Demon-human relationships aside. All of the bullshit aside—and what is left?*

Sylvia genuinely likes Pilkington, enjoys his company, his conversation, and though it makes her face blush to admit it, his looks. He's handsome, of course. She forces herself to recall his demon face, the form he had worn the first time she met him, and even though his skin was blue, and he had horns and a tail, she can still appreciate the dark markings on his arms and torso, the long dark hair that she was sure was silky to touch, the outlines of muscles across his shoulders, chest, and abs.

There is something wrong with me, she decides. *How can I find a creature like that ... attractive?* But she does, and there's nothing she can do to change how she feels.

Is that the bond then? Are my feelings, this pull toward Pilkington, the result of a magical bond? And if so, how is that any different from Theo right now being compelled to stay with his Maker?

She has tried to avoid thinking about Theo and how he must be occupying his time. It's been nearly six weeks since Jolena arrived to claim him, and though both Harald and Oren are searching, they haven't found him. Sylvia wonders if Jolena has taken him somewhere far away. She knows it's a possibility. If the ancient vampire didn't know about the dagger, she had no reason to remain in the city.

Unless she wants to torment him ... by keeping him near his friends ... and me. Sylvia doesn't know much about Jolena, but this fits with what she does know. Jolena likes to play with her vampires. Sylvia wonders if Jolena knows about her or not, if Theo has mentioned his human lover to his vampire Maker. *Would she threaten me? Use me to keep him in line?* Sylvia sighs, knowing that such lies aren't necessary. Theo is compelled to do whatever Jolena asks of him. She doesn't need to threaten him—he will obey regardless.

Sylvia believes that if Theo could escape and return to her, he would have by now. So he must be bound by her will, trapped in place until she changes her mind and bores of him again.

How awful, she thinks, *to lose one's free will.* She thinks about love and how much of herself she has surrendered to the needs and desires of another person—and she compares that willing sacrifice of some autonomy to the overwhelming and uncompromising power that holds both Theo and Pilkington in check.

Well, used to hold Pilkington in check. Sylvia recalls the moment in her shattered apartment, the thrum of power echoing around them both, and the way the demon was able to ignore the rod in Adam's hand. Thoughts of Adam and the rod cause her to picture her ex as she last saw him, eyes open and staring as he lay on the floor with part of the broken rod jammed in his chest.

She isn't sorry that Adam is dead, not really, but she is sad that a person died—two people actually. *But isn't the world a better place without both of them?*

Is it? And who am I to judge such a thing? And what happens if I do start thinking like that? Will I be able to kill as easily as Pilkington did today? Or Theo does?

She takes a deep breath, struggling to contain her swirling thoughts. *You said you needed time to think, and you've had it,* she tells herself. *What now?*

Sylvia nods, knowing the time has come for some decisions. They don't have to be the big questions, not yet, but she needs to decide how she feels about some of this—and more importantly, how she plans to move forward.

Theo. Yes. I will keep looking. When we find him, I can deal with how he is.

Pilkington. She looks up at the ceiling, studying the square ceiling tile for a long moment. *I have no idea. And until we finish this—the dagger, the Greater Demon,*

Theo—I won't know. And that's okay. But for now, the demon is her friend, her companion, and although she doesn't like what happened today, part of her knows it was necessary. As long as that ruthlessly pragmatic part doesn't get any bigger, Sylvia figures she's okay.

She hopes.

And what about me? Where is Sylvia on this list of priorities? She knows her focus has been skewed lately, her existence wrapped up in the supernatural forces that have taken over her life, but she also knows that she will find her way back to herself in the end. She always does.

What do YOU want? She demands honest answers from herself, knowing that this is the real purpose of her coffee moment.

I want ... a life that is my own. Not one determined by fate or the whim of some vampire I've never met. She knows that Jolena is a part of the Theo's life, and that isn't going to change. Even when the vampire does return to her—if he does—he will always be subject to his Maker's call.

Maybe I can free him, she thinks, *like I managed to free Pilkington... Phil.* She thinks of the dagger in her bag, the blade now protected by the scabbard that two men died for. *Could I kill her if that's what it took to free Theo?*

I don't know. She can feel the honesty in her answer, and it reassures her.

CHAPTER 12

HARALD

HARALD WAITS OUTSIDE A DINER, STARING PAST HIS NEW-found reflection in the windows to see Sylvia sitting alone at a booth, nursing what must be a cold cup of coffee in both hands. Her face is serious—a bit sad and a lot wistful—and as Harald stands there, a series of emotions flash across her mouth—laughter, sadness, guilt, confusion. He can identify each one as it passes, but he doesn't know the cause—though he can guess. He glances at Ula standing beside him, the witch slightly nervous about meeting Sylvia for the first time. He takes her hand, reassuring his mate. She gives him a grateful smile, then looks up seconds before Oren lands on the sidewalk beside them.

"You know that's super obvious, right?" she comments. "Humans don't notice everything, but you jumping off a building is eventually going to end up on YouTube."

Oren rolls his eyes, dismissing the witch's criticism as he has since meeting her. "It's dark, and there's no one around but you two," he defends. "And unlike some people, I'm not going to show up on YouTube." He gives Harald's reflection a long look that is both envy and relief. "One benefit of flying solo."

When neither half of the happy couple replies, Oren peers through the glass. "Did you tell her?"

Harald shakes his head. "No. We were waiting for you."

Oren narrows his eyes and grimaces. "Damn. I hoped that long face was for Theo. Apparently not." He looks around the small diner, clearly searching for Pilkington.

"The demon isn't here," Harald tells him. "She's here alone."

"Alone?" Oren exclaims. Harald can hear the same question in his friend's voice, wondering what could have happened to drag the demon from her side.

"Well, not totally alone," Harald adds. "That ... creature is with her." He nods, and Oren follows the line of his gaze to the space beneath the booth where the dark form of Tengo can be seen lying beneath Sylvia's feet. Oren frowns, though Harald is the one who dislikes dogs.

Oren pushes his friend's arm. "Come now, man," he says. "You've little to fear from a dog now, even a demon dog. I can't believe you're still afraid of them after all this time."

"You always ran fast," Harald says to his old friend. "They were never going to catch you."

"And now you run faster," Oren reminds him. "No dog could hurt you now. Besides," he glances at the witch at Harald's side, "no doubt your witch will defend you." He gives Ula a long look. "Don't witches come equipped with cats?"

"Jerk," Ula exclaims, smacking Oren on the arm. "This isn't the Middle Ages. Not all witches have cats."

Harald turns to approach the diner door just as Oren whispers to Ula, "But be honest—you have a cat, don't you?"

The witch winks at him as Harald holds the door open, and she walks through first, entering the diner with her head held high. Oren follows her, and the three creatures approach Sylvia's booth. She doesn't look up right away, a sign of how distracted she is, how caught in her own mind, but Tengo raises his huge head as they get closer.

The server gives them a questioning look, and Oren smiles and nods in Sylvia's direction, a clear signal that they are joining a friend. The woman nods, then lifts the coffee pot in offer. Oren nods and flashes her three raised fingers.

"Sylvia," Oren says as they draw closer, and she looks up, her surprise at their appearance turning to suspicion as she spots Ula. "Scoot over," he tells her. "This is going to take a moment."

Sylvia obeys, taking her purse from atop the table and stuffing it in the small space between her body and the wall before making room for Oren to sit beside her. Harald gestures for Ula to slide into the opposite bench first, then follows her.

"Uhh," Sylvia says, staring at Ula. "Who is this?"

Harald can tell there is something different about Sylvia—a newfound confidence that borders on fear—as if she has discovered new abilities and isn't sure if she can trust them yet.

Harald takes Ula's hand in his, then rests them together on top of the table, in clear view. Sylvia looks down at them, then back at Harald, face expectant.

"This is Ula," Harald says. "She's my—"

"No," Ula says suddenly. "Not like this." She looks up at Sylvia, eyes sympathetic, and Harald knows that his mate understands more of this situation than he does. His witch has picked up clues that he doesn't know to look for, and he decides to let her take the lead. Ula gives Sylvia a long look. "You know what I am?"

Sylvia nods, and then they all look up as the server approaches with a small tray containing three mugs. She lays them down without a word and fills them with coffee, then nods at Sylvia's nearly empty mug. "Need a warm-up, hon?" she asks Sylvia.

Sylvia slides her mug across the table without a word, and then everyone has hot coffee.

"Menus?" the server asks.

"No, thank you," Oren says, flashing his bright smile. "We're fine." He puts just enough power behind his words to ensure the server will not return to disturb their conversation, not until they call for her. She nods, then walks away, disappearing into the kitchen behind the counter. They are alone in the diner now, able to speak more freely.

Sylvia takes a moment to dress her coffee, adding sugar and creamer slowly enough that Harald thinks she is stalling, gathering her thoughts. She stirs everything together, then offers the spoon to Oren, who also takes sugar and cream in his coffee. Harald takes a sip of his black, the way he likes it, then opens a sugar packet and empties half of it into Ula's cup, the gesture earning a smile from his beloved.

"You're a witch," Sylvia says finally. She sits back in the booth, putting distance between herself and the witch across from her. "You're one of ... *those* witches."

Ula nods, and Harald glances at Oren. He hasn't told his friend much about Ula other than the fact that she is his mate. He wonders how his friend will react to her family connections. "I am Suren Tallardy," Ula says formally, "though I prefer Ula."

"Then it's yours, isn't it? You smell like it does now," Sylvia says. "Are you here to claim it?"

Smell like it? Harald says nothing, but he exchanges a quick glance with Oren, who also seems confused by her words. Ula frowns, giving Sylvia a long look. "That was my mission," she admits, "but ... circumstances have changed."

"What—you fell in love with Harald, and you guys are running away together?"

Harald smiles, unable to stop himself, but he still doesn't speak, letting Ula handle this. "I wish we could," his witch says, then pauses, gathering herself for a story. "I was sent here by my family to reclaim the lost dagger. We had word that it was here, but no one knew where or who had it."

"How long have you been here?" Sylvia asks.

"Nearly six months," the witch explains, and Oren gives Harald a sharp look. Ula doesn't miss it, and she squeezes Harald's hand. "Yes," she answers Oren's unspoken question. "I felt him immediately, and I had to find him. That was five months and one week ago on Thursday. We were going to tell you," she explains.

"But then the other demon arrived, and things got … complicated."

"The other demon," Sylvia repeats. "You mean Pilkington?"

"No." Ula shakes her head. "He's always here. I mean the demon Hesperus."

Sylvia winces at the name, the memory of the Greater Demon rushing over her, that burbling voice close as the creature did something to her deep inside. She cocks her head. "What do you mean, Pilkington is always here?"

Ula's eyes widen, clearly not expecting this line of questioning. "The demon Pilkington spends more time in this realm than he does at home. He always comes to this city when he is on this plane." The witch pauses, watching as something shifts in Sylvia's face, some piece of a puzzle falling into place. "I assume he visits you," she adds. "After all, you bear his mark."

Sylvia frowns. "You can sense the bond?" she asks.

Ula shakes her head, then reaches out across the table to lift up Sylvia's necklace. Harald and Oren stare at her in confusion. Sylvia often wears the necklace, though they have both seen her take it off on Theo's arrival. The chain is made of silver and burns a vampire's skin. "Not the bond," Ula says, "though now that you mention it, yeah, that's there too. But I mean this."

Harald and Oren stare at the compass on the chain, the arrow swiveling as the compass shifts orientation, then settling in a direction that is most definitely not north—instead pointing into the street. "What is it?" Harald asks.

"A token," Ula says. "It marks the wearer as belonging to a specific demon. This one is for an arusha though." She lets the compass drop, the token thumping against Sylvia's chest. Her hand reaches down to touch Sylvia's wrist, but finding it bare beneath the sleeve, she lets her go and sits back, lips pursed. "Serious stuff. I didn't know Pilkington had claimed anyone, though now that I see you, it makes sense."

"I have no idea what you're talking about," Sylvia says, fingers holding the compass tightly. "And you need to explain yourself right now." Harald doesn't quite believe her display of ignorance. Sylvia surely knows more than she says, or she wouldn't be sitting in this diner contemplating so seriously.

"You're the one from the cemetery, aren't you? The one my cousin tried to use to summon Forneus?" At Sylvia's wide eyes, his witch continues, "Look, that was awful, what she did to you." She shakes her head. "Esme was never ... all there. Even when I was a kid, I knew she would do something crazy. I saw it, but no one listened to me. Then."

Harald knows that some of Ula's abilities involve visions, glimpses of the future. That was partly why her family had sent her after the dagger—not so much to find it, but to witness that what she had foreseen would come to pass. She hasn't told him anything more than "things will work out just fine," but he wonders how much chaos can occur between now and some future "just fine." Ula had also seen that she would meet him, so she had to come—family wishes or not.

"And now?" Sylvia prompts, letting his witch tell the story in her own way.

"Now, they know better than to doubt my visions."

"What did you see," Sylvia asks bluntly, "for me?"

"I knew you would live," Ula says, "and I knew he would claim you—and that would matter now when we all came together."

"Wait," Harald interjects, "are you talking about when the demon escaped from Wagner's circle? That's when he claimed her. Sylvia was terribly hurt in the process. The demon kept her alive until Theo could get there."

Ula narrows her eyes. "You mean when Charlie Wagner was killed?" At Sylvia's nod, she shakes her head. "Oh no. Girl—you were claimed years ago."

"That night," Sylvia whispers. "He saved me that night."

"Yes," Ula nods. "And he could save you because you were already marked by him."

"Phil," Sylvia mumbles, and Harald gives Oren a look. Neither of them knows a Phil.

"He didn't escape unscathed," Ula continues. "The blade marked him just as it did you." Ula runs a finger up her forearm. "You've seen it, right?" Sylvia shakes her head, her hand unconsciously grasping her wrist and forearm, no doubt recalling how the witch touched her there, looking for something. "You will then." She frowns. "Didn't you go swimming already?"

Sylvia cocks her head. "With Theo?"

"No. That was before ... at the beginning. We're at the end now." Harald watches Sylvia's face fall at the witch's words. Ula shakes her head, her frown deepening. "Sorry, sometimes I get the timeline confused."

"Hold up," Oren interjects, speaking for the first time since his interaction with the server. "Are you saying Sylvia has been claimed by Pilkington before now? That she wears his token marking her as his?" When Ula nods, he turns to Sylvia. "But what about Theo?"

"What about him?" Ula asks, and Oren looks at her, freeing Sylvia from his judgmental gaze.

"Why is she messing around with my friend if she's promised to some demon?" Oren asks, the outrage clear in his voice. Harald understands—Oren's belief in loyalty is fundamental to who he is. Looking at Ula, Harald knows that such things are sometimes complicated, and there are no easy answers.

Ula snorts. "Clearly you haven't spent much time around demons. It's a bond, Oren, not a marriage vow. Sylvia is free to share her time," she glares at Oren, "or her bed with whomever she chooses." She looks at Harald. "Honestly, your friend has very outdated ideas about intimacy."

Sylvia's face had pinked at Oren's question, but at Ula's reply, her cheeks flush crimson.

"What does this have to do with the dagger?" Harald asks, pushing the conversation in another direction and giving Sylvia a moment to compose herself.

"It belonged to my family. It was our burden—when we could find it to bear." Ula gives Sylvia a long look. "But now, I'm not sure it's ours anymore." She pauses, taking a sip of her coffee.

"Why?" Sylvia asks, her voice quiet now. "What's changed?"

"You were cut by that blade that night in the cemetery, right? As a virgin?" Sylvia's face floods with heat, her heartbeat increasing, but Ula ignores her, nodding to herself. "And then it drew his blood, bonding him to you." Sylvia looks like Ula just punched her, but Ula seems not to notice. The witch tilts her head, brows furrowing. "And then it cut you again, this time not virgin blood, but it recognized you."

"Recognized me?" Sylvia echoes weakly. "You make it seem like the dagger is alive." Something in her face makes Harald think this is not the first time she has had that thought.

"It is alive," Ula says, "in a sense. Remember—it's filled with the power of hundreds of witches. All of them live inside it still. They would not forget a virgin bonded to a demon." She pauses, then nods. "I think the dagger may have bonded to you permanently."

"What?" Sylvia asks, the word an explosion of breath. "Can things stop bonding to me, please!?"

"It's not a terrible thing," Ula says, "though I'm not sure yet. You need to use it more, and then I'll be able to tell you."

"Let me get this straight: Sylvia is bonded to someone named Phil who rescued her years ago, and she wears his token, but they were both bonded by the dagger at the same time—and now she's also connected to Pilkington?" Oren looks like his head is about to explode.

Ula nods. "Yes, except the demon Phil and Pilkington are one and the same. Sylvia has been protected for a long time—since that night, in fact."

"That's why it didn't work," Sylvia whispers, as if realizing something. She looks up at Ula. "Is that why Theo's power doesn't work on me unless I let it?" She glances at Harald but says nothing, and he dips his chin slightly in silent thanks.

The witch raises her eyebrow but nods again. "Arusha bonds are strong, and they only grow stronger over time. I imagine very few creatures could affect you now."

Sylvia puts her face in her hands and groans. "I'm so tired of hearing about bonds."

Ula laughs. "I've never met anyone who was triple bonded before. That must be something."

"Triple bonded?" Oren echoes, cocking his head as he tries to work out the third.

Ula holds up her hand and lifts one finger. "Claimed as arusha." She lifts a second finger. "Marked by the dagger." She lifts a third. "And reinforced when he kept her alive with his essence until Theo could arrive to give her blood."

"His essence?" Sylvia chokes.

Ula nods. "How did you think he stopped you from dying? I've read it's like a golden light. It's supposed to be super peaceful. And so close." Harald touches Ula's leg under the table, a small part of him disliking the eager way she describes someone else's experience. His witch glances at him, then meets his eyes fully, clearly catching the hint of his jealousy. She gives him a look that makes him wish they were alone. "And bonds aren't the worst thing, Sylvia," she adds, gripping Harald's hand tighter and lifting it to her mouth for a soft kiss.

"Yeah, you want to tell me about that?" Sylvia asks, jumping on the chance to move the conversation anywhere else.

Harald gives her a goofy grin. "She's my mate."

"Mate?"

Oren answers, "Vampires have a myth about finding mates. We—" he scoffs, "apparently, *I* didn't believe it was true, but seeing Harald here, I'm a convert."

"More magical bonds?" Sylvia asks, her face tired.

Harald nods. "I knew right away. So did Ula. It's unavoidable." He sees the doubt on Sylvia's face, deciding to tell her right away. "And I knew when it happened... because I could see my reflection for the first time since I was alive."

Sylvia gasps, then looks at the window across the diner, no doubt seeing both him and Ula shadowed against the glass. She sits alone on her side of the booth, Oren invisible beside her. Harald watches her put the pieces together, sees the comprehension cross her face in a slide of fear, anger, relief, guilt, and finally resolve.

"So, Theo..." She lets the words trail off. Harald shakes his head no, sorry to be the one to tell her.

Sylvia nods. For a moment, Harald is sure she will cry, her eyes glassy, but then she takes a deep breath, obviously steeling herself. "It doesn't matter," she says finally. "It doesn't change anything. I still need to find him." She looks from Harald to Oren. "Even if he's not my ... mate, we can't leave him trapped with Jolena. We have to find him."

Oren sighs. "Not to pile on to the absolute shitshow of bad news you're getting tonight, but..."

Sylvia stares at him. "No."

Oren nods. "Yes. We found him."

Sylvia begins scooting toward him on the bench, seeming eager to do something instead of talking about more information she doesn't want to know. "What the hell are we doing here then? Let's go!"

"Do you still want to find him?" Oren asks, trying hard to keep his tone neutral. "After all, it seems like you have some other obligations."

Sylvia glares at him. "Of course I want to find him," she replies, her voice cold.

Oren nods, accepting her words, and puts a hand on her shoulder, holding her in place. "There's more," he says quietly.

Sylvia looks at his expression. "Oh fuck," she breathes. "What now? Let me guess—he's trapped in some impossible to escape place. The fortress is surrounded by a hungry army of vampires. That Mirrikh guy has his relatives in town." She pauses, exasperated. "Dammit, Oren, just tell me!"

"It's none of that," Oren assures her.

"But your face says it's *worse* than that," Sylvia says. "What could be worse than that?"

"I found him, and I spoke to him. He's fine," he explains, anticipating her next question.

"Well, what then?"

"He doesn't want to see you," Oren says finally, not able to look her in the eye as he speaks. "He wants us to leave him there and tell you not to wait for him."

Sylvia's face, which had reddened quickly before, now turns a frightening shade of white, her eyes burning in a way that makes Harald think of witch's power and women scorned.

"Um... yeah. No. No fucking way in hell is that happening." She gives Oren a burning look. The vampire stiffens on the bench next to her, surprised by the vehemence in her tone. "Take me to him. Now."

"You sure?" Oren asks.

"Oh yeah," Sylvia says, gathering her bag and taking a final sip of her coffee. "I may not understand anything else right now, but of that, I am absolutely certain."

CHAPTER 13

THEO

THEO MULDAVIAN IS STARING AT THE STARS AGAIN. OVER the long centuries of his life, in times of turmoil, he has found himself staring up into the night sky, identifying the patterns he memorized as a child. His father had told him that the stars would always show him the way home, no matter how far abroad he drifted.

His father had been wrong about a lot of things. Theo had never returned home, not in the centuries since he became a vampire. But there is still some truth to be found in his words—*the stars are eternal*, Theo muses. *Even to one who has lived as long as I have, the stars are the same.*

Maybe they will shift in another thousand years.

Maybe my world will change. Maybe I will be free.

Theo looks down at the rooftop on which he stands, knowing that he has the ability to fly away from here, to run from Jolena, but that it doesn't matter. Jolena chose this place to torment him. She would prefer a place deep underground, a place where there is no danger of the sun, but she has chosen to stay in his penthouse apartment instead, knowing his friends would come to him and try to tempt him to flee.

She hasn't even compelled him to stay with her. His Maker has been very careful about what she says to him, allowing him just enough freedom to tempt him.

He knows it's a false sense of freedom, an illusion. His Maker will snatch him back the moment he tries to leave.

And what is there to leave for? She would only take out her disappointment on those he cares about— Theo has learned that lesson very well over the years. While Oren and Harald would survive such treatment, Theo knows that Sylvia will not. He has no doubt that Jolena knows about his human lover. She is only biding her time, waiting for him to do something foolish so that she can react. Theo hopes that if he does nothing, remains her meek plaything the way he knows she wants and yet also hates, Jolena will bore of the game and leave him alone.

But even if I could leave now, he thinks, staring up at the stars again, *would I?* The last two months have given him a lot of time to think, to seriously examine the life he has in this city. Viking Times is a good thing. His relationship with his friends is a good thing. But they have had such things before and could again, somewhere else, some *when* else—when Theo is ready to face himself in their eyes again. He is rarely glad to not have a reflection, but after Jolena returns, Theo is always glad that he doesn't have to look himself in the eyes. Seeing the pity on his friends' faces is more than enough to remind him that each time she returns, she changes him a little bit more.

He had seen it on Harald and Oren's faces the night before when they tried to talk him into running. They didn't understand. They never would.

It's too easy with her, too easy to become the creature she enjoys, the wild beast, the hunter, the one who rebels against her control but also bows to her whims. Theo pictures Mirrikh, knows that years ago, the werewolf was strong, fighting his Mistress's hold with everything in him, but time has softened his resolve, and now the wolf simply seems spent. Theo wonders if he wants to die—anything to release him from servitude. One look at the man's shoulders reveals his despair.

I want to fight, Theo reminds himself. *I need to fight. But why bother? It seems pointless, especially if that is my future.* He's been in this position before, and it always ends the same way: Jolena gets her way, and Theo spends the next few decades trying to rebuild some semblance of the man he wants to be.

So, what then? I will not give up, not like Mirrikh. But I will not fight either. The warrior in him rebels at the idea, but the strategist in him has already calculated the odds, and he knows this is a long game. It will take time.

Time that Sylvia does not have.

Theo is still learning to let her go. He knows Harald and Oren will see to her protection—they had agreed to that much at least before they eventually left— though the demon makes them superfluous. He wishes he were able to help them find the Greater Demon, or even find out more about the dagger, but he doesn't fear for his human. As long as he gives Jolena no reason to punish him, she should be safe.

Theo is just about ready to go back inside, passing through the sliding glass door back into the kitchen, when a thump on the roof behind him makes him pause. He senses Oren, the only vampire he knows who can fly like he can. Harald can slow himself while falling, but his skills never allowed him to fly. If Oren is here, that means Harald must be coming from inside the building instead, probably after compelling the doorman to let him on the elevator.

Don't they know better by now? Why do they keep trying?

Theo closes his eyes, preparing for another argument. "Oren—"

"It's me," another voice says, and Theo whirls to see Sylvia standing on the rooftop next to the lounge chair she once sat in, the two of them spending the night staring at the stars—and other entertainment. His first instinct is to run to her, to protect her, but at the same time, Jolena's not-compulsion echoes in his veins, and he freezes in place, not wanting to alert his Maker. Oren crouches on the edge of the rooftop, hands on his knees as he studies his old friend.

"You shouldn't have come," Theo says after a moment. He glares at Oren, who should know better. Jolena will kill Sylvia if she catches her here. "You shouldn't have brought her here."

"Tell her that," Oren says, rolling his eyes.

"Yes," Sylvia says, and Theo looks at her, "tell *me* that." There is something different about her, but Theo can't place it. She is still beautiful, her long blonde hair blowing out behind her, the moon streaking it with hints of silver and white. She wears a pair of jeans and a black hoodie, her messenger bag slung across her shoulder just as it was the first night he met her, and Theo catches a hint of her blood, a small taste as if she cut herself recently. *But she is always beautiful,* Theo thinks. *Tonight, she is ... terrifying.* Sylvia has changed in the last months, perhaps had started changing before he left, but he had been too close to see it.

"You shouldn't have come," Theo repeats quietly, hating himself for the words but knowing they are necessary.

"Why?" she asks, her voice just as soft as his own. For a moment, Theo can pretend they are not standing on the roof with his jealous Maker only a few feet away; instead, they are having a quiet discussion with all the time in the world, conversations they have had too few of during their time together. Staring at her now, Theo knows that he can silence her words with a kiss, calm her questions with his body. Or maybe he can't. There is a subtle difference in the way she stands, the way her eyes assess him and the distance between them.

"It's too dangerous," Theo says. It's the obvious thing to say. "You need to go." At his words, the space next to Sylvia begins to swirl. Theo knows magic when he sees it, but he is still surprised to see a large black dog appear at his human's side. Sylvia doesn't even look down, as if the magical appearance of a large dog is a normal occurrence.

She has changed. And so have I.

She reaches down to pat the dog on the head, then her hand slips into her purse. "Come with me," Sylvia says. "You can come with me."

Theo shakes his head, his senses screaming at him to get Sylvia out of there. They can discuss this later

when Jolena is not a few feet away, or better yet—
never. "You need to leave," he says firmly. He turns to
Oren. "Get her the hell out of here."

"No can do," Oren says, looking at his fingernails.
"This one is all you."

Sylvia pulls the dagger from her bag. Theo is surprised at the casual way she holds the blade, though she
has acquired a scabbard at some point. She looks confident, a look he has seen on her face before, but not
like this. She practically glows with magic now. "Please
come with us," Sylvia says again.

Theo feels the order like a jolt through his body,
and he takes a step toward her, unable to stop himself.
He lifts his hands up, pleading with her to see reason.
Jolena will know she is here by now, and he doesn't
know if that dagger will affect his Maker at all.

She will break Sylvia like a twig.

"You have to go!" he grits out, one foot moving forward against his will. He looks up to see that Sylvia
has started to cry.

"You choose to stay here, then?" she whispers, and
the compulsion vanishes as if it had never been. Theo
steps back to where he stood before, putting space
between them. "You want ... her?"

Theo starts to shake his head, but it's more complicated than that. His feelings for Jolena are mostly
disgust now, but he cannot deny that beneath his revul-
sion, there is still love, still that lovestruck obsession
that overwhelmed him when they first met so long
ago—when he woke from delirium to find her face
looking down at him.

"I..." He lets the word trail off, not sure what to say. He knows that he wants Sylvia away for her safety, but is that all?

Is Jolena just an easy way to excuse leaving her behind?

Didn't you always know this was doomed? The soft voice in his mind could be Jolena, but it could also be his own. *Vampires and humans never last. You know that. That's why you never bothered; in all your long years on this earth, you never tried. Because you knew it would end like this. In heartbreak. You, for letting someone get close to you that was never going to be there forever—and them, for believing that you had a future.*

"Just say it," Sylvia whispers, and Theo doesn't think she realizes that she is holding the dagger, that her words still have power over him.

"We ... can't be together," he grits out, hating himself and her as more tears slide down her face.

"Why?" she asks. "Tell me why."

"We're doomed," he replies, and there it is. He can pretend that their differences don't matter; he can pretend that they can overcome the odds, but in the end, he knows the truth.

And even if they did overcome everything and stay together, there will always be Jolena, ready to come in at any moment and yank him out of her life again.

Sylvia nods. "I see." She sniffs, then her gaze shifts to something behind him. He feels his Maker before he senses her, and he freezes in place, Jolena's will holding him fast.

"Well, well, well," the vampire purrs, moving up to stand behind Theo, "what a touching scene." She stands up on her tiptoes, then uses her power to lift the extra few inches so she can whisper in Theo's ear, her breath leaving streaks of pleasure in its wake. "Is this her then? Your little pet?" Theo can hear the smile in her voice as she leans down and kisses his neck. Theo bites his lip, unable to stop himself. "She looks delicious," Jolena continues. "Shall I taste her and see?" She gives Theo a little nip, drawing a tiny line of blood, and Oren hisses, looking away across the city, unable to watch. Theo falls to one knee, feeling Jolena stand tall behind him, her hand on his shoulder, claiming him the way Sylvia's hand touched the dog at her side.

Jolena sighs, scanning Sylvia, who still stands in place, the dagger in her hand, that dog lounging casually beside her. Theo expects Sylvia to be frightened, but he can't sense any fear. Only calm, a frightening calm that he has never seen before.

"So, you're the human," Jolena says mockingly. "I figured you'd be blonde, but I thought you'd be taller." She takes a few steps closer to Sylvia. The dog growls, a low hum, but Sylvia only touches his head, and the creature stops, still staring at Jolena with narrowed intelligent eyes. Clearly, Sylvia makes the decisions in that relationship.

"That's me," Sylvia says, as if they are two women meeting at a coffee shop, her voice casual. "I knew you'd be short. Ancient vampire thing and all."

Theo hears the sharp intake of breath as Jolena gasps, unable to comprehend the insult. How long has it been since someone was rude to her? Theo can't imagine anyone has been anything but flattering to his Maker in centuries.

"Oh," Jolena purrs, "you will be fun to break."

"No one's breaking anyone," Sylvia declares. "Not here. Not tonight." She cocks her head slightly, as if listening to something only she can hear.

"Really?" Jolena asks, glancing over her shoulder at Theo. "I suppose you're right. This one's will broke long ago. He belongs to me now. He always will." She pauses, then continues in a sweet voice, "But you knew that already, didn't you? That's why you're crying on my rooftop, begging him to take you back."

"I won't beg him to take me back," Sylvia says. "But I will fight for his freedom." Now it is Sylvia whose voice turns sweet, quiet, like old friends. "You should just let him go. He doesn't want to be with you—that much is obvious. Don't you want someone who actually wants you? Not someone you have to force to sleep with you?"

Jolena growls, then launches herself across the roof at Sylvia. The human doesn't move out of the way; instead, she holds up the dagger, sliding it free from the scabbard and offering it up to Jolena like a prize, and the vampire skids to a halt inches away. "Is this why you're really here?" Sylvia asks, tilting the weapon so the blade catches the moonlight. "You came to fuck with Theo—I get that—but you stayed because you wanted this." She waves the blade back and forth slowly, a tease. "You want it, right? Take it."

Jolena laughs, rich and throaty. "You think I'm fool enough to grasp a blade made of silver?" she asks.

Sylvia looks down at the blade. "Oh, silly me," she says, flipping the weapon so the leather-wrapped handle faces the vampire. Theo doesn't understand the honesty in her voice, the total lack of fear as she stares down an ancient vampire. "I totally forgot about your little silver allergy. You must be glad you're not into the emo look," she comments, still holding the pommel out to the vampire. "You think you deserve it? Go for it."

The look on Sylvia's face is one that Theo doesn't know, doesn't understand, but in the moment Jolena considers the offered dagger, Theo becomes aware of another presence, the dim outline of the demon Pilkington hovering just above the roof to his right. He tries to signal to the demon without words, but the demon in human form just stays in place, face impassive as he watches the exchange.

Has she commanded all of us to just stand here and do nothing? Theo wonders where Harald is, knowing that his friend would not abandon them. At the thought, he hears a small ruckus coming from the apartment behind him, and moments later, three figures pile onto the roof: Mirrikh, looking apathetic as always, but resigned to his fate; Harald, his hands fisted and red as if he'd been hitting people; and a tiny white-haired pixie that Theo identifies as a witch. *What the hell is happening?*

Jolena had looked momentarily nervous, but with the arrival of the werewolf at her side, her confidence returns. "You're smarter than you look," she tells Sylvia. "Even with your pet demons, you are no match for us."

Sylvia ignores her, turning her attention to the werewolf who has taken up guarding his Mistress's side from the motionless demon. "You're Mirrikh, then?" she says. The creature narrows his eyes at her, trying to judge the level of danger facing Jolena. "I can free you, if you'd like," Sylvia continues speaking as if Jolena isn't standing right in front of her, a deadly vampire with a temper. "Would you like that?" Sylvia presses. "To be free of her?"

Mirrikh gives her a long look, then nods once, swiftly, something flashing in his exhausted eyes. Jolena turns to glare at him, her face promising retribution, but then Sylvia smiles, and Theo feels the power burst from the blade. For a moment, he can see the threads binding the werewolf to Jolena, a powerful spell of compulsion and obedience, and one by one, they snap, disappearing into the wind. Mirrikh shakes his head, looking around as if seeing the world for the first time. He takes two quick steps away from Jolena, moving away from any immediate danger.

"What have you done?" Jolena hisses, turning to Sylvia. "Do you have any idea how long it took to tame him?!" In her anger, she snatches the blade from Sylvia, who doesn't resist. Theo lunges to his feet, ready to fight to defend Sylva from the imminent attack. She may not be his forever, but he will not let her die tonight.

But before he can reach her, Sylvia speaks, her voice eerily calm and quiet amid the chaos. "You know what you have to do," she says quietly to Jolena, who holds the dagger before her with unfocused eyes, though her hands have begun to smoke where her skin touches the exposed silver. "You need to leave this place," she continues. "You've been here too long. You need to leave and never return."

Jolena makes a choked sound, and Theo watches as she turns the blade in her hand, pointing it at her chest.

"Go!" Sylvia orders, and even though the human doesn't hold the blade anymore, Theo feels the magic pulse from the weapon, from Sylvia's will. He watches in horror as Jolena jams the dagger into her chest, stabbing herself through the heart. She falls in slow motion, her face outraged even as her hand continues to push the dagger home, and by the time she hits the roof, she is already beginning to fade away, her body folding in itself. A moment later, and she is gone, the only memory of her an empty green dress on the rooftop.

Theo falls to his knees beside it, the hollow space inside of himself where his Maker had been expanding until he feels like he too will disappear. He is vaguely aware of both Oren and Harald crying out as well, and it is a long time before he is aware of the world again.

A world without his Maker in it.

He is ... free.

The feeling is too much. Too big.

Eventually, he climbs to his feet to assess the situation. Harald is hugging the tiny witch, Oren has blood tears rolling down his face, and Mirrikh has vanished. Sylvia sits where she was standing, hands in her lap, the dagger resting atop the green dress in a pile next to her. The demon dog has vanished, and Pilkington remains where he was, watching everything with that unreadable expression.

Theo stumbles his way to Sylvia, wanting to hold her. He can feel the emptiness inside him swelling, and the lost look on her face says she is feeling the same thing somehow.

"Syl," he whispers, collapsing in front of her. "Are you okay?"

She raises a tear-stained face to his. "I didn't know," she says finally. "I mean, I guess I must have known all along, somewhere deep inside, but I didn't mean it." She looks away from him to the empty green dress, then bites her lip. "I'm lying. I meant it. I knew what would happen, and I did it anyway."

"What are you talking about?" he asks, needing to focus on anything but the space where Jolena was. "You didn't do anything."

Sylvia laughs, an empty sound as she looks up at him. "I killed her," she says quietly. "Don't you get it? I gave her the dagger knowing it would kill her." She frowns, sniffing. "I wanted to set you free," she says, meeting his eyes. "Did it work?"

Theo nods. "I am ... free."

Sylvia wipes her cheeks. "Good. I'm glad." She pauses, raising an eyebrow. "But there's something else, isn't there?"

Theo doesn't know what to say, how to explain it to her. He knows there is something she will understand, though it hurts him to do it. "I can't..." he begins, then takes a breath and continues in a stronger voice. "We can't do this ... anymore."

"Because I killed her?" Sylvia asks, her voice breaking. "Or because I'm not your..." A sob wracks her shoulders, and she looks down, putting her face in her hands. Theo feels a presence at his back, the demon approaching at last.

"Stop," the demon tells him. "Can't you see you're hurting her?"

"I have to hurt her," Theo says, getting to his feet. "Ending things always hurts."

"Are you seriously breaking up with me right now?" Sylvia asks, and the outrage in her voice hurts, but Theo has decided. He knows how this goes. It's better to stop now when everything else is already falling apart. He can feel her anger now, and it is better. She reaches out to snatch the dagger from the dress, snapping into the scabbard with an ease that surprises him. She stands up, jamming the blade into her purse and wiping her face. Her eyes are burning with anger as she looks at him.

"You know what? Fuck you." She turns to the demon beside her. "Take me away from here, please."

"Where?" the demon asks.

"Anywhere he isn't," she says coldly.

The demon nods, gives Theo a judgmental look, then wraps Sylvia in his arms. There is a soft pop, and both demon and human vanish. Theo sighs, then glances at his friends.

"Odin's tits, Theo. You colossal ass," Oren says, hopping off the roof edge to approach him.

Theo sighs, ready to face the wrath of his friends. It's easier than facing what he has just lost.

CHAPTER 14

PILKINGTON

THE DEMON TAKES SYLVIA TO HIS HOME. HE DOESN'T THINK
about it beforehand, hasn't planned to steal her
away from her vampire lover, nor has he any idea how
he will explain her presence to those above him. But
when she looked at him with those pleading eyes, her
heart in pieces after the Muldavian's words, Pilkington
had only wanted to please her.

He knows that part of it is the bond. He must make
his arusha happy: seeing her in pain causes him pain.
The demon understands how bonds work.

But he's beyond bonds now, beyond the realm of
familiar things.

I love her, he realizes, looking down at the seemingly
frail human in his arms.

He has brought them to the front room of the house,
a large open space with a wide staircase leading to the
upper floors behind him and the large front door in
front of him. Sylvia has not let go of him, her face

still buried in his chest, which has lost the layer of the Henley he wears on his human body in the mortal world. Here, in his home, his body has reverted to his normal form, a blue-skinned demon with dark tattoos lining his limbs and chest. He is slightly taller than his human form, but Sylvia's face stays in roughly the same spot on his chest, pressed between his exposed nipples. He is glad that, unlike some demons, he prefers to wear pants at home, so he does not find himself naked with a distraught human pressed against him.

Sylvia had been crying, but now her body stills, her hands that had been pressed hard against his shirt now gently touching the skin of his back. Slowly, she pulls her face free, staring first at the bare skin before her, then craning her neck to look up at him.

"Ummm," she says, "why are you naked? And blue?" She glances around quickly, then pauses to take in the room more slowly. "Where are we?"

"Home," Pilkington breathes, then pulls his hands away from her back, where he had cradled her close to him for the journey. "My home."

"We're in the demon realm?" she asks, her voice rising much less than he expected it to. She releases him and hops to the nearest window. She stands there for a moment, and Pilkington does not speak, letting her see his realm in her own time. He wonders what she makes of the purple sky, the two moons high in the sky this time of night. Pilkington's home is in the mountains, situated near a large lake, the water black in this light. She can probably make out the outlines of what passes for trees in this realm, long skeletal figures without leaves.

A long moment passes without any words, and though Pilkington spies the shadowy form of Billy, his soul-servant, hovering in the doorway to the back room, he waves him away with a hand. Sylvia will have plenty of time to meet his resident ghost—if she decides to stay.

Perhaps she will demand he return her to her own realm immediately. Pilkington would understand. So much has happened in the last few hours. She must be straining under the weight of so many changes.

A soft sound reaches the demon's ears, and he realizes that Sylvia is crying again, her shoulders barely moving as she stands facing out the window. He moves to stand behind her, but he doesn't touch her, realizing that his true form may be one more upsetting thing she doesn't need.

"What can I do?" he asks softly. "Do you want me to bring you back?"

Sylvia lets out a noise that could be a scoff and turns into a sobbing cough as she whirls to face him, launching herself into his arms again. "No," she says, her face pressed against his chest. "No, don't bring me back there."

"We can go anywhere," he tells her, his arms wrapping gently around her back. "Tell me where you want to go."

Sylvia takes a few deep breaths, clearly calming herself, then looks up at him. She reaches out to brush his chest shyly, wiping the spot where her tears have left a tiny wet spot, the sheen highlighting the line of his markings against his blue skin. "Here," she says finally. "I want to stay here."

"Are you sure?" he asks, very aware that she is studying his face, no doubt taking in his long black hair, the two horns that peek out from the top of his head, the tiny fangs he reveals when he speaks. He is not normally a vain demon, but he wonders how his hair looks at the moment. He's been in his human form for a long time now, and though his normal body is more comfortable, he hasn't missed it the way he thought he would. He releases her, tucking his hands in the pockets of his black pants, aware of the tiny trail of hair on his lower belly disappearing beneath his waistband as her eyes slide down his chest, then flash guiltily back up to his face again.

Pilkington has wondered if Sylvia thinks of him in that way, if she ever sees him as an object of desire, but the pulse of confused interest surrounding her answers his question.

"Is it too much?" he asks, gesturing to himself with one hand. "I can change back if you prefer."

Sylvia frowns, then shakes her head. "This is your home," she says. "You can be yourself." She narrows her eyes at him. "Is this you then? I remember you being bigger the first time we met."

"This is me," he tells her. "When we met, I had been summoned, and I always answer a call in my most demonic form."

Sylvia peers at him, and he realizes she is looking behind him. "No wings?" she asks.

"Oh!" Pilkington exclaims, letting the glamour drop. "It's easier not to have them when I arrive home." His wings fade into existence, black webbed with blue patterns.

"What's it like having wings?" she asks. "Like, how do you sleep with them?" She shakes her head. "I'm sorry. That's such a weird question." She sighs, looking down at the floor, seeing the fine carpet. "It's been a really long day."

"I sleep on my stomach," Pilkington replies, trying to ignore the image that flashes into his mind at the thought of his bed: of wrapping his wings around them both as she slept in his arms.

"Sleep," Sylvia echoes. "I think I need some of that. Today just keeps going and going." She glances around the room but doesn't find what she seeks. "What time is it anyway?" She furrows her brow. "I can see it's nighttime, but do you have day?"

"Of course we have day," Pilkington says. "Just because this is the demon realm doesn't mean it's an endless hellscape." He pauses, then adds, "Sunrise is quite beautiful." He takes a few steps through a wide doorway to the left of the staircase, peeking inside to check the grandfather clock against the back wall. "It's 5:37," he calls over his shoulder.

"Oh," Sylvia says, her voice surprising him from just behind where he stands. He shifts sideways, gesturing her through the doorway. She walks through, her jacket just brushing him as she passes into the back room—what Pilkington calls the living room, though that's a human word for it.

The room has three large couches—one faces a large flatscreen TV, one faces a large window overlooking the lake and mountains beyond the house, and one lines the wall to the right, various cushions and pillows tossed here and there. The furniture is obviously different, though, with low backs and wide flat areas—made for the comfort of winged creatures. Sylvia walks across the room, her feet sinking into the soft carpet, and stands before the window. A large fireplace sits in the corner to her right at the end of the couch, and a large stool rests before the slowly burning flames. The clock sits against the back wall near another wide doorway into the kitchen beyond.

"Are you comfortable?" Pilkington asks. "I can make it warmer."

"I'm fine," Sylvia tells him. "Actually, it's nice in here." She tugs her bag from her shoulder, lifting the strap through her hair, then sets the bag on the small coffee table before the couch by the window. She lifts her arms, pulling the hoodie over her head, revealing a lavender tank top beneath. She places the hoodie on the table beside her bag and moves closer to the window. "It's beautiful."

"You should see the sunrise," Pilkington says.

"Can I?" she asks. "When does the sun rise here?"

"Let me see," Pilkington says. "How about a cup of tea?"

Sylvia turns to face him, her face tired, but her smile is genuine. "That sounds lovely."

Pilkington heads into the kitchen, setting the water to boil on the stove. He can conjure hot water and even tea, but he remembers Sylvia's comment about how his conjured food tasted odd, so he is determined to make it for her instead. He wants her to be comfortable here in his home.

"Billy?" he whispers when he enters the kitchen.

The soul-servant materializes in front of the sink. "Master?" he says, bowing his head. "You called?"

Pilkington says nothing at first, knowing that Billy will be unable to maintain his decorum for very long. At the demon's raised eyebrow, the soul-servant explodes, "Who is she?!"

"Sylvia," the demon says, "your Mistress. Do anything she tells you to do."

"A guest!" the ghost squeals.

"Keep your voice down!" Pilkington snaps.

"A lady guest!" Billy continues, his tone suggestive. "I never thought I'd see the day—"

"And you will not see the day," Pilkington threatens, "unless you shut up and tell me what time sunrise is today."

"6:03," Billy replies immediately. "The first moon has already set."

The water in the kettle rumbles, starting to boil, and Pilkington grabs a mug from the cabinet, glad he has made his home like a human one. He scoops loose tea into a cloth bag, then pours the hot water. After a moment, he pulls down another mug and makes himself a cup of tea as well. Before Sylvia, he rarely enjoyed tea, but he has since become a fan. A nice cup of tea before bed is soothing in ways he had not realized. Perhaps all those Canadian women were right about something.

"Thank you," he tells Billy, collecting the mugs and shooing the ghost away. "Now don't let her see you. We can do introductions after she's had some sleep."

The soul-servant salutes, then backs out of Pilkington's way. "Good luck!" he whisper-shouts as Pilkington heads through the door back into the living room.

Sylvia has settled herself on the couch, resting one of the pillows behind her as she stares out the window. Pilkington hands her the mug, careful to give her the handle first so she doesn't burn herself.

"Sunrise is in," he turns to check the clock again, "eighteen minutes."

"Nice." Sylvia brings the mug to her face, letting the smell of the tea waft into her nose. "This smells so good." She pauses, then narrows her eyes at him. "Wait—did you actually *make* this tea for me? You didn't just ... acquire it?"

"You looked like you needed it," he says, standing awkwardly near her holding his own mug.

"Please sit," she tells him.

"Are you sure?" he asks. "I can leave if you'd like to be alone."

Sylvia sniffs, taking a small sip, then winces and sets the mug down on the table to cool. "I should want to be alone, huh." She looks at him. "But I don't want to be alone from you. Is that weird?" When the demon continues to stand, she scoots slightly away from him, patting the cushion near her. "Please sit. You're making me nervous."

"It's not weird," the demon says, settling his large form on the couch. He leans back, his wings lifting over the small edge to hang down. "You've had a difficult day."

Sylvia nods. "You can say that." She sighs. "I'm sorry," she says. "I shouldn't have reacted like that. I was a jerk to you earlier."

Pilkington puts his mug down, turning to face her on his couch. "Not at all," he reassures. "You had a perfectly normal reaction to an unnatural situation."

"Why are you always so calm?" she asks him. "So reasonable."

The demon scoffs, reaching for his tea. "I am not always calm or reasonable," he assures the human on his couch.

Like right now, I am neither.

"I suppose not." She pauses, a sigh lifting her chest. "I know why you did it. I know it had to happen. But it was Adam. I mean, we were close once. I know he wasn't … worth saving … in the end, but still. He was a person. And you killed him so easily."

Pilkington pauses, wondering how to respond. Should he tell her what Adam intended to do to her after he acquired the dagger? He has a feeling that she already knows, having faced her ex once before. But even knowing that isn't why he killed him. Pilkington hasn't been caught flatfooted by a spell in a long time, and even though he is now free from compulsion magic, the boundary on the shop's back door would have kept him helpless while they did as they pleased with him. He is lucky that Sylvia was with him and able to break him free. For such audacity alone, he had to die. The man was a threat. Besides, Pilkington had promised to kill him if he ever saw him again after that day beneath the ground in the subway station when Sylvia nearly died in his arms. Pilkington knows his arusha has a kind heart, but he also knows that she can be practical when it comes down to it.

"I killed him," the demon says carefully, knowing that he is taking a chance, but that it has to be done. "And I would do it again, easily."

"Why?"

"To protect you." The words tumble free, and he can't stop them. He has to get himself under control soon, or he will be useless in his regular dealings. "And me."

Sylvia's gaze slides to her bag, no doubt thinking of the dagger within. "I can protect myself now," she says quietly, as if the idea still isn't quite real. "Ula said the dagger bonded with me, but she also said that we—you and me—have been bonded since I was younger. Since that night in the cemetery. Is that true?" Pilkington nods, not trusting himself to speak. He wonders how long she has known—he knows one of the witches must have told her, but he isn't sure which one. Uncertainty swirls through him. He hasn't lied to her, not directly, but he allowed her to misunderstand, and perhaps that is worse. "So it was you." She pauses, and Pilkington waits, unwilling to sense her emotions. He doesn't want to know yet. Instead of addressing his betrayal, Sylvia says, "She also said that the dagger bound you to me, after it cut me."

This is news to Pilkington. "The dagger?" He shakes his head. "No. I claimed you as my arusha that night on the Ferris wheel, though I did not intend to."

"What does it mean then?" she asks. "Arusha? Is it like the vampire mate thing?"

Pilkington reaches for his mug, taking a sip to give himself time to gather his thoughts. He assumes he is not the first person she has asked about this, so she must have some inkling, but now she is waiting for him to explain it to her. He has imagined this moment, this conversation, though he never imagined it would take place with her sitting on his couch in his home in the demon realm. He never thought she would be willing to come here with him.

"Not quite," he explains. "Vampire mate bonds are soulmates, kindred spirits connected with powerful magic."

"So arusha doesn't mean mate?"

"It does but not in that way. Not always. Arusha means chosen one. Demons choose an arusha, a companion, but it doesn't have to be anything ... more."

Sylvia stares at him. "Wait, that day on the pier, you told me that arusha meant yellow."

Pilkington reaches out slowly, running a tendril of her hair over his finger. His black nails seem too big, too thick next to her delicacy. At least his gloves cover the rest of his hands, the loop over his middle finger holding them in place, the dark fabric covering his forearms to the elbow. "You are my yellow-haired chosen," he says softly. "I wish to make you happy. But you are always free to do as you wish," he assures her quickly. "I will protect you ... if you need it. I will be here if you need me. But you are not obliged to me."

"So, you get to choose me, and then you choose to set me free?" she asks, raising an eyebrow. "Don't I get a say in this?"

"You have all the say in this," he says, sitting back.

"What if *you* didn't choose me?" she asks. "What if it was the dagger all along, connecting you to me?"

"I chose you," Pilkington repeats, certain of himself. "The dagger bond was after my choice."

"But it marked us both, didn't it?" She glances down, and Pilkington knows she is thinking of the scar on her belly, a silvery line he has seen the edges of occasionally when he checked up on her over the years. She reaches over to grab his hand, her fingers gripping the loop holding his glove in place.

"Wait," he says, his other hand closing over hers. "It doesn't matter." He is suddenly shy, not wanting her to see the white scar that runs across the back of his hand and up his forearm. He has worn gloves since it happened because the scar appears no matter what form he wears. Other demons would wonder what kind of weapon could hurt someone like him—and Pilkington doesn't want that kind of attention. He opts for the fashion statement instead.

"Doesn't it?" she whispers, fingers moving again to tug the glove free.

Pilkington grips her fingers, his strength easily stopping her. "It does not," he says again, turning the subject from his arm. "You are trying to say that we are bound by magic, by this artifact, suggesting that I am not free to make my own choices." He gives her a hard look, stretching his hand so her palm fits neatly inside his. "Believe me, I know my own will. I know when I make a choice and when that choice is made for me." He brings her hand to his face, kissing her palm gently. "I chose you."

"Triple bonded," Sylvia says, and Pilkington stiffens, not expecting to hear the words from her lips. He really has to find out more about this new Tallardy witch who seems to know so much about him. "We're bonded over and over again," she adds, "like layers on a cake or something. It just keeps getting stronger." She looks up at him. "Why do you just keep saving me?"

"Why do you keep getting into trouble?" he replies.

"I don't mean to!"

He chuckles. "None of us ever mean to," he assures her. "But still, it happens."

"Is that what you think then—that all of this is just coincidence?" She turns to him. "Do you believe in destiny?"

He sighs, studying her hand in his. "I believe that some things are foretold and unavoidable. But I also believe that our choices can influence events."

"So sometimes you're fucked but ducking helps?" she asks with a chuckle.

He nods. "Something like that." He pauses, then asks the question he thinks she is trying to find. "Do you think our bond is destiny?"

"Do you?"

"I chose you," he replies, squeezing her hand. "Am I destiny then, forging our path in the world?"

"Do I have a choice then?"

He nods. "Always. Just say the word, and I will do anything you wish. I am here for whatever you need."

She nods, accepting his words, but he can tell by her expression that she is still conflicted, that she is unsure of what her connection to him means, but he also knows that she will not come to terms with it tonight. It will take time.

He has time.

"So, what now?" she asks after a quiet moment, looking up at the shifting light in the window. "What happens now?"

Pilkington puts her hand back on her lap, then adjusts his glove so it sits properly on his arm again. "Now we watch the sunrise," he says, "and then you go to sleep. You're exhausted."

"Will you stay with me?" she asks suddenly, her voice very small. "Can I ask that?"

The demon nods, then seeing the lost look in her eyes as the light brightens, he beckons her closer. She slides over to him, scooting into his lap without a word. She rests her head against his chest, curling her body up within his embrace.

Pilkington puts an arm around her back, studying the contrast of his blue skin against her pale hair as she relaxes against him. They watch the sunrise together, the light creeping across the floor until it bathes both of them, but by then, Sylvia is sound asleep in his arms.

CHAPTER 15

SYLVIA

SYLVIA WAKES UP IN A STRANGE PLACE, BUT SHE ISN'T AS worried as she thinks she should be. The bed she is in is comfortable, the sheets soft the way she imagines fancy hotel room sheets must feel. She still wears her jeans and tank top, and she is covered by a dark blue sheet and a soft fuzzy blanket. The pillow beneath her head is fluffy. She rolls onto her back, looking up to an unfamiliar ceiling, white plaster with exposed wooden beams. She can hear the soft crackle of a fire nearby, and she looks to her right to find the fireplace, a simple opening surrounded by gray stones. She can smell the fire, but underneath are two layers of scent: cinnamon red-hots and the ocean breeze. Her brain struggles to connect the conflicting smells.

It's demons, she realizes, knowing the cinnamon is how she thinks of their power.

And the ocean is Pilkington. Phil. He smells like my bedroom in my old room growing up. He smells like home.

Next to the fireplace is a glass door, and Sylvia squints at it, the sunlight filtering through the pane to leave a line on the floor.

This is Pilkington's house. She remembers curling up on the couch next to him that morning, but he must have carried her in here after she fell asleep.

She wants to explore the world beyond that glass door, but first, she needs a bathroom. A look to her left reveals three wide doors, so she crawls out of the massive bed to consider the options. One opens into a closet—stocked with simple skirts, shirts, and dresses in Sylvia's style. She can see the few clothes she jammed in her duffel bag have been unpacked and rest on hangers at the front of the row of new clothes. She flips through the options, feeling strange material and seeing tags with undecipherable letters—though she recognizes the one that says Oscar de la Renta. This one she pulls out, liking the simple sunflower pattern, but then the four-digit price still listed on the tag catches her eye, and she very carefully sets the dress back on the rack, smoothing the sides so as not to damage it.

I'm not sure if this is really sweet or super creepy, she thinks, looking at the closet full of clothing that she would wear. It reflects her style, what little style she has, and it's all in her size.

Maybe I will just call this demon thoughtfulness.

Looking down at her jeans and crumpled top, she sighs, then grabs a pale pink sundress and a black sweater hanging nearby, tearing the tag off the sweater without looking at it. The room has a dresser, and she slides one of the drawers open, not surprised to find a stack of her panties and folded tank tops next to separate piles of similar items in different colors and material. As she selects underclothing, Sylvia wonders if Pilkington actually unpacked her bag and folded everything, or if he used magic. She's not sure which makes her feel better.

Three pairs of socks are tucked into little balls along the edge of the drawer. She isn't sure she remembered to grab socks in her panicked packing session, and she adds them to her pile. She did grab her sandals, and she was wearing her boots last night—they sit next to the bed, the only evidence that someone put her to bed—but her sneakers have been abandoned in her apartment. Glancing back into the closet, she can see a row of various shoes lining the floor. No worries there then.

Sylvia tucks the fresh clothes under one arm, then heads to the next door. This one opens into a hallway, so she shuts it immediately. She's not ready to explore the house yet. The third door opens to a bathroom that is half the size of her apartment.

"Yeah," she says, setting her clothes down on the sink and taking in the room. "Definitely an upper-class demon. Mom would be proud." She begins her routine, a regimen that used to be a morning practice but has shifted to an afternoon process since she started dating a vampire.

Was dating a vampire.

She stares at the enormous shower, recalling Theo's face as he broke up with her. She understands why—mostly—but it doesn't make her feel any better. She turns on the water, then takes a very long shower, trying to unravel the tangled skein of her emotions as the hot water loosens her tight muscles. Halfway through, it occurs to her that the shower is wide because of Pilkington's wings, and she wonders if he showers in this room at all. She tries not to picture it, but her mind is too fast, a flash of water running down his blue skin, his dark hair plastered to his face.

There is definitely something wrong with me, she decides. *Who knew I was into blue people?* A joke about X-Men and Avatar floats across her mind, but she ignores it. She closes her eyes, letting the water hit her face, and the image of Theo's expression fills her mind. Not the look after he broke up with her—before that—the look when he watched Jolena's body disappear into nothingness and fell to his knees in agony.

I did that to him, she thinks. *I freed him, but I also broke him in the process.* She recalls the feel of the dagger in her hand, the weapon seeming to fit naturally into her grip as if made for her hand. There is more—details she doesn't want to think about—but memory floods through her anyway.

There were voices, she remembers. *Quiet whispers as I held it. They told me what to do. How to kill her. And I welcomed their advice, letting them into my mind the same way I invited Theo in so many months ago.* They had disappeared as soon as she returned the dagger to her bag, but she will never forget how it felt to wield so much power over so many strong creatures. *Is that what Ula meant when she said I was bonded to the dagger now? What will happen the next time I touch it? Who will I kill then?* A small sob escapes her at the thought, and she stops thinking about the dagger, her focus shifting to the only other thing on her mind.

Theo doesn't want me anymore.

Standing beneath the water in the demon realm, Sylvia shudders, her tears mixing with the shower as she lets the loss of Theo wash through her.

I knew, she reminds herself. *Of course I knew. But it still hurts.*

Does it hurt because you still want him though? Or does it hurt because you had already started to let him go?

Sylvia pushes the thought away, scrubbing her face and taking in a few deep breaths to clear her mind. After washing her hair with shampoo that smells divine—Sylvia doesn't recognize the letters on the label—and using soap that has actual flowers embedded in the surface, she finally abandons the safety of the shower.

She isn't surprised to find her clothes fit perfectly, and she steps out of the bathroom into her room with a lighter heart. She feels even better after seeing the steaming mug of coffee resting on a tray on the bed. Sylvia wonders if Pilkington was in here while she showered or if his servant had brought her the drink. She remembers him telling her about Billy, the soul-servant who lives in his house. She's not sure what a soul-servant is, except that he's a ghost who works for a demon, but she is sure she will find out.

She spies her purse hanging on a hook next to the door to the hallway, and she walks to it, retrieving her phone and swiping it on. Her battery is low, but since she has no service, she powers the phone down and puts it back in her bag, setting it near the dagger. She can feel the magic of the dagger as her hand brushes past it, the power making the hair on her arms rise, and she hangs the bag on the hook and steps back.

She knows that she will have to return to her world eventually, to face the problems that linger there—but not yet. Right now, she needs a break, and this place is perfect.

Picking up the coffee mug and taking a sip, she sighs. Then she turns to open the door to the outside world. She's seen the demon realm at night under the moonlight, but she is not prepared for the riot of color that assaults her senses when she steps out in the afternoon sunlight. The mountains fill the surroundings in a swirl of blue, black, and white, dotted with greenery of what must be trees, but she can see that closer trees are purple—tall lean branches dotted with few leaves. She stands on a balcony overlooking a crystal blue lake. Leaning on the wide stone banister, she looks down the way she does on her fire escape. Below her is a wide-open space with what looks like grass but is white and silver instead of green. There are paths through the silver, dark places that look like stone, and she follows them with her eyes to the lake. A long dock begins at the water's edge and leads out into the water.

The place is alien and beautiful, and Sylvia takes a deep satisfied breath, the first easy breath she has had in months. She's not sure if the colors are because this world is filled with more magic than her own or if it actually is that bright, but she doesn't care. Her eyes feast on the image, her fingers suddenly itching for paint to capture what she can see.

I will be drawing this place for years.

"Good afternoon," Pilkington says behind her. She turns, resting her mug on the banister, to see the demon leaning in the doorway. His hair is unbound, long waves reaching his shoulders, and two small horns poke up on either side of the top of his head. His skin is blue, though dark lines run across him in patterns. His wings are black, thin membranes scored in blue lines. The tip of a blue tail drifts into view near his side. He wears black fingerless gloves that cover his hands up to his elbow—the ones she had tried to remove that morning, but he had stopped her. She continues to study his demonic appearance. He wears black pants, his feet bare, and she stares at his chest, surprised to see that he has nipples and a belly button as well as a ton of sculpted muscle.

Stop staring, she tells herself, but her eyes refuse to move. She cocks her head, frowning at him. "Good afternoon," she says, "can I ask a really weird question?"

Pilkington raises his eyebrows but nods.

"Um... are demons like ... born?" She shakes her head. "I mean, are you guys born like humans are born?" She tries to remember if the other demons she encountered had nipples but can only recall fur and scales. Demons come in various shapes and sizes, and Pilkington, despite his wings and horns, resembles a human man.

Pilkington follows her gaze to his navel, then looks up at her, catching her staring at the small line of dark hair that disappears into his waistband. Sylvia quickly looks away, reaching for her coffee again, her cheeks heating. "Yes," he replies. "The process is quite similar."

"Oh," Sylvia says, taking a sip and contemplating the repercussions. For a moment, she pictures what the demon in front of her would look like naked, then looks away as her skin flushes with embarrassment.

"Oh?" he echoes, a hint of laughter in his voice. "What did you think happened? Did you imagine that demons just appear fully formed out of the ether?"

Sylvia grimaces, awkward now, hoping she hasn't offended him with her ogling. "I guess not. I just didn't think about it."

"Would you prefer I change my form?" he asks again. "I can be human again if you want."

"How does that work?" she asks. "Is it a big deal?"

Pilkington blurs before her, the blue demon shifting, shrinking, until she is staring at the human man she knows. His wings have vanished, the black pants reappearing as blue jeans and a green Henley covering his chest, and his hair is shaggy but not too long. Sylvia blinks. "That's so cool," she says. "Is that a demon thing or a magic thing? Could you teach me how to do that?"

"It's magic," Pilkington says, stepping onto the balcony to join her at the railing, careful to leave her space between them. He looks up at the sun and closes his eyes, obviously enjoying the feel of his home world. "I can try to teach you if you want. Now that you're bonded with the artifact, you may have some other abilities. Or perhaps you can tap into more of mine."

Sylvia tries not to think about what tapping into the demon's abilities really means. "Is it real?" she asks instead.

"What do you mean?" He turns to face her, hands in his pockets as he leans against the railing, his back to the lake. There's something ... off about the way he leans, something her brain can't figure out.

"Like is this really you now or is it an illusion?" She reaches out to touch him, and Pilkington steps away quickly, the move obviously a reflex. His face falls.

"Forgive me," he says, moving back to her. "It's just..."

"Just what?" she asks. "I don't have to touch you. I'm sorry. That was so rude."

"No," he says, reaching out to grab her hand. Though she can see his perfectly normal human hand holding hers, his long sleeves covering up most of the back of his hand, her senses are feeling something different, a soft material that doesn't feel like skin that she can follow up his arm. She moves her hand in the other direction instead, finding the edge of the gloves on his fingers. She closes her eyes, feeling the glove, then opens them and stares at his naked hand.

"I don't understand," she says. "You look human, but you still feel like…"

The demon nods. "When I shift my form here, it's illusion."

"So, demons can't actually change their shape?"

"Oh, they can," he assures her. "And they do." He pauses, then says with a quiet sigh, "I cannot." He looks down, then continues, "It's a failing on my part… But no one here knows of my issue, so I never let them touch me. That's why I moved away from you. It's a reflex."

Sylvia pauses, trying to understand what he is saying. There is a lot to unpack. She shifts the focus slightly. "When you're in my world, you're still a demon?"

"I'm always a demon," he reminds her, "no matter what form I take."

"That's not what I mean." She bites her lip, staring at him. "I know who you are." Frowning, she adds, "But I've touched you there. And I've held your hand. You're not wearing gloves."

The demon pauses, clearly deciding if he wants to tell her more of his weaknesses. Sylvia waits, not wanting to press the issue but curious despite herself. "When I am in the mortal realm," Pilkington explains, "I am truly the form I take on arrival."

"You're human when you're there? But you're so strong."

"My abilities go with me whatever form I take, and my power is strong. My body is ... ordinary."

"Are you human a lot?" she asks. "Like enough to get used to it, or is it still really weird for you? I can't imagine switching my body."

Pilkington considers, leaning back into the wall. Her brain finally understands what is so off about his stance. Though the demon is relaxed against the banister, there is an inch or so of empty space between his shirt and the stone wall. Sylvia stares at it.

"I'm old, so I have been in many bodies over the years." He pauses, then says definitively, "I am accustomed to my human form, yes."

"Your wings!" Sylvia says, suddenly understanding why he seems to be hovering away from the wall. "They are still there, but I can't see them!"

The demon nods, shifting his body slightly, no doubt adjusting his wings. Sylvia hears the soft sound they make as they touch the wall.

"Wait," she says, "if your form here is an illusion, but your body in my world is reality, that doesn't make sense. Why? Is that just a demon thing?"

Pilkington shakes his head. "No, that's a me thing. Actually, my father's thing, to be honest." Sylvia finishes the coffee in her mug, and her stomach growls quietly. "Time for food?" he asks.

"How about a deal: I'll make us something while you tell me about it?" Sylvia suggests. At his expression, she adds, "You don't have to. It's just... I don't know anything about you. Not really."

Pilkington turns to the door, leading her through the bedroom. "You know how I take my tea," he reminds her.

"True." She nods, following him down the long hallway, past several large doorways, some with closed doors, some open into wide airy spaces, then down a small staircase into a modern kitchen. "But I feel like you know way more about me. You've been caught up in my business for months now."

"I'm not caught," he says. "I am not your prisoner, captured by your whims. I choose to be with you. What are you thinking for food?"

Sylvia considers, setting her mug next to a fancy glass carafe with still steaming coffee inside. She glances at the grounds still resting in the top portion, the air redolent with fresh coffee. She laughs, recognizing the Chemex coffee maker, relieved to see that not everything in Pilkington's house is expensive name brands. "How about breakfast?" she suggests. "I can go for some bacon and eggs, maybe toast of some kind?"

Pilkington nods, heading to the refrigerator to pull out the bacon. Sylvia begins by washing her hands, settling into the routine of making breakfast in the demon's kitchen far more easily than she expects. "Your family?" she prompts, laying the strips onto a pan. Pilkington pours himself a cup of coffee, then hops on top of the island across from her, crossing his legs and settling himself to watch her work. His feet are bare, and Sylvia is strangely pleased to see the demon so comfortable in his own space.

"I don't generally talk about it," he begins.

"It's okay," she tells him. "You don't have to. We can talk about anything else." She raises an eyebrow. "What do demons talk about anyway? Is there some demonic reality show everyone cares about or something?"

Pilkington laughs, and the sound does something to Sylvia's soul, easing her in a way she didn't know possible. "Demons mostly talk about humans," he tells her, "so yes, some of them obsess over television."

"Not you?"

The demon shrugs, taking a sip of his coffee. "Depends. I enjoy watching shows when I'm not working. I'm actually a sucker for Korean dramas."

Sylvia laughs, deciding to leave that detail for later. "What do you do for work then?" It's a strange question, and she looks up, waiting for the answer, hands held in the air before her, fingers shiny with bacon grease.

"I investigate," the demon replies. "When something strange is happening, Forneus sends me to see what's going on, to resolve any issues I encounter." He pauses, then adds, "I am discreet."

"Who's Forneus? Your boss?"

"In a manner of speaking," Pilkington says. Sylvia returns to laying out the bacon, then crosses to the sink to wash her hands again. "He sends me places on behalf of the council."

"The council?" she echoes, drying her hands on a towel. Everything in Pilkington's house is super soft. She opens the oven door, sliding the pan inside and double checking the temperature on the display. Finished, she turns to lean against the sink, watching him. She recalls early conversations with Theo, back when they talked more than kissed. "Am... am I allowed to know this stuff?"

Pilkington smiles, an approving grin. "Absolutely not," he says. Sylvia likes the devilish expression, the rebellion in his tone. She thinks again of Phil, the boy she knew in the man before her.

"So why are you telling me this? Is it because I'm bonded to you? An arusha thing?"

The demon tilts his head. "Yes and no. Yes, because I will tell you anything you wish to know. No, because it's more than that—I *want* you to know. Normally, I would not be able to say these things to a human, an outsider, but since you freed me, I find I can say anything I wish. It is … intoxicating." He dips his head in her direction, an acknowledgement of his appreciation. "I am in your debt, Sylvia."

She watches him, aware that he very rarely uses her name. "I don't want your debt," she insists. "You owe me nothing. I'm just glad you're free. You don't have to tell me anything."

"I know," he assures her. "But I want to."

"Oh," she says, not sure how to reply. The temperature in the kitchen seems to have increased a few degrees, and she pushes her sleeves up. "Let me work on bread." Pilkington nods to a cabinet, and she opens it to find several packages of different bread items: white and wheat bread, English muffins, and an assortment of bagels. She pulls down the muffins, then moves to the toaster on the counter across the room.

She can feel Pilkington's eyes on her as she moves. "So," she says, settling on a topic to break the silence, "want to tell me why you can't change your form here?"

"My father," he says simply. "He can alter his form easily—you can say it is his specialty—and his transformations are always true, no matter where he is. I inherited some of that ability, but not all of it. While most demons are the opposite—their shifts are true here but illusion elsewhere—I can transform anywhere else but in this realm."

"Genetics are a funny thing," Sylvia comments, not sure how demon heredity works. "I have my mom's eyes, but I guess my dad was the blonde." She pauses. "How many realms are there?"

"Many," the demon replies, "though some are more popular than others."

"Is your dad from here then? A demon? Or from somewhere else?"

The demon hesitates, and Sylvia turns to glance at him, letting the muffins brown in the toaster. "I'm sorry," she says. "I'm totally prying again."

"No," he tells her. "It's fine. My father is not from here." He pauses, then shakes his head. "I want to tell you this, but I should not. No one here knows who my father is, and I keep it that way. If you don't know, you cannot be made to tell anyone."

Sylvia nods, recalling her other demon encounters. While Pilkington may be friendly and not a threat to her, those other creatures would not be so kind. "Okay," she says with a grin, "you make it sound like your dad is an angel or something scandalous like that." Pilkington's eyes widen, his mouth falling open, and Sylvia covers her mouth with her hand. "Oh fuck," she curses. "Seriously?"

Pilkington's eyes scan the kitchen nervously, as if checking to make sure no one heard her words.

"New topic!" Sylvia announces, popping out one muffin and adding another. "The important question now." She approaches the refrigerator, hand on the door handle. "Butter or margarine?" She whips the door open, peering inside.

"Butter," the demon says, his slightly offended voice coming from behind her. He has hopped off the counter to stand near her, and his hand reaches past her to grab the carton of eggs as she picks up the small plate with half a bar of butter on it. "Who uses margarine?" He shudders, then heads over to stand by the stove, pulling down a pan from the rack overhead.

"It's easier to spread," Sylvia offers, then giggles, returning to the toaster.

"Heathen," Pilkington says, turning on the burner and heating the pan. "Over hard, right?"

Sylvia nods. "Yes please." She remembers a few times in the small kitchen in her mom's house on the beach: Phil had come over when her mother was working, the two of them cooking a small meal, then sitting on the wooden deck out back to eat, listening to the waves crash or talking of this or that. She watches him cook now, the adult version of the boy she knew, and he still moves the same way.

She has a quick memory of Theo standing at her stove, pulling a pan of lasagna free the first time he had cooked for her. That was the first night they had fooled around, the first time he saw her scar.

And now he doesn't want you, she reminds herself. She knows there are bigger questions—she needs to understand how far she can go with the dagger, and they need to locate the missing demon—but right now, she pushes the angry sadness away and watches the demon make her eggs as if all the years between didn't happen.

"Why didn't you tell me?" she asks quietly.

He looks over his shoulder at her, twisting a little as he does so, and she realizes that he's compensating for the wings she can't see. "Tell you what?"

"Who you were." The toaster pops again, and she flicks the muffins onto a plate, sucking her thumb after to ease the burn of touching hot food. "When you came to help like this, why didn't you tell me you were Phil?"

Pilkington's shoulders sag, and his head leans down. "Would you have wanted to know?" he asks quietly, flipping her eggs. The sizzle fills the room.

"Why wouldn't I?" she asks, putting a small pat of butter atop each muffin half, watching it melt into the surface.

The demon turns around to face her, pan held in one hand. "You mean to say you would have welcomed your old friend Phil back into your life when you were with the Muldavian?"

His honesty cuts, and she looks away, unable to meet his gaze. Theo would not have been happy to learn she had an old demon friend. The vampire barely tolerated her friendship with Pilkington because he knew the demon kept her alive until he could arrive with his restoring blood. Theo would not have wanted to share her with anyone, especially old friends like Phil—the boy who left just when she wanted to kiss him.

How different they are, she muses. *Theo is territorial and jealous, and Pilkington just keeps talking about making me happy. I don't know which I prefer, to be honest.*

Pilkington approaches her, sliding the eggs onto the plate closest to him without a word, then heads back to the stove to make his own eggs.

Sylvia can smell the bacon, and she begins opening drawers, looking for a potholder. She gives up after three, then pulls the towel from next to the sink, and leans over to open the oven door. Pilkington does not move out of the way.

"What are you doing?" he asks, looking down at her disapprovingly.

"Getting the bacon," she answers, hand balling up the towel to use it to grab the pan.

Pilkington shoos her away, opening the drawer right next to the stove and pulling out a blue potholder. "This," he says, leaning down to open the oven, "is a potholder. You use it to pick up hot things, so you don't burn yourself." He sets the pan on the back burner, then closes the oven door. He reaches out to snatch the towel from her hands, snapping it out before hanging it on the oven door handle. "That is a towel, a wet towel, that will only increase the burn you receive when you use it to touch hot things."

Sylvia stares at him, recalling a similar conversation with Theo, except she had judged him for using a towel. The thought makes her laugh, and she rolls her eyes, stepping away from the demon to retrieve her mug. She refills her coffee, then slides her plate over to the stove where the bacon sits. She reaches out greedy fingers to grab a piece, but Pilkington slaps her away with a pair of tongs, using them to place several strips on her plate. "Savage," he mutters, then returns his attention to his eggs, finishing them and flipping them onto his own plate.

"It's bacon," Sylvia says, grabbing her mug and heading for the door to the deck. "Savagery is part of the point." She slides the door open, then gestures for him to precede her outside. They sit at a small table outside, the afternoon light still strong though the sun is lower.

"So," she says as they begin eating, "how about your mother?"

"Lady Asa," he says. "My mother is a demon."

This seems like safer ground. "Do you see her often?"

Pilkington scoffs. "No. My mother would rather forget she has a son, though she does appreciate my skills when they serve her purpose."

"What did you get from her? More shapeshifting stuff?"

"No," Pilkington says, taking a bite of muffin and following up with a sip of coffee. "My mother is an elemental demon. You know—earth, air, wind, fire—that sort of thing. I can control the elements because of her. Comes in handy sometimes."

Sylvia looks around. "I can only imagine," she comments, trying to imagine what it would be like to control elements. The dagger gives her control over other people—which is terrifying enough. *What would I do if I could control the elements?* "My coffee would never get cold," she murmurs. "It must be amazing to have such powers."

The demon gives her a long look. "You too have powers now," he reminds her.

"Apparently," she says, her tone grumpy. "But not cool ones like yours. I just bully people." She sniffs, looking out over the lake, then sighs, the weight of the dagger heavy on her mind. "I made her kill herself," she whispers. "I did that." She pauses, reflecting. "I did it to free him—that's true—but that's not all of it."

Pilkington is silent, letting her decide if she wants to continue. When she doesn't speak, he pushes her a little. "Do you want to tell me?"

She glares at him. "Don't you already know? Can't you sense it? I know you can feel my desire, can smell it like I can smell this bacon. What did I desire last night?"

She looks down at the table for a moment, not wanting to see the shock she is sure covers his face at her outburst, but when she finally does look up, his face is impassive, the same open expression she remembers from her friend.

"Yes," he says finally. "I can sense desire. But this is about you. Tell me—if you wish to unburden yourself. I am here," he suggests.

"I wanted her to die," Sylvia says bluntly. "So I gave her the dagger knowing she would have to use it to kill herself." She sniffs again, tears gathering. "I wanted her to die, but I was too cowardly to do it myself, so instead, I took her will. I added it to the dagger." She pauses, the enormity of what she has done to Jolena sinking in. She doesn't want to think about how it felt to taunt the vampire with the blade—holding it out to tempt her just as the voices said to. "I stole her power and placed it in the dagger. What kind of a person am I?"

Pilkington reaches out to touch her hand. "A human one," he says gently. After another pause, he adds, "She would have killed you. You know that. Vampires like her—they don't let people like you walk away."

"But you wouldn't let her hurt me," Sylvia says, "and I knew that too. I used you—your presence—and Tengo too—to keep myself safe, knowing that I was the bait and trap all at once. I'm a terrible person." She wonders for a moment where the demon dog has been; she hasn't seen him since the rooftop last night.

He's Pilkington's dog. I'm sure he's fine.

Pilkington squeezes Sylvia's hand, pressing it between his own. She can feel the gloves again, though she can only see his human hand. "You are not a terrible person," he assures her. "I've met terrible people. I know how they are. You are not like that."

"But I've done a terrible thing," Sylvia says instead, the guilt eating her up. "I basically killed my boyfriend's ex-girlfriend." She laughs. "My ex-boyfriend's ex-girlfriend." She pauses, an odd grin crossing her face. "Oh my god," she says, "I'm a Lifetime movie plot."

"You are so much more than that," the demon assures her. When she looks up at him, he adds, "HBO, at least."

Sylvia can't stop laughing at his words, and she smiles, a real smile. But it grows watery. "But it didn't matter," she says. "He doesn't want me anyway." A tear tracks down her face, and Pilkington reaches up a hand to wipe it away.

"What do *you* want?" Pilkington asks.

"I don't know," Sylvia says honestly.

The demon sighs. "I probably shouldn't say this, but it must be said at least once: you know your vampire would have you again—if you fought for him." Sylvia looks up, confused hope in her eyes.

"I will not compel him—" she begins.

"That's not what I mean," Pilkington says. He shrugs. "I know desire, and the Muldavian wants you. He's confused now, but give him some time, and he will find his way back to you. You could have him again... if you want him."

"Why are you telling me this?" Sylvia asks, looking at him through a tear-stained face. "I'm your arusha," she says, the word odd to say in front of the demon. "Shouldn't you be... I don't know... telling me to get over him already?"

The demon snorts. "Is that what the witch told you? I want you to be happy, Sylvia. That's what being my arusha means. If being with the Muldavian makes you happy, then I will help you achieve that goal in whatever way you'd like."

"What about you though?" she asks, a sudden thought hitting her. "Do you have some demon chick who makes you happy?" Sylvia tries to picture a tall, blue-skinned demon in a skimpy bikini standing next to Pilkington, a hand on his arm. She doesn't like the idea.

Pilkington looks quickly away, but Sylvia grabs his hand and tugs his attention back. "Tell me—is there someone in your life that I need to support?"

The demon shakes his head, a sharp motion, then tries to look away. Sylvia slides closer to him, reaching up to touch his face, her finger stroking along his chin and up to his cheek. She sees her hands against his human skin, but she can feel smoothness instead of the scruffy human face she can see. Her fingers drift closer to his mouth, and though she knows she should stop, that this is too personal, too much and too close, she can't seem to stop. She drifts her finger across his lips, feeling the thump as she moves over his fangs. His body jerks as she touches his mouth, and he looks down at her, eyes shifting to her lips.

"Tell me," Sylvia whispers to the demon, "what do you desire?"

"I want you—"

"If you say you want me to be happy one more time, I will punch you," she tells him. "Tell me what *you* want."

The demon gives her a long, hungry look, eyes focusing on her mouth. "I want very much to kiss you," he says quietly.

"Then kiss me," she replies. His hand reaches up to touch hers on his face, tugging it down to rest on his shoulder, then he slowly slides his hand down over her hand and wrist, moving down her arm and over her shoulder to press against her back. His other hand reaches up to touch her chin, and he tilts her head to the side just a little, moving his mouth close. He moves slowly, giving her time to back away, to think about what she is offering.

Sylvia stays where she is, enjoying the long moment when his mouth is near hers. She can feel his breath against her skin, and she watches his eyes as they look at her, carefully judging her reaction to his nearness. She thinks of Phil at the beach that last day, his face near hers, his chest hitching as they floated on the waves, his hair plastered to his head. The man before her has the same expression, his eyes focused on her as his arms pull her close.

Finally!

When she is dying just for him to move a little bit closer and press his lips to hers, he pauses, hovering near, allowing her one more chance to stop. "Please," she mouths, no sound escaping her lips, and then he kisses her, his lips warm against hers. Sylvia closes her eyes, and though she pictures Phil in her mind, she can feel the truth of the demon's form, especially when he gently moves her mouth open to deepen the kiss. She sinks into him, into the feeling of slow-burning desire he has kindled in her body. She kisses him back, mouth moving recklessly, not worrying about his fangs nipping her the way she does when she kisses Theo. Blood doesn't matter here—not that Pilkington's fangs seem sharp to her questing tongue—and she lets herself go, mapping the contours of his mouth as he moves with her. The hand on her chin slides around to cup the back of her head, pressing her close, and Sylvia lets out a little moan.

Her hand on his shoulder slides back a little, finding the edge of a wing, and the demon shudders a little in her arms as she runs a finger along the edge, kissing her with more force. Her other hand tangles itself in his hair, and though she wants to reach up to feel his horns, she stops herself, settling for the touch of his satin wing and silky hair.

Finally, when they are both a little breathless, the demon releases her mouth, moving back just a little to look at her. His eyes have shifted from the normal brown to something dark and silver. She can sense the nerves in him now, the usually confident demon uncertain of her reaction. Sylvia licks her lips, leaning in for another kiss, this one fast, then smiles at him.

"Yeah," she says finally, "that was worth the wait."

The demon nods, speechless.

Sylvia knows that she should feel guilty. Theo isn't far from her thoughts, and here she is kissing someone else, but the idea of the vampire only makes her bold.

"I have an idea," she tells the demon.

"Go on."

"Let's go swimming," she says, recalling the words of Ula at the diner. She turns to look at the lake glistening in the strange afternoon light.

The demon nods. "That's a great idea," he says, then follows her gaze. "But not there."

"Why not? You have a secret hot spring nearby?"

The demon snorts. "Not there because that water is freezing right now, and I have a pool in the house."

"Of course you do," Sylvia says, standing up and gathering her dishes. She stares at the back of the huge house, losing count of the windows and rooms above them. She wonders if she will know them all someday, if she will be as comfortable here as she was in her apartment.

CHAPTER 16

PILKINGTON

PILKINGTON WAITS FOR SYLVIA IN THE POOL ROOM. HE still wears the human illusion, his customary long-sleeved shirt and pants replaced by swim trunks, though he is very aware of his wings, the way they will pull when he gets in the pool. One of the things he enjoys in the human realm is his ability to swim without them, his body lighter, but he knows how to use them to float in his own world. He looks down at his arm, where the line of the scar runs up the back of his hand to his elbow, then tucks the arm behind his back, not wanting her to see it yet. He considers the glove, but knows it is foolish—he needs to let her see it, let her see his weakness. The thought unnerves him, and he stands up again, nervously pacing the wide space between the two lounge chairs and the edge of the water. For a moment, he considers going out to find Sylvia and guide her to the room but reconsiders,

201

knowing that Billy will enjoy the chance to talk her ear off on the way.

He had introduced Sylvia to the soul-servant after breakfast, and Billy had been thrilled to tell her all about the house. Pilkington appreciated the interruption, needing some time to calm himself after their moment outside. He has wanted to kiss Sylvia for years, and ignoring the desire made it easier to withstand. But now that he has given in to his passion, it will be difficult to hold himself back. Even now, he can feel his need for her pulsing just under his skin.

Part of the reason he never pushed the issue is because he knows how desire works. Once acknowledged, sampled, it will not be easy to pause. He knows that Sylvia is in a fragile state—her home ruined, her relationship with the vampire broken, her future uncertain. Not to mention her connection to the dagger growing daily and the still missing Greater Demon... Pilkington knows it is only a matter of time before Forneus calls him for an update, demanding he return to the mortal realm to retrieve Hesperus before he can threaten the treaty with the Klaviger.

Hesperus is clever, the demon no doubt holed up away from the city and keeping himself hidden from prying eyes. But the power of the dagger will attract his attention, and once he realizes that Sylvia lives and is bonded to the artifact, Pilkington worries what he might do. They are safe in this realm for the time being, though—Hesperus will not return here willingly. Normally, he wouldn't bother with Pilkington's affairs, finding something else to focus on like the other demons do, respecting Pilkington's position among the aristocracy. But for the dagger and the power it wields, Hesperus will not bow to his rank or influence. The Greater Demon will hunt Sylvia down to kill her. Months ago, Pilkington would have worried more about such a possibility, but Sylvia is stronger now, the power of the dagger behind her.

Not to mention my power, he reminds himself, sitting on the edge of a lounger, feet kicked out on the tile floor, *now that she has embraced the bond. And her abilities will only grow stronger as we grow closer.*

That shared power is only one of the reasons that Pilkington has never chosen an arusha before, though he is far past the age when demons normally name their companions. By now, Pilkington should have an entire harem of chosen creatures, each selected for their position, influence, ability, or usefulness. But Pilkington has never wanted any of that. He prefers to keep his encounters brief and impersonal, relying on traditional demon contracts to earn favors and information.

Now, he has opened the door, allowing himself to kiss his arusha, and nothing will ever be the same. He reminds himself that he cannot let Sylvia see how much one kiss has affected him, how much it has shifted their relationship. For Pilkington, there is no going back now, and though he will still do everything in his power to make his arusha happy, if that means seeing her back with her vampire again, he knows such a sight will be worlds more painful than he can imagine. Before, he could have lied to himself, insisted that they were just friends, that his attraction to her was a passing thing, the result of choosing her while in a teenage boy's body. Now that he has tasted her mouth, Pilkington knows better. He will die still longing for one more kiss from his arusha, the only one he will ever choose.

The door to the pool room opens, and Billy drifts in followed by Sylvia. She wears a red patterned cover-up over a white one-piece bathing suit, her hair down and flowing over her shoulders. Pilkington wants to pick her up, tug her close, and kiss her again. He wants to run his hands along her shoulders and trace the curve of her ears, feeling her shiver in his arms.

"—and that's when he decided to put the pool in the house," Billy is saying. "Good decision, for once," he comments, glancing at the demon.

"You telling her about the storm season?" Pilkington asks, standing up and walking over to join them. The tile floor is cool on his feet, his body warm from desire.

Sylvia nods. "Billy says you have rain and storms for two months every year, and one year, you were adamant about swimming, so you moved the pool indoors. You can just ... do that?"

Pilkington shrugs. "It's only moving matter. That's easy enough."

"Were you training for the Olympics or something? Why the need to swim?"

Pilkington jerks his head hard to signal that Billy should stop talking, but the soul-servant ignores him, as per usual. "It was ten years ago," Billy explains, "back when you were spending all your time in that beach town." He turns to face Sylvia, eager now. "You know he has the wings, right? Well, he had to learn to swim as a human since he was in that body over there." He leans down to whisper conspiratorially. "I'm pretty sure he was trying to impress a lady."

"Ten years ago, huh?" Sylvia echoes, glancing at Pilkington, who looks at his feet. "I bet she was some lady."

"My lord never has any ladies," Billy complains. "You have no idea how glad I am that he has brought you here."

"That'll be all, Billy," Pilkington growls, dismissing the soul-servant.

Billy leans into Sylvia, whispering, "I'll see you at dinner. You like tacos?" She nods, and the ghost drifts out of the room, closing the door behind him with a quick thumbs up to both of them. "You kids have fun!"

Sylvia turns to see Pilkington shaking his head. "Please forgive him," he says. "Billy can be…"

"He's great," Sylvia assures him. "I think he's just really lonely." She steps over to the pool, shrugging the cover-up off one shoulder. "You don't bring people here that often?"

"Never," he tells her, watching her carefully, wanting to see more of her skin as she removes the cover-up.

"Would you have brought me here?" she asks. "When we were younger, I mean?"

Pilkington frowns. "I doubt it," he says honestly. "You were very young. It would not have been right."

"Is that why you left?" she asks suddenly. "Because it wasn't proper?"

"Sylvia," he says, his voice a low growl as she turns to look at him, her chin down as she slides the rest of the cover-up down her body, revealing the bathing suit beneath.

"Is it proper now?" she asks, stepping toward him slowly.

The demon watches her approach, very glad that he wears the human illusion so she can't see his desire. He bites his lip, not trusting himself to speak, knowing he will say something very foolish.

"You know you don't have to look like that for my sake," Sylvia says. "This is your home. You should be yourself here."

"I am always myself," Pilkington tells her, "regardless of how I appear." He holds out a hand to take hers, letting her run her fingers over the skin she sees, knowing she can feel the subtle difference. "It's only magic."

Sylvia reaches behind him to touch his other arm, the one he has casually put behind his back, and twines her fingers in that hand, though her eyes don't leave his. She doesn't sneak a peek, and Pilkington is grateful. "You don't need to hide yourself, I mean," she says, using her other hand to lift his chin. "Not from me."

"I know," he tells her, and her body is just too close. Unable to resist, Pilkington leans down to claim her mouth again, sliding his free hand up her neck and into the hair at the back of her head, his other hand tucking their twined fingers up behind her back. Sylvia arches into him, letting herself be pinned. He knows she can feel the hardness of his body pressing against her, but he doesn't care, allowing some of his more primal nature to show. She doesn't seem to mind, molding her body against his in a way that makes him long for more. After a long moment, Pilkington releases her, some of the wild need in him sated, and he steps away.

"What was that for?" Sylvia asks, a little breathless. "Not that you need a reason," she stammers, suddenly shy as she pulls her hands away.

Pilkington takes a deep breath, knowing that if he doesn't pause now, she will be able to see some of the demon in him. His eyes have probably already started to turn silvery black. He turns his back on her, unconsciously moving his arm to rest against his belly, still out of sight. "I guess," he replies after a long silence, "I wanted to kiss you again while you still wanted me." He sighs, knowing how pathetic he sounds but unable to stop. "Like this."

He hears her step closer, pressing herself against his back. She tries to wrap her arms around him, but instead gets caught up in his wings, her hands framing the invisible lines in the air. Her touch makes him shiver, though the room is warm enough.

"Let me see you," Sylvia whispers. "I want to see you."

Pilkington spins, tall enough in his human form to look down into her face. "Are you sure?" he asks. "It is one thing to kiss your old friend, to act on impulses during this time of upheaval in your life. I understand that entirely." He can see her face fall at his words, but he presses on. "It is quite another to knowingly kiss a demon and mean it, Sylvia."

She backs away, face hurt, and Pilkington can sense the guilt welling up in her. "You think I'm using you?" she asks. "To get over ... him?"

The demon shrugs. "Normally, I wouldn't mind. I am perfectly open to being used." He pauses, frowning at her. "But I know you, and you are not the type," he says finally.

"What type?" she probes. "The type to jump into bed with someone else right after getting dumped?" He can hear the bitterness in her voice, the doubt and self-recrimination.

He reaches out to touch her arm, to reassure her that he is still here. "The type to trust easily," he says. "I know what it means that you trust me. I do not undervalue your faith."

"But do you trust me?" she asks, and Pilkington looks away. Now it is her turn to touch his shoulder, bringing him back into the conversation. He considers the question, knowing the answer already but afraid to say it aloud.

"Yes," he breathes.

"Then let me look at you," Sylvia says. "Don't hide from me."

Pilkington is unable to resist her words, knowing that she is calling out his cowardice, and he lets the illusion fall away. His true form stands slightly taller, so her arm slides down to rest in the crook of his elbow, brushing up against the edge of his glove.

She tugs on it. "You always wear these, huh?"

Pilkington nods. He wants to explain that letting other demons see the scar would reveal weakness, something he cannot afford to do, but the words fall flat, and he watches her reaction to being so near his body instead.

Her eyes dip down to the line of his swim trunks, the material black instead of the blue he wore in his human form. Then her eyes move back up to study his arm and chest again. Her finger slides along the dark line of his markings. "What do these mean?" she asks, tracing the design on his arm. "Are they tattoos?"

Pilkington shivers at her touch, his chin twitching as she slides her finger up his bicep and over to his shoulder. "No," he says. "They're part of me. I was born with them."

"Oh," she says. "A demon thing? Do they do anything other than look cool?"

"They glow sometimes," he explains, "when I use magic."

Sylvia's face lights up in curious wonder. "Can you show me?"

Pilkington calls on the air to lift him a few inches off the ground, knowing the power needed to suspend his body is enough to light his skin. Normally, he uses his wings to fly here. Sylvia gasps as he levitates, and he uses the moment to tug her up with him, resting her feet atop his and holding her around the waist. She looks down at the ground a few inches below them.

"So, you can fly too," she murmurs. "Can all supernatural creatures fly?"

Pilkington shakes his head. "No. Only strong ones like your vampire." He pauses, watching her reaction to the words. Her brows have drawn together, her eyes narrowing as she gives him a pointed look. "And like me."

"Are you strong then?" she asks.

Pilkington doesn't reply. Instead, he lifts them up higher, slowly spinning as they near the ceiling. "In some ways, yes." He looks at her in his arms, marveling at the closeness of her body, the effortless way she fits against him.

"And in others?" she presses.

"In others, I am a fool," he admits, sliding them over just enough that they hover over the pool.

"How's that?" Sylvia asks, glancing down at the water below them.

"I'm a fool for you," he says, leaning down for another kiss, this one barely a brief touch of his lips before he pulls away. "I know..." he begins, then makes himself stop.

"You know what?"

Pilkington doesn't want to answer her, doesn't want to tell her just how much he cares for her, doesn't want to overwhelm her with his emotions. So he changes the subject. "I know you can swim," he says, then drops her into the pool several feet below them.

Sylvia shrieks as she plummets but lands with the expertise of a girl brought up on the beach. She breaks the surface with a laugh, looking up at him. "That was cheating!" she yells.

Pilkington lowers himself a little bit, using his wings instead of magic now, hovering just out of reach. To his surprise, Sylvia slips beneath the water for a moment, then kicks up hard, propelling herself out of the water just enough to catch his ankle, and she yanks him down into the water with her. The demon allows himself to be pulled, surprised and delighted to play with his arusha. His wings are leathery and don't absorb water, but they are heavy, and he uses them to push his head and chest out of the water, a slow wave moving away from him as he surfaces in front of Sylvia.

She watches him swim for a moment, taking in the way his body moves. "You're good?" she asks, checking on his ability to stay afloat.

He nods. "I practiced a lot," he says, "a few years ago."

Sylvia treads water a few feet away, her hair trailing out around her shoulders, and she gives him a big smile. "She must have been some lady," she comments, looking around the huge space, "to warrant all this."

"So much more than this," Pilkington promises her, and she moves closer to him, her body lithe and slippery in the water.

"Can I touch you?" she asks, looking at his head and no doubt thinking about his horns. Pilkington uses a hand to push his hair out of his face, knowing that his actual hair is much longer than the human form she is used to seeing. He nods, and Sylvia reaches out one hand to steady herself against his shoulder. Pilkington keeps moving his wings, buoying them both in the water as she reaches up to touch first his cheek, then sliding up his face to his forehead, and to tentatively touch the horns atop his head. They are only a few inches tall, like his mother's, and a sign of his power. "They're so small," she observes.

"Are you inferring something?" he asks, his tone playful.

"No," she replies, the grin she gives him all woman, "but the demons I saw all had huge horns."

"Big horns are a sign of lower demons," Pilkington explains. "More powerful demons have smaller horns."

"Is that what you tell all the girls?" Sylvia whispers wickedly.

In response, Pilkington reaches out and pulls her closer to him. She wraps her legs around his hips easily, pressing herself against him, letting his wings hold them afloat as his arms settle around her back, one dipping down to stroke her thigh. She looks at him, really looks at him, and Pilkington is very aware of his face, his demon eyes, his fangs. He wonders what she is thinking. He can feel her desire growing as they move slowly up and down with the motion of his wings. He can sense her need for more than this tentative touching through layers of clothing, but he also knows that she isn't ready. Not really.

He lets her look at him, taking in the reality of his body, and when she leans in to kiss him, slowly at first, he accepts her touch, letting her guide their lips and set the pace, though his body aches at her warm lips against his. "Wow," she breathes against his open mouth. "It's nice to kiss you." Her hand reaches up to trace the lines of his fangs behind his lips. "I didn't know how these would feel."

"And?" the demon prompts, curious. He hasn't kissed many humans before, and certainly not in his body. He wonders how it feels to kiss someone with fangs.

She knows what it's like, he thinks, suddenly picturing her with her vampire that night at the hot springs, when he saw them kiss before he left them alone. The memory fills him with an odd feeling—he knows it must be jealousy—and he pushes it away. A jealous demon is never a pretty sight.

"It's interesting," Sylvia says, and Pilkington is back in the moment again, his arusha in his arms of her own free will. "Different." She tilts her head, studying his face again. "I like it."

"I'm glad," he replies, then tugs her close again, kissing her thoroughly, exploring her mouth and claiming it for himself. "I like it too," he says into her mouth. His mouth drifts away from her lips then, dipping down to nuzzle her shoulder. He avoids her neck, knowing that will only remind her of the vampire who no doubt bit her during sex, and the thought spurs him on to move more aggressively, the rational part of him warring with the demon determined to claim his arusha once and for all. His hand grips her hip, pressing her against him, and she reaches down into the water to pull his hand between them. Pilkington's lust clears a little as she tugs his hand free of the water, and he watches as she slowly begins to tug the glove free, starting with the loop around his middle finger and sliding the wet material over his hand. Her eyes do not leave his as the glove pulls free, and she tosses it aside. The demon hears it land somewhere on the floor with a wet splat.

"May I?" she asks, still meeting his eyes. The demon nods, then follows her gaze down to his hand, watching her eyes trace the scar. She traces the line with her finger the same way she followed his markings, though the one on his forearm is badly misshapen, the result of the dagger's power. The skin is white, a glaring contrast against his dark skin, a reminder of how close he came to death.

"I'm sorry," she whispers. "It must have hurt so much."

"Yes," he replies. "You know exactly how much." His other hand brushes against her stomach, and she shivers in his arms, eyes going distant. "Sylvia," he says, calling her back to the present. She looks up at him, biting her lip. Pilkington can feel the conflicting desire within her now—her need to be closer to him and her need to hide from him. He puts both hands against her sides and slowly lifts her up, leaning in to kiss his way down her chest, between her breasts and then over the bathing suit covering her belly where he knows the scar is. Her hands rest atop his head, fingers touching his horns. He pauses, knowing that part of her wants him to continue while another is afraid.

She squirms a little, and he releases her with a small splash, letting her settle back into the water and move away from him.

"I think…" she begins, then kicks her feet, putting more space between them. "I think I need a minute." She swims away, heading to the other side of the pool. Pilkington pushes up with his wings, lifting out of the water with a push that sends waves splashing against the edges of the pool. He lands on the edge, giving his wings two powerful thrusts to shake the water free, then smooths his hair back from his face, wiping his eyes. He looks at the pool to see Sylvia watching him closely, her eyes studying his body with obvious lust. He stands there a moment longer, allowing her to ogle him, then turns to the lounge chairs, retrieving a towel and drying himself.

Sylvia swims the length of the pool three times, then climbs the steps at the shallow end to get out. Pilkington opens her towel, wrapping it around her shoulders and rubbing her back as she stands on the edge, hair still dripping.

"So," he says, moving to stand in front of her, "are you ready to talk about what happens next yet?"

Sylvia's eyes glance at his lips. "Next?" she echoes.

"Yes," the demon nods, realizing that she doesn't know what he means. "Like when do you want to return home? Or discuss your connection to the dagger? Or find the Greater Demon?"

Sylvia groans, stepping forward to bury her face against his chest. "Don't talk to me about all that," she begs. "Not yet." She leans back, looking up at him. "Give me the day," she suggests, then glances at the windows which show that the sun has set and night has arrived while they were swimming. "I mean, the night. Give me one night to just … be."

"To be," the demon says, "…with me?" He raises an eyebrow, his meaning clear. He knows what her answer will be, but he has to ask, to let her know what he wants.

"Can we just be?" she asks, then gives him a speculative look. "Maybe be … but with more kissing?"

The demon laughs, taking her hand and tugging her close. "I am always available for more kissing," he promises her, bending down to taste her lips again.

CHAPTER 17

SYLVIA

SYLVIA SITS IN A SWINGING CHAIR IN PILKINGTON'S library, her sketchpad forgotten on her lap as she stares out the window, taking in the colors of his world. She has been here for three days now, her time spent talking with her old friend, filling in the gaps of missing time between them and getting to know him in his element. Pilkington is the same demon she got to know in her apartment, and yet he is also the boy she had known for those few summers, the one to whom she has compared every other love interest in her life.

Being with Phil is easy, comfortable, and still she feels a little guilty for moving on so quickly after Theo ended things. She is also angry with herself for feeling guilty at all. She is trying not to think about the future, but when she does, it's easier to imagine than one with Theo—although the demon will also outlive her, he can be human, and she doesn't have to worry about either of them losing control over blood.

Pilkington is a demon, she reminds herself. *No doubt he can lose control too—just over something else that you haven't discovered yet.*

She wonders how she can fit into his world—but not how he fits into hers. Though she has tried not to think about her ruined apartment, she knows that eventually, she will have to find a new place to live, to get a new job and return to the normal business of living. *Maybe I can do something at the Lyceum,* she thinks suddenly, making a mental note to contact Jeremy when she returns to her world. *At least they would understand if I had to miss a day due to supernatural weirdness.*

And she knows Pilkington would support her urge to work. Even now, the demon is in his office, catching up on some work of his own. She knows he has been neglecting his duties to entertain her, and that morning—more like noonish—he had left her in the library while he went to answer some letters. She had left him sitting at a large desk, a literal feather quill in hand as he handwrote replies.

Is this what life could be like? She wonders at the routine, her sketching in the library, him working a few hours in the office. *Maybe we can have an apartment in the city and travel back and forth ... like demon tourists.* She knows that Pilkington is allowed to travel between worlds fairly often, though she hasn't asked the specifics yet. Ula had said he spent a lot of time in her world—looking after her. The idea should be creepy, like a supernatural stalker, but if she had known where Phil was all those years, she would have wandered by his house too, hoping to catch a glimpse into his life.

So, am I seriously thinking about doing this? She pauses, her pencil tracing idle symbols on the page as she considers. *Maybe,* she decides. *Baby steps*, she tells herself. *No getting caught up in the moment and finding yourself in bed with a blue demon.* The idea intrigues her though. She wonders what it would be like, what he would be like naked and vulnerable in her arms. A rush of desire fills her, and she decides she is ready for one more little baby step.

Climbing out of the chair, she leaves her sketchpad and pencil on the small table nearby, takes a sip of the water, then heads out of the room and down the hall to where she knows Pilkington's office can be found. She knocks softly on the open door and peeks her head inside. Pilkington sits at his desk, head bent to his work.

"Can I come in or is this a bad time?" she asks, lingering in the doorway.

Pilkington finishes a sentence, then looks up at her, an eyebrow raised. She wears shorts, a tank top, and a light sweater, the same outfit she wears to lounge in her own home. "Not a bad time at all," he says, gesturing her to come inside. His office is comfortable: a large desk in front of the window overlooking the mountains behind the house, a round stool that he sits on, a few potted plants against the walls, bookshelves with a jumble of old and new manuscripts against the walls. He has a few paintings on the walls too, landscapes of places she can't quite imagine, and one of a stern-looking, blue-skinned woman with tiny horns wearing a black dress. Sylvia looks at it, seeing the echo of Pilkington's eyes, the shape of his jaw.

The demon stands up and walks over to stand behind her, one hand resting on her shoulder as the other settles at her waist. She leans into him, enjoying his touch. "My mother," he explains, leaning down to rest his head atop hers. "The Lady Asa."

"She's beautiful," Sylvia says, studying the lines of the painting, the brushstrokes and use of color. "Who painted her?"

"I did," Pilkington says, pointing to a small, stylized P in the bottom corner with one nail. Sylvia tilts her head to look up at him.

"You? I didn't know you painted."

He shrugs, wings fluttering with the motion, then settles his head next to hers. "Occasionally," he admits. "More when I was younger."

"Can I see them?" she asks, reaching up to put her hand over his on her shoulder, very aware of his other hand on her hip, holding her close.

He nods, the motion stirring her hair as he turns his head to kiss her cheek. "Of course."

She turns and he moves with her, both of them facing the large window and the glorious view. "Have you painted that?" she asks, nodding at the view.

"Yes," he says, leaning down to nuzzle her shoulder again.

She sighs at his touch, wanting more. Taking the hand on her shoulder, she lifts it, bringing it to her mouth to kiss his palm. Pilkington takes the invitation, his lips warm as he traces the line of her collarbone, pushing her sweater and then the strap of her tank top aside. Sylvia shivers, loving the feel of his touch, pressing back against him. The hand on her hip slides forward to rest over her belly, waiting.

She takes the hand at her mouth and slowly moves it down, settling it atop her breast. Pilkington does not hesitate, his hand cupping her round fullness, fingers moving to brush her nipple through her shirt. His breath is warm against her shoulder when he whispers, "Tell me what you want."

"I want you to touch me," she replies, a little surprised at the bold words as she speaks.

"Like this?" he asks, hand squeezing her slightly, and she moans, tilting her head to find his mouth.

"Yes," she says, kissing him hard, body aching for more. The hand on her belly moves, fingers inching near the waistband of her shorts. His body is hard behind her, his skin smooth where he presses against her bare legs, and she steps on top of his feet, making herself taller so he can reach more easily. His fingers slide beneath her shorts, stroking her lightly, and Sylvia moans again.

"Like this?" he asks again, his voice deeper now, gruff with the desire engulfing them both. His hand cups her gently, finger sliding against her sensitive skin.

"God yes," she moans, nipping his bottom lip with her teeth, her tongue exploring his mouth as her hand tangles in his hair, fingers wrapping around one of his horns. She lifts her hips, giving him more access, then her other hand slides behind her and between their bodies, skirting along the edge of his pants.

What was that about not jumping into bed with a demon? The voice is quiet, and Sylvia ignores it, fingers searching for the tie she knows is somewhere between their bodies. She finally finds it, fingers twisting to get it free, and then her hand is snaking down inside his pants, eager to discover what the demon wears beneath.

She has barely grazed bare skin when the sound of the door opening interrupts them both. Pilkington turns his body, shielding her from view with his wings as he abruptly stands up straight, his hands pulling free from her clothes with a curse. "Daughter of Lilith!" he exclaims. Sylvia stumbles a little as she steps off his feet back onto the floor, and the demon catches her hip easily, steadying her with one hand while the other tugs at the waistband of his pants, which hang very low on his hips now, that line of hair very visible as she faces him. Sylvia tugs her shirt and sweater back up her shoulder and straightens her own pants.

"What?!" Pilkington barks, hand leaving her body to tie his pants. He whirls to face the intruder. "Don't you knock?"

Sylvia can see the priceless expression on Billy's face as the soul-servant realizes what he has interrupted. "Pardon me, my lord," he says, bowing formally, no doubt to hide the grin he cannot stop. "I didn't know we were knocking now."

"We are," Pilkington tells him, still annoyed. "We have a guest staying with us."

"Of course," Billy agrees. He gives Sylvia a tiny nod of acknowledgement. "My Lady."

Pilkington stares at him, clearly waiting for his servant to continue. "Well?" he prompts when it becomes clear that Billy is perfectly content to simply stand there ogling them and enjoying their flushed faces.

"Well?" the ghost echoes, then his expression shifts as he recalls his purpose. "Oh! Of course." He straightens, sniffing and extending another bow.

"If you interrupted us to deliver a letter, Billiacus..." The demon lets the threat trail off, frowning at his servant. He gives Sylvia an apologetic look.

Billy shakes his head. "Forgive the intrusion, my lord, but you have a visitor."

Pilkington's attention shifts immediately back to his servant, eyes narrowing. "A visitor?"

The servant nods. Sylvia watches the exchange curiously. Apparently, Billy wasn't exaggerating when he said Pilkington rarely had guests.

"Who?" Pilkington demands.

"It's him," Billy says, voice very soft. "Lord Forneus."

"Lord Forneus is here?" Pilkington asks, running hands through his hair and straightening his pants. He glances down at himself, frowning as he sees his bare hands, the scar a white line across his skin. "Where is he?" he asks, turning to fumble with the drawers of his desk.

"He's waiting in the front room," Billy says. "I offered tea, but he refused. He wants to see you immediately."

"Billy, was there a letter? Did you forget to give me a letter again?"

The servant shakes his head. "No, my lord. I am sure of it."

"How does he seem?" the demon demands, finding a pair of gloves in a drawer and hastily dragging them up both arms.

"Interested," the servant replies.

"That's not good," Pilkington says, then turns to Sylvia. "Wait here. Don't let him see you." He seems to recognize the harshness of his tone, and his voice softens. "Forgive me. But Forneus can't know you're here. Not yet. Please stay out of sight."

Sylvia nods mutely, curious about this side of Pilkington, the nervous subordinate before a master. She wonders just how powerful this Lord Forneus must be, to make Pilkington revert to a scuttling servant.

"I will wait here." She leans up on her tiptoes to give Pilkington a quick kiss, pushes his hair behind his ear, then steps away. "Good luck."

The demon follows his servant out without a word, closing the door softly behind him, and Sylvia plops onto the wingback chair in the corner, unfulfilled desire mixing with apprehension as she tucks her legs up under her. The velvet feels nice against her bare feet, and she leans her head back, recalling the feel of Pilkington's hands on her body.

What are you doing? Is this what you want?

Yes.

The reply is so swift that it startles her, and she closes her eyes, biting her lip as she allows herself to relish the feeling of rightness, the satisfaction in her soul. A soft touch against her foot lets her know that Tengo has arrived, the large dog resting his head next to her on the chair, and she reaches a hand down to pet him absently, wondering what caused him to appear but glad to have the company as she analyzes her situation, trying to take stock of her feelings.

Theo was fun, definitely a good time, but this—this is something altogether different. She has been longing for Phil since she first started longing for anyone in that way, and the strength of her desire is startling. For once in her life, facing her desire, Sylvia isn't afraid.

CHAPTER 18

PILKINGTON

PILKINGTON CHECKS HIS APPEARANCE ONE FINAL TIME IN the mirror, making sure he does not look like what he is—a demon interrupted in the middle of a heated moment. His hair is smooth and his expression neutral, the look Forneus would expect of him. He still wears pants and gloves, his feet bare, but he thinks the Lord will forgive his lack of formality. Forneus is the one surprising him at his home, after all. Pilkington takes a long, deep breath, settling back into the demon lord his superior would expect, then steps into his parlor.

Lord Forneus stands at the window, hands behind his back. He wears his human form, the old man innocuous in his simple red robes, but Pilkington knows how deceptive that packaging can be. Forneus is a formidable foe, stronger than Pilkington in some areas—though he would never tell the Greater Demon that. Pilkington has worked under Forneus for a long time, serving as the Lord's eyes and ears in other realms, performing tasks that require a certain level of discretion. Pilkington is particularly good at retrieving demons who overstay in other realms—one of the reasons no one questions his frequent trips to the mortal realm. Serving under Forneus allows him certain privileges, and Pilkington is not willing to disrupt their working relationship until he must.

If the Greater Demon knows about Sylvia, however, Pilkington will be forced to reevaluate his loyalties.

"My lord," he says, bowing to the old man, though his back is still turned. "You honor me with your presence."

The Greater Demon chuckles, the sound a rasp that Pilkington does not trust. "You flatter me with frivolities, Lord Pilkington," the demon says. "Now I know something is amiss."

"What is it?" Pilkington asks, tucking both hands into his pockets as he adopts a casual stance. "Did my foolish servant miss a letter from you?"

Forneus turns around, face placid as he studies Pilkington, eyes scanning the demon from the tips of his wings down to his bare feet. "Tell me," the demon lord says, ignoring Pilkington's questions, "why is it that I have yet to receive a status update on Hesperus?"

"I have not located him yet, my lord," Pilkington says. "There is nothing to report."

The demon lord nods, then looks around the parlor, keen eyes taking in the details of Pilkington's taste. "And yet you are here and not there still searching for him. Curious."

"An issue arose that needed my attention," Pilkington explains vaguely. "I will resume my hunt very soon."

"I see," Forneus says, nodding his head slowly. "These things do happen. Issues arise all the time, of course." The Greater Demon eyes the waistband of Pilkington's pants, and he resists the urge to follow the look down.

Lucifer's balls, are my pants not fastened properly? On the heels of the thought, Pilkington's heart speeds up. *He knows. I don't know how he knows, but he knows about Sylvia.* He gives the demon an appraising look, running through the last few days in his mind. *He must have someone watching me.* He thinks of that first afternoon when he kissed Sylvia sitting on the deck. Outside. Where anyone could see. He remembers their conversation and curses internally. He's been such a fool, neglecting the habits that keep his secrets safe, so caught up in his arusha that he has made several stupid mistakes.

"I assume this issue has been resolved," the demon continues, "and you will be back in the mortal realm immediately, then, yes?"

"Nearly," Pilkington replies, not wanting Forneus to send him now. The demon has the ability to push Pilkington into the mortal realm with a thought. He's done it before—a convenience. But Pilkington is not ready to leave yet, and certainly not if it means leaving Sylvia behind. "I will return tomorrow."

"Tomorrow," Forneus echoes, his tone disapproving. "Pray tell, what is so vital that you would put off a direct request from your superior?"

"I am looking into the background of a certain arti-fact," Pilkington says, the words mostly truthful. He already knows the background of the dagger, but he is legitimately researching Sylvia's bond with it.

Researching it with your mouth, a snide voice comments, and Pilkington restrains the grin that tries to twitch across his lips at the memory of her lips. His face doesn't move, but Forneus must have sensed something because the demon's expression turns even darker.

"This can be done after Hesperus has been returned," Forneus declares. "He has been away far too long. You will find him now, Pilkington. I will not ask again."

"My research on the artifact will lead me to him," Pilkington argues, needing to convince the demon to let him stay for a few more hours—just enough time for him to get Sylvia settled somewhere safe.

"Are you saying you cannot find him?" Forneus demands. "You, who can find any creature in any realm at any time?" The demon scoffs, another glance taking in Pilkington's pants, then his face, specifically his mouth. "Is something wrong with your powers, boy?"

"Hesperus has managed to elude me thus far because of the artifact," Pilkington lies, knowing the risk he takes. Usually, he cannot lie to Forneus, needing to skirt the truth with clever words, but since Sylvia freed him, he is not bound to obey the Greater Demon. He doesn't know if Forneus will sense the lie though, doesn't know the true extent of his powers, but he cannot have the Greater Demon thinking him incompetent or useless.

"I see." Forneus nods. "An impasse then, though it explains your delinquency." He looks around. "What it doesn't explain is why you've been in this realm for three days and didn't see fit to report your ... difficulties. Instead, I had to find out you were here through other means." He sighs. "Do you have any idea how awkward it is to find out one's top investigative demon has been lingering home instead of working on an important assignment?"

Pilkington says nothing, mind frantically going through the list of possible spies Forneus may have sent to watch him. *Who would have told him?* "I expect better from you, Pilkington," Forneus says with a sigh. "I'd hate to think you've fallen prey to the distractions that plague your fellow demons. You always seem immune to such frivolities."

"I am working on it, my lord," Pilkington says quietly, not sure what else to add.

"Are you?" The demon nods, then moves his head toward the rest of the house. "Show me what you've discovered then."

"What?" Pilkington asks, surprised and confused.

"Show me what you've found out about this artifact," the Greater Demon insists, walking through the door into the front room and heading up the stairs. "I presume your notes are in your office, yes? Let's discuss what you have learned."

Pilkington hurries behind the Greater Demon, not sure how to stop him. "Wouldn't you be more comfortable in the library?" he offers. "Most of the books are in there. I can have my servant bring us tea—"

"I have no need of tea," Forneus snaps. "You are stuck. Allow me to help free you."

Pilkington does not miss the implication in the demon's words and follows him to the second floor. He wonders how Forneus knows the location of his office, then curses his own predilection for windows, knowing the spy must have been watching him for far longer than just this week. "Thank you, my lord,"

Pilkington says. Forneus waits at the top of the stairs, allowing Pilkington the illusion of control as he leads the Greater Demon down the hallway to his office where Sylvia is waiting.

"Of course," Forneus says, raising his voice just a little as they approach the closed office door. "Let us sit and you can tell me what you know of ancient daggers."

Pilkington reaches out to open the door, hoping for a moment that Sylvia will have somehow managed to leave the room despite his orders to stay put. He sees immediately that she is still there, curled up in the chair in the corner with Tengo at her side, the demon dog alert to the danger Forneus presents. Pilkington watches Forneus to gauge his reaction to the human woman as well as the dog. He doesn't think Forneus will recognize Tengo, not as he is now, trapped in this form until his arrangement with Pilkington expires, but he still breathes easier when he sees the Greater Demon dismiss the dog in favor of his arusha.

"Why, hello!" Forneus greets Sylvia warmly, turning to give Pilkington a rueful look. "You didn't say you were entertaining, Pilkington. I would have returned later."

Sylvia's eyes widen at the sight of the old man, and Pilkington knows that she senses Forneus's true form, a Greater Demon who manifests as the Leviathan, a monstrous creature of the deep ocean. She says nothing, watching Pilkington for clues.

"It's nothing," Pilkington says. "She can wait."

Forneus chuckles. "Clearly. But can you?" Pilkington glares at him, and the old man laughs again. "Give me some credit," he says. "It may have been some time since I played with the humans, but I recall such pleasures."

"It's not like that," Pilkington argues.

"What is it like then?" Forneus asks. Pilkington doesn't reply, not sure what to say that won't put Sylvia in danger. The Greater Demon turns his attention to Sylvia, studying her. "What about you, then?" he pushes. "You want to tell me what this is?"

"This is his office," Sylvia says quietly, and it takes Pilkington a moment to realize what she said—and he winces, afraid of Forneus's reaction to such sass, and yet so proud of his arusha for standing up to the demon lord.

Forneus scoffs, glancing around the room, eyes catching on the portrait of Lady Asa. His gaze softens. "I was young once too," he says. "I know the power of such distraction."

"It's not—" Pilkington begins, but Forneus cuts him off.

"Please do not insult my intelligence again, boy. I can smell her on you." His glance drifts back to Sylvia, who has brought both legs down to rest on the floor, her back straight as she sits in the chair. "And him on you." He shakes his head. "Is this why you have failed in your duties? Frolicking with a human?"

"I have not failed," Pilkington insists.

"No," Forneus agrees, "and you will not." He gives Sylvia a long calculating look. "Perhaps you need proper motivation to keep you focused," he muses. "I'm sure some time with the Palici brothers will make her think twice about bargaining with demons in the future." He looks over at Pilkington. "You'll get her back … after you return Hesperus. I'm sure she won't be permanently damaged."

Pilkington's vision goes white, then red, as he imagines what the Palicis would do to his arusha given the chance.

"She is my arusha," Pilkington blurts, claiming her as his chosen before the Greater Demon. He knows that labeling her puts her in greater danger in the long term, but if he doesn't say anything, Forneus will send Sylvia to the Palicis as a treat to enjoy until Pilkington fulfills his geas—and he cannot allow that.

Forneus's eyes widen, and he turns to face Sylvia again, this time studying her from bare feet to blonde hair. "Is she now? How curious." He narrows his eyes. "I fear I did not get your name, my lady."

"Lady Pilkington," Pilkington says quickly, moving to stand next to the chair, putting himself between Forneus and Sylvia.

"Really?" Forneus asks. "Forgive me. I seem to have missed the Tethering Ceremony."

"I have not had a public ceremony yet, my lord," Pilkington explains. "I have been occupied with my duties."

"Not occupied enough that you didn't find time to secure a mate, though," Forneus observes. "I simply must hear the story of how you met." He focuses on Sylvia again. "And of the private ceremony that bound you together."

"I…" Sylvia begins, bending under the pressure of the lord's demanding gaze, but her voice trails off as she glances up at Pilkington. "We…"

Forneus tilts his head, looking from one to the other, eyes missing no details. "Or did I interrupt before you could conclude your contract?" he asks. He shakes his head disapprovingly. "That's why you have public ceremonies, Pilkington, so others know when not to disturb you. Tethering a mate is tiresome business."

"I am perfectly well," Pilkington says.

"Yes, you are," Forneus says. "And so you shall remain." He turns to Sylvia. "Your pardon, my lady," he says to her, "but you must wait a little longer. I have need of Lord Pilkington on an urgent matter." His attention focuses on Pilkington again, and Sylvia's foot reaches out to touch the back of Pilkington's calf, forging a physical connection between them. Her hand remains on Tengo's head, but the other, partially hidden behind Pilkington's wings, moves to quickly grasp hold of the edge of one wing, her grip revealing her fear.

"Lord Pilkington," Forneus orders, "you will return to the human realm immediately and locate the demon Hesperus. You will return him to this realm in whatever manner you deem fitting, using your normal discretion. In the meantime, I will entertain your arusha."

Sylvia's grip tightens on Pilkington's wing, and she abandons Tengo's head to grasp his hip with her other hand, pressing both feet against the back of Pilkington's legs, touching him as much as she can as Pilkington feels the power begin to engulf them both. He wants to speak, to stop Forneus from pushing him through into the other world, but Sylvia is clinging to him now, and they both vanish from the office with a soundless pop.

CHAPTER 19

SYLVIA

THEY BOTH APPEAR IN THE LIVING ROOM OF AN UNKNOWN apartment, Sylvia hooked on to the demon's body. He is in his human form, and since the wing she was gripping has vanished, she thumps to the floor behind him with an audible yelp, the hand still clinging to his hip nearly jerking his jeans down in the process.

"You followed me," he says, awe clear in his tone as he stares at her.

"Of course I did," she says from the floor. "You're not getting rid of me that easily."

Pilkington twists his upper body to grab her hand and jerk her to her feet, then yanks her roughly into his embrace. "I'm never letting you go," he murmurs.

Sylvia allows herself to be jostled, sinking gratefully into his arms as her heart slows its frantic pace. She was sure the other demon could hear her heart pounding as he questioned them, and she is so glad to be away from him.

"You're okay," Pilkington whispers against her hair. She reaches up to hug him back, surprised for a moment to find the material of a long-sleeved shirt instead of bare skin and wings.

"He is awful," she says against his chest. "Are all demons like that?"

Pilkington doesn't reply for a moment, then says, "I am not like that."

Sylvia pulls away enough to look up at him, the feat much easier since he is human again. "I didn't mean it like that," she says. "You're nothing like him."

"In some ways," he agrees, then adds, "but I am in others. Demons are just like humans, Sylvia. We are all different, bound by our desires, trapped by our passions."

"Is that how you see it?" she asks. "Desire is a trap?"

"It can be," he admits with a sigh. "Look at us, for example. My desire for you caused me to be careless, and now Forneus will be after you when we return."

He'll have to get in line, Sylvia thinks sarcastically, then focuses on what the demon just said.

"When we return," Sylvia echoes. "You plan to take me back to your home again?"

Pilkington's mouth drops open, and he eases his grip on her, allowing her to step away. "I did not mean—" he begins, then cuts himself off, saying instead, "You do not have to return. Your life is here. I understand. You owe me nothing."

"Hey," she stops him, reaching up a hand to cup his cheek, "slow down. Take a breath." She looks around the room, seeing the simple couch and coffee table, a small kitchen along the back wall, and two doors that probably lead to a bathroom and a bedroom. "Where are we?"

"My apartment."

Sylvia wonders why she never thought about where the demon lived when he was in this realm. Since they started researching the dagger, he has spent most of his time with her at her apartment or briefly returning to his home in his world. But now that she knows he has been visiting her for years, she should have thought about the logistics. Looking around at the apartment, Sylvia is glad to see that it isn't much larger than her studio, though big enough to have an actual bedroom with a door. "It's nice," she tells him, far more comfortable here than she ever was in Theo's penthouse. "How about we sit for a moment and figure out what to do next?"

"Forneus—" he begins, but she slides her hand over his mouth.

"Forneus can wait," she declares. "We need to talk."

Pilkington nods, silent now, and allows her to lead him to the couch and sit down. His face is blank, clearly bracing himself for bad news.

He totally expects me to break up with him, she thinks. *Wait, are we even dating?* She recalls the feel of his hands on her body. *More than dating,* she decides. *Sort of. We'll figure it out later.*

"Tell me about this Tethering ceremony," she says bluntly.

"What?" He is clearly caught off guard.

"Whatever Forneus was talking about," she prompts. "Clearly, it's important to demons. What is it?"

The demon's words come out slowly, halting, as if he doesn't want to tell her what he told his superior they had already shared. "The Tethering... It's a binding ceremony," he explains. "Sometimes, demons will ... connect with their arusha, sharing their powers. For the stronger partner," he continues, "it can be quite ... exhausting."

"I got that," Sylvia says wryly. "Let me guess the rest—it probably involves sex, right? And then some kind of magic?" When Pilkington only nods, she asks, "But we're already sort of sharing powers, aren't we? So did we actually do this ceremony and I missed it?"

Pilkington bites his lip, then says, "No, we have not bonded in that way. We can share powers because we have been bonded for a long time, and over time, such things can happen."

"But if we did this Tethering thing?" she pushes.

"If you agreed to be my arusha and consented to the ceremony, you would gain access to all of my powers," Pilkington tells her.

"And what about you? What do you get out of it— other than a good time?" she asks.

Pilkington meets her eyes, his expression soulful. "I get an equal," he says softly.

"So, it's not redistributing your powers," she realizes. "It's just leveling up the partner to your level?" She pauses, still not understanding part of what Forneus said. "Does it hurt?"

"Not you," he says quickly. "I mean, if you decided to... it wouldn't..." He lets his head hang, words failing him. Sylvia smiles, delighted to see the normally unflappable demon completely confounded.

"So what?" she asks. "You exhaust yourself with sex or something?"

"After Tethering," Pilkington says, "the stronger partner is weakened, at the mercy of any foes who wish to attack. Most powerful demons will gather a small band of protectors to watch over them afterward, though for some strong demons, their new partner can be enough to protect them."

Pilkington doesn't strike her as the kind to have many friends. He seems very much alone. Sylvia wonders who he would trust to keep him safe while he was vulnerable. "So," Sylvia says, trying to picture it, "you have a group of protectors lined up already?"

"Daughter of Lilith!" he exclaims, the outrage clear in his tone. "No!"

Sylvia giggles at the expression, recalling the last time he said it. She wonders if they can recapture the moment here instead. "Then you're relying on me to protect you?" she suggests, knowing the question will make him answer her.

The demon stares at her, face serious. "I have no plans of Tethering," Pilkington insists, "so I have no need of protection—from anyone."

"Really?" Sylvia says, calling his bluff. "So you don't want to be Tethered to me?"

"You don't know what you're asking," he huffs.

Sylvia scoots over to where he sits on the couch, climbing onto his lap and pressing him back against the couch. She takes his arms and pushes them up onto the back of the couch. "Have you done a poor job explaining it then, if I don't know what I'm asking?"

Pilkington looks up at her, clearly surprised and infatuated with this side of her. "It's a permanent connection," he says. "We don't have to—"

"I know," she says with a sigh. "We don't have to do anything at all." She frowns. "Trust me—I get it. You've made it very clear that I don't have to be with you." She dips down to kiss his neck. "I don't have to do this," she says, sliding his hand back so his arm bends at the elbow. His shirt slides down to reveal his wrist, showing the scar on his hand, and she kisses that next. "Or you can tell me to stop." She pauses, looking down at him, echoes of Phil in the curve of his mouth. "Do you want me to stop?"

"No," he breathes, his other hand slipping down to rest against her hip. The hope in his face nearly undoes her.

"Do you want me?" she asks bluntly, hiding her nerves under aggression.

Pilkington takes in a sharp breath, the hand on her hip pulling her forward so that she rests atop his hard length, the implication clear. "I want you, Sylvia," he assures her. "I've wanted you for ages."

"Then stop trying to get rid of me," she says, her voice smaller now, her fear rising. He has left her before and just when she needed him to stay.

"I'm not trying to get rid of you," he assures her, sitting up and flinging his other arm around her back. "I'm trying to give you a choice."

"I have a choice," Sylvia says, "and I choose you." She frowns, then adds, "It's always been you... even though you left."

Pilkington leans forward, burying his face against her chest. "I'm so sorry I hurt you," he says, then looks up at her with tender eyes. "You understand though, right? You know why I had to leave?"

"Tell me," she says, her heart beginning to pound again. She waits for the voice in her head to speak, to insist that he had tired of her, that she wasn't good enough, that everyone would always leave her behind in the end. But Pilkington catches her face between his hands, forcing her to look at him.

"I had to do right by you," he explains. "You were so young. Too young. And you needed to see the world on your own, without me holding you back. You needed to do things on your own."

"What, like Adam?" She sighs. "I probably could have done without that."

"Could you?" he asks, face serious. "Think, Sylvia, not about how it ended, but about how it began. Remember how he made you feel at the start." His hands brush through her hair, a finger tracing the edge of her ear the way Adam had done when they first started dating. "Close your eyes," he says, and Sylvia obeys.

"Remember how it felt?" Pilkington whispers, his mouth close to hers, hovering the way Adam sometimes did when they kissed in those early days before he grew too eager and started demanding things she could not give him. When he kisses her, his mouth moves the same way Adam's used to, and Sylvia's toes curl despite herself.

"Fine," she admits, shivering in Pilkington's arms though her mind is lost in the memory. "I remember." *And it wasn't terrible. It was ... nice.*

"You've known human kisses," Pilkington purrs, "but there's more to life than that. As you know." His mouth moves away from her lips, finding the line of her jaw and kissing his way over to her ear, nipping her earlobe.

"I know," Sylvia says, the hair on her arms rising as Pilkington runs a line of kisses up her neck the way Theo would do. "Vampires," she adds. At the words, Pilkington sucks on her neck, and Sylvia tumbles into a memory of Theo biting her, her body contracting in ecstasy. "That's not fair," she moans.

"And how do you know I'm not playing fair right now?" Pilkington asks, and Sylvia opens her eyes to look down at him. She narrows her eyes, knowing she has lost.

"Because I have something to compare it to," she admits. His words make sense, but she doesn't have to like them.

"I didn't want to go," the demon assures her. "But I would not steal your life like some demon in a fairy tale claiming a child bride. You needed to live without me." He sighs, adding, "And if I'm honest, I never truly left. I've always been near, Sylvia."

"How do you do it?" she asks, thinking of all the things he must have seen her do over the years, watching her from the shadows. "How could you see me with them and not be jealous?"

Pilkington leans up to kiss her, his mouth strong and sure on hers. "I like seeing you happy. I wasn't jealous," he says into her mouth, "not then."

"Now?" she breathes.

"Now," he growls, hands gripping her hips and sliding beneath her shirt, "you are mine."

"Am I?" she gasps, her hands finding his waist and pushing his shirt up to reveal his muscles and a light dusting of hair across his chest. "I thought I was free to leave at any time."

Pilkington wraps his hand in her hair and tugs on it, forcing her to look at him. She can see the demon in his eyes, and though she thinks she should be frightened, the look only excites her more. "You are mine," he says again, more forcefully this time.

"Then take me," she challenges. "Claim me. Make me yours." She pauses, then whispers, "Tether me."

Pilkington's eyes narrow, and she can see the demon in him warring with the human form he wears. "Don't tempt me," he says, "not until after you've bedded me first. Don't make promises you can't keep. You don't know what you will want tomorrow." The hand in her hair eases as he traces a finger down her cheek. "Desire waxes and wanes like the moon."

"'Oh swear not by the moon,'" Sylvia quotes, the words creeping in from her subconscious, an echo of an English class where she read *Romeo and Juliet*. "'The inconstant moon'?" She frowns, sudden anger joining the flood of desire. "You are so arrogant." She recalls a similar conversation with Theo, when the vampire also insisted that she was too young to know what she wanted. "You think you know my mind better than I do?"

"No," the demon says, leaning in to kiss her neck again, sucking hard, "but I know more about desire than you do, and I know how things change with time." He bites her then, hard, and though he doesn't have Theo's fangs, or even his own demon fangs, the sensation is enough to send her back into another body memory, and she shudders again with remembered passion. "You wanted him like this not so long ago," the demon whispers against her skin, "and when you see him again, you may want him like this again." He pauses, moving to look in her eyes. "But once you have chosen to Tether with me, you will not be free anymore. I will not share you again." His eyes darken, a hint of black and silver overtaking the brown, and Sylvia shudders, feeling the echo of his magic in her skin. "That's what Tethering with me means," he growls.

"And until then, you would share me?" she asks. She knows she is pushing him closer to an edge, but she cannot stop herself, needing to know.

"Our definition of sharing is quite different, Sylvia. You speak of sex, but I'm talking about something more."

"Would you share me for sex?" she asks, running her hands through his hair.

He shrugs, kissing her neck before looking up at her, his expression wicked with carnal desire. "I would enjoy watching you find your pleasure, yes." She can't deny the thrill that shoots through her at the promise in that look. Sylvia wonders how much of what she has heard about demons is true.

"And what about beyond the physical then?" she pushes. "Would you share my love with another?"

Pilkington grimaces but nods. "I would not like it, but I would... if that's what you wanted."

"And do you expect me to share you?" she asks, challenge clear in her voice as she tugs his head back by the hair. "If you wanted?"

The demon shrugs, dismissing her concerns. "It doesn't matter," he replies. "I do not want anyone else."

"Right now. But as you said, time changes everything."

"Yes," he agrees, "but I'm a demon, and I'm old enough to know that I only want you. No amount of time can change that."

"Exactly," Sylvia agrees. "It's always been you. Now stop stalling and bed me already."

"You think I am stalling?" he says, sitting up straighter on the couch.

"You keep talking," she observes. "So many warnings..."

With ease, the demon lifts her body and spins her around so she sits on his lap facing the room, her legs splayed over his, his chest pressed tight against her back. "Maybe I'm just savoring the moment," he says. "Enjoying having you all to myself." His hand drifts up to her breast, and she gasps as he squeezes a nipple, much more forceful now after their heated discussion. "Now where were we?" His other hand moves slowly across her belly, then slides just below her waistband, pausing just above where she wants him. "Was I here?" he asks, nuzzling her neck. His hand creeps lower, his long finger sliding against her wetness. "Or here?"

"There," Sylvia moans, pressing back against him as his finger begins to move. "You were right there." She begins to squirm against his hand, heat building in her belly, and she twists her head, needing his mouth on hers. He obliges, and she reaches up to bury her fingers in his hair, surprised for a moment not to find his horns. Her other hand presses atop the hand over her breast, squeezing hard, and the wave of pleasure crests, bringing her along with it. She gasps into the demon's mouth, heart pounding as the wave recedes. The hand between her legs pauses, still cupping her but giving her a moment to recover. "Yeah," she mumbles. "Right there."

Rallying, she turns her body a little, giving her hand room to run along the top of his jeans. "I'm pretty sure I was about here," she says, then turns around. Pilkington's hand slides out of her shorts as she moves, running over her butt and cupping her hip as she settles herself on his thighs, facing him. She pushes up his shirt again, leaning forward to kiss his very human nipple. Her hands work at his waist, unbuttoning his jeans and slipping her hand within to grasp his length. "I was trying to get here," she comments. Pilkington gasps, leaning over to kiss her as her hands work to free him from his pants. She strokes him, very aware of his human body, a form that is truth here but isn't the real Pilkington.

She wonders how this form compares to his demonic form and stops herself. *Be here now,* she thinks. *Be with him, like this, now.*

Pilkington groans at her touch, his head tilting back as she finds a slow rhythm. He is hard in her hand, his body eager, and suddenly, he sits up and lifts her again, this time pushing her to the side so that she lies on her back on the couch, her legs still twisted around his hips. He kneels between her legs, looking down at her with eyes glinting silver with desire. He watches her face as he bends down, his hand slowly sliding her tank top up, revealing her scar. Sylvia waits for the urge to hide from him, to cover herself, but it never arrives. Instead, she looks down at her belly, the line of silvery flesh just another part of her now, and Pilkington leans down to kiss her skin. He doesn't move along the length as Theo did, outlining the wound, instead the demon treats her scar like any other part of her body, making his way up her belly to nuzzle her breasts, pushing the tank top off her arms and over her head. Sylvia reaches out to pull his shirt over his head, biting her lip at the sight of his bronze skin, the muscles of his back and shoulders clearly defined.

He really is beautifully made.

Watching her, he slides back down her body, pulling her shorts off slowly, then he bends to kiss her sensitive skin, holding her tight when she would pull away, forcing her to endure wave after wave of pleasure.

"How do you know exactly what I want?" she gasps. "It's like you can read my mind."

"Not your mind," he replies, face resting atop her thigh. "Your desire."

"So, it's magic then?" Her hand finds his head, fingers stroking his hair. "One of your powers?"

"I'm a demon," he reminds her. "Desire is what I do." His finger trails up her thigh, pausing just shy of where she wants him to touch her, despite her still recovering heart. "You still want more," he says, moving his head so his tongue can stretch out to lick her. She shivers, pleasure shooting through her as he brings her over the edge again, this time slowly, lazily. After, she lies there, sweat coating her skin as she gasps, then opens her eyes when he chuckles quietly.

"What?" she manages.

"We can pause," he tells her. "You look like you need a break."

Sylvia rallies, sitting up on the couch and reaching for him. "No pause," she says, hands sliding down to push his pants off his hips. "I've waited long enough for you. No more."

Pilkington stands up, letting her pull his pants free and steps out of them. Sylvia stares up at him, hunger silvering her own gaze. Wordlessly, Pilkington reaches down and lifts her up, holding her easily. Sylvia wraps her legs around his waist, her thigh muscles promising retribution when she stops long enough to feel them again and settles her arms around his shoulders. He presses against her, hard and eager.

Sylvia moves her hips, about to slide onto him, when a thought hits her like lightning. "Oh fuck," Sylvia says suddenly, "you're human."

"What of it?" Pilkington asks, taking the few steps to hold her against the wall, taking the strain off her protesting thigh muscles.

"Babies," she breathes, trying to think through the haze of desire clouding her mind. This is something she didn't have to worry about with Theo. Vampires couldn't have children—not through sex anyway.

"You want babies?" Pilkington asks, pausing just beneath her.

"Yes," she says, "eventually. But no—not now. Definitely not now." She frowns. "I don't have anything." She thinks of her purse back in Pilkington's house, but even if she had it with her, it wouldn't matter. Sylvia has never owned condoms, has never had sex before Theo—and he didn't need them.

"I will not give you a child tonight, Sylvia," Pilkington promises, his length pressing against her.

"How do you know that?" she asks, wanting so badly to slide down atop him.

"I'm a demon," he replies. "We choose when we have young."

"Seriously?" she asks, shocked out of the mood by the revelation.

"Seriously," Pilkington assures her, leaning down to kiss her neck.

"That's so cool," she says, leaning her head back into the wall, giving him more access. "Your magic is amazing."

"Absolutely fantastic," he says dismissively, mouth moving up to kiss her hard. Sylvia wraps her arms around him, adjusting her hips for the right angle, hard smoothness rubbing against her in a delicious tease. "You know what is even better?" he asks, pressing himself into her, aligned with her body. "Finally bedding you." Without pausing, eyes watching her face, he slides deep inside. Sylvia moans, surrendering to the feeling, and when he begins to move, she loses herself completely, her body a slave to the desire the demon wields like a weapon, wringing pleasure from her with each shift of his hips.

She becomes aware of time again long after, finding herself on the couch, Pilkington resting atop her, still inside her, their bodies slick with sweat and his hair covering his eyes. She groans, body completely drained, and he shifts, rolling them so that she lays on top of him, her head resting against his chest. They rest there for a moment, catching their breath, just feeling the other's heartbeat, and then Sylvia shivers, the air cool on her naked back. There is the low hum that she now associates with magic, and then a soft blanket is covering her.

"That was awesome," she breathes into him. The demon kisses the top of her head. She snuggles closer into him, kissing the clavicle beneath her mouth. "Seriously. So worth the wait."

"I'm glad to hear it," Pilkington says, nuzzling her hair.

"And I know we have things to do," Sylvia says, her voice slurring as satisfied exhaustion creeps over her. "I just need..."

"I know what you need," the demon assures her, his arms closing around her. "Sleep, arusha. Rest."

Sylvia's body twitches, and she tightens her abused muscles, aware that he is still inside her. "Wait," she manages, "how are you possibly still hard after all that?"

"I'm a demon," he says, his voice very male. "You didn't think everything you've heard about demon lovers was a lie, did you?"

Sylvia chuckles, the words following her down into sleep. *I have a demon lover. Phil is my demon lover.*

CHAPTER 20

PILKINGTON

PILKINGTON LIES ON THE COUCH, LISTENING TO SYLVIA breathe as she rests in his arms. The sun has set outside, the stars visible now, and he knows he will need to wake her soon. Forneus's words echo in his mind, and he wonders how to resolve the mess he has left behind.

He has already retrieved Sylvia's purse and the dagger, pulling them through the worlds almost immediately after Sylvia fell asleep, relieved that Forneus didn't find it first. He wonders if the Marquis searched his house after they left or if Billy was able to maintain his property. The ghost isn't strong compared to demons, but his position as soul-servant binds him to the house—and the laws of hospitality grant him certain abilities when protecting his home.

He's probably rearranging the books in the library while Forneus uncovers my secrets, Pilkington thinks bitterly, cataloguing the places the Marquis might find compromising information. There aren't many, but the more pressing problem is how much the spy may have learned in the last three days. Pilkington recalls the two conversations he had with Sylvia outside that could have been overheard—one on the balcony about his inability to alter his appearance and one on the deck about his family. The first is bad, but Pilkington can work around it, especially since he is now free from the compulsion to obey Forneus. What is worse is them knowing about Sylvia. Claiming an arusha is one thing—shocking for him to do but nothing more than gossip that will pass in time—but telling Forneus he planned on Tethering was the height of foolishness. Beyond the issue of Sylvia's willingness to participate in such a ceremony, Pilkington understands the risks it poses.

He is a powerful demon, respected for his mother, but feared for his unknown father as much as for his connection to Forneus, a Marquis of the Realm. If he were to lose the protection the Marquis's good will affords him, Pilkington knows he has many enemies who would use a Tethering to attack him. Sylvia would have access to all of his powers, but without Forneus to keep the others at bay, Pilkington wonders if he is strong enough to defend himself.

He sighs, chest rising with his breath, and runs a hand over Sylvia's head, stroking her hair.

It's worth it, he decides, knowing he would give up everything he has to stay near her. *No matter what happens now, she is worth it.* He studies her, memorizing the image of her body in his arms, knowing he is experiencing a moment he has long dreamed of, especially since they started spending time together researching the dagger. He knows it is foolish, but he is thankful for the artifact—even grateful for the scar on his arm—because it gave him a reason to be near her again.

He knows that they will go to the vampires tonight, to see what they've learned about Hesperus in the last few days, and he knows there is a chance that his arusha will reconnect with her vampire lover. He trusts her word when she says she has chosen him, but he also trusts that desire is a strange power, often enthralling people beyond conscious thought or control.

Even if I lose her tonight, he thinks, *it is still worth it. And I would do it again.*

"You are thinking very hard." Sylvia's voice rolls up from his chest, and she lifts herself up on one elbow to peer at him. "Want to tell me what has you making that face?"

The demon dips his head down to kiss her softly, gently. "What face is that?" he asks, leaning back but still looking at her.

She narrows her eyes at him, suspicious, then nods her head slowly. "So we're not talking about it then? Just avoiding questions tonight instead. Got it."

"I was thinking about my life," he says honestly.

"What about it?" she probes, resting her chin on her hand as she looks at him. "We talking the future or the past?"

"The past, specifically how I just blew up my life back home," he admits, eyes scanning the ceiling as if the answers hid there. "I can't go back until I figure this out."

"We can't go back until we find the demon," Sylvia adds. "I imagine returning with Hesperus will please your boss, right? Maybe he will forget about the other stuff."

Pilkington glances at her use of the word "we." He doesn't want to believe her, to imagine a life with her—at least not before she sees her vampire again and he knows how she feels. "It's more complicated than that," he tells her.

Sylvia sighs, moving to sit up. "Yeah," she says sarcastically, "not like I would know anything at all about blowing up your life." She tosses the blanket aside as she gets to her feet. "I mean, I just spent the last months entirely engulfed by the supernatural, had my apartment trashed, saw my ex killed, and reconnected with my childhood crush—who's a demon and bonded to me—and there's a magical dagger that wants—"

Pilkington stands up, tugging her to him for a kiss and cutting off her rant. She looks up at him, eyebrow raised. "We'll figure this out," she promises him, then glances down at her naked body. "First, I think I need to get some clothes." She looks around the apartment. "Any chance you have a fancy Sylvia-sized closet of clothes in this apartment, too?"

Pilkington smiles, then gives her an appreciative once over. "I'm not minding the view," he comments.

Sylvia slides her eyes down his naked body and then back up to his face. "Neither am I," she says, "but I'm pretty sure we have things to do tonight." She laughs, then adds, "I'm going to need pants if I want to continue to fight evil tonight."

"Jeans then?" he asks.

Sylvia nods. "A shirt and a hoodie, too." She glances down at her bare feet. "And my boots, if possible, or sneakers?" She smiles. "Have I mentioned how incredibly handy that ability is?"

The demon chuckles, reaching into the space between worlds to collect the items. He pulls them from the room in his house the same way he retrieved the dagger, but before handing them to her, he gives the hoodie a long sniff.

Sylvia eyes him warily. "Um... that's creepy, Phil." It's the first time she has used that name, and they both pause to acknowledge the moment, locking eyes over her clothes.

The demon speaks first, breaking the spell. "Just wanted to make sure the house wasn't on fire," he tells her. "I'd be able to smell the smoke."

"I'm sorry," she says, taking the bundle from him. "I hope your house is okay. I didn't mean to make your boss mad at you."

Pilkington moves away as she dresses, heading into the bedroom where he keeps a few changes of clothes. "It's not you," he assures her from the other room. "Forneus was always looking for a reason. You were just ... convenient."

"How flattering," she says, and he looks up to see her standing in the doorway. Her hair is wild around her face, blonde tendrils running over her shoulders and the black tank top she wears. Her feet are still bare, but she wears her jeans. "You sure know how to make a lady feel special." She steps over to sit on the bed and begins sliding socks onto her feet. Pilkington tugs the Henley over his head, then moves over to push her down onto the bed, a place they have yet to explore together.

"You," he breathes, kissing first one cheek and then the other, "know you are special, Sylvia Copland." He kisses her chin next, and her nose, before smothering her face with butterfly kisses. "My arusha," he says, admiration in his voice as he finally finds her lips and kisses her thoroughly. Sylvia wraps her legs around his hips, and he feels the desire spiral out from her center.

She groans, frustrated, and lets her legs fall aside. "Why do we always have to do things at night?" She frowns, then sits up as he releases her. "It would be nice to use the dark for something else for once."

"I'm sure your vampires will disagree," Pilkington comments, settling himself next to her and sliding on his own socks and shoes.

"Hey," she says, reaching out to touch him. Pilkington pauses, giving her his full attention. She gestures between them, a quick motion that melts the demon's heart. "You and me—we're doing this. Vampires or no. Greater demons or no. Daggers or Leviathans or no. We are doing this together. You and me."

"I love you," the demon says, the words tumbling out before he can stop them.

"Good," Sylvia says. "It's about time." She stands up, heading out of his room to sit on the couch and lace up her boots, leaving Pilkington sitting on his bed and staring after her, unable to believe his luck at finding the perfect arusha.

CHAPTER 21

SYLVIA

A FEW TEXTS ON SYLVIA'S PHONE ALLOW THEM TO ARRANGE a meeting with the vampires at Viking Times, the building empty on a weeknight, and they arrive with the night still very young. Sylvia approaches the back door slowly, recalling how not so long ago, she had fled through these same doors—trying to escape the strange man who captivated her.

Yeah, and then I ran right into the demon. Glancing behind her, she spies a different demon, this one sworn to protect her. *He said he loves me.*

The idea makes her want to burst out into giggles and throw herself into his arms, but she does neither, aware that the space between them is fragile, especially since they are about to go see the vampires again.

Own it, Copland, she thinks. *You're going to see Theo— and he'll probably be able to smell Phil on you.* She marvels at the name, how easily Pilkington has shifted in her thoughts, her old friend and long-time dream companion coalescing into the demon in human form standing behind her. *Do I care?* She wonders at the thought, debating how she will feel when she sees him again. *I don't want to hurt him.*

He hurt you.

Yes, but he's been held by Jolena for almost two months. He's different—and so am I.

"So, do you plan on knocking or shall I just open the door?" Pilkington asks, the demon leaning forward to speak near her ear. Sylvia starts, realizing she has been standing in front of the door, motionless, for a long moment. She studies the door, not seeing a handle on this side of the exit.

"I guess we knock?" she suggests, raising a hand to tap gently on the door. She doesn't hear a response, but the demon scoots her gently to the side so the opening door won't hit her.

"They're coming," he explains. A moment later, the door opens, the steel slab pushing slowly out into the dark back alley.

"Hey," a voice says, and Sylvia recognizes Ula, the witch giving her and Pilkington a quick once-over. Her face relaxes. "Finally!" she exclaims, turning to Sylvia. "You went swimming, right?"

"Oh yeah," Sylvia replies, oddly comfortable discussing this with the witch. "Jumped right in the deep end."

Ula giggles, the sound delightful despite the tight sensation in Sylvia's gut, and something inside her relaxes. She looks over Sylvia's shoulder. "Lord Pilkington," she greets, bowing formally before bouncing back up and waving them inside.

"Lady Tallardy," he replies, his voice cordial.

"Perfect," the witch says, turning around and heading back down the hall. Her voice drifts back to them as they step inside. "It's tonight then!"

Sylvia glances at the demon over her shoulder, mouths, *Tonight?* and follows the witch inside. Sylvia remembers the hallway, though she was only back here once—the night she met Theo. Looking up, she sees the light fixtures she glimpsed while being carried over the vampire's shoulder like a prize. The memory is funny now, tinged with a hint of sadness but nothing more. Sylvia waits to see how she will feel when she sees him.

They turn a corner and step through thick curtains onto the soft dirt floor of the arena. In the wide-open space, two long tables are still resting where the performers drag them for the final scene of the show, long benches on the back side of the arena. Harald is pacing slowly in the dirt on the other side of the table, swinging an axe and warhammer in a choreographed routine that reveals the bulging muscles of his chest. Oren sits atop one table, legs crossed and eyes closed, and Sylvia wonders if the vampire is meditating. He does not look at them as they enter, face impassive.

Sylvia takes a deep breath, then turns to see Theo. She heard him already, knowing that the red-headed vampire is practicing like Harald, but where the fair-haired vampire's moves are slow and steady, Theo is flying through his steps, the long sword a whirlwind around his head. Sylvia has seen him perform in the show, but those moves are practiced, choreographed. This is wild, yet she can still see the order in his motion, the swings and steps perfectly balanced. He doesn't pause, though she knows he must sense their presence.

Ula stands at the end of the table, catching Harald's eye first. The big man stops his practice, stepping over to stand next to his witch, dropping a soft kiss on her forehead as he places both weapons on the table and grabs his discarded shirt to wipe his face. Sylvia and Pilkington pause, not sure where to stand, and Oren opens his eyes, giving Sylvia a pointed look before cutting his eyes at where Theo continues to move. He rolls his eyes, giving a small shoulder shake, then hops off the table in a display of lithe grace. Approaching Sylvia, he drops to one knee in the dirt before her, placing her hand on his forehead.

"My eternal gratitude," he says formally, "for freeing me."

"Uh," Sylvia stutters, not expecting the gesture, though she remembers that the last time she saw Harald and Oren, both were crying tears of joy.

Theo had not been so pleased with his freedom.

"You're welcome," she manages, urging him up with both hands. "Please get up. This is too weird."

The vampire obeys, releasing her hand as he stands. His nose twitches, and his eyes skate over her shoulder to the demon behind her, but he says nothing, his jaw tightening slightly as he meets her gaze. "Do you realize what you've done for us?" he asks.

Sylvia nods. "I do, and I'm sorry." At Oren's horrified expression, she adds, "I mean, I'm sorry it had to happen. I'm not sorry you're free. You should have always been free." Sylvia looks over at Ula, the witch watching their exchange. "Are they free from the dagger, then?"

"Oh no," the witch says. "The artifact still controls creatures." At Sylvia's frown, she adds, "But they are free from their Maker, something that rarely happens for vampires, so I too, thank you." She gives Harald a loving look. "He is mine, you know, but he would never have been all mine—not while she lived. As soon as she realized we were fated, she would have called him to her. And I wouldn't have been able to stop it."

"So, Maker powers are stronger than fate bonds?" Sylvia asks. "But neither is stronger than the dagger?"

Ula nods. "There is a balance to the world, Sylvia. You must understand now, having bonded so thoroughly." When Sylvia's brow furrows and she glances behind her at the demon, Ula adds pointedly, "With the dagger. It's yours now."

"Is it?" Sylvia asks, wondering how much the witch read into the look. Did everyone in the room already know she was with Phil? Eventually, she would have to hang out with normal people again, so she could have some semblance of privacy. She wonders what Jeremy and Miriam would say to all this, though they aren't entirely normal either. Sylvia wonders what normal means at all.

"Test it," Harald suggests, tugging his shirt back on over his head and leaning back against the table's edge.

Sylvia sighs, never comfortable with the dagger's power, but she pulls the blade out of her bag, hand resting on the pommel as if she's been wielding daggers for her entire life. The quiet voices are back in her mind, whispering softly, but Sylvia does not focus on them, does not want to hear what they have to say. "What should I do?" she asks.

"Perhaps a different test from the one you gave me," Pilkington says behind her, and she blushes, recalling that her last dagger test had been to ask the demon to kiss her—a request he had been able to refuse. Sylvia chuckles, unable to stop herself.

"Raise your hand," she suggests. Harald's arm moves up immediately, Oren's a split second later, and the sound of Theo practicing a few feet away stops suddenly. There is a muffled curse, and she looks over to see the sword held aloft above the vampire's head, her order encompassing all three vampires easily. She follows Ula's glance behind her to see that Pilkington has not moved, his arms still resting casually at his sides. The witch's eyes widen, and she squeals, jumping up and down in her excitement.

"You did it!" she yells, stepping forward to grab Sylvia's free hand. "I knew you could do it!"

"You knew..." Sylvia's voice trails off. "You knew I would free him?"

Before Ula can reply, Theo's voice cuts across the space. "Mind letting us go then? Since you're so keen on setting people free?"

Sylvia winces at the bitterness in his tone, and she looks over at him. "Put your arms down," she tells them, returning the dagger to her bag. "I thought I was helping you," she snaps, unable to stop the words, though she knows she is only poking the bear.

"Spare me from any more of your help," he retorts, spinning back into another move.

Sylvia purses her lips, turning her attention back to the friendly vampires. "So... that's not awkward or anything."

Oren shakes his head, eyes narrowing in disapproval as he studies his friend. "It's hard," he admits, "and I get that. It's always hard coming back—but it doesn't excuse what he did to you." He glances at Ula and Harald, who both are studiously ignoring the red-head. "Or what he's done since."

"Look," Sylvia says, "we can work out our differences another time. Right now, we're in a bit of a time crunch." She meets Pilkington's eye, and he nods slightly, granting her permission to share his situation. "There's a demon." When Oren opens his mouth, no doubt to make a "duh" sound, Sylvia continues, "A different demon back in the demon realm. A Lord of the Realm. A Marquis, I think." She catches Pilkington's eye again, and the demon nods. "Yeah, a big deal—and he demands we return Hesperus immediately."

"Your Master?" Ula asks.

Pilkington flinches a little at the word. "I serve no master," he says. "My ... employer."

"Okay, so this boss compelled you to find Hesperus immediately?" At the demon's nod, she narrows her eyes. "But you can't be compelled anymore."

Both vampires stare at the demon, who raises his eyebrows and bares his teeth in a goofy grin. Sylvia hears Theo stop moving, the third vampire turning to stare at the demon as well.

"Wait, you freed him from all compulsion? All the time?!" Theo's voice is ragged. Sylvia recognizes the blend of awe, anger, and fear.

"I did," she says simply, not knowing what else to say. After a long moment where everyone continues to stare at her, she swallows audibly, then says, "But his boss doesn't know that—and we'd like to keep it that way."

"You," Theo says, "as in both of you." He cocks his head, still standing several feet away from where they are clustered. "You planning to go back to the demon realm then?"

Sylvia frowns, then shrugs. "Yes?"

Theo scoffs. "Let me guess—the demon has a glorious castle on a mountainside."

"Actually, it's on a lake," Sylvia snaps, "and it's a mansion—not a castle."

"You wouldn't let me buy you a mansion," Theo accuses.

"It's not my mansion," she replies. "And I don't need one. I was fine in my apartment, which—if you didn't know—has been ransacked and destroyed by Adam." She can see from his face that Theo knew that her apartment had been broken into, but not by whom. "Oh, don't worry," she adds, watching the fury build on his face at the idea of Adam returning to her home. "He's dead. We had to kill him after he tried to steal the dagger."

"I didn't know," Theo says quietly.

"No, you didn't," Sylvia snaps. "You don't know anything about the last months because you haven't been here!" She pauses, catching her breath, then adds, "Crazy me, I thought you may want your freedom back. You'd want to see them at least." She gestures at Oren and Harald. "But none of that matters now," she says finally. "We need to find Hesperus and send him home." She looks at Oren and Harald. "Any leads?"

Both vampires shake their heads. "We think he's staying somewhere outside the city," Oren shares. "But he's hiding himself somehow."

Pilkington nods. "I thought the same thing."

"So," Sylvia says, looking at everyone—even Theo—in turn, "any theories on catching a Greater Demon?"

"You can lure him here," Ula says.

"Me?" Sylvia asks, hand to her chest. "Why me?"

Ula nods at the bag at Sylvia's hip and the dagger within. "You wield the Tallardy Dagger," she says. "Call him. He cannot resist."

Sylvia furrows her brow. "What? You mean I could have called him at any time? Why didn't we do this sooner?"

Ula shakes her head. "No, you couldn't do it before. Not until you fully bonded with the blade. Now it's yours to command."

"I really don't understand what you mean when you say I bonded to the blade," Sylvia admits. "I mean, I feel like it's mine somehow, but is that … it?"

Ula smiles. "Artifact bonds are particular to each item, depending on the magic used to create them. The dagger was created for vengeance, intended to be wielded by a virgin."

Sylvia grimaces, eyes skating to Theo before she can stop them. "Um, I don't know how to tell you this, but I'm not—"

"But you were," Ula insists. "The first time the blade tasted your blood, you were." She looks up at the demon. "And then it tasted you—and the parameters for the next bond were set. It took a while, but both of you needed to acknowledge your bond before the dagger would truly recognize you."

"Bond?" Theo asks, and both Oren and Harald look away.

"You didn't tell him?" Sylvia asks.

"He wasn't much for talking," Oren says neutrally.

"I asked you to fill me in," Theo snaps. "You said nothing of demon bonds."

"You didn't want to hear anything about her, man," Oren replies, "and you know it."

"He speaks truth," Harald adds. "You are not yourself."

Theo says nothing for a moment, and Sylvia sees the Theo she knows struggling with the stranger standing before her. Her vampire lover was reasonable; he would listen to arguments—but this Theo is too angry, too conflicted to hear details of her life without him. Finally, he sighs, and says, "You should have told me."

"How about I tell you now?" Sylvia offers. At his expectant look, Sylvia gestures to Pilkington. "Theo, meet Phil."

"Phil?" Theo echoes, not comprehending for a moment, then realization crosses his handsome face. "Wait—your Phil?"

Sylvia nods. "I didn't know," she explains. "Not for a while. Not until we went to the Lyceum."

"You were at the Lyceum?" Theo's anger is rising again as he looks at his friends. "Odin's balls! Why would you bring her there?"

"They didn't," Sylvia continues. "Phil did." She takes a breath, then summarizes the main features of their visit to the supernatural school—meeting Jeremy again, learning the dagger's history, then ends with their ill-fated trip to the magic store.

"Wow," Theo says when she has finished. "That's ... a lot."

"Tell me about it. Then add in a pissed off demon lord showing up at his house and sending us back here."

"How pissed off?" Harald asks, looking at Pilkington. The demon shrugs.

"Pissed enough to want to give me to some other demons as entertainment for proper motivation," Sylvia shares.

"That's bad," Oren says. "But you escaped?"

"For now," Sylvia says. "I don't know what he can do to me since I'm an arusha, but—"

"A what?" Theo asks.

"A—" Sylvia opens her mouth to explain, but Ula interrupts her.

"It doesn't matter," the witch says. "Not if we can call Hesperus to us."

"What then?" Harald asks. "If she can call the beast, how can we contain it? I've heard tales of Greater Demons. We are not strong enough to fight it."

"Leave that to me," Pilkington says softly. "If we can get him somewhere, I can do the rest." He looks at the three vampires, the witch, and Sylvia in slow succession. "I'll need a few moments though. We can try a circle, but if he gets free..." His gaze returns to the vampires. "Can you ... keep him occupied?"

Harald picks up the warhammer resting on the table beside him and flips it easily. "I thought you'd never ask."

CHAPTER 22

THEO

THEO STANDS AT THE EDGE OF THE ARENA, WATCHING AS the demon, the witch, and his former lover move around the circle they have created in the center of the open space. They had debated location for a little bit but eventually decided that calling Hesperus here to Viking Times made the most sense. The building is closed for the next few days, far enough from residential areas that a fight wouldn't attract too much attention. The arena is spacious enough too, especially after they moved all the tables and chairs out into the front area near the gift shop. If the place survives the demon battle, they can put everything back together before the next show this weekend.

Watching them carefully draw lines and symbols on the smooth dirt, Theo has his doubts about the circle. He knows demons are supposed to be bound by such things—the price of their power much as his was forfeiting the sun and relying on blood—but he also knows that demons escape from such circles often enough. Hesperus himself escaped when he was conjured here—and nearly killed Sylvia in the process. Without the demon to heal her, she would have died before Theo could reach her.

He doesn't want to be grateful to the demon, doesn't want to think about his feelings for Sylvia at all, but watching them together hurts somewhere deep inside. He knows it's better this way, knows she's better off without him, but beyond the swirling chaos Jolena's influence has left behind, he still aches at the loss of his sweet Sylvia, the first human to intrigue him enough to stay more than a night or two.

And it's her Phil, he thinks, recalling what she had told him of her childhood friend when she'd shared her sketches with him. He'd recognized first love when he saw it.

What of me? Would I even recognize my first love? He thinks back to his human life, trying to call forth the face of the first girl he had loved, but the image is hazy, dark hair and a smirk as they snuck away to watch the stars away from the village. *Signe,* he thinks, a name he hasn't thought of in a long time. *I think a better question is whether she would ever recognize me. I wouldn't recognize me.*

Especially not now.

But he knows that it takes time to come back to himself after Jolena. She forced him to act on his baser instincts, making him nothing more than the creature she made him, and it is hard to put the monster away after indulging for so long.

One good thing, he muses, *is that I'm still strong, glutted with blood and power.* Oren and Harald had left to hunt, bolstering their strength the same way, while the others created the circle to trap the demon. When Harald had asked why Pilkington expected them to fight if they were using a circle, the demon had only shaken his head, reminding them that Hesperus had already escaped a circle easily enough.

Of course, that was a Charlie Wagner circle, the summoner barely passable in his skills, and Ula seemed much more competent. But Theo still remembers the amount of blood on the floor beneath where Sylvia lay in the demon's arms when he arrived, and he's prepared to take every precaution. He wanted Sylvia to leave immediately after conjuring the creature so that she wasn't in danger, and though Pilkington looked like he wanted to agree, he said nothing, and Ula explained that Sylvia needed to be there to control the demon until Pilkington could send him home.

Watching them complete the last inspection of the summoning circle, Theo hopes the magic holds and the demon can be returned without trouble. His long life tells him that such fortune is not likely, not with his luck.

Harald and Oren return, the vampires glancing at the circle before walking around it and moving to stand near Theo. "Are you with me, brother?" Harald asks, looking at Theo intently.

Theo nods. "I am." He sighs, then adds, "Please forgive me … for what I said. I am not myself."

Harald nods, and Theo can see his friend recalling Theo's reaction to the news about Ula. He had not been his best self. Instead of congratulating his friend on finding a mate and the peace that entailed, Theo had snapped and snarled, calling Harald a besotted and bewitched fool for believing such nonsense. Even seeing Harald's reflection had only made him silent, the implications sinking in. "I know," Harald says. "Already forgiven, man."

They embrace in the old way, shoulder to shoulder, arms slamming against backs. Both separate to see Oren, who is smiling at his friends, glad to see a glimmer of the old Theo in the gesture.

"We know, dude," Oren adds. "And it will be fine. Let's just get through tonight, shall we?" He sniffs, studying the space again with a critical eye. "Can he fly?"

"Not sure," Harald says, then faces the circle, shouting, "Can Hesperus fly?"

"Not well inside here," Pilkington replies. "He's too big for his wings to work well." He glances at the roof. "He could fly free if he made a hole." He cocks his head. "Though he probably won't leave until you are all dead."

"And you?" Theo asks.

The demon shrugs. "He knows what killing me means for him when he does return. He will try not to offend me."

"Who exactly are you?" Oren asks, head tilted as he stares at the seemingly normal human man.

"I'm no one to be trifled with," Pilkington replies primly. "And if I can get close enough to him for him to recognize me, this should go smoothly enough."

Theo reminds himself to research the demon far more when all this is over. "Why hasn't he already returned home if he knows you are hunting him?" Theo asks, adding, "If you're such a big deal among your people, why can't you control him?"

The demon side-eyes him carefully. "Given your disposition these last few days, how easy has it been for your friends to corral you, Muldavian?"

Theo looks away, embarrassed both by his behavior—which he still cannot control—and the observation that he is stronger than his companions. Harald is a better fighter in terms of strategy and Oren is more clever, but Theo's combined fighting skill and understanding of his opponent has always given him the edge. He knows exactly what to say to defuse a situation if he wants, to agitate a foe into a foolish fight, to hurt a friend with barbed words, and he admits ruefully—to break a human's heart.

"When he arrives," Oren asks, picking up the thread of Theo's question, "will you be able to control him?"

Pilkington frowns. "In my true form, perhaps. He would recognize me then." He glances down at his human body. "Like this, he will need to sense my magic to recognize me—and he may be too angry to try." He shakes his head. "I'm starting to wonder if I wasn't sent here like this to die."

"What happens ... if you die?" The question comes from Sylvia, who hasn't said much during the preparations, no doubt focusing on what part she will play in the battle.

The demon shrugs, running a hand through his hair and giving the human a reassuring look. "I go home," he says simply.

"Can you come back?"

"Assuming he is willing to allow it, yes. Technically, if I die before sending Hesperus back, I must return to complete my geas. But I will return human again because my task was to locate the Greater Demon, and that is easier done by blending in." He rolls his eyes. "The Marquis just wants me to suffer for my defiance. It's no matter. I've died before, and I'm sure I'll die again."

"Like when you ran off the cliff," Sylvia murmurs, and Theo listens despite himself, feeling like an intruder on their conversation but unable to stop. "And you returned like this."

The demon nods. "I did not know that the dagger could summon Hesperus," he admits. "If I had, this would have ended long ago."

Something about the way he says that makes Theo think the words aren't exactly the truth. He recalls those long hours at Sylvia's apartment, the three of them researching, or just Sylvia and Pilkington researching while Theo hunted with Oren and Harald. *I think maybe you didn't want to know*, he thinks, *so you could spend more time with my human.*

His human. His—what was it Sylvia said? Akursha?

"What I don't get," Oren says, "is why there's a Greater Demon running around this realm, and we haven't heard a single word about it. Don't demons delight in slaughter and mayhem? Why is he lying low?"

Pilkington shrugs, his attention back on the finished circle, eyes scanning the symbols with detached evaluation overlaying a tiny part of disgust. *He must hate it*, Theo realizes, *using a circle at all. Like I would hate using Jolena's abilities for anything in my life.*

"Some demons don't want death and chaos," he explains. "Some just want something different." He pauses, eyes narrowing as he leans down to adjust a line in the dirt ever so slightly. He stands up, wiping a hand on his pants. "Though if he wanted to sightsee, Hesperus could have simply applied for a permit and arrived the normal way in a human body."

"You make it sound like getting a visa," Oren says. "Is that really how it works?"

"Some demons sneak through the portals," Pilkington explains. "Some are summoned and linger after they are freed—or free themselves. But if you know someone in the right place, you can always travel the realms."

"You've got a guy in customs who lets you through." Oren nods.

"I've got a guy who sends me through," Pilkington corrects. "I'm an investigator."

"Were you sent to find Sylvia?" Theo asks. "All those months ago, was it you?"

"I was sent to investigate the vampire who killed a demon," Pilkington admits, giving Theo a pointed look, "and to ensure that the truce with the Klaviger remained intact."

Theo nods, recalling the surprise visit from the Vig the night he met Sylvia. "They were here to see you," he muses.

The demon shrugs. "No doubt they had more business than just a meeting with me," he says. "That Gabrielle was very interested in vampire movements in the city."

Oren snorts, giving Theo a look, and for a moment, Theo is himself again, complaining about the obsessive vampire he has yet to escape. *And now that Jolena is gone,* he thinks, *she will be even worse.* He groans, shaking his head and swinging his sword a few times to loosen his muscles.

"We are not talking about the Vig right now," Theo announces. "We're summoning a demon and sending it home. Let's focus on one problem at a time."

He can feel Sylvia's gaze on him, the human no doubt wondering who Gabrielle is—and what she means or meant to him. *Not her problem anymore,* he thinks bitterly, then stops himself. It's his fault she doesn't know ... because he didn't tell her things. Not after his initial confession of being a vampire. He'd given her snippets of his human life, but nothing of himself in between. If there hadn't been a powerful physical attraction between them, Theo wonders what would have happened even if Jolena had not shown up. Sylvia is human, and she wants to stay that way. Sooner or later, Theo would slip up, his vampire side making a mistake, biting her in a passionate rage, and then she would resent him for turning her.

Seeing her now with the demon, he feels relieved. The demon is also strong, like he is, but he doesn't pose a threat the way Theo does. He won't snap and accidentally hurt her.

Though I do wonder how they will manage if he's in his demon form. His nails are sharp, not to mention the tip of his tail. He cuts off the image forming in his mind immediately, swinging his sword more violently and pacing a little in the dirt.

He may be relieved to see her with someone better suited, but he does not enjoy picturing her with her new lover. He's not that nice of a guy.

"It's ready," Pilkington announces, taking a few big steps away from the circle. He speaks a few words in a foreign tongue, the consonants hard and the vowels slippery, and Sylvia winces, but they all see the magic spring forth, a wispy wall of power coalescing around the circle, forming a tube that shrinks as it reaches the high ceiling.

CHAPTER 23

PILKINGTON

PILKINGTON FORCES HIMSELF NOT TO CRINGE AWAY FROM the circle magic. He knows how to summon demons, but he has always hated it, hated the feeling of robbing another demon of their free will. This time, however, he is not summoning Hesperus. The Greater Demon is beyond his reach with a name secret even to Forneus. Pilkington has no doubt that if Forneus knew Hesperus's true name, he would never have sent him here to retrieve him. The fact that Hesperus has been here this long is starting to make the Marquis look bad to certain demons back home. That's part of the reason why Forneus was so quick to threaten him. If the Marquis's reputation were not in danger, they would have worked out some arrangement.

Pilkington still hopes they can find mutual ground when he returns, especially if he can return Hesperus tonight. Forneus will see reason. The only question is what it will cost Pilkington to keep Sylvia safe. Until now, he hasn't had anything worth threatening.

His mother's powers are a deterrent, not to mention her position among the elite, and the mystery of his father is enough that most demons leave him alone. Forneus finds his skills useful, and Pilkington has enjoyed the arrangement, taking advantage of the frequent trips through the worlds to check on his arusha.

He wonders how frequent those trips will be after all this. He's about to begin cataloguing the lists of possible favors that he can redeem to ensure easy passage back and forth, then the magic before him shudders, and he returns to the moment at hand.

Sylvia is holding the dagger aloft. She isn't speaking, but her lips are moving, and he can see that she is deeply attuned to the artifact, unaware of the outside world. If Ula wasn't standing behind her, the witch perfectly capable of pulling his human to safety when the demon appears, he would move closer. But he stays put, hoping the enraged Hesperus might taste his magic and recognize him when he arrives in the circle.

This is a bad plan, he thinks, the thought skimming across the surface of his mind, and then all he can feel is the summoning. The call is not for him, but he is still a demon, and the magic burns against his face and hands. He winces, eyes narrowing as the magic nearly blinds him. When he can see again, the Greater Demon Hesperus stands within the magical summoning circle before them. The creature lets out a bellow of rage as his arms begin striking the magical wall, streaks of magic trailing after his movements. The Greater Demon is huge, easily fifteen feet tall with massive wings pressed tight against his back, long tail whipping around, searching the circle for any signs of weakness.

Pilkington can't help but sympathize with Hesperus. He knows that feeling—those first few moments after the summoning when everything in him would fight against the circle, against the power holding him captive, against the loss of his free will. He does not enjoy putting another demon—even one like Hesperus who was known for his delight in tormenting his prey—in such circumstances.

Sylvia stands before the circle, the dagger held before her body, face deep in concentration as she wields the artifact. Pilkington tries not to remember the last time he was in the same space as Sylvia and Hesperus, but he cannot stop the memory from flooding across him, the warmth of Sylvia's blood on his legs as she nearly bled out before him.

Any sympathy he has vanishes as the rage begins to burn. *He tried to kill my arusha*, he thinks, the dark part of him he tries to ignore flaring to life. *He cannot live.*

A quick glance at the Muldavian shows that the vampire has the same thought. The demon catches the vampire's eye, and they share a brief moment, united in their memory. Pilkington sees the resolve in the Muldavian's eyes, the way the vampire settles himself, ready for the fight they both know is coming.

It is decided, then, he thinks. *Hesperus must not be sent back. He must die—permanently.* Pilkington knows the idea is foolish—there will be consequences if he fails to deliver the Greater Demon—but it doesn't hurt to imagine the possibility. He cracks his neck, a foolishly human gesture, but one he has seen many men make before wading into a fray. His human body will not help him here, but his powers should.

"Little bait," Hesperus whispers, using his demonic voice to unnerve the humans. Pilkington sees Ula wince, but Sylvia doesn't seem to notice the small flex of power. The witch hunkers down, well out of the way of the demon and the probable fighting.

"Hesperus," Sylvia says, but the voice is not her own. It is her voice overlaid with dozens of other voices. *The victims of the dagger,* Pilkington realizes. *All those witches.*

With dawning horror, Pilkington realizes that he never asked Professor Dilmun which demon had destroyed the original Ardy family. From the look on Sylvia's face, he has a sinking feeling in his very human gut that Hesperus may have been involved.

"You have grown strong," the demon says, adding more push to his voice. Ula sinks to one knee, Harald moving in front of her protectively, but Sylvia only stands before the circle, seemingly unfazed by the power.

"You have grown careless," Not-Sylvia says, "allowing yourself to be captured so. The mighty Hesperus falling prey to a silly little artifact."

The Greater Demon lets out a bellow at the taunt, but Sylvia does not move. The three vampires all look at her, and Pilkington realizes that her ears are bleeding.

No more time, he thinks. *I have to move now.*

The problem with moving at all is that Pilkington must release the demon from the circle in order to send him back to the demon realm. And he is not going to release Hesperus with Sylvia standing so close.

"You are mine," Not-Sylvia says, and the hairs on Pilkington's human arms stand on end, his scarred forearm bursting into sharp pain. This is not his Sylvia, and if he doesn't separate her from that dagger soon, it will be hard to get his arusha back from whatever grip the artifact has on her.

I should never have let her do this, he realizes, *not without researching what a bond with that artifact meant.* A snatch of conversation plays in his memory: Sylvia in his apartment listing her recent trials. "A dagger that wants," she had said, and he had been too distracted by his desire to bed her that he hadn't asked what she meant. He knows some artifacts are sentient and can possess their wielders. Of course, the Tallardy dagger would work that way, especially since it contains so many victims within.

I am an idiot!

"I command you," Not-Sylvia continues. "You must obey. Kneel before me!" Pilkington can feel the power in the words, and for a moment, he almost drops to a knee, the urge to obey deeply ingrained. All three vampires have fallen to their knees, though Theo is straining against the command. Pilkington hesitates a split second, then falls to his knees as well, not wanting Hesperus to know that he is not bound by the dagger.

Eventually, the Greater Demon will be back in the demon realm, and such knowledge is too precious to share. Pilkington does not want to have to murder Hesperus for real to keep his secret safe—but he will if he has to.

Hesperus slowly sinks to one knee inside the circle, body straining but unable to stop the motion.

"You destroyed everything," Not-Sylvia says. "You will suffer as I have."

A wave of pain whips through the room, and all three vampires moan in agony. Pilkington can sense the power, but it does not affect him. He shuffles forward on both knees, moving slowly, hoping Hesperus does not notice him.

"As you tore my family apart," Not-Sylvia shouts, "so shall you be torn asunder!"

Oh fuck, Pilkington thinks as he has a terrible idea of what her next words will be. He abandons his ruse, standing up and running over to Sylvia. She turns to face him as he approaches, her attention leaving the demon for a second, and he sees no recognition in her face. "Sylvia," he says, holding his hands up. "Come back to me."

Not-Sylvia shakes her head, fighting herself. Her eyes have gone full black, the power of hundreds of witches' fury possessing her body.

"Arusha," he says quietly, his voice calm and controlled, unlike the noise echoing through the room: Ula whimpering, the vampires moaning, the demon growling. Not-Sylvia looks up at the word, hissing. Pilkington stares into the black abyss of her eyes. "She is my arusha," he repeats. "You cannot have her."

"We do not recognize demon laws here," Not-Sylvia insists, her voice layered with others.

"You treat with a demon right now, Lady Ardy," Pilkington reminds her. "You use demon laws to keep him captive." He pauses, letting reason seep through her anger. "Breaking the most sacred demon law renders your power useless."

The blood that was slowly dripping from Sylvia's ears slows and then stops, the witches using their power to heal her human body. "We will not harm her,"

Not-Sylvia agrees. "Your law is met." She turns back to the demon, but Pilkington clears his throat, a quiet sound that cuts through the noise again.

"And her companions?" he prompts. "Your power affects everyone in this room. Punish the demon if you must but leave them alone."

Not-Sylvia cocks her head, studying him. "Not you," they say. "Why doesn't it affect you?"

Pilkington grins, spreading his hands. "The power of love, my lady!" He cuts his eyes to the Greater Demon, who watches the exchange with interest. *So much for secrecy,* Pilkington thinks. *I will have to bribe him, or kill him, or find his true name when I get home. Or I could always just kill him for real...* He chuckles, letting the charming part of himself free. "You should try it sometime. You'd be amazed how freeing it can be."

"Don't speak to me of love, demon," Not-Sylvia hisses. "You don't know what the word means."

"Is that a fact?" he asks. "You claim demons cannot love?"

Something in her face shifts, and Pilkington senses the change. Something he said has struck a nerve, loosening the artifact's hold on Sylvia. "Demons only lie," Not-Sylvia whispers.

"No, my lady," Pilkington replies, voice calm and pleasant. "Demons cannot lie. We can embroider the truth, but the only lies are the ones you tell yourself."

Not-Sylvia turns to look at Hesperus. "He lied," she insists. "He wore a different form, much like you do now, so handsome and human," she spits the word, "but none of it was true. None of it was real."

"I do not know the particulars of the agreement your family made," Pilkington says, stalling now, waiting for the weak spot to reveal itself as it always does when he works on a contract.

"I didn't make the agreement!" the voice snarls, but it is no longer layered with hundreds of others, the tone settling into something Pilkington thinks may be the original Sophia Ardy. "Esme did it, but she promised we would be safe!"

Pilkington wants to ask what the arrangement was, but it isn't time yet. She's closer now, but not there yet.

"But then he showed up like that!" she snarls, turning to stare at the Greater Demon again. "And he killed her. And everyone else." Her voice turns cold. "He must suffer." Before Pilkington can speak, she is talking rapidly. "Hesperus," she says, and Pilkington feels the power that has been holding the entire room in thrall shifting, focusing on the creature in the circle instead. "You started by tearing Esme in half. I'll never forget the sounds. Tear off your arm."

Pilkington turns in time to see Hesperus reach over with his right arm and begin yanking at his left. The sound of tearing ligaments is terrible. He returns his attention to Not-Sylvia. "This is barbarous, my lady. Did it not occur to you that he may have been compelled to destroy your family?"

Not-Sylvia looks away from the demon currently pulling off his arm to study Pilkington. "How?" she asks.

Pilkington lifts his chin in the direction of the demon currently trapped in the circle. "He could not have stopped himself from obeying, no more than he can stop himself now."

Not-Sylvia's eyes narrow, and Pilkington feels the power filling her. A drop of blood runs from his arusha's nose, and he snaps, "Stop it! You are hurting her!"

"She will live," Not-Sylvia dismisses coldly. "For which you should be thanking us." She frowns, considering the possibility that Hesperus may have been compelled to attack. "Who would do such a thing?"

Pilkington shrugs. "No doubt Esme had many enemies," he comments. "Your family was powerful. There are always those who seek more. Even you," he adds.

"I seek nothing," she snaps.

"Nothing? What of your revenge?" He turns to watch the spectacle inside the circle, the Greater Demon's left arm a disfigured tube of bloody sinew. As Pilkington watches, the muscle holding it attached gives way, and his arm comes free in a splash of gore that stains the magic of the circle in gray and black. He turns back to Not-Sylvia, trying to judge her next move, but any chance of reasoning with Hesperus has gone.

Pilkington sniffs. He didn't want to treat with the demon who had nearly killed his arusha anyway, but he also doesn't like giving up advantages when he doesn't have to. Hesperus is a liability now, and he must be destroyed—not only here, but at home as well. He will figure that out another time.

A look at Not-Sylvia shows that she is ready to have the demon tear another piece of himself free, but before Pilkington can interject, the demon stands, and with a roar that makes the other creatures tremble, the Greater Demon throws his arm at the edge of the circle, where the magic meets the ground. Pilkington understands the move at once, but there is no time to shout a warning.

"He's fr—" he manages before the magic circle explodes outward in all directions, the power knocking them all flat, even Not-Sylvia. The Greater Demon has used his arm to damage the symbols drawn into the dirt floor. Normally, the creature within a circle can't affect it with anything they have, but by detaching his arm from his body, Hesperus introduced a foreign body into the circle, still a demonic body part, but not connected to the demon the circle was intended to hold. The breach is enough to destroy the entire circle.

Pilkington is on his feet immediately, moving to shield Sylvia, but Hesperus is already blocked by the vampires, all three finally free from the dagger's compulsion to kneel. Oren reaches him first, the small vampire leaping in with his staff, landing a hit against the demon's legs intended to trip him, but the staff simply bounces off, the demon's body too strong for such tactics. Theo is there next, and having learned from Oren's failure that the demon's body is too strong, the Muldavian slashes at Hesperus's broad wings, the webbed material much more susceptible to damage. As the Greater Demon turns to face the Muldavian, having deemed him the greater threat, Harald steps up behind and lands a crushing blow to the back of his exposed neck. Oren swivels, using his staff to leap up and then bringing it back down incredibly fast between the demon's back and wings, pushing the demon off balance as he pries them apart.

Pilkington drags Sylvia behind him, moving a few feet away. The vampires have Hesperus well enough in hand. Now, Pilkington only has to use his power to send him back. He takes a deep breath, calling the magic to him. It will only take a few seconds.

And then he feels the cold steel of a blade against his neck. He looks down, not surprised to see Sylvia's hand holding the dagger. "Don't you dare," she hisses in his ear. "I have waited too long for this moment."

Pilkington laughs, the sound genuine. "Kill me then," he tells the witch. "I'll be back in a few moments." He hopes she is too distracted to realize the bravado in his words. Based on the scar on his arm, the dagger could unmake him, but now that his arusha has freed him, he isn't so sure. Still, it is enough of a diversion as he begins calling his power again, ready to bring the Greater Demon home, focusing on the palace in the desert where the Marquis Forneus likes him to return wayward demons.

The blade at his neck leaves, and the voice says, "You will. But she won't."

Cold rushes through him, and he turns around to see Not-Sylvia holding the dagger against his arusha's throat. Her eyes are normal again, his Sylvia back enough to realize, but she still isn't in control of her body. "You wouldn't," he says, everything in him focusing on the thin line of blood where the blade has already cut her skin.

"She has no vampire blood to save her this time, demon," the witch possessing Sylvia's mouth says. "You will watch your arusha die."

What happens next isn't something Pilkington planned—and he is a demon who plans a great deal of his existence. Using the powers from his mother, he can control the elements with a brief concentration. His demonic abilities allow him to seal contracts and, when under a geas from Forneus, return lingering demons back to their home realm. Those powers take a brief moment of concentration to engage.

The power from his father is not so particular in its use. Seeing his arusha under a direct threat, the buried part of him roars to life, and he has only one thought—to destroy the thing threatening Sylvia. He retains enough sense to know it is the dagger that threatens her and not her body, so the power that spills out of him is aimed at the blade—and ancient grudges from virgin witches are nothing compared to the destructive power of his divine heritage. The blade glows bright blue for an instant before shattering. There is an awful wail as the witches are destroyed, ages of captured magic freed, and Pilkington notes the blood on Sylvia's neck, patches soaking through her hoodie from the shards that have cut her, but he is cold now, distant.

She will live.

He senses the vampires behind him, the creatures drawn to the scent of her blood, and he turns, the destructive power yearning for another target. He aims a bolt at Hesperus, and the demon's wings disintegrate where the bolt hit them, the creature letting out a terrible scream.

Destroy him, Pilkington thinks clearly. He knows a simple death here will only return the demon to his home, but that is not enough. He will use his power to unmake Hesperus one piece at a time.

The vampires are staring at him, but he can sense their hunger, their desire to feed on his arusha.

No.

He shoots a bolt of power at the redhead, the one who seems most drawn to her blood, and the vampire only manages to dodge because the skinny vampire uses his staff to knock the redhead's legs out from beneath him, knocking his head and chest below the magic.

It doesn't matter, Pilkington thinks. *I will destroy them all eventually.*

CHAPTER 24

SYLVIA

SYLVIA RETURNS TO HER BODY SLOWLY, AWARE OF A painful ringing in her ears and an awful headache that she can feel in her teeth. She has a vague idea of what's been happening, but she feels like a bystander, watching another use her body, speaking with her mouth. When Hesperus's arm broke the circle, she regained some control, able to see events from within herself instead of hovering nearby, but she cannot stop the hand that reaches around to threaten Pilkington with the blade, nor can she stop herself when her hand turns the dagger on her own neck.

She is very aware of the moment that her demon lover surrenders himself to the insane power within him. She sees it in his eyes, the familiar brown disappearing in a blaze of golden fury, and then the dagger shatters, the voices in her head silenced with a final shriek of defiance.

The pain comes next, hot stinging flesh, and she looks down to see patches of blood soaking through her hoodie. She doesn't feel like she's dying though, and Pilkington has turned his back to her, walking over toward Hesperus. She gets clumsily to her feet in time to see a beam of white light streak from the demon's palm and take out a huge chunk of the Greater Demon's wing.

Oh fuck, she realizes. *That's not demonic power... That's...*

She recalls the conversation in the kitchen when she had jokingly suggested that Pilkington's father was an angel.

That's divine magic, angelic power. And apparently, that beam of white light disintegrates things in its path. She watches as Pilkington turns slightly, sending his next attack at Theo's head. Relief floods her as Oren manages to trip Theo just in time, sending the vampire to his knees so the magic flies over his body.

I have to stop him! But how?

She takes a deep breath as Pilkington sends another beam at Hesperus, the Greater Demon running for cover and attempting to escape through the door to the gift shop out front. Pilkington scores another hit, the white light taking out both legs, and Hesperus slides to the dirt floor in a heap of mangled wings and one arm. Sylvia doesn't have time to sympathize with the pathetic creature, though later, she knows she will feel guilty for his fate.

But Sylvia knows that Hesperus is already dead—Pilkington just hasn't delivered the final blow yet. And after that threat is gone, he will turn to the rest of them.

Not me though, she thinks. *He'll kill everyone in this room except me.*

So I can do this.

She runs to the demon just as another blast takes out Hesperus's head, the tangle of gore that was a demon lying still. Tackling Pilkington from behind, she uses her momentum to roll them so she lies atop him, her hands searching for his face as they both tumble in the dirt.

"Stop," she says softly, knowing he can hear her. Her hands cup both of his cheeks and she looks down into his face. His eyes are still that golden blaze, and he doesn't seem to see her. His hands move to lift her off, and without thinking, Sylvia leans down to kiss him, her mouth gentle, calling him back to her. He lies frozen for a moment, and Sylvia stays where she is, eyes closed, not deepening the kiss, just lying atop him with her lips pressed to his.

You, she thinks. *Always you.*

Slowly, his hand reaches up to touch her face, and Sylvia opens her eyes to see the Pilkington she knows and loves underneath her. He kisses her softly, tenderly, then closes his eyes, breathing deeply. Sylvia moves slowly, sitting up carefully, not wanting to disturb him as he recalls himself.

She takes several deep breaths of her own, trying to calm her racing heartbeat. When she opens her eyes, she sees the three vampires and Ula are standing in a line a few feet away from them.

Theo's body is tense, but he only looks confused, not angry.

"Someone want to tell us what the fuck that was all about?" Oren asks conversationally.

Pilkington rubs his face, then sits up, drawing up a knee as he studies the creatures surrounding them. "That," he says, "was divine retribution."

Ula puts it together first. "You're part-angel," she whispers. "But—"

"Wait—what?!" Oren yells. "How could you not tell us that?" He gestures at the remains of the Greater Demon. "I mean, we could have taken this guy out months ago!"

"It's not something I do often," Pilkington says, clearly uncomfortable. He looks at Theo, guilt clear in his expression. "Forgive me," he says. "I was … not myself."

Theo nods. "Nothing to forgive," he insists. "Believe me, I get it."

"But I thought angelic power would be like, I don't know, rainbows and light and stuff," Oren muses. "I never thought it was like a science fiction death ray."

"It's destruction," Pilkington explains. "Angels were often used as tools of destruction in the old days. I don't use it because—as you saw—it tends to take over."

"Dude, I gotta know: do you have feathery wings?" Oren asks, eyes wide. "A halo? Tell me you have a harp. I can't believe you're an angel."

Sylvia snorts, unable to stop herself. "No, no, and no," she tells the vampire, taking Pilkington's hand where they sit in the dirt. "He's not an angel. He's my demon."

CHAPTER 25

OREN

OREN SITS ATOP THE REMAINING TABLE, LEGS CROSSED IN his favorite position as he takes in the aftermath. The gory remains of the demon Hesperus are gone, taken by Ula and Harald to be disposed somewhere Oren doesn't want to know. The witch seemed to know what to do, and after a brief conversation with Pilkington, she and Harald bundled the chunks into a tarp and headed out the back door. There is still an hour or so before sunrise, so he doesn't have to leave quite yet.

Since Jolena's death freed him, Oren has been thinking about the sun a great deal, wondering if maybe he should watch the movies Theo and Harald use to remember. He has no desire to meet the sun and end his existence, but it would be nice to think of the sun without the painful memory of a world without Morena in it. He fingers the chain around his neck, the silver burning him as it always does, but he wonders if someday soon he will take it off. Seeing Harald with Ula, and even Theo and Sylvia, he's started to wonder if maybe there is someone out in the world for him again. He doesn't like the idea of surrendering control ever—even to the idea of fate—not since he has only just gained his freedom from his Maker.

But maybe, he thinks, *it's a possibility. Someday.*

He can wait. Watching the awkward trio remaining in the arena, Oren decides he can definitely wait.

Pilkington stands off to one side, doing something to the dirt where Hesperus fell. Oren can sense magic, and before he would have said it was demonic power, but now he's not sure. Pilkington's power had always seemed different to him, the demon slightly distinct from the other demonic magic he has felt—and now he knows why. He had thought it was because Pilkington was a strong demon, but actually, he had been sensing angelic magic.

I really need to pay more attention to my abilities, he thinks. *We all should.* He watches the demon's back for a moment, debating. *I could ask him what he's doing,* he thinks. *He would tell me.*

A glance to his right reveals Sylvia and Theo standing awkwardly apart as they talk quietly. He can see that Pilkington is trying to focus on whatever he is doing, trying to give them privacy, but he can hear their conversation plainly with his vampire ears, so he's sure the demon can hear it too.

"How do you feel?" Theo is asking Sylvia. She has changed out of her bloody hoodie, trading it for a clean one from the gift shop, the words Viking Times emblazoned on the back and a horned helmet printed on the hood, which rests against her back. Oren wonders if she's naked underneath the zipper, then catches himself. He doesn't often fantasize about the women he knows, but now that he's contemplating the possibility of a companion again, the door seems to have flung wide open. Sylvia is not for him. He likes her well enough, definitely respects her strength, but she's not his type—and a good thing since she's doubly spoken for.

Oren has a good idea which creature she will be leaving with in the morning though.

Sylvia shrugs, pulling her hair up into a ponytail. She reaches into her pocket, searching for a tie, but finding none, frowns and tucks her hair into a loose bun that immediately falls apart, her hair sliding down into her hood. "I'm not sure," she replies. "I've never been possessed before." She cocks her head, looking at the vampire. "Have you?" she asks. "Did it have lingering effects?"

Theo sighs, shaking his head. "I've been controlled by magic," he admits, "but that's not the same thing. I never lost myself—just my ability to control my body." He pauses, then shakes his head again. "No—that's not true. Not exactly. I have lost myself."

Sylvia nods, ever the understanding one. "With Jolena," she says. "What..." Her voice trails off, and Oren wonders if she will ask the question he knows must be burning her inside. "Do you want to talk about it?"

Theo shakes his head once, hard. "No." His voice softens, and he continues, "Not now. Maybe not ever." He pauses, body language awkward as he shifts from foot to foot, hands moving from his sides to his pockets and back to his chest, not sure if they want to cross or not. Oren has seen this dance before, but not since they were young and Theo had to apologize to his mother for doing something foolish. "I ... am sorry," he says finally, head down.

"You don't have to be sorry," Sylvia tells him. "There's nothing—"

"I am sorry because I was awful," he interrupts, "to you. You freed us—freed me—and I was ... not kind."

Sylvia shrugs. "You don't owe me anything, Theo," she says quietly. "You have a right to react however you feel. I don't blame you for being angry. She was your Maker."

Theo nods. "She was. And I don't know how to thank you for setting us free. I don't think you realize what it means."

Sylvia's gaze shifts to Pilkington, then back to Theo. The vampire's body tenses, and Oren knows he saw the look. "I think I do," she says. "Or at least, I understand more than I did before."

There is another awkward pause, and this time, it is Sylvia who shifts on her feet, clearly searching for words.

"So," Theo says casually, shoving the conversation to the question he needs answered, "Phil, huh?"

Sylvia's head jerks up, and she bites her lip, the look adorably guilty. Oren knows that Theo will ache for his human lover long after she is gone—but not forever. "I didn't..."

"Neither of us did," Theo says, his tone soothing. "Do..." The vampire stands up straighter. "Do you love him?"

"Yes," she replies. "I'm sorry," she adds, as if ashamed of answering so quickly. "It's just... it was always him, you know?"

Theo nods. "I know." He chuckles, a genuine smile crossing his lips. "And we had a good run, didn't we?"

Sylvia grins. "We did." After a moment, she adds, "Thank you, Theo. I don't know if I would have been able to do this ... with him ... if it hadn't been for you."

"Glad to help," Theo tells her, and Oren can hear the old Theo in his voice. "He better be good to you."

"He will," she says. "So, do we like hug now or what?"

"Come here," Theo says, gathering his human into his arms for an embrace. He whispers into her neck, but Oren can just make out the words. "Thank you, too," Theo says, "for showing me it's okay to... to let someone in."

"I thought I invited you in," Sylvia quips, and they both laugh, easier now that the moment is over.

Theo releases her. "You did. And I'll never forget it. Or you."

Sylvia narrows her eyes at him. "Sure you won't," she says. "I fully expect a farewell visit when I'm on my deathbed, Theodore Muldavian."

"You have my word," the vampire promises.

The two make their way over to the table where Oren sits, staff across his knees, and Pilkington joins them.

"So," Oren begins, "is this where we part ways?"

Sylvia glances at Pilkington, who gives her a nervous look, his eyes skipping back and forth between her and Theo. "Is it?" he asks.

"Well, I assume you have to return to your realm now," Oren says. "Doesn't your visa or whatever expire now that you've completed your task?"

The demon frowns. "I haven't completed my task. I was to return Hesperus to our realm. Instead, I..."

"What will you say?" Theo asks. "What can you say?"

Pilkington sighs, the demon seemingly out of ideas for once. He seems very tired—but Oren suspects his distance has more to do with Sylvia hugging Theo than his demon situation. Maybe Pilkington couldn't hear what they said after all.

"Blame it on me," Sylvia says. "Tell him I did it." When Pilkington opens his mouth to protest, she continues, "Tell him the dagger took control of me, and I destroyed him and the dagger in the process."

The demon looks at her, then his eyes skate over to Theo again, assessing. "That's a possibility," he says quietly. "If you're going to stay here, of course, I can—"

Sylvia reaches out a hand to touch his arm. "Wait, what?"

Pilkington looks at the hand on his arm and then at her. "I can tell him you are dead. The Muldavian can take you out of the city and then—"

"Hey, hey, hold up!" Sylvia snaps. "I'm not leaving the city—and definitely not with Theo. We can figure out something else."

"We?" Pilkington echoes, and Oren hides a smile at the raw vulnerability on the demon's face. *Will I look that foolish one day? That happy?* "You mean ... to stay with me?"

"Of course I'm staying with you, you idiot," Sylvia tells him. "I told you—you aren't getting rid of me that easily." She frowns. "Unless you really mean to leave me here and return to your normal life?"

The demon grabs her shoulder and tugs her to him, framing her face with his other hand. "You are my life," he whispers, then kisses her softly. A moment later, they part, both embarrassed in front of the vampires.

"Yeah," Oren says, hopping off the table. "That's our cue." He reaches out for Theo, putting an arm around the taller man's shoulder. "Come on, Muldavian."

The two take several steps away from Sylvia and her demon, then turn as one to face them, both dropping into the formal bow they used as human men. "We are in your debt, my lady," Oren tells her. "I mean that, and I know what it means to owe the lady of a demon." He smiles at them both. "Give me a call when you're in town. Maybe we can hang out when we're not dealing with a crisis. Grab pizza or watch a movie sometime."

He glances at Theo, watching his friend's reaction to his offer. Theo doesn't seem to mind the idea. "You know," he adds, nodding his head, "I've been thinking about maybe taking some classes at the Lyceum. Maybe learn more about some things. Maybe I'll see you around."

Sylvia laughs. "I do make a great pot of tea," she says. "Great for research parties."

"Good luck, you two!" he says, then turns Theo and heads for the exit. "Don't worry, man," he says to his friend. "We can fix this place up tomorrow, and Grace will never need to know about our demon extracurricular activities."

CHAPTER 26

PILKINGTON

THE DEMON KNOWN AS PILKINGTON STARES AT HIS ARUSHA, not sure what to say. He doesn't want to break the spell that somehow has her choosing to stay with him, to face the mess he left back home together.

"So," she says, "what's the plan then?"

The demon frowns. "I honestly don't know," he tells her, then winks. "But give me a few minutes, and I'll come up with something."

"Well," she says, "I always find that I have better ideas when coffee is involved." She yawns, the stress of the night catching up with her. "Let's go sit somewhere and make a plan."

The demon takes her hand, marveling at the feeling of her skin against his, then raises it to his lips for a brief kiss. He decides to take a chance. "How about my apartment?" he asks.

"I thought you'd never ask," she replies, following him down the street to his place in the human realm.

They don't talk much on the way back, each lost in their thoughts as the sky starts to lighten. By the time they reach the door into the building, Pilkington has the rough outline of a plan that might work, freeing his thoughts to focus on Sylvia again.

As they take the elevator up to his floor, Pilkington wonders if Sylvia likes his apartment or if she would prefer something more lavish like the Muldavian's penthouse. Watching her face as they enter the small living room, he decides that his arusha does not want fancy apartments. Sylvia likes simple things. Her gaze takes in the room again, and he catches a wave of desire from her as she sees first the wall and then the couch. He grins, moving to the small kitchen to start making coffee. They don't have a lot of time before they need to return with a plan, but it has been a long night.

Sylvia explores the small space, looking at the two paintings on his wall—one of the mountains behind his home, the other of a very familiar beach. Pilkington returns with two mugs, hands one to Sylvia, then moves to open the curtain, revealing a lovely view of the mountains beyond this city.

"Wow," Sylvia gasps, standing up to approach the window. "I didn't know you could see them from here."

"We're near the edge of the city, beyond the taller high rises," he says. "It's why I picked this place."

"Do they remind you of home?" she asks, gesturing at the distant line of mountains. When Pilkington nods, she asks, "Do you miss it?"

"Sometimes," he admits. "I do love my house."

"How often are you away?" she asks, taking a sip. Pilkington senses the nature of the question. If she plans to stay with him, she needs a better idea of how he lives his life.

"It depends," he tells her. "Sometimes only a few days. Sometimes a few months."

"Oh," she says, and he can tell that she doesn't like his answer.

"But," he insists, grabbing her free hand, "if you want to stay with me, I don't have to go. Forneus can find a new investigator."

"You'd quit your job?" she asks, her eyes wide. "That's not what I'm asking!"

"I want to be with you," he says simply. "I don't need to work."

Sylvia stares at him. "So why did you? Before this? Why not just be a demon of leisure and hang out painting and reading or swimming all day?"

Pilkington shrugs, sipping his own coffee and watching the sunrise over the mountains. "I did," he tells her, recalling the ages spent working on his house, painting, swimming in the lake, and reading the old tales. "For a time, I did just that. But then I got bored, and traveling the realms seemed interesting. And then..." He looks at her. "And then I met you, and I had a reason to travel even more."

Sylvia smiles at him, then sips her coffee again. "Do you like it?" she asks. "Finding lost demons?"

Pilkington nods. "I do. I'm good at it, and it lets me see new places and meet new people. And I can pick up the odd favor here and there." There is a pleasant silence as they both drink their coffee and watch the sun rise. The golden light hits Sylvia's face, her hair shining like honey as she looks at him.

"What are we going to do?" she asks, her voice serious now. "Have any theories on how to explain all this?"

Pilkington nods, taking another long sip of his coffee before setting it down on the table behind them. "I do," he says. "The truth." At her wide eyes, he adds, "Well, most of it anyway."

"How much is that?"

"I will tell him what happened: we found Hesperus, we trapped him in a circle, but he had a magical artifact in his possession, a dagger—and it possessed you—but then something went wrong and it exploded, destroying him in the process." He holds up his arm, sliding up his sleeve so that she can see the scar, the line stark white against his skin, evidence of his encounter with the blade. "I was even hurt in the process."

"You think he'll buy it?" she asks.

Pilkington tips his head from side to side, considering. "For all the rush for me to return Hesperus, I don't think Forneus actually wants him back, so his true death is a boon. It also reinforces the rules against lingering in the realms without permission. Hesperus paid for his transgression with his existence. And the fact that I was wounded reminds the others that I am not infallible, and they will ease their scrutiny, seeing my perceived weakness and forgetting anything they may have overheard." He lays out the benefits of his solution, nodding his head. "It's likely, especially if we return soon."

"How soon?" Sylvia asks, finishing her coffee and setting the mug down next to his.

He feels the low stir of her desire, and he bites his very human lip. "That depends," he tells her. "Why?"

"Well, you seem to have this all figured out," she says, stepping closer and lifting a hand to her zipped hoodie. "And I'm not wearing a shirt anymore, so I should probably change into something more presentable before we face your boss." She frowns. "Maybe I should have kept my bloody clothes as props, though."

The demon reaches out to touch her, slowly drawing the zipper down to reveal her bare skin. His fingers move around the small cuts she has on her neck and chest, evidence of the dagger's explosion. "I'm sorry I can't heal these," he whispers.

"I'm fine," she tells him, cupping her hand over his and reaching her other hand around his neck.

"I should have protected you," he says, guilt in his voice.

"I'm fine," she repeats. "It's over. Now we just have to face the other demons."

"Not yet," he tells her, leaning in for a kiss. "We have a little time."

"Good," Sylvia whispers into his mouth, and he can feel the desire pooling around her, surrounding them both, and he surrenders to it.

They are in the shower when Sylvia brings up the Tethering ceremony. "What are we going to tell him about that?"

Pilkington groans, leaning back into her touch as she rubs shampoo into his hair. "I forgot about that."

Sylvia grabs his head and tugs it back, meeting his eyes with a raised eyebrow. "No, you didn't," she tells him.

Pilkington leans his head forward, letting the water rinse the shampoo from his hair, then turns to face her. "No, I didn't."

"Well?" she asks. "What will you tell him?"

Pilkington sighs. "I cannot lie about that."

"Why not? I thought you could lie to him now."

"I can," he says, motioning for her to turn around so he can wash her back, careful of the small cuts on her shoulders. "But the Tethering is ... more. Demons can sense it."

"I figured that. You said it gives the partner access to your powers. It's pretty obvious I don't have that—not the way you described it." She frowns. "Will he be so grateful about Hesperus that he won't bring it up?" she asks, looking over her shoulder at him.

Pilkington huffs. "Maybe, but it would only be temporary. Likely, he will hold it over my head, using you as a bargaining chip any time he needs something."

"Well, that doesn't work," Sylvia says, backing up so the water rinses her, offering him a small smile as their bodies touch before he steps out of the way. "You know, the shower in your house is much bigger. I bet we wouldn't have to dance around like this."

"I would love to test your theory," he says, leaning down to kiss her. His hands find her skin, and they are in danger of distraction again, but Sylvia rallies.

"This isn't going away, Philk," she says against his mouth. "What are you going to do?"

Pilkington pulls away, cocking his head. "Did you just call me Philk?"

Sylvia snorts, a hand going to her mouth. "Oh crap. Yeah, I did. It's kind of what I started thinking of you as now … Phil and Pilkington. Philk." She frowns. "I'm sorry."

"I love it," he tells her. "Don't be sorry. I've never had a special name before. Do I need a nickname for you now too?"

Sylvia curls her lip. "Meh. I'm not loving my nicknames so far."

"What are they?"

"Adam called me Sylvie, so please no. And Theo..." she pauses, "Theo called me Syl."

"Sylvia then," Pilkington says, turning to face the water for a final rinse. "Unless you prefer your middle name?"

Sylvia shakes her head. "Nah. It's just Jane. Sylvia Jane Copland."

Pilkington stares at her for a moment before recalling that for her, names aren't important beyond the sounds they make. She probably tells strangers her name all the time. Human names hold no more power over them than any other word—not like demons and fae.

It's such a silly thing, he muses, *to have such power and yet be rendered powerless by a series of syllables.* He knows some witch powers work with words, so he understands that magic works that way, but sometimes it seems so arbitrary. *Like so many other things in the world,* he decides. *How am I to believe in the power of fate in such a random existence?*

But I am not longer subject to my name, he remembers, looking at Sylvia. *Or am I?* She seems to follow his thoughts.

"Do I know your real name?" Sylvia asks suddenly, and Pilkington freezes, hands in his hair. He slowly turns to face her. "I feel like I do." At his expression, she reaches out to touch him. "I would never tell anyone," she promises him. "Or use it." She shudders at the last words. His arusha has had enough control over creatures to know better. "Does it even matter anymore? If you can't be compelled, can you be summoned with your name?"

"I don't think so," Pilkington says, "but I won't know for sure unless someone tries."

"I get the sense that doesn't happen very often."

"No," he assures her, moving so that she can rinse one more time. When she nods that she is done, he turns off the water, and they step out into his small bathroom, fumbling with towels and giggling on the small bathmat as they try not to get water everywhere.

"Clothes?" Sylvia asks, looking down at the towel she wears.

"What would you like?" Pilkington asks, opening a drawer in the dresser and pulling out a pair of black shorts. When he looks up, Sylvia is watching him curiously. "What?"

"You have clothes here?"

Pilkington looks around the small bedroom. "Why wouldn't I have clothes here? I live here when I'm in town."

"But I thought you always just magicked your clothes, like you did for me."

"I did that because I don't have anything here for you. I didn't know you would come here."

Sylvia laughs. "Oh. Yeah. I see that now." She pauses, then adds, "So the closet back at your house?"

Pilkington turns his back and drops the towel, stepping into the shorts. He can feel her eyes on him. "That was just in case," he says quietly, turning to hang the towel on the hook by the bathroom door.

"Just in case?" Sylvia echoes. "In case I happened to stumble naked into the demon realm someday?"

Pilkington shrugs. "Your life tends to take odd twists, arusha." He smiles at the name, loving the feel of it on his tongue. "I just hoped to be there if you needed anything."

"You've always been there," she tells him, "even if I didn't know it, haven't you?" When he nods, she shakes her head. "I should be totally creeped out by that, but instead, it just makes me feel better. Safer." She pauses, as if debating her next words, but then they spill out, as he knew they would. Sylvia rarely keeps her thoughts to herself, especially around him. "With Theo, I felt safe from the world—but not from him. I didn't think he would hurt me, but he never let me forget how easily he could. It was always this careful dance to watch himself. Or watch myself so I didn't make him do something he'd feel guilty about. I didn't worry about him hurting me, but I did worry about the aftermath, about watching him wallow in guilt." She frowns. "And the funny thing is that you're just as strong as he is—stronger, probably, with that whole destruction thing—but I never wonder if I'm going to do something to set you off or anything. You seem more in control of yourself." She pauses, staring at him. "Am I wrong? Should I worry about you like that?"

"I would never—" he begins.

"I know that," she interrupts. "I know you wouldn't want to hurt me." She looks down at the floor, then back up at him again. "But I also saw you in the arena." Now, it is Pilkington's turn to look away as he recalls the emptiness that filled him, the rage and need to destroy everything and begin anew with a clean slate. "You wouldn't have touched me," she continues, "but you would have killed everyone else—and that would have hurt me anyway."

"I understand," he says quietly. He doesn't feel guilt for his behavior, not even for the possibility of hurting Sylvia by harming her friends. When the witch threatened his arusha, he had to react. He is sorry that Sylvia was cut by the shattering dagger, especially now seeing the scratches scattered on her collarbone and shoulders—but he wouldn't change what happened even if he could.

"I don't know if you do," she says, walking over to sit on the edge of the bed, face deep in thought. "You've always been strong." She looks at him. "Have you ever been truly afraid?"

Pilkington pauses, giving the question the consideration it deserves. "Not in the same way," he says finally, crossing the room to sit beside her. He knows she is thinking of that night in the cemetery when she nearly died. "Tell me," he pushes, sensing she needs encouragement as she untangles her thoughts. It has been a very chaotic few days: her former life is gone, her home destroyed, her sense of stability remade in the vampires. Her connection with him may be old, but her relationship with him is new, and they are still figuring out the dynamic.

"I was afraid that night," she says. "I didn't want to die, but even more, I was afraid of not living. Does that make sense? I didn't know what I wanted to do, not really—but that I wanted to do something. Or the chance to do something." She looks at him, eyes sad. "Have you ever felt that way?"

"Not here," he tells her. "Or in any other realm but my home." He pauses, the memory of that morning flooding through him. "But when I was young, I lived in my mother's palace, Karakul." At Sylvia's raised eyebrow, he translates, "Black Lake." He can see it in his memory, the dark water so still despite the creatures that live below the surface. "I had seen others jump into the lake many times. They changed their forms to remove their wings so they could swim easily." He looks away, the ghost of water-soaked wings heavy on his back. "So, I waited until I was alone, and I jumped in. I didn't know how heavy my wings would be, and I sank immediately." He sniffs, remembering the inky water around him, the space going on for what seemed like forever. "In my world, I can die—even from something simple like drowning."

"How did you get out?"

"A water nymph saw my struggle. She thought I was playing, so she tugged me around a little bit, bringing me to the surface for little gasps. I still wonder if she knew just how lost I was. Eventually, she grew bored and abandoned me on the shore. I lay there for a time and cried ... so afraid that I would never grow old enough to swim properly."

"But you swim fine now," Sylvia says. "You use your wings to help you. Don't other demons do that?"

Pilkington shakes his head. "Hells no. They simply change their shape into one more suited for the water."

Sylvia nods slowly. "But you can't change your form there. So, you had to learn to swim another way."

The demon laughs. "Yes," he agrees.

"But why bother at all?" she asks. "If you almost drowned as a kid, I'd think you would just avoid water altogether."

He shrugs. "I did, for a time, but then I found a reason to learn." Sylvia narrows her eyes at him, seeming to follow where he is going. "What?" he says. "You practically dragged me in the first time at the beach."

"You could have said no," she tells him. "You could have said, 'Hey Sylvia, I nearly drowned as a child and would rather not relive that painful memory.' I would have understood."

"I know you would have," he says, leaning in to tuck her hair behind her ear, "but I was trying to impress you, and being afraid of a little water isn't very impressive, is it?"

"Well, you still managed to make an impression," she snaps.

"Yes, clearly it was all because of my swimming prowess."

Sylvia snorts. "You were a terrible swimmer, Philk. I was always a little worried you'd drift away from me and start flailing."

"I had to learn how," he explains. "In that body and then again in my own."

"But you did it," she says, reaching out to touch his arm, "for me."

He shrugs. "But it's not the same thing here," he reminds her. "Even if my body drowned, I would survive and return in another body."

She strokes his arm. "So, is this body real then? Or magic?"

"It's real," he assures her. "I cannot change my form in my own realm, but whatever form I adopt in any other is always truth."

"So right now, you're just a regular mid-30s human man?"

"A regular mid-30s human man with access to powerful magic, yes," he corrects.

"Will you age?"

Pilkington chuckles. "If I stay in this body, I can age in it, yes. Worried about being the older woman eventually?" He says it as a joke, but he can see he hits home, then curses himself. Of course, she would have thought about their ages. She just finished dating a vampire.

"How old are you, exactly?"

Pilkington frowns. It's not a simple question. Demons don't measure their age the way humans do. "I was born before your vampires, but that's not a good reference because demon time passes differently. I've seen some realms created, and others destroyed, so by those standards, I'm ancient. Yet, my people still consider me a young demon, still a little rebellious, a bit green, not yet come into my full power."

"Give me some context then. In human terms, how old are you, roughly?" she tries.

"Late-20s," he replies. "Old enough to know how the world works, young enough to still have some hope of changing it, experienced enough to know who I am and what I want."

"How old was Hesperus?" she asks. "Same scale."

Pilkington considers what he knows about the Greater Demon. "Mid-30s," he replies. "Old enough to know that he shouldn't hide from Forneus." Seeing her next question, he adds, "Forneus is much older. Think early-70s. He is massively powerful." He pauses, then adds, "And he will do anything to hold on to his power in our realm."

"Will he hurt you?" she asks, her voice quiet.

Pilkington looks up. "Only through you," he admits. "Being my arusha gives you certain rights, but he's powerful enough to take you from me, if he wants."

"But you can destroy him," Sylvia says.

"I can. And I would." He sighs. "And then everyone would know about my power, and I would never be able to sleep through the night easily again. They would come for me, and eventually, they would kill me. I could rule them," he suggests, "but I don't want to. And they will never believe that."

"What do you want?" she asks, leaning her head on his shoulder. He wraps an arm around her back.

"I want to take a shower with you in my house," he says honestly, "without worrying about who is watching my windows and planning their attack."

Sylvia sighs. "I'm sorry. I didn't mean to mess up your life."

Pilkington sits up a little, lifting her head so he can look in her eyes. "Don't say that," he tells her. "You are not a burden to me, Sylvia. I am so thankful to have you with me."

"But before I made you bring me there, your life at home was fine. Now..."

"Nothing has occurred that would not have happened eventually." He sighs, not wanting to say what he has to say next, but he has to offer. "Sylvia, I can leave you here. You will be safe. You can rebuild your life. You do not need to return with me."

"You want to leave me here?" Her question isn't needy, only interested in his motivation.

I should, he thinks, *but I don't want to.*

Pilkington shakes his head. "No, but I will if you wish it." He pauses, then says, "If you choose, though, I would have you face it with me—as my arusha."

"I choose you," Sylvia says simply. "Whatever that means. Whatever happens next. I'm with you."

Pilkington says nothing, the love swelling his heart making words impossible.

CHAPTER 27

SYLVIA

THEY RETURN TO THE DEMON REALM WITH A QUIET PULSE of magic, Sylvia opening her eyes to see the familiar walls of Pilkington's front room. She can feel the magic dissipating around them, recognizing it as demonic power, a scent she now associates with cinnamon and the zing of red-hot candies on her tongue.

She glances down at her body, glad to see that her clothes have come with her, the simple shorts, tank top, and sweater she left Pilkington's apartment wearing still intact. Her demon stands in front of her, his blue skin contrasting with the dark pants he wears, his large wings appearing and then tucking against his back as he looks down at her.

"I'm fine," she answers the unspoken question. "Just getting used to traveling like that."

Before he can reply, Billy rushes into the room and Tengo appears at Sylvia's side, the large dog putting his head under her hand. Pilkington gives the demon dog a look, then says, "Yeah. We're going to have to talk about that at some point." Sylvia doesn't think he's talking to her, and she gives the dog a few friendly scratches. Pilkington looks at Billy. "What has happened since we left?"

Billy shakes his head. "They didn't find anything," the soul-servant tells them. "He searched your office and your bedroom but didn't stumble into any of the hidden spaces. I think they were afraid to poke too hard, thinking they'd set off a trap or something."

"Good," Pilkington replies, nodding. "When did they leave?"

"Last night." Billy cocks his head to the side, ghostly hair swaying to the side. "I am to inform you that you are to contact Lord Forneus as soon as you return." He gestures in the direction of Pilkington's office upstairs. "You have a message on your desk. I didn't touch it."

"Well done," Pilkington tells him. "I need a few minutes before we inform him of our return."

Billy clears his throat. "Might I suggest my lord prepare himself for such a meeting this time?" He nods at Pilkington's bare chest and simple pants. "The Marquis of the Realm expects more ... decorum from those who beg him for mercy."

Pilkington scoffs. "I have no intention of begging for mercy."

"Did... did you return Hesperus as he commanded?" the ghost asks.

"No."

Billy nods, putting his hands behind his back and slowly floating out of the room. "It has been a pleasure, my lord, to serve you these last years—"

"You're not finished serving me, Billiacus," Pilkington snaps. "And I will deal with Forneus as I am."

"Wait," Sylvia adds, looking from the demon to her own clothing. "Maybe he's right. What do demons wear when they dress to impress?"

Pilkington gestures at his pants and Billy laughs, a full belly laugh. The soul-servant looks at Sylvia. "At least Lady Pilkington has some sense." He draws himself up. "I can lay out some dresses for my lady, if she wishes."

Sylvia nods. "Yes, please. That would be lovely, Billy." As the soul-servant leaves, she turns to Pilkington. The sight of the demon in his skin is enough to take her breath away, the alien nature of his beauty still making her heart pound. But now she gives him a critical look. "What do demons wear to dress up?"

Pilkington sighs, running a hand through his hair. "I don't know. I never follow fashion." When she raises an eyebrow and gives him a look, he wilts a little, then sags, head tilting back. "Some wear nicer pants or fancy shoes. But it's really about the designs."

"Designs?"

Pilkington gestures at the black markings on his skin. "Some demons will add designs to accentuate their patterns," he admits.

"Show me a picture," she demands. At his expression, her tone becomes sterner. "I know you have one somewhere."

"I am not—"

"You want to impress Forneus, right?" she interrupts. "You want him to be impressed by the 'accidental' removal of a thorn in his side?"

"I do."

"And this Marquis is an old-man demon who likes the finer things in life, right?"

"He is."

"So, you showing up all decked out would be unexpected—"

"And ridiculous," he manages.

"And oddly impressive, like you're finally taking that stuff seriously for once?" She frowns, biting her lip. "Now, we can't go too wild because we don't want him to think you're angling for a promotion or anything, but you need to remind him of who you are. You may work for him occasionally, but he is benefitting from your skills, not the other way around. You could be someone of power here if you wanted to, but you don't choose to, so he doesn't see you as a threat. But maybe you need to remind him that you aren't a threat to his position, but you are still your parents' son, and he needs to respect you."

Pilkington sniffs, thinking through the logic of her words.

"Philk, he went through your house. He had spies watching you. You need to push back—and now—before he goes even further." She pauses, then adds, "Besides, it will totally fuck with him if you show up all fancy, especially if you normally don't. He'll wonder what your game is."

The demon nods, shoulders slumping as he accepts her argument. "Let me find a picture for you."

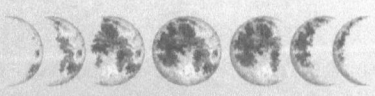

Two hours later, Sylvia and Pilkington stand before the large mirror in his bathroom. She wears a red dress that hugs her curves but covers all of her skin, her hair piled atop her head, just enough makeup to highlight her elegant features. She has Pilkington's compass tucked under the dress, the necklace invisible beneath the high neckline. Her feet are tucked into fashionable boots. She looks pretty good, but standing next to her is a vision of devilish temptation.

Pilkington wears black leather pants tucked into simple back boots and gloves cover his forearms—red to match her dress. His hair is wild around his face, the horns peeking through more obvious because Sylvia has highlighted the tips in silver and blue. The dark lines that cross his body are complemented by swirls of silver, the lines highlighting his muscles, reminding viewers of the strength of his body. She has done the same on the outside of his wings, but much more subtly, not adding to his natural blue lines across the black webbing but using shading to emphasize them. The result is a demon who looks sexy, badass, and powerful as hell.

Pilkington nods at his reflection, then watches her face as the hand on her back slides slowly down the line of her spine.

"Hey now," she teases, "we have somewhere to be."

"And all I want to do is get you out of that dress," he growls. "It's so prim and yet so provocative all at once."

Sylvia snorts, reminded again that for all that she is dating a demon, he still just a guy. "That's the point," she tells him. "I'm so covered, it leaves more to the imagination, makes people wonder what I've got under here." She cocks a hip, highlighting her curves.

"But there's enough to suggest that the underneath is definitely worth checking out." She frowns. "It won't work on Forneus at all. He's too old and knows better. Will anyone else be there, though?"

Pilkington frowns, then shrugs. "I do not know. He will not be alone because he rarely is, but he knows I am coming and will want an audience for my supposed disobedience. I'm not sure who he would choose to witness my punishment."

"Does he hang around with younger people? Men like you?"

The demon narrows his eyes at her. "I'm not thrilled with the notion of you setting yourself up to be ogled by others, arusha."

"Hey, it's fine to look," she reminds him. "Just no touching."

"Stay by me."

"I will," she promises, "and if I can't, Tengo is with me."

Pilkington nods. He had seemed reluctant to bring the dog with them at first, but she had argued that he may be distracted and could focus more if he knew she was protected. An expression flickers across his face that she doesn't understand. "Eventually," she tells him, taking his hand as they leave the bathroom, "you're going to have to tell me the deal with your dog."

"He's not my dog," Pilkington says. "He's Tengo. And that's a long story."

"Next time," she agrees. "So, how do we travel there? Are there demon rideshare apps or what?"

"We could travel there physically if you want, but it is easier to teleport."

"I'm sorry—did you just say teleport? Like poof?"

The demon gives her an odd look. "What do you call the way we traveled to this realm?"

Sylvia shrugs. "I don't know. Portaling, I guess. That's through dimensions. I didn't know you could just pop off places in your realm."

Pilkington laughs, kissing her hand as he leads her into his bedroom, pausing at the dresser to open a top drawer. He pulls out a silver swirl of metal about six inches long.

"Uhh?" Sylvia asks, looking at it and trying to figure out what it is.

"May I?" he asks, reaching out for her arm. She watches as he slides her hand into the metal sleeve, then pushes it up her arm so that it rests along her forearm, the metal overlaying the sleeve of her dress.

She holds her arm up, studying the odd bracer. "Is it jewelry?"

"It's the mark of an arusha," he tells her.

"Cool," she says, remembering how Ula had touched her wrist, searching for something. The witch had seen this too. "Much more obvious than a ring or anything. Does the color mean anything?"

"Silver signifies long-term agreement," he explains.

"And gold?"

"Gold means temporary arrangement."

She grimaces. "That's lovely. Why not just stamp 'by the hour' on someone? Are there other colors?"

He nods. "Black."

"That sounds ominous."

"Depending on your perspective. It means permanent arrangement."

"What, like Tethered?"

The demon nods but says nothing else as Sylvia looks at her forearm, now covered in swirls like Pilkington's body.

"Are you ready?" he asks.

Sylvia takes a deep breath. "Let's do this."

They arrive in the parlor of Forneus's palace surrounded by other demons in finery. Sylvia gasps, tucking herself close to Pilkington as a red-skinned demon with huge horns and elaborate black markings brushes by them. He turns to see who has arrived, stares at her with interest, then immediately hurries away after seeing her companion.

"Damn," Pilkington curses quietly.

"What?" Sylvia mumbles, glad for Pilkington's arm around her shoulder as he studies the room. Her hand hovers, waiting for Tengo's reassuring head against her palm. When nothing touches her, she looks down. Tengo is not with them.

"He's having one of his parties," Pilkington says. He gives her a squeeze. "Good call on the clothes." Seeing her searching hand opening and closing, he adds, "Unfortunately, that means no dogs allowed."

"Not even Tengo?"

"Especially Tengo."

Sylvia swallows, trying to calm her pounding heart as she looks around to spy other demons. A tall skinny demon with green skin and medium sized horns wearing bright green pants, his yellow wings bigger than Pilkington's, gives them a cordial nod, then continues through the doors into what must be the main room. A curvy woman with red skin, tiny horns, and huge black wings flutters her eyelashes at Pilkington, her tail sliding suggestively up her leg to the slit at her hip, then her eyes find the silver bracer on Sylvia's arm, and she nods respectfully, her manner shifting.

"Lord Pilkington," she greets, her voice low and sweet and sexy in a way that makes Sylvia want her to speak again.

"Lady Kamika," he replies, nodding at her. "How lovely to see you, as always."

"I didn't expect to see you at one of these," the demon comments, a perfect eyebrow arching, and she turns her attention to Sylvia, "and with a companion."

Pilkington moves a little away from Sylvia, still holding her hand, and bows sideways oddly, the move somehow showcasing her at his side. "Lady Pilkington," he introduces. Sylvia doesn't say anything, not sure what to say. They already agreed that this was her name if anyone asked.

Kamika's eyes slide to the bracer again, then back to Sylvia's face. "My lady," she greets, bowing gracefully, her long arms held out to her sides and her tail hovering just over her right shoulder. "Am I to expect an invitation then?"

Pilkington pauses, and Sylvia leaps into the conversation. She assumes the demon is asking about the Tethering ceremony, and she wants to avoid putting Pilkington in an awkward position with his people. "We're still working out the details," she says, then smiles at Kamika. "Your dress is absolutely stunning," she flatters, then adds, "and that necklace is beautiful."

She pauses, then asks, "Can I ask if it has any significance? I'm still learning the rules here."

Kamika gives her a conspiratorial smile, then lifts the green gemstone from her neck so Sylvia can see it more closely, the motion putting her large breasts directly in Sylvia's face. "Of course, my lady," she coos. "It's an Emerald Star, a gift from a dragon lover. For them, it's a mark of protection—as if I needed it from a simple dragon—and a sign that I am connected to a specific tribe."

"And here?" Sylvia prompts, giving Pilkington more time to collect himself and craft a different plan. They had not expected to meet Forneus with so many other eyes present. "Does it mean something else?"

The demon winks at her. "That I play well with dragons," she says, her eyes moving to Pilkington again. "Your lord probably has a Star of his own somewhere in that empty house of his," she adds, "though he would never tell any of us about it. I'm surprised he shared you with us at all."

"Lady Pilkington is not to be shared," Pilkington says softly, his voice just the cordial side of menacing.

Kamika's smile lights up her face. "Ooh!" she squeals. "Touchy too! It must be the real thing then. Lovely to meet you, Lady Pilkington. May we meet again when we have more time to get acquainted." She executes another bow, then departs in a swish of fabric and sexiness.

"Wow," Sylvia breathes, "what is she?"

"Succubus," Pilkington replies, "but you already knew that."

"She's beautiful," Sylvia says, a little wistfully.

"I'm sure she would entertain you if you asked," he suggests.

Sylvia scoffs. "What? No!" She snuggles against his side again. "I can appreciate her, but you're the only one I want."

"Want has a different meaning in this realm, arusha," he explains. "I would not judge you for exploring your options."

"Well, I would judge you for exploring other options," she snaps, "though you apparently enjoy dragons in your spare time."

Pilkington laughs, the sound loud enough to attract the attention of the few remaining demons in the room. He leans down to whisper in her ear, the feel of his breath stirring her desire despite her annoyance at the idea of Pilkington with a sexy dragon woman. "Kamika is just trying to get a rise out of you, arusha. I have contacts in the dragon realm, it is true, but I do not earn my Stars the way she thinks."

"Oh," Sylvia says, the sound falling out of her as his touch makes the hair on her arm stand up beneath the dress she wears, and she wishes, suddenly, violently, that they were alone. "Are we going to run into any of your exes here?" she asks, unable to stop herself. Sylvia is confident that Pilkington is with her, but after seeing Kamika and knowing the power demons have over desire, she just wants to be prepared.

"Here?" he asks, scoffing. "No. Would-be lovers, perhaps, but no successful partners." Sylvia decides to interpret this to mean that he has been approached but hasn't taken anyone up on the opportunity. She wonders about Pilkington's history, which must be long given how old he is, and she decides she will ask another day.

"Oh," she repeats, and he gives her a meaningful look, as if knowing her thoughts exactly.

"They will wish to be you tonight," he says, "and the rest will wish to be me."

"You think so?" she asks.

"Oh yes," he breathes, and she shivers. "Kamika would have you up against that wall if you gave her any indication you want her."

Sylvia swallows, wondering how she will navigate this new world of demons and desire. She had barely gotten her feet in the vampire world of blood and hunger, and now she is in a new arena. "Well," she says, standing up straighter, her voice prim, "I have no plans of anyone 'having' me against any walls in this place tonight."

Pilkington raises an eyebrow at her and chuckles. "We shall see, Lady Pilkington."

She smiles politely as Pilkington greets a few more demons, and Sylvia tries to categorize them based on what she already knows, attaching their level of deference to physical cues like horn size and elaborateness of their dress. After a few minutes of observation, she reaffirms that Pilkington is a person of some importance in this community, a loner or rogue whose presence at this event has caused a minor stir. She's not sure what this means for them and their predicament, or the ramifications for his place in demon society, but she pays attention to details, studying the behavior and situations like she did when she waited tables, enjoying her theories and seeing if her predictions are accurate.

They move through the doors into a larger room, and Sylvia is reminded of the ballrooms she has seen in movies. Couples whirl around the center of the space, performing complicated moves that seem choreographed. A waft of magic hits her, the scent of desire she is learning to identify, and she tries to narrow it down to individuals. Near them, a tall, blue-skinned demon who resembles Pilkington moves with a different red-skinned demon, this one a male judging by his bare chest, but the sex appeal radiating from him allows her to identify him as a succubus, too.

Wait, she thinks, *incubus? I need a guidebook.*

As they pass, the blue demon seems to notice Pilkington and abandons his partner, much to the red demon's dismay. He follows his former partner with his eyes, his gaze filled with longing.

The blue demon approaches, then claps Pilkington on the shoulder. "Pilk!" he says, his voice loud and cheerful. His hair is long, twisted into a braid that disappears into the darkness of his wings. Like most of the men in the room, his chest is bare, except for two silver hoops through his nipples. The dark lines on his skin are highlighted with silver and gold paint. Sylvia doesn't know how to judge demon ages, but he seems to act younger than Pilkington, though they look roughly the same age. "I haven't seen you in ages! What in the realms are you doing here?" He notices Sylvia, eyes widening when he spies the silver bracer. "And who is this?"

Pilkington shakes his head, but a small smile covers his lips. "May I present Lord Saren?" he says to Sylvia. "And this is Lady Pilkington."

"What?!" The demon's handsome face breaks into a shock followed by exuberant joy. He smacks Pilkington on the shoulder again, harder this time. "Daughter of Lilith! I never thought I'd see the day!" He turns to face Sylvia, executing one of those fancy bows the demons seem to favor. "The pleasure is all mine," he insists, reaching for her hand. Sylvia is about to let him have it when Pilkington intervenes, collecting her hand with his own and holding it against his side.

"She is all mine," Pilkington warns quietly, and the grin on Saren's face spreads even wider.

"Well," he laughs, "cry your pardon, cousin mine."

"Your cousin?" Sylvia echoes, the resemblance making more sense if Saren is a relative.

Pilkington nods. "Saren is an elemental demon, like my mother."

"Lady Asa is my mother's sister," Saren explains. "This one and I spent lots of time together as imps." He leans down and whispers to Sylvia, "He was always pulling me out of trouble, you know."

"I believe that," Sylvia says with a laugh. Pilkington knows how to have fun, but she can imagine him being more serious than his cousin. "Did he start the trouble though?"

Saren winks. "Sometimes." He gives them both a once over, then shakes his head. "So, when can I expect the invitation?"

Sylvia sighs, tired of everyone asking, feeling like the last unmarried couple at a wedding. "We're still working on the details," she says quickly.

"Oh," Saren says, smile fading a little as he glances at Pilkington, and Sylvia knows there is an entire conversation in that look, the way family can say something without any words at all. "I see." He shakes his head. "What I don't see is what in the realms you are doing here at all, cousin."

"I have dealings with the Marquis," Pilkington says quietly.

Saren tilts his head, raising an eyebrow. "I had heard you were to retrieve the Greater Demon Hesperus from the human realm. Have you returned him then?"

"It is ... complicated," Pilkington admits.

Saren nods his head, and the light in the room catches on the silver hoops that line his ear. "Hesperus never was the wisest," he murmurs. "I have no doubt you will accomplish your goal."

"How is the Marquis tonight?" Pilkington asks, voice pitched low so the others can't hear over the sound of talking and quiet music.

Saren moves his head from side to side. "Not the worst night ever," he says, "but not the best either. I don't think you're at a disadvantage." He glances at Sylvia again, eyes lingering on the silver bracer. "Does he know about ... that?"

"He does," Pilkington tells him. "He was ... not impressed when last we spoke."

Saren's smile returns, and he puts a friendly hand on Pilkington's arm. "I have every confidence that you will restore your esteem in his eyes. You always figure out a way." He pauses, then adds, "Though bringing her here in silver is risky, Pilk. I get you want to make a statement, but this is nearly a challenge. I hope you know what you're doing."

"Is this a planned party?" Pilkington asks, and when Saren looks confused, he adds, "Earlier today, did you

know this was happening tonight? Or is this a spontaneous event?"

"This has been planned for at least a week."

"So, he knew when I contacted him," Pilkington
muses, "that we would have an audience for my report.
Interesting." He tilts his head. "Saren, how many of
those here are loyal to Hesperus?"

Saren grimaces, then scans the crowd. Sylvia takes
the moment to do the same, seeing a kaleidoscope of
colorful demons amid a handful of humans—who all
wear bracers in various colors. She tries to assess the
relationships that matter—Pilkington said smaller
horns meant more power, so she dismisses those
near the huge horned creatures, focusing on the few
remaining demons—mostly red and blue—elemental
demons and succubi. *And incubi,* she adds, seeing the
same man Saren had abandoned lingering near the
dance floor again. He leans against the far wall, still
watching them with longing.

I get it, she thinks. *He's hot. But I didn't realize that
an incubus could pine for someone like that. I really need a
guidebook.* Sylvia's Guide to the Demon Realm: A One-
stop Source for Survival among the Supernatural. *I can
illustrate it and everything.*

She continues her perusal of the scene, counting
around thirty demons in the main room. She gasps
when she sees a familiar demon standing near another
door at the far end of the room, recognizing the furry
body and claws of the Balaam demon—the creature
that was first sent to retrieve her for Charlie Wagner
so long ago. She knows that the Balaam do not speak
in her realm, and this one seems to be wearing livery of

some sort, its bearing that of a servant, and she spies another one near the door they passed through.

Balaam demon, she thinks, making an entry in her mental guidebook, *limited intelligence? Servant to aristocratic demons. Commonly summoned to other realms for menial tasks.*

"Teran, Korus, and Rekar, for sure," Saren mumbles. "Maybe a handful of other Greaters might have a grudge. I'd say seven, eight max."

"And the others?"

"Illius will be near Forneus, as always," Saren adds. "She is never far from his side. And likely Kivan as well, though he does more spying than fighting for the Marquis these days. A dozen others looking to curry favor for this or that may join in. You looking to start trouble, cousin?"

Pilkington shakes his head, frowning. "I seek to avoid trouble," he says.

"I will back you," Saren says, and Sylvia is proud to see that Pilkington does have more than just allies in his world. He has loyal family. "Kamika and Kimo would side with us as well. Though they would expect us to fuck them in exchange at some point." He glances at Sylvia. "Kamika might trade you for her. She'll negotiate."

Pilkington shakes his head. "Demons always negotiate," he complains. "That's why I avoid these kinds of things."

"He told you to come then?" When Pilkington nods, Saren takes a deep breath. "He's plotting something then." He nods. "Let me collect the 'buses and we will back you."

"Wait," Pilkington says. "I may not need them."

"Better to ask now and not need them. You worried about owing them?" Saren laughs. "If it means that much to you, cousin, I will take the debt. Miko has been chasing me for months now. A threesome would be sensational. You should watch."

Sylvia wonders if she will ever get used to the casual way the demons talk about sex. She knows it's part of their nature, their culture—Pilkington's primary power is desire after all. He has other gifts from his parents, but his demonic nature is all about what creatures want. Sylvia doesn't think of herself as repressed—more inexperienced. This is a whole new world in so many ways.

Instead of terrifying her, the idea is exciting—not the proposed threesome, but the idea of learning her way in this new place.

"I will take it under consideration," Pilkington replies evenly, his eyes scanning the room. In the very back, seated on a raised dais, she sees another demon with smooth gray skin decorated with white lines. He is bald with large horns on both sides of his head, and his white wings are huge even as he is seated.

"Who is that?" she whispers. "The white wings?"

Pilkington frowns. "That is Forneus."

"But ... his horns are huge! I thought you said—"

Pilkington scoffs. "Forneus is very very old. If he were my age, he would not be quite so powerful. Even demons born with a modicum of power can grow strong given enough time." He pauses, then adds, "Also, he has a habit of absorbing power from those who displease him."

"Like the d—" Sylvia cuts herself off quickly, glancing at Saren. He may be a trusted ally, but Sylvia doesn't know much about him. "Wait," she says, turning to Pilkington. "He won't—"

"No," Pilkington assures her. "He won't."

"I'm getting the 'buses," Saren says, shaking his head at them both.

Pilkington ignores him, lifting Sylvia's hand to his mouth for a kiss. "Shall we?" he asks, nodding at Forneus across the room.

"Let's do this," she says. "I stand behind you, right?" She's been watching the other humans in the room, most of whom wear gold bracers. She's seen two silver like hers, and no black at all.

"You stand at my side," he tells her. "Always." He begins leading her through the crowd. "Unless I shove you behind me."

"I figured that," she snaps, following him. The crowd seems to part as they move, the other demons subtly shifting their focus to the drama about to unfold.

"Shut it," Sylvia overhears a female black demon say to the green demon standing next to her. "I have a bet on this one."

"I went with the Marquis," the green demon replies, "and you're definitely losing this time. Did you hear his rant last time about insubordination? The rogue lord is a lost cause."

"We'll see," her companion says, moving in to occupy the space Pilkington and Sylvia pass through. By the time they reach the other side of the room, most of the conversation has died down, the attendees stretching necks to see the confrontation.

Sylvia sees that Saren has moved to the right, standing behind the two red sex demons, head down between them, mouth moving quickly. As she watches,

Kimo's wings fade from existence, and the incubus pushes back against Saren, the elemental demon's arm wrapping around a more easily accessible shoulder to hold him close. Kamika laughs, and Sylvia can hear the sound from where she stands at Pilkington's side, the succubus's voice still capable of giving her chills.

They are so powerful, she thinks. *I bet they could degenerate this party into an orgy in a matter of minutes.* She frowns, keeping the thought as a possible back-up plan if this goes badly. The sex demons exude lust like a scent, and Sylvia has learned to push smells around a little bit. It's not a great plan, but if things go badly, she and Pilkington could escape out the back door while everyone is overwhelmed by desire. She wonders if it's a tactic that has been used before. They are demons, after all. Sex is a skill and a weapon for them.

They reach the empty area before the dais where Forneus sits in his demon form. She stares at him, wishing she had asked Pilkington exactly what kind of demon he is. She recalls something about the ocean when the witches had tried to summon him back in the cemetery. She represses a shiver, remembering the sense of vastness of whatever they tried to summon that night.

But that wasn't Forneus, she realizes. *They wanted Pilkington's master, his ... father.* That would explain the huge power she had sensed gathering before Phil had broken free.

I really need a guidebook.

Standing behind Forneus is a large green demon wearing a white dress that highlights the white lines drawn on her yellow wings. A large circle is on a chain around her neck, and Sylvia wishes she knew what the symbol on the necklace means. *Is this the Illius Saren mentioned earlier?* Her body language suggests she is a familiar, a follower of some kind, her clawed hand resting casually on Forneus's shoulder. The Marquis is one of the only demons in the room wearing a shirt, the white fabric bright against his gray skin. His eyes are also a bright white without any color in them, a sight that makes it hard for Sylvia to look at him. She would almost prefer the terrifying old man she met at Pilkington's house.

"Ah!" Forneus says in greeting, the word loud and boisterous. "The Lord Pilkington deigns to grace our little gathering with his presence. To what do we owe the pleasure, I wonder?"

Pilkington executes the formal bow Sylvia has seen others give him, and she follows awkwardly, her movement quick and obviously clumsy. "My Lord Forneus, Marquis of the Realm," Pilkington greets, "I am humbled by your request for my presence. I had no idea the honor you bestowed upon me."

Forneus's eyes darken, the white fading into normal pupils again, and Sylvia watches the demon look them up and down, taking in the appearance, their clasped hands, the bracer she wears. "Obviously," Forneus says dryly. "What news have you to report? Have you returned the demon Hesperus to our realm?"

"I have not," Pilkington replies, and there are small gasps and an undercurrent of talking around the room as the guests begin commenting.

"I see," Forneus says, voice cold, but Sylvia senses something awful in the words. Forneus is pleased that Pilkington has defied him, happy to see her demon fail.

I need to learn way more about demon politics. It's all going in that guidebook.

"And why have you chosen to return without completing your assigned geas?" Forneus asks. "In fact, how have you returned at all? I believe I was quite specific in my instructions. Were you slain in the human realm?"

"I was not," Pilkington says, answering the second question and avoiding the first. Again, more gasps surround them.

"Then why have you returned without Hesperus?" Forneus demands.

"Hesperus is not available to be returned," Pilkington says carefully.

Forneus frowns, his eyes narrowing as he considers the demon before him. "Explain yourself. Where is Hesperus?"

"The Greater Demon Hesperus is no longer with us," Pilkington says, and now a few voices cry out in anger and surprise. "An artifact exploded near him, and he was obliterated." Sylvia keeps her face impassive at his words. Technically, what Pilkington says is true—except those were two separate events—not cause and effect.

"What artifact is this? Where is it?" Forneus demands.

"The Dagger of Tallardy," Pilkington explains, "and it too, was destroyed."

"How?"

"I am not entirely sure," Pilkington admits, and though he knows his power destroyed the artifact, he doesn't know exactly how or why it worked, so there is enough truth in his words to pass any sensitive demons in the room. Pilkington has told her that Forneus reads body language and tone to catch lies, but others use magic, and they don't know who is in attendance here. "It exploded," he repeats.

"And yet here you are before us," Forneus says, "unharmed—while poor Hesperus is not."

"The explosion caused quite a bit of damage," Pilkington explains. "My arusha suffered many wounds." There is another ripple at the word arusha. He begins tugging off the glove on his left hand, revealing the long white scar on his forearm. "Even I was wounded." The hush that follows the sight of his scar is eerie, the only sound that of wings moving gently and sharp gasps.

"Is that ... a scar?" Forneus asks. "On your demon form?"

"It is a scar on every form," he admits, and another swell of talking fills the room. He pauses, waiting for it to die down again. "The dagger cut me before it exploded, and I was nearly unmade by it. I had to find a healer before I could return."

"Interesting," Forneus says, nodding his head. "We are grateful that you survived such an ordeal." He glances at Sylvia, then adds, "And your lady." He sniffs, then cocks his head. "How is it that I did not know of this Dagger of Tallardy, nor what it is capable of?"

"Was capable of," Pilkington corrects gently. "The artifact is no more." He pauses, then adds, "You are welcome, my lord."

There are a few titters at his cheekiness, but Forneus ignores them, continuing his questions. "You required a healer. Whom did you use?"

Pilkington swallows, clearly calculating his response. Sylvia wonders where Forneus is going with this. And Pilkington hadn't needed a healer—but months ago, she had—after an encounter with Hesperus. "I engaged the services of vampires," he says after a moment. Sylvia doesn't look anywhere except Forneus's shirt, afraid her face will give something away. Again, Pilkington isn't lying, but they were both healed from the dagger years ago, not that morning. *He's combining events, muddying the truth without lying.*

"Vampires, you say," Forneus repeats. "And will the Klaviger now be involved in this debacle?"

"No," Pilkington assures him. "It was a fair exchange freely given, no debts owed."

"I see," Forneus says. "No doubt you utilized one of your many favors in the human realm to gain aid." He smirks, adding, "I understand the dragons hold you in high regard. Perhaps you should have used Samson instead. The dragon operates a surgery in that city."

"My lord is wise," Pilkington says, flattery obvious. "I should have thought of that."

"Well if, as you say, there is no harm done to our treaty with the Klaviger, then all is well." He frowns again. "Though this does mean that your arusha must be full of vampire blood at the moment, doesn't it? Should you want to keep her humanity, I would be very careful for the next few days, lest she have an accident and return one of them instead."

Pilkington stiffens at the obvious threat.

"Speaking of your arusha," Forneus continues, and Sylvia's heart begins to pound, "I see you have claimed her in silver. My understanding was that you planned a Tethering ceremony after the business with Hesperus was completed. Now that is over, when should we expect an invitation?"

Pilkington's grip on her hand tightens, and he pauses. She knows they never really worked out a solution for this question. "May I speak?" she blurts out, bowing at the waist and looking at the floor, waiting for the word to proceed or for the yelling to start.

"Very well," Forneus says, clearly amused. "Lady Pilkington, please, grace us with your words."

Sylvia stands up, scanning the room as she gathers her courage for the crazy idea she just had. Spotting Saren with Kamika and Kimo still across the room, she meets Saren's gaze, and then pushes with the new power she has gained from bonding with Pilkington, thinking about cinnamon lust flooding the room, slowly building up desire in the crowd. Saren blinks, and both red demons inhale sharply, nostrils flaring.

My work is done there, Sylvia thinks. *Now for the rest.*

"My lord," she begins formally, "I am still learning your ways."

"Obviously," he says dryly, "or you would not be speaking at all. But you amuse me, and I will allow it, little arusha."

"Lord Pilkington and I have agreed to the Tethering ceremony," she says to a round of gasps around the room. Sylvia is pleased to note that some of the sounds coming from the side of the room with the succubus and incubus are more like moans of pleasure than gasps of surprise. Pilkington's grip on her hand is hard. "But," she continues, "we are still working on the details. I understand that such agreements are complicated, like any demon contract, and I asked him to wait for me to get a better sense of this world."

"What are you saying, Lady Pilkington? What else do you need to know?"

"Well," she blurts, "for starters, I'd like to see what he does for work." There is some laughter at this, and more quiet moans as that wave of desire creeps across the room. "I mean, I'd like to accompany him on one of his investigative missions for you. I want to see how I would be properly utilized in his everyday routine."

Forneus nods, and Sylvia thinks she may have struck a nerve in the demon, admitting her desire to be useful to Pilkington. Forneus wouldn't understand anything else. She can try to speak of love, something she hasn't actually said to Pilkington, though she shows it in so many ways, but she doesn't think that will sway the old demon. *It might sway the rest of the room though,* she thinks.

"How ... fitting," Forneus comments. "And if I agree to this arrangement, what will I receive?"

"Another strong supporter," she says, "eventually. We don't want to rush into Tethering immediately. But in the end, it will be worth your while."

Forneus studies Pilkington, no doubt recalling the demon's skill set. "Lord Pilkington is quite resourceful," he says. "Having another with his powers could be incredibly useful..." He lets the words trail off, then gives her a sharp look. "I do require one thing from you, little arusha."

"What is that?"

"The truth."

Pilkington squeezes her hand in warning, but Sylvia is already in too deep. She's so close to the end now. A whisper of desire from the crowd brushes against the back of her leg, hitting the bare skin above her boot, and she nearly pulls a muscle repressing the shudder that wants to rush through her. The soft undercurrent of talking has shifted to other sounds from around the room, and Forneus glances up, eyes narrowing as he sees the shift in the room's atmosphere.

"One question," she allows.

"Very well," he agrees, and she feels the agreement snap over them both. He says nothing, studying her intently.

"Well?" she says, unable to stop the word from spilling out, nerves and desire making her impatient. "What is it?"

"Oh, I'm not asking you anything tonight, Lady Pilkington," he says with a soft chuckle, hand stroking absently against Illius's thigh as the power in the room finally hits him too. He gives her a hard look from his perch atop the dais. "But at some point, I will demand truth from you, and you will give it, Lady Pilkington."

Fuck.

"Okay," she says. "So, can we go now?" Forneus nods, waving a hand in dismissal, turning to look at the woman now stroking his shoulder. "And you're not going to burn down our house?" she asks, the question exploding from her mouth.

"How delightful you are, Lady Pilkington!" Forneus chuckles, glancing at her again. "No, I will not burn down your house." He pauses, adding, "Not tonight, anyway."

Pilkington's voice is rough in her ear. "Let's go," he says, tugging her away. They stumble into the midst of bodies, and the full power of unleashed succubus and incubus powers floods her senses.

"Oh wow," she moans. "Did I do that? That is just... wow." Her hand finds skin, any skin, and she runs her finger along it, not caring that it's the arm of a complete stranger, the human man wearing a gold bracer as he stares at her with lust-dazed eyes.

Pilkington tugs her again, and she moves another few people, this time getting caught against a pale gray demon who slips her fingers into his mouth. "Oh fuck," she says, part of her knowing that she should be disgusted, that she isn't someone to let a stranger suck her fingers, but the sensation just feels so nice. She closes her eyes, surrendering to it, and then her hand is being yanked from the warmth as Pilkington lifts her up into his arms and bodily carries her through the crowd.

They pass through a doorway, and she is vaguely aware of bodies everywhere in this new room, people on the floor and against the walls, the haze of magic like a cloud over everything. Pilkington groans, and she lifts her hand to his face, needing to touch him, to satisfy the magic smothering them both.

Stumbling through another doorway into what looks like a grand foyer, perhaps the actual entrance to Forneus's palace, Pilkington doesn't hesitate as he carries her up a set of stairs. Flinging open the first door he finds, he scans the room, finding it empty, and kicks the door shut. Sylvia catches the hint of a canopied bed in the center of the room, an old-fashioned dresser against one wall, and then Pilkington is setting her feet on the floor, bending his mouth to hers and kissing her fiercely. She returns the kiss, eager hands sliding across his skin, not caring about his fangs or his wings or the little horns she grips in his hair. He pushes her back, hands working at her dress, sliding it up to her hips.

"I—" he pants, pressing her against the wall. "It's the—"

"The magic," she says into his mouth, hands tugging on his pants, freeing the tie and shoving them down. She hooks her leg around his hip, needing to be closer to him, to satisfy the wild passion racing through her. "I know."

"You ... want ... me ... like this?" he grunts, lifting her other leg around his hip and situating himself at her entrance. Sylvia doesn't pause. She knows what he's asking—he's in his demon form. They've never had sex like that before. Her desire swells again, and Sylvia decides that she doesn't care. She wants him in any form.

"For fuck's sake, Philk," she grunts, jerking his hips forward and shoving him into her, "just fuck me already!"

"So demanding," he croons, hips moving now as they kiss again.

"Always," she replies, clutching his shoulders tight. One hand reaches out to touch his wings, and he shudders against her.

"You wanted to be properly utilized, did you?" he says against her mouth. "I told you you'd be up against a wall by night's end."

"We really should explore more beds," she agrees, and then the magic washes them both away with it.

CHAPTER 28

PILKINGTON

A WEEK LATER, PILKINGTON AND SYLVIA SIT ON THE COUCH watching the sunset over the mountains, a mug of tea in their hands. There have been no further instructions from Forneus, no threats from strange demons, and seemingly no repercussions from the events at the party. They have settled into a careful rhythm, trying to plan a life together. Pilkington is giving her space, knowing that they narrowly escaped severe penalties.

"So, should I just be prepared for all parties to end like that here?" Sylvia jokes as Pilkington holds out a paper filled with fancy script inviting them both to a gala in four days.

The demon shrugs. "I don't go to many, but those that I have, maybe. Like I said, desire is what we do here. Sex is a fun way to explore that."

"I'm happy to explore that," she says, "with you." She pauses, adding, "Just you."

Pilkington nods. "I understand. Just let me know if you change your mind. Saren is dying for us to watch him pay his debt to Kamika and Kimo." He chuckles, shaking the invitation. "I will send our regrets." He gives her a serious look then, recalling how she had encouraged the demons to push lust into the crowd, a distraction from the show Forneus had planned. "How did you know to do that?"

"Do what?" she asks, sipping her tea.

"Spread desire into the crowd?"

Sylvia shrugs. "It seemed like a good distraction. I'll admit I was totally stereotyping demons at the time. I thought we could escape during the orgy."

"We did," he reminds her. "Upstairs."

"Yes," she replies, a blush coloring her cheeks.

"Something else for your guidebook," he jokes.

"Yeah," she agrees.

They sit in companionable silence for a bit, then Sylvia asks, "Are we going to just stay here for good now?"

"You did call it our house," he reminds her, thinking of the swelling in his chest at her words, claiming him in front of everyone. He smiles at his arusha, happy to be near her in any realm, and she returns the look, face thoughtful. "We can go where you want," Pilkington tells her. "Now that you're approved to travel with me on jobs, the worlds are open to us. Where do you want to go?"

Sylvia grimaces, sinking back on the couch. "I think I should go home," she tells him. He nods, but she adds quickly, "I need to call my mother, and I should probably tell Miriam what I've been doing. And I was serious about taking some classes at the Lyceum about supernatural creatures. I need to learn so much."

Pilkington nods. "Do you want to live there then?"

"For now?" she asks. "Is that okay? I know you like it here."

"Here will be here," he tells her. "I like it wherever you are, and until Forneus sends me somewhere else, I can be with you there as well as here."

"Well, my apartment is gone," she says, "so that's out, but how about your place?"

"How about we find a place together?" he suggests. "I know you like a fire escape to sit on."

"You seriously want to go apartment hunting with me?" she asks. "I don't have a job. My references are from shitty buildings."

"You can get a job," he assures her. "Until then, I can cover things."

"You are not buying me a building," she warns him, and he remembers her independence, her need to support herself even though he can easily provide for them both, with actual money and with magic.

"I will not buy a building," he promises her. "But I would like to buy you a new teapot, if that is acceptable."

Sylvia smiles, a soft giggle escaping her lips. "That will do. We'll need a kettle too, for the stove."

Pilkington nods, thinking of the shopping trips they will have together, decorating the home they make in the city. "You want to do this," he asks, "with me?"

Sylvia sets her mug down on the coffee table, moving over to straddle his lap, eyes meeting his. "I want to do this with you," she says. She pauses, then says quietly, "Can I ask you something?"

The magic jolt surprises Pilkington, the old promise jerking to life inside him, and his response spills out without conscious thought: "Anything."

"Why do you keep asking me if I want to be with you?" She pauses, as if sensing that she has finally asked the question she requested so long ago that night on the Ferris wheel when they first met. He owes her honesty, and while he never lies to Sylvia, he also keeps some things to himself, protecting his heart.

"I need to know that this is your choice," he tells her, but it's not the whole truth. "And I keep asking because I just can't believe I could be so lucky that you would choose me of your own free will."

"Are you so unlovable, then?" she asks, cupping his chin with one hand as she stares at him.

"I'm a demon," he whispers.

"You're my demon," she replies, kissing him softly on the lips. She pulls away, love bright in her eyes, and he soaks in the image, capturing it in his heart forever. "I love you, Philenliel," she says, and the use of his true name strikes a chord in his soul, binding them ever closer. "I have always loved you."

"I love you, Sylvia Jane Copland," he says, kissing her again.

"Finally," she says, sighing as she leans into his chest, her arms wrapping around his shoulders. After a moment, she says, "You know, we should probably talk about my name. Am I just Lady Pilkington now? I know names are a big demon thing..."

Pilkington chuckles, pulling his love closer. They have plenty of time to figure out those details.

EPILOGUE

Theo

THEODORE MULDAVIAN HASN'T BEEN BACK TO THIS CITY IN several decades, but when Oren told him about Sylvia's 90th birthday party, he knew it was time to return. He has seen Sylvia Pilkington a few times over the years, watched her grow older with her demon by her side, his dark hair graying just as hers turned white.

Standing in front of the white three-story house just outside the city, he looks through the windows, seeing the many people inside. He hasn't been to this house yet. The last time he saw her at home, she and Pilkington were in the apartment, their two children still young enough to require playpens. He knows they built this house when those children married and had children of their own, the Pilkington family needing more space to gather, and the two dogs wanting more grass to explore. For the first time in a long time, Theo wonders about the demon dog he had seen with her the night Jolena died. Perhaps that creature lives in their home in the demon realm.

He takes a deep breath, knowing that he will see many aged human faces, and it will hurt to see the marks of time, knowing that he will still be here when they are all gone.

But Sylvia won't be gone, he reminds himself. *She's Tethered to Pilkington; she will remain in his world after her death in this one. She won't be able to return to the mortal realm again, but she can still travel the other realms if she wants.* Oren and Harald have told him some of her adventures in the other realms, hunting rogue demons with Pilkington.

He walks up the path from the street to the front steps, clenching his fist only once, the cool band of the wedding ring on his left hand a reminder that he is not alone.

Not anymore.

Thinking of his beloved, he knocks, and a small boy of about six answers. He has black hair like Pilkington, and Theo can see the echo of his great-grandfather in him.

"Pilkington residence!" he announces. "You here for great-grandma's party?"

Theo nods.

"Well, come on in!" the child invites, waving him inside.

"Who is it, Aaron?" A blonde woman in her early 30s turns the corner, wiping her hands on a dish towel, and spies him in the doorway. "Who's this, then?" she asks, looking him over. "Wait!" Her hands go to her mouth in surprise, and she shouts "Harald!" into the room. "Is it really you?" she asks.

"I'm Theo," he says, not sure how to react to being recognized.

"Of course you are!" she says. "I've seen you in her paintings!" She waves him inside, and he enters the home, the magical protection rescinded at the invitation. He stands inside a warm parlor, a few comfortable chairs scattered about between small tables laden with finger food and walls covered by bookcases. "You were her model for the first vampire in the Klaviger guide."

At Theo's look, she laughs, then walks over to a bookcase against one wall, tugging a book free. She hands it to him, and Theo reads the cover with a chuckle: *Sylvia's Guide to Supernatural Creatures: with useful illustrations!* He flips it open, scanning the alphabetical entries, then skips to the back to find V. His face stares back at him from the page, his red hair perfectly rendered in Sylvia's confident style, his clothes those he wore the night they met—his Viking Times outfit. They have long stopped participating in that venture in this city, but others took up the mantle, and the show still sells out on weekends, Grace's great-granddaughter running things now. He moves to put the book back on the shelf, smiling as he reads the other titles there: *Lord and Lady Pilkington's Guide to Dragon Society: including dance steps, Sylvia's Guide to the Demon Realm: with useful species chart,* and a handful of other titles next to another series of books called *Billy's Collected Haikus.*

The woman smiles at him, then points to the staircase he can see through the door. "She's upstairs. I think she's been expecting you."

Harald walks through the doorway, and Theo gives him a quick embrace. "Good to see you," Theo tells his friend. He still sees Harald, Ula, and Oren, but he has been busy the last few years with his own life. Finding a mate tends to upend everything, as Harald has told him, and Theo finally understands. But he has time to reconnect with his vampire friends. Sylvia, however, only has a few years left in this place, and Theo doesn't think he will travel to see her anywhere else.

"She hoped you would come," Harald tells him, then points up the stairs. A small gaggle of children run by as he moves to climb the stairs, followed by an exasperated man in his mid-40s, probably one of their first grandchildren. "Please don't run!" he implores, giving Theo a quick cordial nod before disappearing into the kitchen. Theo spies a dozen humans in there, most bearing the look of Sylvia or Pilkington's human body.

Who knew they could create so much life?

Theo smiles at the sight, knowing that Sylvia made the right choice in her life. They had needed one another—her to learn to trust again, him to learn to take a chance—and he is a better vampire because of her.

He climbs the stairs slowly, soaking in the sounds of a houseful of life, of a family he will never have, not like this. He knows that Harald and Ula have a son, a man they rescued from death and eventually adopted as their own, but Theo doesn't know if he's ready for any children, vampires or not.

Listening to the sound of small feet pounding through the bottom floor of the house, the laughter and giggles as a small blonde clone of Sylvia leads the pack, he wonders if maybe it's time to consider such possibilities.

He reaches the top of the stairs and turns to the sound of quieter voices, these casual and laughing. Walking into a large open space, he spies familiar faces sitting on couches arranged around the room. Oren sits on the arm of one couch, his arm casually around the shoulder of a young human woman. Next to her sits an old couple, but Theo recognizes Sylvia's friend Miriam in the old woman's face, and after a moment, he can see her friend Jeremy, the one from the school, in the old man's expression. Across from them on another couch, Sylvia sits next to Pilkington, the two still holding hands as they drink from mugs in their other hands. Sylvia's hair is pure white now, still long over her shoulders, and though she is old, she sits up straight, her back unbowed by time. Pilkington looks old as well, but he lacks the frailty of the old man sitting across from him. Theo can sense the strength in the demon even now.

Seeing Theo, Oren stands up. "Theo!" He smiles, and Pilkington sees he isn't wearing the silver necklace anymore. His neck still has lines of scars from years of silver burns, but Theo is relieved to see his friend so free. "Glad you could make it, man."

"Wouldn't miss it," he says, crossing the room. Sylvia puts down her mug, then pats the empty seat next to her.

"Sit, Theo," she says, then chuckles. "That's not an order."

"I know," he tells her, taking a seat and looking at her. She is an old woman now, but he can still see the Sylvia he knew in her face. "You can't order me around anymore."

"You're so young," she breathes, staring at him with wide eyes. "I mean, I guess I knew that," her gaze drifts to Oren, "but I just … didn't think about it. You look great."

"So do you," he replies.

Sylvia scoffs. "Please! I'm ancient. I know what I look like." She looks at the young woman sitting next to Oren and waves at her face. "Remember this, Callie, if you mean for that to last." She gestures between herself and Theo. "This would have been hard to explain eventually."

Theo shrugs, smirking. "We could have figured it out. I have magical persuasive powers. No one would question anything," he assures her.

Pilkington leans forward and wraps an arm around Sylvia's shoulders, tugging her back into him with a laugh. "Now, now, Muldavian," the demon growls. "That's my arusha you're talking to."

Theo laughs, lifting his hands in surrender. "I am well aware," he says.

Sylvia looks at his hand, then at his face, then back at his hand. Eventually, she grabs his left hand, tugging it close so she can see the wedding ring there. "I think someone else might question us," she says, giving him a pointed look. "You want to tell me about this?"

Oren stands up again, gathering the teapot and mugs from the table. Callie helps him, along with Miriam and Jeremy, the others getting up.

"You don't have to go," Theo says, but they ignore him.

"Let's give you some time to talk," Pilkington says, giving Sylvia a gentle kiss before following the others out of the room.

"So," she says once they have all left, "how's married life?"

He looks at the ring on her finger, then his eyes follow the lines of the black tattoo around her left forearm. "It's nice," he says. "How's Tethered life?"

"Nice," she echoes. "Are we going to talk about anything real today?"

"Do we have to?" he asks.

"Well, you did promise to show up at my deathbed, so I'm starting to get a little nervous here. Something you want to tell me?" She raises an eyebrow, the expression so familiar he laughs.

"You've got some years left in you," he tells her. "Here."

Sylvia nods. "I figured they told you."

"Are you excited then?" he asks. "To live in that realm forever?"

Sylvia sighs. "I've been so many places, Theo, that one is as good as another." She pauses, her eyes skipping to the doorway and the voices echoing around the house. "I will miss my family," she says wistfully, "though I may see some of them."

"Do they know?" he asks.

"Charlotte, my daughter, does. Her husband Kivan is a demon, so I will see her there eventually. Her son knows too, but not her daughters." She takes a deep breath. "It's a difficult decision. Pierce, that's her son, inherited some of his father's abilities, but the girls are perfectly human. It's a burden she doesn't think they want or need. It's easier for Miriam and Jeremy—not for her, of course, when she first found out about all this—but all of their kids are witches, so it just makes sense. I think the others suspect something, but unless they ask, my family doesn't automatically tell them. I wonder sometimes what is better."

"Would you want to know? If you were human like those girls?" he asks.

"I think I would, but I'm also speaking from years of living like this. I'm bonded to a demon, so of course I want to know, but right now, maybe it's easier to think that grandma's guidebooks are just funny fiction." She shrugs. "I can't make that choice for them." She sniffs, then gives him a long look. "Would you," she asks, "if you had children?" She pauses, then adds, "Wait, do you have children?"

Theo chuckles. "No. I do not. But maybe I'm more open to the idea than I thought."

"And how does your partner feel about that?" she asks neutrally.

"I'm not sure," he replies. "We haven't really talked about it." Sylvia nods, and he can read the look on her face. "Don't give me that look," he snaps.

"What look?" she asks innocently.

"The look that says you're thinking I spend too much time fooling around and not enough time talking."

"Well," she says, "that's what we did. Do you now?"

Theo shakes his head. "No, actually. We talk all the time, about everything."

"But not about kids?" she prompts.

"It's complicated," he replies. "Not like you. I can't just have sex and have a baby a few months later."

"Theo," Sylvia says, leaning in, "I hate to be the one to tell you this, but even if you weren't a vampire, you wouldn't have been having the baby anyway."

He snorts, glaring at her, but her comment breaks the tension that had been building at the serious discussion. "I'm well aware of that, Syl."

She smiles, and he remembers how long it's been since he used to call her that. "Well, I hope you figure out what you want and then make it happen." She pauses. "Wow, that sounded like an inspirational poster. I've gotten so cheesy in my old age."

"You were always cheesy," he reminds her. "It's why I liked you."

"I'm glad you liked me," she says. "I liked you, too. It was a good thing, right, us being together, even though it didn't last?"

Theo nods. "It was." He wags his eyebrows suggestively at her. "We had a good time." When she snorts, he continues, "I'm so happy for you, Syl." He gestures around the room, suggesting the house and the family filling it. "This life suits you."

"Thank you, Theo. I'm so glad to see you found happiness. You deserve it." She narrows her eyes at him. "I just hope they deserve you!"

He grins, warmth flooding him, then simply nods, words failing him. He leans in and Sylvia hugs him, her body still wiry strong despite her age.

A throat clears, and he looks up to see Miriam in the doorway. "It's cake time," she announces. "They're herding the kids to the kitchen to sing happy birthday."

Theo and Sylvia stand up and walk over to the door. The old woman gives him a raised eyebrow as he passes, no doubt judging that embrace she walked in on.

"You know," he says casually, unable to stop himself from poking the bear, "you could come visit in the other realm, Miriam." He grins. "If you wanted. Jeremy's a witch. He could go too."

"Oh hell no," Miriam says, taking Sylvia's arm and leading her to the stairs. "I've enjoyed watching your crazy adventures from afar—no need to join in now. I'll stay in my armchair at home, thank you very much!"

Theo laughs, then follows the women downstairs to enjoy some very human birthday cake.

Sylvia and Pilkington will return!

BOOK CLUB QUESTIONS

1. Theo and Sylvia spend most of this book apart, and each uses that time to examine the relationship. Do you think that they would have stayed together if Jolena had not arrived?

2. Harald and Ula are mates, a magical connection that bonds them together. Do you believe in soulmates like that? Is there someone for everyone?

3. Oren spends a lot of this book thinking his friends have lost their minds. How well do you think he copes with their behavior? What would you do in Oren's position?

4. Pilkington is determined to give Sylvia choices in her life, to that point that she wonders if he's looking for a reason to leave her. What do you think of his supportive nature?

5. When Adam dies, Sylvia faces the fact that demons are just as dangerous as vampires, and she wonders if she has traded one monster for another. What do you think about this comparison?

6. Sylvia breaks many bonds during the story, including the Maker bond Jolena has over the vampires. What do you think of Theo's response to this sudden freedom, as opposed to Oren and Harald's behavior? Why do they react in such different ways to this change?

7. As Sylvia is drawn deeper into Pilkington's world, she learns about demon society. What do you think of the party they attend and the cultural practices they observe?

8. Pilkington is expected to Tether with Sylvia, a ceremony that comes with a certain amount of risk. If you were Pilkington, would you consider Tethering? How about if you were Sylvia? Why or why not?

9. You knew it was coming: who is better for Sylvia— Theo or Pilkington? Why?

10. This book ends with an epilogue that contains spoilers for future stories in the series. What revelation surprised you the most? Why?

AUTHOR BIO

AUTHOR OF THE *KLAUDEN'S RING SAGA* AND THE *CONJURING Fascination* series, JM Paquette writes fantasy and paranormal romance novels. When she isn't writing, she can be found teaching English to college students as Dr. Paquette or watching her favorite Russian shifter romance movie, *I Am Dragon*. Her areas of expertise include the history of the English language and the intricacies of grammatical rules, but her favorite class to teach is on *Lord of the Rings*. (If you've ever wondered why English is a crazy language, watch her video series on YouTube under Editor JMPaquette!) She enjoys editing manuscripts for academic and creative writers alike, and she adores tabletop roleplaying (THAC0, anyone?) where her halfling ranger/Twi'lek adept/vampire wizard/[insert race and class here] is often underestimated. You can also find her guest co-hosting the podcast Drinking with Authors—even though she doesn't drink, she loves getting to know fellow authors! Check out JM Paquette at authorjm-paquette.com and 4horsemenpublications.com and as Author JM Paquette on Facebook and Instagram.

Discover more at
4HorsemenPublications.com

10% off using HORSEMEN10